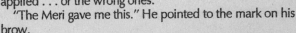

Wyth pulled him
Osraed."

"Yes . . . but by wha

"The Kiss cannot be

"*Anything* can be .... are
applied . . . or the wrong ones."

"The Meri gave me this." He pointed to the mark on his
brow.

Ealad-hach shook his head. "Perhaps you believe that.
I am almost persuaded that you do. But, *if* you do, you have
been misled. Betrayed, as we are all being betrayed."

"No."

"Your mistress is strong. *Osraed* Wyth, but she is not
invincible. The Meri will out."

"Yes, She will."

"I pity you."

"And I, you."

Ealad-hach shivered, but covered the twitching movement by coming to his feet and pushing his stool back
beneath his workbench. "Where is Catahn?"

"In the small audience chamber."

"Very well, I'll go to him. Have the others been
informed?"

"They will have been."

Ealad-hach approached the door, but was loath to pass
near Wyth. He paused, quailing a little beneath the
younger man's gaze.

"You're wrong," said Wyth. "You're wrong about
Taminy, about Bevol, about me. Caraid-land is in danger
— we are *all* in danger — but not from her. She may be
Something we don't understand, but she is not evil."

"You're blocking my path, Osraed Wyth." Ealad-hach
raised pale eyes, trying, with every ounce of himself to
pierce Wyth Arundel's poise. He felt a thrill of victory
when the young man dropped his gaze and stepped
silently aside.

Toward the light we ever turn.
Her knowledge is the lamp we burn.

Baen Books by
Maya Kaathryn Bohnhoff

The Meri
Taminy
Crystal Rose (forthcoming)

TAMINY

MAYA
KAATHRYN
BOHNHOFF

BAEN

TAMINY

This is a work of fiction. All the characters and events portrayed in this book are fictional, and any resemblance to real people or incidents is purely coincidental.

Copyright © 1993 by Maya Kaathryn Bohnhoff

All rights reserved, including the right to reproduce this book or portions thereof in any form.

A Baen Books Original

Baen Publishing Enterprises
P.O. Box 1403
Riverdale, NY 10471

ISBN: 0-671-72174-7

Cover art by Darrell K. Sweet

Map by Eleanor Kostyk, from a sketch by the author

First printing, June 1993

Distributed by Simon & Schuster
1230 Avenue of the Americas
New York, NY 10020

Printed in the United States of America

Dedication

To Stan Schmidt, for giving my writing career a quick launch and for helping me exceed my own expectations. In gratitude for his kindness, his patience, and for his being the kind of editor who makes a writer find her own solutions.

To Bahá'u'lláh for plaguing me with the irresistible desire to write.

Acknowledgements:

I would like to gratefully acknowledge the following folk, without whom my efforts would have been much less productive and rewarding: my best buddy, Vern McCrea, for helping me generate brainstorms; my husband and first reader, Jeff, for his tireless patience in wading through the downpour; Jim Baen, for seeding the clouds.

I would also like to thank the Sub-Space Cadets (Suburban Writers' SF enclave) for their invaluable friendship and loyalty and the Bahá'í Community of Nevada County for its loving support.

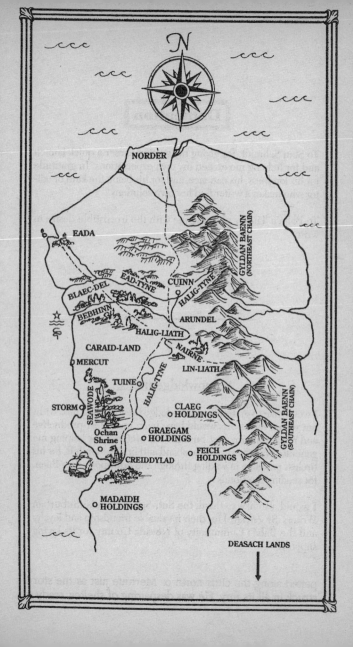

A TELL OF THE FIRST PILGRIMAGE

Osraed Tynedale's Brief History of the Cusps

❖   ❖   ❖

The Meri first appeared on the western shore of Caraid-land during the fifth year of the reign of Malcuim, called the Uniter for his consolidation of the noble Houses under one lordship. His truce with the two most powerful of the Houses, Feich and Claeg, was uneasy at best, and often as not the two were, separately or together, seeking to undermine his authority.

On the eve of what might have been a disastrous day for Malcuim, an eve which saw the Claeg and Feich plotting an assault on the Castle Mertuile, a great storm assaulted the country's Western shore. This storm not only shattered the plans of the conspirators, but it began an adventure for a boy named Ochan-a-Coille which would revolutionize the history of Caraid-land.

Ochan, from a Forester's family in the wood north of Mertuile (near the present-day town of Storm), was a young man of great virtue, but he had a penchant for daydreaming. Though he loved the woods of his childhood, by the age of fifteen he was uneasy and eager, chafing to expand his knowledge of the healing arts, praying to use his native abilities for more than grafting branches.

His father, thinking him unfit to follow the family trade, and having several sons much better suited to Forestry, sent his youngest boy to the Cyne's castle to seek a more studious calling. So Ochan, travelling to that end, happened along the cliffs north of Mertuile just as the storm struck in all its fury. He was despairing of shelter, ready to give himself up as lost, when he saw the lights of the Castle glittering in the distance. He began to run and, in careless haste, he fell down a shaft in the cliff.

The shaft fed into a deep cave, breached by the sea and filled with enough water to break the boy's fall. When he rose from the salt pool and cleared his eyes, Ochan found himself surrounded by glory. For a moment, he thought he must have died, but when the chill of the cave penetrated his disorientation, he could only stand gawping at the place. In a chamber where there should have been no light, there was light in abundance. It seemed to come from everywhere and from nowhere, amplified and refracted and colored by the thousands upon thousands of crystals — large and small — that studded the walls and ceiling of the huge chamber.

It was as he rose from the freezing pool that Ochan saw what lay at his own fingertips, gleaming in water no less pure and clear than the crystals. It was the largest, most perfect crystal in sight — lucent invisibility, tinted with just enough color that his eyes could perceive it. He took it in his hands and held it up to the omnipresent light. And the light grew brighter.

Before him, the water bubbled and frothed, brilliance breaking from its surface and roiling in its clear depths. And while he stared, clutching the great crystal, a Being rose from the pool, wrapped in radiance so intense as to be nearly blinding. White-gold was the Light and, in its embrace, moved a form like a maiden's — the core of a flame dancing above its wick. Ochan trembled, but did not run, for the Being breathed gentleness and peace.

He waited awe-struck for its approach and nearly melted away when a sweet voice embraced him. "Ochan," it said. "You have reached your goal. I am the Meri — the Star of the Sea. I am the Gate between God and Man, the Bridge between Heaven and Earth. Open the Gate, Ochan-a-Coille. Step across the Bridge."

She came to him in the shallows, golden-eyed and gleaming, and held out a hand of light. He took it, hugging the crystal to his breast, and shivered with joy as the brilliant Being bent and kissed his forehead. He was flooded at once with light, with knowledge, with love, with peace. And he knew, when he left the cave in the morning's light, that the crystal he held was both a tool and a symbol of the Meri's power.

Ochan went straight to the Castle Mertuile and gained an audience with the Cyne, claiming to have a marvelous story to tell him. And Cyne Malcuim, rough, unlettered and battle-calloused, was wise enough to listen to the words of the radiant young man. He gazed upon the crystal, which Ochan called Osmaer — meaning, Divinely Glorious — and watched Ochan focus, through it, unheard of powers.

The Cyne made Ochan his Durweard and covenanted to listen to his words of guidance. "What are you to be called?" the Cyne asked him, and Ochan said, "I am to be called Osraed — which is to say, Divine Counselor. I am to heal the sick and educate the hungry and be companion to the Cyne."

Cyne Malcuim was cheered by those words, taking them as a sign that he was favored by the Meri over the Chiefs of the other Houses. Upon the sea shore, over the mouth of the crystal cavern, he raised a Shrine to mark the spot where the Meri had first appeared.

Osraed Ochan advised the Cyne well and helped him consolidate the realm of Caraid-land, bringing the rival houses together, freeing Caraidin slaves, and holding the first Assembly of Peoples. Based upon the success of that first Assembly, Malcuim instituted an annual gathering, whereat the Chiefs of every great House and the Eiric from every settlement came and consulted together before the Cyne, to discuss their needs and offer the goods and services of their people. A settlement arose around the Cyne's Castle and, because of the great crystal of Ochan, he called the place Creiddylad, which means Jewel of the Sea.

Ochan taught the most promising young men of Creiddylad and the surrounding villages what the Meri had imparted to him in Her Kiss. They transcribed Her teachings as they fell from Ochan's lips and recorded the Tell of his accidental Pilgrimage.

The fifth year of Ochan's residency at the Castle Mertuile, the Meri gave him a vision which caused him to send the eldest of his students to the sea shore, to seek Her out. Of the five that went, two returned as Osraed, each bearing a golden star-like mark upon his forehead.

After ten years, Ochan had collected a dozen fellow Osraed, and the Meri bid him set up a school away from the Cyne's center of power. Taking a handful of Osraed and Prentices with him, Ochan followed the Meri's call up the Halig-tyne to a great bow in the river, in the wooded fringes of the Gyldan-baenn, whose peaks formed the eastern frontier of Caraid-land. In the shadow of a gleaming cliff was a tiny settlement, too small, even, to have a name. Atop the cliff was the ruin of an old fortress.

Here, on the war ruin, Ochan raised Halig-liath — the Holy Fortress — with help from every able-bodied and artful man, woman and child at the Cyne's command. And as the work on the holy place progressed, a village grew at the bottom of the cliffs, lining both sides of the curving river. The village was called Nairne because it was built in a grove of river alder.

For many years thereafter, Ochan resided at Halig-liath and taught. He instituted the Osraed Council, ordained the Triumvirate and determined the succession of the head of that Council — the Apex. Each year Cyne Malcuim would journey to Halig-liath at the summer Solstice to fête the departing Pilgrims as they left on their trek to the Meri's Shore. And when the new Osraed would return from the Sea, the Uniter would call them to Creiddylad to hear their Tell.

Thus began the traditions of the Farewelling and the Grand Tell — traditions that remained inviolate until the six hundred fifth year of the House Malcuim.

PROLOGUE

The Meri is not reachable by the weak, or by the careless, or by the ascetic, but only by the wise who strive to lead their soul into the dwelling of the Spirit.

Rivers flow to the Sea and there find their end and their peace. When they find this peace and this end, their name and form disappear and they become as the Sea.

Even so, the wise who are led to the Meri are freed of name and form and enter into the radiance of the Supreme Spirit who is greater than all greatness.

— The Book of the Meri, Chapter Two, Verses 5-7

❖   ❖   ❖

On the darkened shore, the girl froze — a wild thing in the act of bolting. But she did not bolt. She wavered for a moment, then dropped back to the sand, her face set. She did not see the Watcher in the waves.

Stubborn. Loyal, too, or she would not have made it here — would not be sitting there. Stay, Sister Meredydd, you have met your Goal.

On the shore, the girl Meredydd turned her face downward into darkness. Tiny rinds of flesh sifted down to lie on the cloth of her tunic. She lifted a trembling hand to her cheek, stroking it with her fingertips. The flesh crumbled and fell. She stared at her fingers, eyes wide. The fleshy remnants clung to them and they, too, glowed.

She did not take her eyes from her hands as she rose from the sand. Once on her feet, she rubbed at her cheeks, at her arms — her movements desperate, fevered. Robbed of its covering flesh, the substance of her arms gleamed gold-white in the darkness of the night, brighter than the gold-white heart of the fire where her young companion, Skeet, lay in sodden sleep.

The girl removed her tunic, her boots and leggins, her shirt. Then, after a moment's hesitation, she stripped off her undergarments and stood, naked, upon the beach. She would not be cold, the watching Being knew, for heat radiated from her pied body, leaking, along with the light, from patches where flesh had come away with cloth.

Ah, I remember. How well I remember.

With hands that no longer trembled, the girl continued her task, shedding what was left of her outer self, shaking her hair to free the flame hidden within the drab chestnut strands, until finally she was bare of flesh, blazing and lustrous like a tiny sun — like a star.

The Watcher recalled Her own moment, a hundred years past — Her moment of terror and wonder. She'd shed the husk to find, within, a Jewel — a becoming vessel for the Star of the Sea, a fitting home for the Meri.

Joy, She sent the girl. *And peace.*

When the last scrap of slough had dropped, when the once-girl had surveyed her new body with eyes garnet-bright with wonder, she raised those eyes to the Sea and found the Meri's green-white flame beneath the waves. It filled the water with glory and washed, like translucent milk, upon the shore.

The girl stepped down to the waterline, letting the Sea lap at her gleaming toes. She waited calmly now, her eyes sparkled, expectant.

The Meri rose, then, from water that seethed and roiled, shedding emerald fire on froth and foam, sending it in questing trails to the shore to kiss the toes of the gleaming Pilgrim.

"Beautiful Sister." Her voice came from nowhere and everywhere, and filled the cloudless sky and covered the milky waters. "I have waited long."

The girl of gold opened her mouth, found her voice,

and though a thousand questions burned in her breast (the Meri knew), said only, "I have traveled far."

"I have traveled with you, Sister." The Meri lay a welcoming carpet of brilliance before her golden twin. "Come home, Sister. Come home. This is that for which you have been created. Not to be Osraed, but to be the Mother of Osraed. Not to carry the torch of Wisdom, but to light it."

The girl bled a great sense of unworthiness through the touching streams of gold and green. She was disobedient, inattentive, stubborn —

"You are kindness; you are compassion; you are obedience tempered with love; you are justice tempered with mercy; you are strength of purpose; you are faith and reason. You will be the Mother not of the bodies of Osraed, but of their spirits — the Channel of the Knowledge of the First Being. For this you have proved worthy." The Meri extended radiant "arms." She laughed again, filling sea and sky and shore with Her voice. "Come into the water, Sister, and do you get wet."

The girl laughed too, then, and raised her own arms of Light and stepped from the shore into the milky Sea. The Meri met her in the surf and embraced her, drawing her down beneath the waves. She felt the girl's wonder that she could breathe here just as she had above in the air — was amused by her realization that she no longer needed to breathe. For a moment they floated, wrapped in luminescence — the girl's gold, Her own green.

Great emerald eyes locked with eyes like garnets. *Now, Sister,* said the Meri without sound. *Now, hold the knowledge of all that has been.*

The banners of their individual radiance mingled — green and gold — and the girl from the shore ceased to be Meredydd-a-Lagan and began to be Something Else.

When at last the brilliance separated — the gold and the green — the two which had been One floated apart, still touching.

Emerald eyes caressed eyes like garnets. *The Lover and the Beloved have been made one in Thee.*

The Meri smiled a smile that could be felt and heard, if not seen. *And I had wondered what that verse meant.*

Now you know.

Now We know.

The green radiance withdrew, separating completely from the gold. *Farewell, Sister Meredydd.*

Farewell, Taminy.

Toward shore, she went, the green luminescence fading from her as she neared the beach, dying as she stepped out onto the sand — merely a glimmer now, only moonlight on wet skin and pale hair. There was a boy there, sitting beside a fire. Waiting, with his eyes on the milky gold water. Beside him sat a little girl with moonlit hair, and beside her was a man — a copper-bearded Osraed — holding out a robe.

Taminy-a-Cuinn took a deep breath of winy sea air and laughed. "Ah, Osraed Bevol! I have not breathed for a hundred years!"

CHAPTER 1

One walks upon the Shore;
One glides beneath the Sea.
In the water meet the twain
Who never met and meet again.
In the water they combine
The human soul and the Divine.
Humanity is glorified,
Divinity personified —
The dance of glory to and from
One to return, One to become.
One glides beneath the Sea;
One walks upon the Shore.

— *The Meri Song, Book of the New Covenant*

❖   ❖   ❖

There was no moon. Yet there was light — laid out upon the surface of the water like a stole of palest green. No, not on the water, beneath it — *within* it — as if the very nature of water had been transmuted.

The old man writhed upon his couch, struggling to turn his head away from the vision, desperate to close his eyes to the dream, but dream eyes are forever open. That brilliance — he had seen it before with physical gaze, a young man, then, at the end of a long Pilgrimage. But on this shore stood a girl, waiting for a favor from the Divine, a favor to which she had no right.

Usurper! She lingered to commit heresy.

The radiance of the water grew and held out ethereal arms to the one who waited. They stretched toward the shore, wave-borne, beckoning. The girl moved closer to the water, closer, until it kissed her toes, until her face caught the brilliance of the waves and reflected it back, mirror bright. Her dark eyes glittered with it. Even her hair, blending into the mahogany night, was woven with emerald threads.

The Inhabitant of the waters called and the girl answered, stepping into the waves' embrace.

To your death! cried the old man's soul, shivering. *To your* death, *Meredydd-a-Lagan!*

But the girl did not die. Transformed she seemed to him — not flesh upon bone, but light upon light. She melted into the liquid glory, her hair fanning out on the waves in banners like sunbeams. The spectral lumines-cence that wrapped her was mottled now — pale green, dappled with amber, the hues fusing to a whorl where they pulsed and wheeled.

Through eyes that would not close, the old man watched as the amber and green whirl clotted and sundered, drawing at last apart. An eternity the waves lapped, muted, at the shore, trailing gleaming foam along the colorless sand. Then the girl reappeared, rising from the Sea, dripping glory from her naked body. Clad only in the glittering jewels of salt spray, she waded ashore, a luminous green stain spreading in her wake.

Her brow! He must glimpse her brow. Did it bear the Kiss? Had the Meri accepted her? He strained incorporeal senses toward the girl and found himself gazing into her face. The face of a stranger.

The Sea ceased its whispering as the girl stepped ashore, blinking eyes the color of the waves she quit, shaking back a mane of flax.

He knew her, yes, he was certain of it. But he could recall no name, no circumstance. Dread gripped him in cold claws and shook him. Fear her, it whispered. Fear that hideous beauty. You thought Meredydd-a-Lagan a Wicke; meet this, the Cwen of Wicke.

The old man whimpered in his sleep. A cool hand came to caress his brow and his wife's voice petted his ears.

"Ealad . . . Ealad, do you dream?"

I die, he wanted to answer, but had no voice. Instead, he nodded.

"Poor soul," she murmured, stroking the sweat from his face. "I wish I could lift your burden."

The Osraed Ealad-hach took his wife's hand and pressed it between his own. If all women were like this woman, he would dream only pleasantly of things that augured well.

"Bevol is here this morning." Osraed Calach glanced over from his workbench in the sun-strewn chamber, pen poised above his papers. "He's taking his first year class back as of this morning."

"And so?" Ealad-hach did not return the glance. He pulled his Rune-journal from the shelf over his bench and pointedly stuck his nose into it.

"I hoped perhaps he was ready to recommence his Council duties. It's been weeks since . . ." He left it unsaid: since Meredydd-a-Lagan walked into the sea and drowned.

Ealad-hach turned the chill that coursed down his back into a gesture of disdain. The Rune-journal snapped shut. "Would you appear among your fellows in the face of such disgrace?"

"I do not think he takes it as disgrace, Ealad, but as loss," said Calach reprovingly.

"Pah! He doesn't even seem to take it as that! All that talk of — of transformation. The girl drowned and it's unhinged his mind."

Calach put his pen aside. "I don't believe Bevol's mind is *unhinged*, Ealad."

"Then what? Do you believe his claim that Meredydd-a-Lagan was transmuted into an Eibhilin being? Perhaps to become a member of some mythic honor guard, escorting the Meri about the Sea?"

"It is possible."

"Bevol saw exactly what he wanted to see. The fact of the matter is that that smug girl-child went into the water and did not come out. Presumptuous creature! If she was transformed, it was a sea snake she became."

"There is no such animal, Ealad-hach. I am surprised at you — a scientist — uttering such complete nonsense."

The Osraed Bevol stood just inside the doorway, arms folded across his velvet-clad chest, sunlight glittering warmly in the silver-copper haze of hair that floated, cloudlike about his head and shoulders.

Ealad-hach rounded on him, ready to snap, wishing he would make some noise when entering a room. Their eyes met in what once would have sparked a clash of wills, but Ealad-hach had no will but to dissemble. Bevol's eyes were too knowing, as if he could see into his crony's darkest corners and snatch out what hid there.

Don't look at me, thought Ealad-hach. *Don't tug so at my thoughts; I will spill them. I will spew out that damned dream.*

But Bevol, perversely, persisted. "I really ought to take offense that you so baldly accuse me of falsehood. I ought to call for the Council to settle it once and for all time."

"I do not accuse you of falsehood, Bevol," objected Ealad-hach. "Merely of the wishful interpretation of events."

"I am not interpreting anything. Since my return I have done nothing but tell you what I saw up to the time that Meredydd entered the Sea. That she was transformed is the unambiguous truth. That the waters were splendid with the Eibhilin light of the Meri is also undeniably true. Now, if you would know more than that, call upon the Meri to send you an aislinn vision . . . if She has not done so already."

Ealad-hach felt the blood drain from his head and fancied he could hear it trickling through his ears.

"Has the Meri sent a vision to you, Ealad-hach?"

He could not lie. Why *should* he lie? He had no reason. "I have dreamed," he admitted. "I have dreamed of a great danger to Caraid-land."

Calach stirred uneasily. "And have said nothing?"

Ealad-hach aimed an arch glance down his well-proportioned nose. "I have not yet interpreted the aislinn images. I had thought to wait for the return of Prentice Wyth. His knowledge of the Dream Tell coupled with the knowledge he will receive from the Meri — "

"If She accepts him this time," interjected Bevol.

"Yes, *if* She accepts him, of course."

"Why didn't you bring your dreams to us?" asked Calach, his voice sounding stung.

"I doubted Bevol could be objective, given the tenor of the vision, and besides, his grief — "

"I'm not grieving, Ealad. And don't pretend you hadn't noticed that. Meredydd is not dead. And how objective do you expect Wyth Arundel will be when he is still in love with her?"

Ealad-hach pulled out his chair with a long, ear-shredding scrape, and set himself in it. Barely soon enough, his legs wavered so, his soul shuddered so. "Love had nothing to do with it, Bevol. Your Prentice Wove a bonding on him. She played his body. Don't imagine she laid hands on his soul."

"Ah, but she did," Bevol answered him. "She laid hands all over his soul while trying to push him away. The boy was needy, Ealad. He was starving for love, for approval. If anyone *tried* to Weave a bonding, it wasn't Meredydd. Your star pupil wanted her strength to lean on. You may thank her she didn't let him, but got him standing on his own feet, looking to his own approval. He was heartsick when he left here on Pilgrimage, but he was his own man."

Bevol waited a moment, then, receiving no reply from Ealad-hach, made a dismissive gesture. "Beside the point, all that. What are you waiting for, Ealad? Tell us your dream as is your duty. There are other Osraed besides myself well-versed in the Aislinn Tell. Share your vision with them, if I won't do. What are you hiding?"

Osraed Ealad-hach thought the returning blood would burst from the top of his head in a narwhal spout. "I hide nothing. Nothing! And I shall not justify myself to you, Bevol-a-Gled."

He had to pass Bevol to leave the room and did it with as much haste as he could muster. When he had gone, the two remaining kept silence, until his wake had settled. Then Osraed Calach took up his pen once more.

"I have also dreamed," he said.

"And what have you dreamed, old friend?"

Calach looked up to catch Bevol's eyes. "I dreamed a

great, deep chasm opened up through the heart of Caraid-land, splitting it from Sea to Mountain. The Sea filled it."

Bevol nodded, his gaze going unfocused, losing its waggish glint. "I've seen it too," he said. "And have not wanted to know its meaning."

"Has it to do with Meredydd's transmutation, do you think?"

Bevol's brows rose. "You say transmutation. You don't believe she was drowned?"

Calach became distracted by the light glinting from his pen. "Even death is transformation, is it not?"

Laughter rippled from Bevol's lips. "A pretty diplomacy, Calach. I never know what side of the the wall you fall to."

"The top of the wall offers a superior view of both sides," observed the elder Osraed. "But then you know that. I sense it is not all you know."

Bevol sobered. Sobriety did not sit well on him and so made Calach uneasy. "Sensible, sensitive man," Bevol murmured. "Stay atop your wall as long as you may."

Gwynet-a-Blaecdel sat in the high-ceilinged classroom and wondered whatever had made her new guardian think her capable of grasping these lessons. The portly Osraed at the head of the room went on about runelore and the historical use of crystals in Weaving inyx while Gwynet watched dust motes wheel, golden, against a shadowed recess above his head. She lowered her eyes once, only to have them collide with her teacher's. Thereafter, they stayed aloft.

If the Osraed thought of surprising the obviously distracted child with a question, he did not, and she was grateful. She sighed as she left the classroom with her little satchel of books and slates and papers. She couldn't yet read the books and expected never to be able to absorb the knowledge in them. Tomorrow, the Osraed had said, they would be tested on the history of crystals in the Art. All she could remember of it was the heart-stopping tale of a boy who fell, feet first, into a sea cave full of natural treasure.

Shoulders stooped, eyes floor-crawling, Gwynet ran

head on into Osraed Bevol. "Maister!" she cried and dropped a clumsy curtsey.

Bevol responded with a chuff of exasperation, which sailed over the girl's fair head. "None of that, Gwynet. I'm your guardian, not your Cyne. Save your curtseys for Colfre, if you should ever meet him."

The very thought of that eventuality flung her into two more hasty genuflections. "Oh, I'm sure I should ne'er meet the Cyne."

"Eh, well, with the infrequency of his visits to Halig-liath, your chances are more slender than they once might have been. . . . How have your classes been today?"

Gwynet's eyes skittered sideways to poke at the tiny crevices in the stone walls. "Oh, well . . . " She shrugged one bony shoulder.

"Yes?" he prodded.

She raised her face then, her brow a map of consternation. "It's all so *thick*, Maister. Or, that is, *I* am. I cannot seem t'stick my mind to't. All them Cynes and Cwens and Eirics and Osraeds by the bushel. And as to the Crafts — " She rolled blue eyes in exaggerated distress. "The Rune-craft class is set to cull crystals tomorrow. I'd not know a good Weaving crystal from a lump of coal."

The Osraed's eyes seemed strangely watery and he squinted them up crookedly and bit at his lip. "I'm sure that's not true, Gwynet. We'll work together on crystal selection and I'll see that you get your history as well." He patted her shoulder, then turned her in the direction of her next class. "Go on, now, child. Osraed Calach is likely anxious about you already. He tells me you're first in the classroom every day."

"Oh, aye, Maister. I do like Osraed Calach, he's a sweet soul."

Bevol chuckled. "He is that, so you're well matched. Off, now."

She went running. Against the rules, of course. There was nothing about her that was not against some rule or tradition or widely held belief. Bevol grimaced privately and stepped into Osraed Tynedale's empty history class-room. "Well, Dale, how are we doing today?"

Tynedale's bird-bright eyes fluttered to Bevol's face. He should have been named Robin, Bevol thought. It suited. Especially in moments when, as now, the round, cherubic face matched Robin's red breast for color. The Prentices called him "Dumpling" and sniggered that he was a poor specimen with only two raisins and a prune to the bun.

"I assume," he said, his voice all bristle, "that you refer to that wafer-brained would-be Prentice of yours."

"Wafer-brained? Gwynet? I admit, the child is timid — "

"Timid? She cowers, Bevol — *cowers*. And when she's not cowering, she's daydreaming. Whatever happened to that child to make her so impossibly *blank*?"

"A good deal more than has happened to any other child at Halig-liath. Meredydd . . . extracted her from an abusive household. It's been weeks since her last beating; she still limps a bit."

"Shuffles, actually," corrected Tynedale, his face losing its Robinesque shading. His brow knit ferociously beneath his thinning curls. "I understand your feelings of sympathy for her, Bevol. She . . . can't help reminding you of Meredydd." The twin currants disappeared for a moment in a wrinkling of doughy flesh. They glistened a bit more when they appeared again. Tynedale cleared his throat. "Yes, well, the point is this — she hasn't Meredydd's talent. She's a vague child, unfocused."

"Ah, and Meredydd, if I recall, was self-absorbed, glib and stubborn."

Tynedale reddened again. "She was all those things. But she was also immensely gifted."

"I wish Ealad-hach had been as charitable in his assessment of her. She might not have suffered so much."

"Ealad-hach recognized her talent," said Tynedale, gathering up his texts. "His Tradist indoctrination simply refused to allow him to accept it. I find nothing wrong with educating cailin of outstanding ability. But as long as Ealad and his brother Tradists view it as tantamount to heresy, we must not encourage it." He paused in his gathering and snorted delicately. "Whatever must he think the God is about — to give a girl child so much ability and expect her not to use it? Whatever would the purpose be?"

Bevol pursed his lips. "Oh, to teach her humility, no doubt."

"Meredydd-a-Lagan did not need to learn humility. She needed to learn self-acceptance. I pray she did not perish aforetime."

"She didn't perish at all, so you needn't worry on that account."

Tynedale eyed his fellow Osraed uneasily and grappled his books. "Must go," he murmured. "Have a seminar 'cross court." He waddled energetically from the room, leaving Bevol to chuckle in his wake.

Gwynet lay sprawled upon the braid carpet before the fire she had built for her Master's homecoming. Before her, between supporting elbows, and triangulated with her nose, was a crystal. It was a blue crystal. She liked those best because they reminded her of water and evening skies . . . and her own eyes. And with the firelight playing so, each facet formed a tiny world in which it was always just sunset. She liked this crystal especially well because Taminy had given it to her, saying it was a very pure crystal — a good crystal for Runeweaving.

Gwynet grimaced, squinting her eyes against the blaze of a multitude of roseate sunsets. But what *made* it good? Its facets seemed no smoother or glossier than any other crystal she'd pored over in the last week or so. It was no bigger, no sharper of corner, no clearer than any of those crystals. It was not as grand-looking as the one Aelder Prentice Aelbort had used in her Weavecraft class that afternoon. It was arguably truer of color.

She stared at the symmetrical little cluster of worlds until her eyes blurred them into a wheeling montage of azure and gold. Fire in the sky. Bright, clear fire; growing hot and sweet and pure; pouring out of the sky in a river —

"Oh!" Gwynet scrambled to her knees as the flames from the hearth licked out and over the gleaming fender like a hot tongue and poised, tip drooling, as if to taste the azure stone. In a gasp, it had flicked back again, shedding sparks across the carpet while Gwynet scrambled forth again to pat at them.

She had assured herself that all were cold and sat back with a shudder and a sigh when she heard a soft chuckle behind her. She jumped and spun. "Oh, Taminy! I'd such a start. Did you see?" Her hand trembled toward the homey fire, docile again within its grate.

"Aye." The older girl faded from the shadows, her long, flaxen hair catching fire sprites and Weaving them through its length.

"What was it, please?" the child begged. "Say, mistress, were't demons?"

Taminy's laughter lay pleasantly against Gwynet's ears despite the fright she'd had, for the older girl was usually so muted and wistful.

"Demons? Of course not, Gwynet. It was *you*."

"Me? How? I've ne'er called fire up like tha'. I swear it."

Taminy came to stand on the hearth rug and reached down to pick up the blue crystal. "You've never used a rune crystal before, have you?"

"*Used* it? Oh, mistress Taminy, I wasn't *using* it. I don't know how."

The other girl sat beside her on the braid rug, the crystal still in her hand. "You mean you're not *supposed* to know how. And the Osraed won't deign to teach you for another year or more. You'll cull them, sort them, type them and codify their uses, but you'll not Weave one tiny inyx through them, oh, no. And *that*" — she nodded toward the innocent flames — "is probably why. Half the houses in Nairne and the Cirke stable, besides, would be burnt to the ground the eve of the day you lot were turned loose with these."

Gwynet blushed. "But what'd I do?"

Taminy held the crystal up before her eyes and frowned into its faceted depths. "What *did* you do?"

"I was just picturing."

"Picturing?"

"Aye. Like I used to do in leaf dew. I pictured the crystal was all these little worlds with bright, hot waters flowing out the skies and then — " She shook a hand at the fire and peeked up at Taminy's pensive face. "Are you sure it weren't demons? Dew never done that."

"There are no demons, Gwynet."

"My old guardian, Ruhf said —"

"Your old guardian Ruhf was making excuses, Gwynet. There are no demons, only wicked people . . . and weak ones."

"Am I wicked, Taminy?"

"No. You're not. But even innocence can be dangerous. You must be very careful with this crystal. Careful not to 'picture' in it without Osraed Bevol about to guide you. You wouldn't want to burn Gled Manor down."

"No, mistress!"

Taminy fell silent then, her eyes locked on the stone in her hand. Puzzled, she seemed to Gwynet, as if she grasped for something that eluded her; as if she had lost something and thought the crystal must contain it. And she wilted just a little, like a flower set too long on a sunny sill. Then she blinked, shook her head and handed the rune crystal back to Gwynet.

"What you just did, Gwynet, without meaning to, was start a Weaving. You reached through the crystal and wove your will to the flames and pulled them to you."

Gwynet was stunned. "I did. I . . . ? But, mistress, I don't know any — any spells — any inyx, I mean. And I don't know any of the runesongs — the duans. How could I Weave when I don't sing and I don't know the words?"

"You said your dewdrops never did anything like that. What did they do?"

Gwynet studied the other's firelit face and tried to remember. Remembering was hard sometimes. It was all bound up in pain and feeling like a rabbit in a hunter's snare. But she remembered going to the rill in the early morning to bathe and she remembered the dewdrops.

"They . . . they made me feel all wonderful. Like I were happy. Sometimes I might wish that the sun'd shine all day and Ruhf'd not be like to lay hands on me." She lowered her head and blushed. "Sometimes I let myself fancy it worked. That he were lookin' askew at me and might will to touch me, but couldn'a. I'd pretend my wishing done it."

"Perhaps it did."

Gwynet puzzled that. "But how?"

Taminy stood, her face fading back into the shadows of the dusky room. "Ah, Gwynet, some people are born singing duans. They breathe them in from the ether and breathe them out into the world."

"Meredydd was like tha', weren't she?"

"Yes, she was."

"And you. Are you like tha'?"

Taminy was already moving toward the door, receding completely from Gwynet's firelit patch. "I was once," she said, and was gone.

Osraed Bevol arrived home a bit late that evening, his mind still picking its way through the signs and portents of his last meditation. Gwynet was engaged in the sage pursuit of practicing her alphabet, while Skeet, upon seeing him, commented reproachfully on his tardiness and began scurrying to put the meal on the table.

"Where is Taminy?" he asked the boy, watching him ferry pots of hot food into the large dining chamber.

"Upstairs." He cocked his head, flicking his eyes upward. "She did come down today, though. Roamed about the house a bit. . . . Spoke to the Little One about crystals."

"Did she?" Bevol nodded. "That's encouraging."

Skeet's eyes dropped to the bowl of vegetables in his hands. "Aye, I do suppose. . . . What must it be like, Maister Bevol? What must it be like to be dumped back upon the earth after living in the Sea? What must it be like to have to walk where before ye've darted like a silkie?"

Bevol shook his head. "That, Skeet, is something you and I will never know. Nor is it something Taminy could describe to us even if she would." His gaze went to the ceiling of the dining room as if he could see through it into the chambers above. "But we will do all we can to help her adjust, for she must do more than walk, Skeet. She must run. She must fly." He sighed volubly. "I sometimes wonder if Mam Lufu might not be better suited to this."

Skeet cocked his head pertly. "Mam Lufu weren't the one summoned."

Bevol pointed at the tip of the boy's nose. "Get on with

the supper, Impertinence." He left Skeet's grin unanswered and went up to see Taminy. She was in her chambers — chambers that had so recently been Meredydd's — gazing out over the fields at the front of the house. She turned from the window as he entered the open door and sat facing him on the window seat.

"How was the day?" he asked.

"It was a cool day for Eightmonth," she said and toyed with the fabric of her skirt. "Gwynet drew fire this afternoon. Through that blue crystal I gave her. She has a natural Gift."

Bevol nodded. "I suspected as much. And did you instruct her in its use?"

"I?" She laughed self-deprecatingly. "I've not been able to croak so much as a Sleepweave. You know that. I simply explained to her how the crystal worked. She found it hard to believe the talent that drove it was her own. I told her you would show her the use of it and not to 'picture' in it until then."

"Picture in it?"

The girl's porcelain pale face lit in a tender smile. "She paints a picture in her mind, focuses it in the crystal and makes it real. Just like that. She's been Weaving with dewdrops . . . to keep from being beaten and to make herself not mind the abuse." Taminy shook herself visibly. "She'll be expecting you to speak to her about the crystals. Perhaps after supper — "

"After supper would be a good time for *you* to speak to her about them, yes."

The girl glanced up sharply. "But Osraed, I cannot."

"Have you forgotten your history? Your culling standards? Your technical knowledge?"

"No. You know I haven't. I remember everything about the Art, except how to use it. I can't Weave. My duans are just unfocused ditties. I'm an empty vessel, Osraed. I poured myself out into the Sea and the Meri took all of me. I don't begrudge Her that," she added. "I don't."

"No, child, of course not. But don't discount yourself so harshly. You had a native Gift. That will return, if slowly. Those who have gone before you are proof of it."

Her eyes held such a roil of frustration and hope, of doubt and faith, that Bevol was moved to go to her and gather her into his arms, awfully aware of what he held there. A unique being was Taminy-a-Cuinn. A singular meld of young woman and aged saint, of earthly frailty and divine virtue. She was a dust mote with the properties of a star, a drop of the finite that had been breathed upon by the Infinite. What did a man, even an Osraed, say to that?

"You are Taminy-a-Cuinn," he said. "You were chosen by the Meri to be Her Vessel. Trust that She will not allow you to remain empty for long."

"I will trust, Osraed Bevol," she murmured against his shoulder. "And I will try to instruct Gwynet, if you desire it."

"I do. I do desire it. As I desire that you eat a good, healthy meal this evening. At table with the rest of the family."

She leaned back from him and smiled. "I do like the sound of that word, dear Osraed — 'family.' You make a duan of it."

"So, Gwynet, you've learned the use of a crystal this evening." Osraed Bevol broke bread into his stew and passed Taminy a secret wink.

"Oh, *no*, sir!" the child came back immediately. "I did something by accident complete. I was only picturing and . . . " She glanced at Taminy for assistance.

The older girl smiled. "You summoned fire."

"Oh, *no*, mistress!"

"A natural," said Bevol, nodding. He speared Gwynet with sharp eyes. "But you'll have to learn control. Discipline. Taminy will teach you that. You'll show that old Tynedale a trick or two before you're a Pilgrim."

Gwynet bowed her head, acquiescently. "Yes, Maister," she murmured and didn't quite hide her secret smile.

Skeet set out a bowl of greens and slid into his seat, eyes jet-bright. "I did the bartering in town today, Maister, as ever. I've wonderful cream scones for breakfast.

"And wonderful gossip for supper, I've no doubt." Bevol's expression was wry. "What's today's portion?"

The boy served up Gwynet's greens, then heaped up his own plate. "Nairne's agog over Meredydd, still."

"Of course. And likely will be till I'm in my grave and they can safely say I was mad."

Skeet passed the bowl to Taminy. "Ah, well, the Backstere has it you're poor in the head — torn by the talons of grief. Popular tale is she was magicked into a sea snake or some'at. That's the Backstere's go at it. Lealbhallain the Loyal heard none of that. He believes you, Maister, bow and bind. 'She's transformed,' he says, 'made over out of Light.' Brys-a-Lach, now, he says it's *all* heresy, either way: snake or silkie. Said she deserved to drown, he did." He scowled with sudden fierceness. "Called her a heretic . . . and worse. Said the Moireach Arundel was right about her seducing her boy, Wyth. Said she tried to seduce *him* too." He paused and glanced at Gwynet. "I'd've liked to cast a Wartweave on him."

"I've no doubt," said Bevol mildly. "Don't let it upset you. When it's old news it will be supplanted by the new."

"Aye!" Skeet brightened, waving his fork in the air. "Has been. 'Speaking of heresy,' says the Backstere, 'have you heard the rumors from the capitol?' 'Which ones, says,' Arly Odern, and the Backstere gives the tell of his uncle from Creiddylad and some strangeness with the Cyne."

"This isn't about those murals again."

"Ah, no. This is that tell you bid me keep my ears up for. Though, to all earfuls, those murals are an eyeful."

Bevol shot the boy a warning glance. "You were giving a tell . . . ?"

"Backstere's uncle goes to the Castle Cirke in Creiddylad once a moon. And at last Waningfeast, the Cyne just up and does this ceremonial."

Taminy looked up from her plate, eyes waitful. "What did he do?"

"He up in the midst of the recitation of the Covenant and sips the Holy Water right out of the Cup. Tells everyone the Meri moved him to it."

"That's all he said?" asked Bevol.

"Well, that's all the Backstere said, anyway. Might've said more but for Marnie-o-Loom. It'll be all over the

village by morn, like as not. Once the Backstere's got it — "
He shrugged eloquently.

"Aye," Bevol agreed wrly. "Gossips nearly as well as he
bakes."

"You'll want to hear about Marnie," said Skeet. "She was
abroad the night we came home from Meredydd's Pilgrim
Walk."

Bevol was all attention — for his supper. "Was she?" He
glanced at Taminy, a sop of stew-dripping bread in one hand.
"And what did she see on this night of nights?"

"Cat smug, that one," opined Skeet. "Looks me over
grand as a Moireach and says, loud, so the whole shop
hears, that she thought Meredydd had come home with us.
'Two girls I saw,' she says. 'Bevol, and that boy and *two*
girls — one little, one big.'"

"Ah," Bevol nodded. "So now I'm hiding a humiliated
Prentice under my roof, is that her tell? I thought they'd
all settled that Meredydd was dead or inyxed into a myth."

"Marnie'd have none of that. Here she'd been, chewing
on this tidbit for weeks and just biding till she might uncork
it. All a-sudden, Backstere's got this sucky bit about the Cyne
— Marnie'd *have* to best that."

Bevol shook his head, chuckling. "Well, now. I wonder
how long it will take for Marnie to get her sly chatter up to
Halig-liath?" He sighed, set aside his napkin and eyed
Gwynet's near empty plate. "Sop that up, child, and you
and Taminy will begin a study of rune crystals."

CHAPTER 2

What is seen in Nature in a flash of lightning — That is Wonder. That comes to the soul in a flash of vision. Its name is Tighearnan, which means "Lord"; and Halig, which means "Holy"; and Caoim-hin, which means "the lovable, the gentle."

As Tighearnan, That should have obedience. As Halig, That should have reverence. As Caoim-hin, That should have adoration.

All beings will love the lover of such a Lord.

— The Corah, Book II, Verses 51, 52

❖   ❖   ❖

"I'm not made happy by this, Lealbhallain. If I'd my will in this, no son of mine would go into such a den of ambiguity."

"But it isn't your will I serve, father. I serve the Meri's will."

Giolla Mercer could not help but find his boy a constant source of amazement. If anyone had told him his timid, chuckle-headed child would return from his Pilgrimage a diminutive but solemn adult — an Osraed, by the grace of God — he would have pronounced that person daft. Leal's new aura of quiet confidence seemed to extend even to the tips of his unruly hair.

Now, under the intense paternal gaze, the boy blushed right to the roots of that, red on red, but continued to fold clothing into the hidebound case that was his family's farewell gift.

Giolla Mercer sighed volubly and glanced about his

son's attic room. It would be empty soon. "I know you're right, boy. And I couldn't be prouder of you, or more sure of your path, but I can't help but worry when I hear such things from Creiddylad as are being whispered through Nairne these days."

Leal's green eyes glinted. "Oh, I wouldn't say they were *whispered*, da."

"Should have been. The tale of the Cyne's artistic pursuits doesn't bear repeating." He hesitated a moment then added, "Nor, I'd say, does Marnie-o-Loom's tell of seeing Meredydd-a-Lagan home from Pilgrimage." He watched his son's usually expressive face and felt a sense of loss in its new opacity. Not even out the door, his boy, but no longer at home. "You don't believe it, Leal?"

"That Meredydd's here and hides? No, da. She wouldn't hide from me. The Osraed Bevol wouldn't let her hide. I believe the Osraed's tell. But I don't pretend to understand what it means."

Giolla Mercer nodded and did not betray his own beliefs. If Osraed Bevol was mad, it would come to light in God's own time. "So," he asked, managing a conversational tone, "have you heard when you are to give the Pilgrim's Tell? Will you go before the Cyne?"

Leal shook his head. "I've heard we may give the Tell at Halig-liath this year. The Cyne's a busy man, according to the Osraed at Court. He wasn't at Farewelling." He didn't say "again," thinking it too critical. "Though there was a letter from his Durweard, bidding us good journey."

Giolla frowned. "Last Season he sent up a man, at least, to say that he was ill. There was no excuse given for that letter. Merely, 'urgent business at court.' What can things be coming to in Creiddylad that our Cyne can't even be bothered to meet his new Osraed face to face? Over six hundred years the Cyne's been hearing the Tell at Castle Mertuile. An age of tradition and Colfre sneezes it away in two years."

Leal grinned. "Well, there, you see? That must be why the Meri assigns me to the capitol. I'm to keep an eye upon the Cyne for Her. Yes, I can see clearly that Creiddylad needs Osraed Lealbhallain-mac-Mercer desperately."

Absurdly pleased to see the impish glint in his son's eye, Giolla Mercer laughed aloud and tried not to think how much he would miss the boy when he was gone.

Taminy saw the Osraed Bevol and his small would-be Prentice off to Halig-liath after breakfast, then retired to the garden behind Gled Manor. The sun shone on the heights above Nairne, warming the centuries-old stones of the Academy and dusting the eons-old rock beneath it with a blush of rose. She could just make it out through the garden's clustered trees — the rounded walls of the central rotunda, a bit of slate grey roof, a glisten of aged pines.

Memory. Odd, how it could evade you when you reached for it and overtake you when you glanced aside. She could hear Halig-liath in mind's ear; the scuff and clatter of dutiful feet — fewer now in the summer months when only the first year students attended; the chatter and laughter of young voices; the atonal song of the morning bells calling assembly.

She could see, too, the upturned faces, a myriad eyes raised to the Osraed Gallery, waiting to hear invocation from the lips of the Apex of the Triumvirate, Convener of the Divine Council. Osraed Kinsel had been at Apex in her time at Halig-liath, a position Osraed Bevol now held. She had never been able to please Osraed Kinsel — or so she'd thought. Yet, when others had decried her as Wicke, he had been the only one to reserve judgement. The only one to suggest that the Meri should condemn or absolve her of the charge.

She listened to the drowsing silence. Yes, she could hear them now, the bells; like the shimmer of sun on water, translated to sound. In a moment, the small aspirants to Prenticeship would gather for prayer and morning song.

Lift up, lift up heads, hands and hearts.
The Meri wills the day to start.
Raise up, raise up heads, hearts and hands.
The Meri wills us understand —
Toward the Light we ever turn.
Her Knowledge is the lamp we burn.

She found herself humming the pretty little melody and broke off, smiling, but rueful. Oh, the things one remembered . . . and oh, the things one forgot.

She rose and crossed to where a climbing white rose twisted itself about a thick oak. Dew sparkled in its petals — gems for the dawn, her mother had always called them. A heart-thorn of pain pricked her. Mother and father were gone now — their bodies returning to the earth, their spirits loosed in Realms she could no longer reach. They had been so near not that long ago, but in shaking the Sea from her flesh, it seemed she had shaken their souls from her embrace.

Blinking back tears, she turned her eyes from the roses and sought the Sun in the green of Bevol's garden. It was there, lying amid a veritable platter of jewels — emeralds most of them — scattered in the grass. The lawns blurred to velvety splendor for a second, but a blink made it be grass again. No, self pity was unforgivable in a place of such beauty and peace. Doubly or triply so for one who knew what Taminy knew, had been where she had been.

She returned her gaze to the rose bush, reached out a hand and broke off a new bud. Carrying it to a gilded patch of green, she sat there, heedless of the effect of dew on skirts, and focused her all on the flower.

The bloom became her world. She narrowed her gaze to one folded petal. The petal became her universe. She narrowed her gaze to a dewdrop on that petal. The dewdrop became a Cosmos. She let it fill her completely.

Think you are but a pitiful form when entire universes are wrapt within you? That passage from the Corah had once comforted her. Now it seemed only to mock.

Yes, I am pitiful! A lake severed from its river; an errant ray of light shuttered from its Sun.

Entire universes . . . and she had seen them, each and every one, ablaze with Light.

Perhaps I am not shuttered, but only temporarily blinded. Anyone who looks into the Sun spends a moment in darkness.

Here was a cosmos in a dewdrop . . . on the petal of a rosebud . . . in a hand that quivered with half-forgotten power.

Taminy felt the swelling of her heart and soul, the quickening of her blood, the sudden acuity of her senses. She heard the distant Halig-tyne passing regally between her banks with lady-skirt rustle as the children atop the cliffs sang their morning songs and a falcon cried somewhere far above and the Sun chimed softly in the dewy grass, riffling among its jewels for the fairest and finding it on Taminy's rose.

Here was a cosmos in a dewdrop . . . on the petal of a rosebud . . . which opened slowly to full flower in a hand that quivered with half-remembered power. A myriad tiny worlds sparkled on each pale, spreading petal. In each world a rose had reached sudden maturity at Taminy-a-Cuinn's gentle urging.

It was the long outflow of another's breath that pulled Taminy away from the place she had been. She turned her head and, just for an instant, saw herself through the eyes of her watcher; a pool of vivid blue in the velvet sward, a banner of pale golden hair, paler skin and paler rose, petals spread wide.

"Mistress," soughed Skeet, "that was *wonderful*."

She glanced back at the rose. "It was a start. Only a start."

"You feel better now, though."

Taminy nodded and rose, brushing at her dewy skirts. Something tugged at her mind, then — an odd little tickle. She turned and glanced up over the wall and through the trees toward Halig-liath.

"What is it, mistress?" asked Skeet, eyes following.

"Curiosity," she said and, cupping her rose, hurried inside.

"I am ready," said Osraed Bevol, "to resume my duties at Apex."

The members of the Council glanced at each other, eyes showing relief, caution, uncertainty, disbelief.

"Pardon, brother," said Osraed Faer-wald, "if I do not seem in whole-hearted agreement, but you have recently sustained a terrible loss."

Bevol looked at him straight. "Pardon me, brother, if I

contradict you, but I must tell you, *once again*, that I have sustained no loss but that of Meredydd's physical presence. I do miss her, but I am not, as is popularly believed, suffering and grieved. I am ready to resume my duties at Apex. There is nothing to keep me from them."

"I'm not sure this is wise," persisted Faer-wald. "You began teaching classes again only yesterday. Surely, you wish to wait until you have readjusted yourself to that schedule — "

"I am not a frail old man!" Bevol's eyes sparkled with pale fire. "It would please me no end if you would cease treating me like one. There is no law or right by which you can deny me a return to my duties if I declare myself to be fit . . . unless, of course, you are prepared to challenge either my integrity or my sanity."

The council chamber echoed with the tiny shufflings of discomfiture — a cough, a scrape, a rustling of meticulously rearranged robes.

"We are not prepared to do anything of the sort," said Calach firmly. "Are we?" His eyes circled the room, resting on each face in turn. All signaled the negative. "Then I believe we must take our brother at his word. We welcome your return, Bevol," he added and sent his sincerity through warm eyes. "I gladly relinquish the Chair to you."

The move was a literal one. Calach rose from the central seat at the crescent table occupied by the Osraed Council and moved to the one he had traditionally held to its left, the third of the seats reserved for the Triumvirate composed of himself, Ealad-hach and Bevol. Bevol, for his part, stood down from the center of the room and resumed his place at Apex. He had no sooner settled himself into the high-backed chair than he turned the attention of the Council to business.

"You have all heard the rumors from Creiddylad," he said and waited for affirmation. It came, reluctantly, via mumbles and head-nods.

"Rumors," repeated Ealad-hach. "Do you honestly believe they are significant?"

"Yes, I believe they're significant. Especially significant because of their source."

"I heard about the murals months ago," said Ealad-hach dryly, "from Niall Backstere. What's significant about that? He's the biggest gossip in Nairne."

Several of the other Osraed chuckled.

"What is significant," said Bevol, "is that we have heard *none* of this from our brothers at Ochanshrine."

A murmur circled the crescent table.

"I wonder, myself," said Calach, with obvious trepidation, "if we need to be concerned about the lack of official news from the capitol. The communications from the Brothers of the Jewel have been both sporadic and uninformative."

"The time element involved — " began one of the two junior Osraed, Kynan.

"This latest incident with the Holy Water purportedly took place at Waningfeast *last* moon," said Bevol. "A Speakweave could have been performed or a bird could have been dispatched or a messenger could have come up with the teamsters. The point is, we should have been informed by the Osraed at Creiddylad, not the village chat."

Ealad-hach cut across the murmur of assent, his voice waspish. "*What* incident with the Holy Water?"

"According to Niall Backstere's uncle," said Osraed Kynan, "Cyne Colfre performed a . . . new rite at Waningfeast that involved his, em, sipping Holy Water from the Star Chalice."

Ealad-hach's face paled. He opened his mouth and spluttered. "An outrageous report! By the Kiss, if it were true, the Abbod Ladhar would surely have let us know. Look, Osraed, if the Backstere's uncle is anything like his nephew, he's not likely to let the truth get in the way of a good story. He must be exaggerating the event."

"Can we be certain of that?" asked Osraed Tynedale.

"Perhaps the question should be," suggested Bevol, "*how* can we be certain of that?"

Osraed Faer-wald snorted. "I wager you have formed some opinion about that."

Bevol nodded. "We have a new Osraed, Lealbhallain, leaving for Creiddylad directly after Pilgrim's Tell. I suggest that we authorize him as our official agent to the capitol."

"Lealbhallain will have his own mission to tend to," said Ealad-hach. "We should not burden him with another. Besides, which, I know Osraed Ladhar. If there were anything worth mentioning going on in his bailiwick, he would mention it. He has not. I say we must disregard the rumors as the work of a bored imagination. We are Osraed; if our brothers were disturbed by any goings-on in Creiddylad, we would know of it."

There was an awkward moment of silence, during which throats were cleared, robes rearranged and glances exchanged. It was Osraed Calach who destroyed the silence.

"I don't know how disturbed our brethren in Creiddylad are, Ealad, but I will admit to some anxiety. The night before last, I dreamed a horrible chasm opened up in the heart of Caraid-land. I intended to bring it to this meeting — now seems the appropriate time. It wasn't clear whether the disaster was a physical or spiritual one. I begin to believe it is the latter."

"Aye," agreed Osraed Tynedale and was echoed by at least one other voice. "I too, must admit to some peculiar unease of late. I have no aislinn to report" — he dipped his head toward Calach, who was charged with recording such visions — "but I am not content with these rumors, no not at all. It distresses me to hear them. We have never had a Cyne like Colfre — "

"He is a little eccentric," objected Faer-wald. "Surely that is preferable to someone of Earwyn's ilk who would throw Caraid-land into senseless battles with her neighbors."

"Is it his eccentricity," asked Bevol, "that causes him to repeatedly postpone the General Assembly?"

"I have also been visited by visions," announced Ealad-hach and, with his somber, elegant bass, drew the attention of the entire seven man Council. "I would speak of them now, if you please. They are pertinent." When all had consented, he rose and circled the Triumvirate's long table to stand at the center of the room — a place where light and shadow struggled and found, each, its own level. Sun from the high windows dappled his green robe, makng him appear to be clothed in a sylvan sward.

A tree, thought Bevol. *An oak — knotted of thought, rooted in habit, covered with lichen. They do not bend, these knotty old oaks.*

"My aislinn was crystalline," said the deep, ringing voice — crystalline, itself. "The images, fearfully clear. They had nothing to do with Cyne Colfre. They were not of murals or of the drinking of Holy Water or even of chasms. They were of Meredydd-a-Lagan."

"Meredydd!" exclaimed Osraed Kynan and the slightly elder Eadmund echoed.

Bevol gazed at the table top, noticing how fine was the grain. Ealad-hach, in turn, gazed at him.

"They were visions of a monstrous heresy," he finished dramatically.

Bevol nearly applauded the performance, but restrained himself. "Describe them to us, Ealad. We cannot interpret what we haven't seen."

"*You* saw." It was an accusation delivered to Bevol on the tip of a finger that trembled with emotion.

Fear, Bevol thought, though Ealad-hach was holding it severely in check behind a shield of anger. He spread his hands, palms up. "Tell us what I saw."

"I'll do better. I will Weave it for you." He paced the invisible perimeter of a circle, etched in the pattern of dark and light by the tapping of his feet. He stopped where he had begun the circuit. "She awaited the Meri, as woman was never intended to do. She waited in the darkness for the Light. And the Light came. . . . " From the tips of his outstretched fingers, colors flew and danced into the circle, becoming a shore with a lone occupant, and waters suffused with emerald and spangled with bits of fire.

Calach gasped and Tynedale breathed out sibilantly.

Ealad-hach divined the reason for their excitement immediately. "Oh, yes, it came! *She* came and drew the heretic into the water . . . to *drown*."

"You suppose," murmured Bevol and the woven image wavered like smoke.

Ealad-hach pitched it more fuel. "She walked beneath the waves and was sucked from sight." Indeed, that was what the watchers saw. "And then, the most puzzling, horrific image of all — a girl rose from the waves, shedding light as a bather sheds water. She came from the waves naked, and stood, laughing, on the shore, flaunting herself."

"Meredydd?" asked Calach in a whisper, squinting at the misty face. For the image of the girl was watery, vaporous, and dark.

"No. *Not* Meredydd. Another, older cailin. A girl with pale hair and eyes like the sea."

"Pale hair?" repeated Tynedale. "What are you saying? Gwynet-a-Blaecdel has pale hair, surely you don't think this is her." He waved a meaty hand at the ambivalent form.

"It was not her. She's a child. This was a young woman. A stranger to me." The figure lengthened, but showed no more solidity.

"Who then?"

"Not who, I think, but what. Woman, she was, and Wicke. The Cwen of Wicke, my aislinn self knew her to be."

"*Knew* her to be," echoed Bevol, sounding faintly amused.

"Without doubt."

"I had thought," said Bevol quietly, "that you were at a loss to interpret this vision. That you were waiting for Wyth to come home so that he could give the Tell."

"I still intend that he should do so. But I was moved to speak here and now." He glared at his peer. "I do not question the promptings of the Meri." Within the half-light circle, the aislinn folded in on itself and disappeared.

"No, no, of course not."

"If," said Calach, "the figure in the vision is symbolic of all women, do you take this to mean that we must expell Gwynet-a-Blaecdel from Halig-liath?"

Ealad-shrugged. "I would have it so, but that is at the discretion of the entire Council. However, an issue such as the presence of cailin at Halig-liath could be the source of the rift you envisioned in your aislinn."

Calach pondered, frowning, then shook his head. "The logic is sound, but the tell refuses to fit."

"I dreamed," murmured Kynan, almost defensively, "that one of the Cyne's murals came to life."

"You've never *seen* one!" Faer-wald exclaimed.

"In the dream it was most vivid," continued the young man, "although . . . when I awoke . . . I couldn't remember much about it. Which is, more or less, why I neglected to mention the dream in the first place. And also . . . well . . . I was ashamed. It was such a — a sensual image, I thought . . . I thought it must be a personal test. But now, when I hear the Osraed Calach speak of chasms — "

"It is *Wicke* we must fear, not our own Cyne! Not even his outrageous murals!" Ealad-hach's voice was belligerent. "Let us deal with the issue of Wicke."

"In Nairne?" asked Kynan. "Where in Nairne will we find a Wicke? Meredydd-a-Lagan is *gone*."

Bevol ignored the barb, focusing his eyes entirely on Ealad-hach. "Oh, yes. But there is Gwynet. Perhaps she must be a Wicke to have survived her master's ill treatment. Perhaps our brother has seen Gwynet in the *future*. . . . Well, surely we must banish the child then, or perhaps imprison her in the Cirke cellar."

Tynedale snorted loudly. The sound reverberated gratingly from every hard, polished surface in the vaulted room. "The wee cailin, a Wicke? Ludicrous. She's as sweet and gentle as a morning breeze. Besides that, she hasn't the Gift. I'm sorry, Bevol, but it's true. She's got not a midge of talent, not a morsel."

"You're wrong, as it happens," said Bevol, "but don't apologize, you may have just saved her life."

Ealad-hach exploded in a controlled rage. "I am not suggesting we do anything heinous to Gwynet! Not even that we eject her from Halig-liath. Gwynet is a child. She's not at issue, here."

"Then who is? *What* is?" Bevol stood, facing his sudden adversary across the gleaming expanse of the Triumvirate bench, his arms outstretched in entreaty. "You say we are in danger from Wicke — the very Cwen of Wicke, according to your aislinn self. You equate my Prentice, Meredydd, with this Wicke Cwen, and accuse her of heresy — *monstrous* heresy. You identify this monstrous heresy with allowing cailin at Halig-liath, yet you balk at equating Gwynet, a cailin at Halig-liath, with this monstrous heresy. Are you suggesting, Ealad, that you will only fight evil as long as it is faceless? Why will you not put a face to this heresy? Why will you not put a name to it?"

"Because I have none!" Ealad-hach trembled like a tree in a stiff breeze, every leaf shifting. "The only name I know is Meredydd-a-Lagan. The only face I see is one I have never met. My soul tells me this is the foulest evil. But it is nameless, faceless, without identity!" He dropped his eyes to perform a feverish search of the darkness near the floor, as if that might yield some answer. "It cannot be a person, surely," he murmured. "No, no, it must be a construct. A metaphysical construct."

"A *construct*?" repeated Faer-wald. He shook his head. "We must have more than *that*."

"I have no more." The whimper of defeat was followed by silence.

A chime sounded, brassily, and a light glowed above the door.

Saving us, thought Bevol, *from having to know what to do next.* "Come!" he said, aloud.

An awed-looking Aelder Prentice thrust his head into the room, his adam's apple bobbing like a fishing bouy. "Pardon, Osraed, but I have just come from the front gate. Prentice Wyth — that is, Osraed Wyth — has come home." His face split in a sudden and unashamed grin and he ducked out of sight.

"*Osraed* Wyth," repeated Bevol. "Well, Ealad. Perhaps now we'll get a sensible tell for your aislinn."

"Now then, Gwynet . . . " Aelder Prentice Aelbort smiled sweetly and tapped his pointer gently into one lanky hand. "What is the most important quality of a good Weaving stone, eh?"

Gwynet blinked. Aelbort's habit of ending nearly every question that way made him sound like Ruhf Airdsgainne's aged mam — an association neither pleasant nor funny. Yet, she nearly giggled when the student behind her mimicked a squeaky hinge.

She poked herself mentally. That would never do —
to be thought disrespectful of her betters. Her mouth a
straight, solemn line, Gwynet said, "Why, purity,
Maister."

"Once again," said Aelbort gently, "I am not your
'maister.' 'Aelder' or 'Prentice' is quite sufficient."

Gwynet's brow wrinkled. Sufficient. Yes, well, whatever
that was.

"But you're right, of course," the Aelder Prentice
continued. "And how is purity determined? Anyone?
Anyone?"

No one.

He turned his benign, canine gaze back to Gwynet. "If
you please, child."

Did the Prentice *want* to be old, she wondered. Would
he be pleased to waken one morning to discover his hair
gone white and his firm young cheeks, just now showing
more than adolescent down, sunken?

"I asked," he reiterated when she continued to gawp at him,
"if you would tell us how we determine the purity of a crystal."

"Pictures," said Gwynet immediately. "Em, 'imagey,' I
think Osraed Bevol called it."

"Huh?" grunted the boy to her right and, "No, it isn't,"
insisted another. "It's refractive precision."

Aelder Prentice Aelbort smiled with sweet irritation and
bent his golden head toward the speaker. "I didn't ask you,
Tam-tun. I asked Gwynet. I'm sure you'll answer me many
questions before the year is out. Now, Gwynet, what do
you mean by 'imagey,' eh?"

"Well, Aelder Prentice, just tha', don't you see? 'If in the
stone, you see the mirrored mind, then it be the truest of
its kind.'" There! She had remembered! She smiled,
momentarily pleased with herself.

The Prentice was also smiling. "Very good, child. A
delightful saying. Where did you get it?"

"Oh, Tam— " Gwynet's blue eyes blanked. She wasn't
supposed to mention Taminy. Taminy wasn't ready,
yet, to come out. "A friend . . . em . . . once taught
me tha'. To help me word out what I was

thinking. And I was thinking that in the crystals, there are these little bits of the world and when a crystal's pure, the little bits become mirror glasses for your imagey."

Tam-tun tittered. "She means imagination!"

"Yes, sir. Tha's the word." Gwynet blinked up at the Aelder, ingenuous and wide-eyed. "Imagey-whatsit."

Aelbort's smile edged toward the beatific. "A mirror for the imagination," he paraphrased. He put a hand on Gwynet's shoulder and gazed about, spraying the other students with his delight. "A perceptive comment. Which proves something I have always believed — that education can release perception, but it cannot *produce* it." His eyes fell at last to Gwynet's upturned face.

She smiled, trying not to show how little she understood what he had just said.

"Gwynet, do you think you could show the class how to select a pure crystal?"

"Oh, *no*, Maister!" she said, aghast.

"No?" He moved briskly to his workbench and removed two stones from its polished surface. Holding them out on the flat of his hand, he advanced toward Gwynet, tiny spots of red and purple light dancing about his palm.

She ought really look away, she thought. Ought to screw up her eyes or close them altogether, but there was some horrible fascination in those two colorful shards and a perverse little demon wondered if she could really tell which of them would make the finest focus. Compromising, she drew back, her eyes fastened, out of focus, on the Aelder's hand.

"Come, Gwynet. See if you can't decide between these two specimens. There, there! You can't be afraid of them."

"Well, I'm not afraid, quite, Aelder, sir. It's just . . . " She paused to lick her lips. "Well, my maister Bevol said I oughtn't be too free with imagey around crystals as I might burn down a house or some'at."

Tam-tun let out a crack of ribald laughter. "She must think she's Wicke! 'Burn down a house or some'at!'"

Aelbort did not censure his student. He merely stared at Gwynet owlishly and continued to hold the crystals out in her general direction.

She thought, *Now I've done some bad business. If only I knew what it was.*

Aelder Prentice Aelbort had no opportunity to tell her what she had done, for while he froze in mid-aisle, a younger Prentice popped into the room as if on a spring and said, "Have you not heard! Wyth Arundel is come home an Osraed! He's in the courtyard this moment. Won't you come *see*, Aelbort?" And he was gone.

Half the class jumped to their feet, the other half wavered between sitting and leaping.

"Might we go, Prentice Aelbort?" begged one boy. "Might we go and see?"

Aelbort, his beatific smile vanished, nodded a stiff assent. The boys disappeared as swiftly as the Aelder's smile, leaving Gwyent to wonder if she should have joined them.

"Aren't you going too?" The question came out in a petulant rush, destroying the Aelder Prentice's pretense of maturity.

Gwynet put out a hand and grasped his empty one. "If you will come, too, Aelder."

The benign smile returned. The crystals stuffed into a pocket and forgotten, they went down to the courtyard hand in hand.

Gwynet did not quite know what to make of the scene on the sunny cobbles. A tall young man was making his way slowly through a small throng of students and Prentices, answering questions in monosyllables and working toward the staircase where she and Aelder Prentice Aelbort stood. It certainly *looked* like the Wyth Arundel she had met, but she was amazed at the change in him.

She'd thought him a somber old thing and had wondered through the wee hours of several mornings what had made him that way and if anything could be done about it. Osraed Bevol had spoken of his family — his dead father, his regal mother, the estate he would inherit, but didn't want. He had told her, too, that Wyth Arundel had loved Meredydd-a-Lagan, and Gwynet thought it sad that he would never see her again in this life.

And that was the miracle, so far as Gwynet was concerned; this Wyth Arundel smiled and laughed and accepted his congratulations with back-slapping joy. Her eyes went to his face and clung. Radiant as that was, more blazing, still, was the stellate mark between his brows. A star of rose-gold, it was — of blushing amber — not unlike the one of emerald tint on the foreheads of the Osraed here, but newer, sharper, brighter.

Oh, wonder, she thought. To have such a Being as the Meri press Her burning lips to your brow and breathe knowledge into your soul! To no longer be ignorant and slow — aye, that would be the greatest favor of all: knowledge. She longed for it with every fiber of her young self.

Then and there, as she gazed up into the triumphant face of the new Osraed Wyth Arundel, she knew he possessed something she must have for herself.

CHAPTER 3

There is a sign from God in every condition. The sign of intelligence is meditation and the sign of meditation is silence, since it is impossible for one to both speak and reflect.

This is truth: that when one reflects, he speaks with his own spirit. In that condition, one can question the spirit and receive its answers.

— *The Book of the Meri, Chapter One, Verses 24, 25*

❖　❖　❖

His insides were quivering, but not with fear or dread or even timorousness. Not this time. Reborn — that was how he felt. Recreated and given new eyes and ears and mind, and a new, brave heart to go with them. He stood in the vaulted chamber and watched the Council rise to greet him and thought, "I am one of them now. I am a Divine Counselor."

The Osraed Bevol came forward to meet him and draw him into the half-circle and seat him in a tall carved chair at its center. He accepted the elder man's embrace with delight and shared a glance which spoke volumes about their common bond.

Seated, Wyth watched Bevol return to his own chair at the Apex of the Council and recalled an earlier time when he had stood, quaking here, while his mother's voice accused him of being bewitched by his fifteen year old student, Meredydd-a-Lagan, labeling Meredydd a Wicke. He *had* been bewitched, he realized, and it was as pure and clean and holy an inyx as had ever been woven. He was bewitched now, too. Possessed by the Possessor of all things. In thrall to That. Fear was a memory, only.

Did they, he wondered, gazing at the seven Osraed arrayed about him, feel as he now felt? Or had the years between now and their Moment of Great Light dimmed the flame of their faith? His eyes were drawn to the Kisses they wore, to a man, between their brows — emerald to his rose-amber and seemingly dimmer. They varied, he realized in bemusement. Some were a smudged-looking peridot, others like Calach's and Tynedale's and especially Bevol's —

"Welcome, Osraed Wyth," said Bevol, beginning the formal Pilgrim's Greeting. "The Meri has crowned you with Her Kiss — the culmination of your Journey. Speak to us, Pilgrim, of that Journey."

He did speak — of spiritual trials and tests of wisdom and patience. Of being sent by the Eibhilin Gwenwyvar, the White Wave, to be the easing of a child's pain. And at last, he spoke of reaching the Meri's Shore.

"Indeed you have reached the Shore of faith, Pilgrim," said Bevol. "Indeed you have found the end of the Path of steadfastness. Speak to us, Pilgrim, of your Vigil. What dreams were you given? What visions, what gifts?"

Wyth blushed. "It wasn't much of a vigil," he admitted, and wondered momentarily if they would believe what he had to tell them. But, of course, they had to believe him; he wore the Kiss of the Meri on his brow. "We reached the sands, Prentice Killian and I, and he went to gather firewood. I sat and watched the sun set and recalled a dream I had had once — a horrible, arrogant dream of entering the Meri's Ocean without getting wet. Meredydd told me I had missed the point of my Pilgrimage. I thought of that as I sat there in the sand and laughed at myself." He smiled at the looks of disbelief that admission garnered. Wyth Arundel had laughed at little, once, least of all himself. "I suppose that is one gift I took from the Shore — the gift of laughter. I had no visions."

He paused a moment, then continued. "The sun set and the moon rose over the water — or so I thought. But the moon, I recalled, was behind me in the East and this was the Light of the Eibhilin world — the Light of the Meri. Bright and golden, it came, flooding the water with glory. The Sea was like a golden broth or a cup of spring wine. I could see every pebble beneath the water — jewels, all of them — and garlands of seaweed. And then, the waters began to froth and foam. I thought I would faint, but I didn't. I thought the brilliance would blind me, but it didn't. Then She slipped from the waves and stood before me."

He realized his hands were stretched out toward the Triumvirate — toward its Apex. He lowered them and went on. "Her eyes were like jewels," he said. "Like garnets in the Sun."

"Aaah," said one of the other Osraed, "indeed She has changed Aspect," and others nodded.

"I felt," said Wyth, "as if I knew Her. And of course, I did. I have spent my life learning Her ways and singing her duans and longing for a day when She would give me one of my own. Overwhelmed, I threw myself to the wet sand and . . . She laughed at me." He smiled again, eyes watering. "It was music. And out of the music came Her voice saying, 'Rise, Wyth Arundel. Rise and come to Me.'" He stopped, passing eyes over the faces of his listeners. *Here, now, they will cease to believe me.*

" 'Come to Me'?" repeated Faer-wald. "She bid you come . . . into the water?"

"Those were Her words, Osraed. I spoke them just as I heard them. I swear I will never forget them."

"And . . . did you — ?" Ealad-hach's voice was white as his crown of hair.

"I could scarcely believe I'd heard Her right. I've studied the Pilgrimages all my life. No one has ever been summoned into the waters. I thought She must be tormenting me on account of that dream. So, I asked if She meant I was to come into the Sea. 'The Water of Life, Wyth,' She said and laughed again and said, 'Come into the Water of Life and see if you do not get wet.' I was horrified — certain I must be punished for my arrogance. But She told me that I wasn't arrogant, only ignorant." He chuckled. "I hadn't thought arrogance to be a worse offense, but of course it is. For in ignorance, one simply doesn't know; in arrogance one knows, yet refuses to understand. I understood the Goal, then — the End of Longing: to get wet. To drown in that Water; to absorb that knowledge; to let it permeate every atom. And as I understood that Goal, She held out Her radiant arms to me and I stepped into the Sea."

Ealad-hach gasped, seeming to strangle, momentarily, on the air he breathed. Wyth glanced at him, then went on.

"It was warm. She was warm. Her radiance embraced me, surrounded and engulfed me. Warm as sunlight, comforting, loving. She *is* love!" he added suddenly, his expression going from dreamy to zealous. "We teach laws here and histories and dreams and inyx. I tell you, what we must teach, above all else, that She is love." He paused and looked about at the circle of faces old and older. It had been years since a new Osraed had been willed to Halig-liath. Years since any doctrinal changes had been made. "We must teach that," he repeated and knew Calach would record it faithfully as the first doctrinal utterance of his Mission. "We must make it part of the morning invocation."

"Now," Wyth squared his shoulders and sat as tall as his body would allow. "I am coming to a part of my Tell which . . . " Something like fear fluttered beneath his breast- bone. He must have no fear. He must continue. He must give the whole Tell. He glanced at Ealad-hach, trying to gauge, from the old hawk face, what effect his story was having. But Ealad-hach was little more than a shadow, sitting far back in his tall chair. Wyth looked to Bevol and found an eager gaze. He delivered the rest of his tale directly to Meredydd's Master.

"The Meri held me in Her arms and drew me beneath the waves with Her. And, as they closed over my head, I had no fear. She smiled at me. I couldn't see Her smile, but only feel it. And then, She kissed me . . . first on the lips, then on the brow."

A whisper wafted in a circle about him like an eddy of wind, invisible and cool.

"And She called me Her son."

The wind was sucked from the room leaving it soundless and motionless.

"You — you jest." Ealad-hach half-rose from his place, his hands, on the table, supporting him. "You're playing a game with us. No, testing us. The Meri has commissioned you to test the Osraed."

Wyth shook his head. "No, Osraed Ealad-hach. I do neither."

"This — this is unprecedented!" exclaimed Eadmund. "For centuries the selection of Osraed has followed a prescribed pattern. For *centuries*! Never in the history of the Divine Arts has the Meri drawn an elect into the Sea, never has She kissed him upon the mouth and *never* has She referred to him as Her son! What can you possibly mean by all these things?"

Osraed Bevol rapped quietly on the tabletop, stopping the flow of questions. "We are out of order. Our new brother, Wyth, brings us a Tell that is stunning, to be sure, but we have no reason to doubt his words. Indeed, to do so would be tantamount to sacrilege. It is certain from the reports of both our new Osraed, that the Meri has changed Aspect. I seem to recall that the last such Cusp brought some significant changes in the Laws and Observances."

"But not like this!" objected Eadmund. "This is outrageous!"

"Who are we to judge the Meri's decree outrageous? Look at our young brother, Wyth. Can you doubt that he has been touched by the Meri? Can you doubt that he speaks only what the Meri commissions him to speak?"

The entire assemblage turned, as a man, to peer at the Kiss, brilliant, on Wyth's brow. They could not doubt, and Bevol knew it. The Apex nodded at Wyth. "Tell us, Osraed Wyth, what were the words of the Meri to you after She bestowed Her Kiss?"

"She said, 'Am I not the Mother of Osraed? From this night you are no longer the son of the woman who bore you. This night, you have become my son, for I have given life to your soul.' She did that."

"And did She extract from you any promises?"

"That I would use the knowledge She gave me

well, and . . . " He grinned at the memory, causing several of the Osraed to wriggle uncomfortably. "And that I would learn to laugh."

"And what is your Mission, Wyth Arundel?"

"I am to be attached to Halig-liath. I am to protect the Covenant between man and Meri. I am to bring about certain . . . reforms in Divine Doctrine. I would prefer not to speak of these things until I've rested. I haven't slept for several days — "

"What sort of reforms?" asked Ealad-hach sharply, ignoring Bevol's chairmanship. "Have they do to with admitting cailin to Halig-liath?"

"Ealad, *please!*" Calach stared at his compatriot in bemusement. "The poor boy is exhausted. Look at him. What an experience he has had! He has obviously been singled out for great honor."

But Ealad-hach would not desist. "Does it mean nothing to you that, according to the testimony of Osraed Bevol, Meredydd-a-Lagan entered the Sea as this boy claims to have done? Does it mean nothing to you that I have dreamed of that event?"

"Meredydd?" echoed Wyth as Osraed Tynedale repeated, "Claims?"

Wyth scarcely heard what was said for the next few seconds. He cared only that Osraed Bevol would know what had really happened to Meredydd. "Meredydd was transformed," he murmured, unthinking. "The Meri told me."

They heard him and poured out as astonished a silence as when he had spoken of the Meri kissing his mouth.

"Transformed?" Even in the semi-dark that hovered protectively about his head, Ealad-hach's face was pale. "In what way, transformed?"

Wyth looked to Bevol. "She said you knew, Master. She said if I asked, you would tell me."

Bevol sat placidly at the center of attention, glancing from face to face, his lips not quite smiling, his eyes revealing nothing. "Yes," he said, "I do know. Meredydd-a-Lagan was transmuted into an Eibhilin form. I saw it happen. Skeet saw it happen. Even Gwynet saw it, though

I doubt she understood what she saw, any more than our brother Ealad understands the implications of what he dreamed. I don't doubt the two things are related." Bevol turned his eyes to Wyth then. "I will tell you of Meredydd's last moments on the Meri's Shore, but later, when you are rested. Then we must discuss the changes the Meri wishes to be made here and your inclusion on the Council."

Wyth felt an odd prickle in the core of his mind. "No, Osraed Bevol. I . . . I am not to serve on the Council. I am . . . to be Weard to the Covenant."

"Weard to the Covenant?" repeated Faer-wald. "Why? Why does the Covenant need such protection?"

"It simply does or . . . it will." The prickle was waning. "I'm not sure yet, exactly," Wyth said apologetically. His head dipped in a moment of habitual self-deprecation. "I can only say it will soon become clear."

"What is clear," said Osraed Faer-wald later, "is that we are once more at a Cusp. A dangerous Cusp." He shook his shaggy, greying head and watched the first-year students scurry cross-court toward the Refectory for the afternoon meal. "The Meri has changed again — in both Aspect and behavior. Such a change is always accompanied by calamity."

"Surely knowing that, we can do something to ameliorate it," suggested Eadmund. "Isn't that most likely to be our role in this — to discern where the tests lie and to rise to them? Imagine, brothers, what blessings would be forthcoming if we can but successfully navigate this treacherous period."

"What?" asked Ealad-hach peevishly. He rubbed his temples and cringed from the glare of sun in the cobbled yard below. "Blessings? How can you see blessings in this situation?"

"I've studied the past Cusps," Eadmund began.

"As we all have," interjected Faer-wald.

"Of course, but I think we must dimly understand their significance. You say that changes in the Meri's Aspect have always been accompanied by dire calamities. Why so? In Cyne Earwyn's time the reason was obvious. He had engaged in war against the Deasach. Cyne Liusadhe wrought unjust vengeance on the innocent kinsman of a traitor."

"And," said Faer-wald, "lest we forget, the Osraed had so completely lost the spark of their purpose that the Meri caused nearly every one of them to be replaced."

"Are you suggesting that's happened again?" asked the Osraed Kynan.

Eadmund shook his head. "No, but we must consider our own responsibility for this event, if we have one. Have the Osraed displeased the Meri in some way — angered the God that sent Her? Or is the problem somewhere else — among the people, within the other arms of government, perhaps? Consider the reports we've heard from Creiddylad. Consider how the Cyne has repeatedly postponed the General Assembly. Isn't it possible we are being warned of some calamity arising from evil elsewhere so that we might take some action? Or that the whole thing is a test of our spiritual awareness? These things are not mutually exclusive. And consider this: if the Meri was displeased with us, surely She would simply tell us through Her new elect. Yet, She has chosen two Osraed this season and has warned neither of any such displeasure — "

"Ah," interrupted Faer-wald, "but that's not strictly true. She did express displeasure with the socio-economic situation in Creiddylad and is sending Lealbhallain-mac-Mercer there to look into it. And, dare I say it, She is obviously desirous of having female Prentices at Halig-li-ath — though why She should wait all this time — "

Kynan waved that aside. "Obviously, women haven't had the capacity until now, regardless of what men like Osraed Bevol say. I want to hear Eadmund's point."

"My point is that these Cusps, these periods of difficulty, must be tests, otherwise the Meri would simply and forthrightly tell us what was Her will. The fact that there is any mystery at all supports the idea that we are being willfully placed in a position wherein we must fall back on our spiritual resources." He glanced about at his listeners for approval and Ealad-hach gave it.

"Osraed Eadmund is right. This outrageous claim of

Wyth's can only be understood in that light. Sonship — what is that? A concept without precedent. The Meri is, Herself, the offspring of God. What can it possibly mean to say that Wyth is *Her* son — that he is God's grandson? Pah!" He gave his temples one last impatient shove, then lowered his hands almost forcibly, shaking the sleeves of his robe down over them. "What disturbs me most, Osraed, what troubles my soul day and night, is that these Cusps always involve women. *Always*. Every time a female goes to the Sea, there is calamity. I have dreamed of an entire train of women, going back to antiquity, who have visited the Shore. Some were convicted of the Wicke-craft by the highest courts of the land, and yet marched themselves down to the Sea to wait for the Holy One. Night after night, I see them. Condemned by the very act of taking Pilgrimage without leave of —"

"Except for Meredydd-a-Lagan," murmured Eadmund.

"What?"

"Except for Meredydd-a-Lagan, who took her Pilgrimage *with* the permission of the Osraed Council." His eyes were back-lit with hope. "This is significant, brothers. I know it is! Don't you see? Women have gone to the Sea without sanction, without permit, and calamity has always followed. But this time, a cailin went forth with the agreement of the Council, if not," he added, glancing at Ealad-hach, "the blessing of all its members, and almost in response, we are suddenly to be instructed to enroll women at Halig-liath."

"Meredydd-a-Lagan *died* in the commission of heresy," said Ealad-hach. His voice was a dry old rope, twisted and frayed.

The others glanced at him and tried not to show their discomfort at his open denial of Wyth's Tell.

"Are we to take the position, then, that Wyth Arundel and Bevol are lying?" Osraed Faer-wald's broad brow wrinkled ferociously. He shook his head. "No. No, it's inconceivable. An Osraed lie?"

"An Osraed can be misled by strong emotions. Bevol is an old man — not as old as I, to be sure, but old. He has lost his wife, his child, and a Prentice who was like a daughter to him."

Faer-wald waved his hands as if to ward off the thoughts his crony was voicing. "No, Ealad, I reject that. I *reject* it. Bevol may be aging, but I will not swear that he is tetched. And Wyth is fresh from the Meri's touch. Her Kiss is almost unbearably luminous on him. How can you accuse him —"

"I do not accuse him," said Ealad-hach testily. "And you're right, of course. It is inconceivable that one of us should lie. No, we must assume that Wyth is giving the Meri's Tell. What we must use all our resources to determine is what that Tell means. We must pray, brothers. We must pray for guidance. Our brother Bevol is right in one thing: we cannot suffer this evil to remain faceless. We must name it before we can fight it."

Eyes closed, the Osraed Wyth savored the caress of wind on his face. Laden with the spices of the river and the silken cool of approaching autumn, it teased and tempted him. He could smell the Backstere's; he could taste the river. He opened his eyes and let them wander the long, high, verdant valley — a bed of green velvet upon which the Halig-tyne and her sentinel woods lay like a necklace of emeralds and silver.

"I feel as if I've been gone a lifetime," he said. "I think I half expected to come home to find my house empty and Halig-liath covered with vines. I thought everything would be changed."

Beside him Bevol smiled and leaned elbows on the sun-warmed parapet. "Everything *is* changed, Wyth, because you are changed."

Wyth followed his elder's gaze to the bottom of Halig-liath's great mount where the Holy River wound about its base, and where, bright-hued and clean, the doll-sized houses of Nairne cheerfully cluttered her banks. He felt as if he could reach down and snatch that villager just leaving the tavern. Snatch him up and plop him down onto the deck of one of those little, toy fishing boats bobbing along the quay.

"That isn't enough. Not for Her. Not for the Meri. She wants Halig-liath to change — and soon. She wants the order of things to change."

"You will give a full account tomorrow, if you are able."

"Will I also give the Pilgrim's Tell before Cyne Colfre at Mertuile? Or will he send his ambassador up again this year?"

"Ah." Bevol's gaze went down the river and out to Sea, making Wyth suspect he could see all the way to Creiddylad. "Well, as a matter of fact, we have heard nothing from our Cyne about this year's Grand Tell. A message from the Privy Council told us only that our monarch is involved in delicate negotiations with a delegation from the South. That the royal Court may not receive us again this year. There was no mention of any ambassador. I believe you will have to give the Tell to only these hallowed walls and the good citizens of Nairne village." His hands gestured up and back toward the Fortress above them, then swept the panorama below. "If you've no objection, the Osraed Council favors this coming Cirke-dag. Lealbhallain is eager to be off on his mission."

"I'm agreeable," Wyth said. "Will you now tell me about Meredydd?"

Bevol did not take his eyes from the valley. "When you are more rested."

"Please, sir. Don't put me off. I want to know."

Bevol glanced at him askew, then nodded. "Very well. I will tell you of her last moments, as I promised." He took a deep breath. "Come into my sanctum and I will Weave it for you."

Wyth followed the older Osraed back along the parapet and into the cliff face through a doorway laboriously hewn there centuries before. There had been colorful little tiles around it once, but they had discolored in high wind and hard winter or fallen away.

Through dim, cool passages smelling of earth musk and time, Bevol led the way to his private chambers, the place he studied and wove inyx, prayed and meditated. With a tingle of delicious longing, Wyth knew he would soon have such a place of his own. He ran a hand along the cool walls — walls that had seen the passage of hundreds of Osraed and felt the caress of their fingers as they went to and fro in the Holy Fortress's secret heart of hearts.

It was to a circular inner chamber within his offices that Bevol led his guest — a room that took light from a series of arcing shafts cut through the native stone above, and ending high on the roof top of the Academy's South Wing. Light cascaded down the paneled walls, leaving the core of the little cell in partial darkness. A palpable darkness, Wyth thought, that seemed to pace the heart of the chamber like a restive cat.

"Please sit," invited Bevol, and Wyth did, finding the padded bench about the perimeter of the circle a more than adequate perch.

Seating himself, Bevol placed something on the floor at the heart of the living darkness and sat back, his eyes on the spot. It was a crystal. One of the largest, clearest crystals Wyth had ever seen — a crystal that seemed to suck the timid light away from the safety of the walls to trap it within.

"I have already described Meredydd's Pilgrimage to you. She did well, though she didn't know it. She chose wisdom as her guide, found the Gwenwyvar, saved Gwynet-a-Blaecdel from certain destruction and found, in herself, the ability to channel healing. Yet, her greatest test came during her vigil."

Bevol's hands moved, drawing Wyth's attention down to the great, clear stone. The thick, light-spangled darkness around it began to eddy. "It was a long, difficult vigil, tested by wind and rain. She confronted loss, guilt, vengeance, self-loathing and love. Do you see her waiting, Wyth?"

"Yes!" he whispered and didn't lie. In the darkness before him, she sat, woven from the warp of the crystal and the woof of Bevol's mind. She sat conversing with ghosts, consorting with her own spirit, expelling her own demons. He saw her mother and father in the parade of wraiths. He saw himself.

"She fought her own exhaustion and lost; she fought a storm to a draw. And when it was over, when she thought herself lost, the Light came into the water. She had been preparing to leave, but there the Meri was."

"Green!" exclaimed Wyth softly. "The Light is emerald

green. Leal went the next week and said it was amber. It was amber when I went."

"So it was. . . . Watch." Bevol directed his gaze back to the pool of vision. "The Light excited Meredydd beyond joy and she leapt up to see if Skeet was watching her Great Moment. But Skeet was watching naught but his own soul slip away."

Wyth could see the boy as Meredydd had seen him, face down in the shallows like a sodden doll. He felt the tearing of her spirit between the advancing Light and the boy's advancing darkness. He watched her make a choice of which he could only say that it was just like her — just like her to use every ounce of herself in one inyx. To sing all of her soul into one duan. Huddled over Skeet's limp form, she drew Light from the ether and poured it into his failing heart. Then she breathed life into his lungs.

Wyth was amazed to the core. If he had always known Meredydd-a-Lagan was exceptional, he had never suspected she was invested with that powerful a Gift. "But . . . " he whispered, "only an Osraed can restore life, and even then . . . Has she been accepted without ever having seen the Meri?" He shook his head and spread his fingers toward the aislinn pool in a gesture of bemusement. "What am I seeing?"

"A birth," said Bevol. "Watch. What do you see?"

He saw a darkened empty strand and felt his spirit fall heavily. "The Light is gone. The Meri has abandoned her."

"Ah," breathed Bevol. "Ah, but see — she returns to her post. Steadfast, disciplined, she waits once more until . . . "

Until she began to shift uneasily in the sand and rub at her arms as if chilled or in some other discomfort. Until the chafing became fevered and turned to anguished clawing. Until scrapes and scraps and ribbons of cloth began to come away in her hands and fall to the sand. Until there was no cloth left to rend.

Horrified, heart plummeting from throat to stomach, Wyth watched the aislinn Meredydd shred first her clothes, then her flesh until . . . until . . .

He was astonished and ashamed, rocked by waves of wonder and fear. Her naked, golden radiance was beyond beauty, as if, with clouds torn back, he glimpsed a corner of heaven. He felt as if he had stolen a look at God's face. No, not *God's* face, but . . .

Wyth's breath caught in his lungs as the golden, gleaming Being that had been Meredydd-a-Lagan stepped into a Sea that throbbed with emerald glory to meet a second Eibhilin creature face to face. Together, arm in radiant arm, they slid beneath the waves.

Wyth dared breathe, the air leaving his body reluctantly as if it might never return. "Then it's true. Meredydd is a Being of Light — one with — "

Bevol raised a hand. "But it's not over. Watch."

The waters within Bevol's aislinn pool of tame darkness pulsed and flickered with ghostly lightnings of gold and green. Then, from the roiled brilliance stepped a Being of verdant luminosity. She came to shore, losing her radiance drop by drop until she stood in naked humanity, peering out of the vision pool with laughing green eyes.

"Oh, Master Bevol," she said, "I haven't breathed in a hundred years!"

The image floated, static, the words echoing softly from the girl's parted lips while over one white shoulder, Wyth glimpsed a Face in the gleaming waves — a Face of holy flame with garnets for eyes. His senses blew past the already fading image of the strange cailin and collected themselves before that Face, clinging until nothing remained but translucent darkness, prowling in silent circles like a black cat seeking a resting place. And Wyth sat watching it, waiting for his soul to return from a journey it hadn't, perhaps, been ready to take.

Bevol leaned toward him across the circle. "What did you see?" the elder Osraed asked, eyes tight and watchful.

"A birth," said Wyth. "I believe I have seen a birth."

Bevol nodded. "Of more than you know."

Wyth at last made his eyes focus on the other's face. "Then . . . " Dare he put it into words? "Then Meredydd has become . . . the Meri?"

Bevol smiled. "Essentially correct. She hosts the Meri's

Spirit and gives substance to Her Essence."

"But this is what Osraed Ealad-hach has dreamed, is it not?"

"Yes."

"*He* believes it is death."

Again Bevol nodded. "It is that, too," he said.

He was utterly exhausted by the time he reached Arundel. Exhausted and overwhelmed by his new knowledge. There were still things he didn't understand; who the girl was that came out of the Sea as Meredydd entered it; how Ealad-hach could find so much to fear in the idea that a female might be Osraed; and how he had not recognized Meredydd in the Meri when he saw Her. Dear God, when She kissed him!

What was he to do now, he puzzled. In light of all he knew, what must his next task be? She would tell him, of course. He knew that as surely as he knew he breathed. But his certitude was underpinned with white terror; given what he now knew, what would the touch of the Meri's spirit feel like when it next came over him?

It was darkening as Killian, in his last task as Wyth's Weard, drove the new Osraed out to his family estate. No longer bored, the younger boy was still agog with the events he had witnessed. He would return to his own family and regale his relations and friends with tales of how a great, gleaming creature plucked Wyth from the beach and attempted to devour him. But he would have to give his tell soon, for every night of sleep would separate him further from the already corrupted memory. In a week he would remember the Pilgrimage as only marginally eventful and pray his would be more spectacular.

Deposited before Arundel Manor, Wyth stood and listened to the creak and rattle of the Nairne-bound carriage. He stood, staring at the house's brick facade as a moon peeked shyly over the eastern hills. Dim lights went on in several first floor windows, dashing his hopes that his mother might not be at home. He inhaled deeply of the cool, fragrant air and followed Killian's progress across the Bridge to Lagan.

His errant thought of Meredydd he withered where it bloomed, ears groping for the rush of the Halig-tyne. She crooned in sweet sibilance, pulling his thoughts away downstream to wash them.

Wyth stirred and considered picking up his pack and opening the door. But the door was already opening, he realized, and he stood, dumb, peering into the dark entry way.

"Who is it, please?" asked a familiar, scratchy voice, then, "Oh, but it's Master Wyth — oh!" And the manservant ran, leaving the door wide open.

Smiling, Wyth shouldered his pack and stepped inside, closing the heavy carved door behind him. The hall was dim, lit only by the wicks of two floor lamps on either side of the stair. The servants hadn't gotten to lighting the door lamps yet, nor any of the upstairs lights, it seemed. But the dark was soothing to Wyth. It was muted, peaceful. He desired peace and quiet above all things just now.

He was not to have it. He was at the center of the large entry when the servant reappeared from the direction of the dining chamber, followed closely by the Moireach Arundel.

"Wyth! Wyth, you're home! Dear God!" She slipped past the ogling servant and hurried to her son's side. Her eyes went at once to his forehead and read his success. She stopped, hands hovering halfway to her mouth, eyes huge and flowing with a slurry of swift-passing emotions. Wyth could not read any of them with external senses, yet knew them to be ambiguous.

Pride won out, and the Moireach waved at the gawping manservant. "Lights, Adken! Lights! All must see my son's triumph!"

It was then that Wyth realized Adken was not alone in the dining room doorway. Silhouetted there were at least five other individuals who must have been dining with his mother.

That lady was beside herself with excitement. And, as the wicks' glow brightened the entry way, Wyth found himself surrounded by family and friends. He was overwhelmed once again. Deluged in their expressions of delight and amazement. It took him a moment to realize that he was being overwhelmed by more than the mere expression of those things. Deep inside, a door had opened, allowing their emotions to walk through his soul.

Agape, he stood, fielding this one's awe and that one's astonishment that someone *they* knew could have possibly seen the Meri. His eldest sister's jealousy cut through all, tormenting him; her pledge-bond's amazement was tinged with disbelief. Neither of them, he realized, had expected him to come home an Osraed. As for his mother . . . He looked at her beaming face with its glittering eyes and marveled at how pride and grief could dwell together behind that facade. He had won her an honor; he had lost his family an heir.

"Oh, do come join us, dear Wyth!" she gushed, tugging at his arm. "Do tell us all about it."

"Yes, indeed," agreed one of the male guests — the Eiric of Cinfhaolaidh. "It'd be a rare experience to hear of a Pilgrimage from the lips of the newly chosen! Was it near as magical as they say, or is that all myth?"

Wyth's sister, Brann, laughed brittlely. "Myth, I'd wager. What of it, Wyth? What's the Meri like?"

Gazing around at the circle of expectant faces, Wyth was torn. For several of his mother's guests this was a matter of faith, for others it was merely a matter of entertainment.

"Come Wyth," said his sister, her eyes over-bright. "Come, boast to us of your exploits along the Pilgrim's path."

Rousing from what must seem to all like a stupor, Wyth smiled at her, ignoring the acid in her voice. "I've nothing to boast of, Brann," he said. "But I would gladly answer your questions were I not so weary. I give the Pilgrim's Tell with Lealbhallain-mac-Mercer next Cirke-dag at Halig-li-ath."

"What? You'd make us wait? How terribly rude."

"I'm merely tired, Brann. Please, return to your supper. I crave rest more than food right now."

Brann, on her betrothed's arm, laughed and tossed black curls. "Yes, do sleep, Wyth. You look that ragged. Perhaps you'll be up for it tomorrow and can tell us all at breakfast. I suppose the rest of you will have to be content with seeing the Kiss." She bobbed her head toward the others, then drew her pledge-bond away, jealousy passing as she began to consider what advantage might come to the sister of an Osraed. The other guests followed.

Wyth felt his spirit sag, pulling his shoulders and the corners of his wide mouth down with it.

"Well." The Moireach, his mother, still stood beside him. "I *am* disappointed that you couldn't be persuaded to give a special Tell to our dear friends. But I suppose if you're *that* tired . . . " She shrugged, her eyes searching his face with an odd mixture of hope and reproach.

"Thank you for being so understanding, mother. I'll no doubt see you in the morning." *And by then I'll have decided how much not to tell you.* Hefting his pack, he started for the stairs, wondering at how heavy it suddenly seemed.

Adken was at his side in an instant. "Do let me carry that for you, Master. Are you hungry? Shall I bring you up a tray? I'd be *most* happy if you'd allow me that. Oh, and some hot tea. That'll be wanted, I'm sure. Nothing like hot tea to soothe the wearies. Oh, it's good to see you, Master, and none too soon. We knew you'd make it this time, the wife and I. Surely we did. Said some special prayers at Cirke, too. Oh, it's a great day, it is. A *great* day! Those who didn't believe, sir, they'll swallow a bitter pill, indeed."

A great day, thought Wyth, as Adken prattled on about their faith in him. It was a real faith, the new Osraed marveled. He could put out mental fingers and touch it, hold it, feel the strength and weight of it. A great day, yes. But still, a day he wished, desperately, would end.

Alone in his room, he lit a candle and sat on the bed to meditate. He did not think about how different he felt from the last time he'd sat in this room. He did not think about how different his homecoming had been from the way he'd imagined it. He did not ponder his time with Osraed Bevol in the dark aislinn chamber. Instead, he stared at the dancing flame and tried to meditate upon the Meri.

In a moment he was all chagrin. How could he meditate

upon Her without *thinking* about Her, without *feeling* about Her what he now felt. Love. Love entangled with love. He loved the Meri and he loved Meredydd, who had become the Meri. And now they refused to be separated. They could *not* be separated. Or, if they could, he did not know how. He thought of Her and felt the rise of more than spiritual devotion.

No wonder the gleaming face had seemed familiar. My God, how could he have not known who faced him in that trembling water? How could he have kissed her lips — Her lips! — and not known at once, that She was Meredydd? *The lover and the Beloved have become one in Thee.* What a unique truth that verse now held for one Wyth Arundel. It was his last conscious thought before he slept, falling over into the down mattress and giving up his exhaustion in prayer as he gave up prayer in exhaustion.

He woke some hours later, feeling as if someone had summoned him to consciousness. The candle had burned nearly in half. He extinguished it entirely. He felt it then, as he settled himself into the warm, close darkness. He felt the tears of the woman in the suite of rooms above. Tears, not of thanks-giving, nor of motherly loss, nor of swelling pride. There were selfish tears, tinted red by a sense of martyrdom. How great was her sacrifice, how ungrateful his pursuit of the spiritual, when she had struggled to give him everything material.

Sadness brushed over him like a veil of spider-silk — clinging, but lightly — and he marvelled with a strange, detached awe. How had he lived in this house for eighteen years and never known how much bitterness it contained?

CHAPTER 4

Fire is not seen in wood, yet by some power it comes to light as fire. In such a way the Spirit of the Universe and in man is revealed by the power of Its Word.

— Prayers and Meditations of Osraed Ochan, Number Four

✧　✧　✧

The breeze was from the high passes of the Gyldan-baenn this evening, and carried in its perfect cool a tang of pine and heath. Summer waned quickly, evening by evening, welcoming the long autumn. Wyth welcomed it too, as part of the experience he was about to embrace. Standing upon the ageless battlements of Halig-liath, he inhaled the fragrances that eddied up from the great courtyard below — smells of baps baked only minutes ago and trundled up the road from Nairne, and sweet porridges and stews, and meats turning slowly over pits of blazing rock. There were sounds to be drunk, as well, of laughter, song, the tuning of pipes, the shouts of neighbor to neighbor from stall to stall.

Halig-liath had sprouted this day a great village bazaar; ringed round in the shadow of the great walls were the booths and wagons of Nairne's merchants, craftsmen and artisans, all preparing to do their part in the celebration of the Pilgrim's Tell. For when the ceremonials were over and the rituals fulfilled, the celebrants would flood the courtyard to eat and drink, dance and sing and tell stories through the night.

Did I ever believe this day would be mine? Wyth caressed the horizon with his eyes, drinking in the deep greens, the winy reds and violets, growing intoxicated and flushed.

He jumped when someone tapped his arm.

A small third year Prentice he recognized from his Dream Tell class bobbed awfully at his elbow, eyes drawn to his forehead. The boy blinked repeatedly, ducking his head in reverence. "Osraed Wyth, it's time," he said. "The pipers are ready and your robes are laid out."

Wyth smiled and nodded, giving the worn parapet a loving pat. Ruanaidhe's Leap they called this spot. It was a point of tragic history, but Wyth could not find it in himself to feel tragic. Tonight, his own history would be forever woven into the stones of Halig-liath.

He followed the Prentice down from the wall and back across the cobbled yard, wending behind kiosks and wagons to the Academy's rounded central structure. Glowing orbs lit the hallways with warm gilded light; musicians gathered in noisy knots here and there and gave him glances eloquent with amazement.

They're more excited than I am, he thought and wondered at that. He had in the last hours welcomed into himself a great and alien contentment. He savored it, yet knew it to be momentary. He wondered if it would last the night.

Osraed Calach and Lealbhallain (*Osraed* Lealbhallain, by the Kiss!) awaited him in a small annex to Halig-liath's sanctum. One paced, the other smiled contentedly.

"Ah, there you are, Wyth!" Calach's smile expanded to embrace him in warm welcome, while his Prentice-companion scurried to fetch his robe. Like Leal's, it was a deep, ruddy gold.

Beautiful, he thought. *Beautiful, but faded-looking compared to —*

"Will this night *never* end?" Lealbhallain ceased his pacing and stood, worrying his prayer chain, eyes on a window of frosted and colored glass through which he could see nothing but patterns of fitful light.

Calach laughed. "Dear boy, it's barely begun."

"Why beg it end?" asked Wyth, shrugging into his robe. "Isn't this the night of nights? Isn't this to be savored? Remembered?"

Leal's hands flung upward, flying from his voluminous

sleeves like flushed birds. "It's only a doorway, Osraed Wyth. A passing point." He speared his fellow Chosen with zealous eyes. "I long to be through the door, past the point, on my way to Creiddylad."

"Ah, yes." Calach nodded approvingly, bustling to straighten Wyth's white stole and arrange the links of his prayer chain upon it. "An arduous mission you have drawn, Leal, if I read news from Creiddylad right. I admire your zeal for it."

"It's not zeal," said Leal oddly, turning the pendant crystal of his chain in one hand. He glanced back at the window. "It's fear."

Calach made a quick and nearly indiscernible gesture to the attending Prentice to take up his slate and bluestick. "Fear of what?" he asked, while Wyth could only stand idly by, his mouth open. A sudden, prickling awareness told him another Presence had slipped into the room; Lealbhallain was brushing the Meri.

"Disintegration," Leal answered then said, "The hand that caresses keeps what it holds; the hand that seizes, crushes what it hopes to mold."

They waited silently, all of them, while the Prentice's bluestick skittered over its slate. Then Leal shook himself and stared full into Wyth's face. Amazement. The smile started tentatively and spread to his entire body, freckle by freckle.

Only puppies smile so, thought Wyth, then chided himself for the inane thought.

Before he knew what was happening, they were in the hall again and stepping in measured time to the courtyard.

Awash in a swirl of sights and sounds and smells she'd never before experienced, Gwynet clung to Taminy's hand and tried to drink everything in. When she thought her eyes could get no wider and her senses could not absorb one more fragrance or sound, the bells of Halig-liath began to peal and sing in a great, iron-throated chorus.

She cried out, but the sound of her small voice was lost as it left her lips, swallowed in the deep, bright music. The air shivered with it, and all around her, people began to hurry to places about the courtyard's vast, open center.

Taminy tugged at her hand and bent to peer down into her flushed face, her own all but concealed by the cowl of her shawl and the bright scarf tied over her forehead. "Shall we find a place to watch, Gwyn?" she asked and Gwynet could only nod.

The place Taminy chose was away from the pressing throng of villagers, halfway up a worn flight of stone steps that mounted to the walk along the inside of the high outer wall. From this vantage point, Gwynet's eyes could scoop up their share of wonders.

The bells ceased their lusty duan now, and a new, alien sound rose in its wake. From a stone arch across the yard and halfway down Halig-liath's massive flank, pipers appeared, two abreast, stepping in time to the deep, hollow rhythm of unseen drums. Gwynet all but held her breath as piper after piper emerged from the archway to parade down the center of the court. They were escorted, in their turn, by other musicians, playing feidhle, drum and pat-a-pat, rib-stick and tambourine.

Gwynet had never in her life heard such a sound. It was like the keening of wind in the tall pines. It was like the march of thunder across the hills and the music of rain on leaf and stone. And the melody was at once joyful and sad and spritely and grand.

It took her a moment to realize the tune was playing closer at hand, as well. She glanced up at Taminy, who sang along in a clear voice, adding words to the music, her eyes glinting from the shadow of her cowl.

Caught in this, the older girl lowered her eyes and laughed. "I once was certain as certain could be that they'd play this song for me when I came home from the Sea. That I'd step to the piper's duan with the Meri's Kiss on my brow. How strange life is." She laughed again and stroked Gwynet's hair. "Listen well, Gwynet-a-Gled. That may be *your* tune someday, and your dance." Her hand measured the two long rows of musicians that now formed a euphonious avenue down the center of the Great Court, ending before the broad steps that mounted to the Osraed Gallery.

Gwynet turned her eyes to that path and imagined that what Taminy said might be true — that she might someday be accepted by the Meri. She took the idea into her heart. Taminy had come from the Meri's Sea, she reasoned. Taminy must possess the Meri's wisdom. She didn't understand all she'd heard of Eibhilin Beings and transformations or all she'd seen on a beach not that long ago, but she did understand that Taminy-a-Cuinn was like no one else in the worlds of Blaec-del or Nairne.

She watched and listened with fascination as the pipers and drummers and feidhlers faced each other down the court and began a new melody. From the stone arch came Prentices carrying glowing orbs of liquid flame mounted on tall, finely carved poles. There were six of them, and in their midst were the new Osraed — Wyth, the Tall and Spare; Lealbhallain, the Small and Freckled. The two walked together, down the avenue of song, in step with their escort. At the end of their walk, they mounted to the Osraed Gallery and were greeted by the men who had been their masters and were now their peers.

The crowd below Gwynet's perch burst into noisy celebration. Grown men capered like boys; old women twirled like maidens on a dancing green, their bright skirts and panel coats sailing about them on the air. Osraed Bevol took some time to quiet them; Gwynet thought he must be enjoying the sight of all those souls acting out childways, swarmed by bright light. But at last they did hush, their attention soaring to the glowing Gallery where Osraed, new and old, collected.

Now Gwynet's ears were stormed by silence, for every man, woman, child and babe within the hallowed walls hushed to stone stillness. It seemed they must even have ceased to breathe and, so, did Gwynet.

"At dawn," the Osraed Bevol said, and his voice rang clear as the bells, "we walked with the Spirit of the Universe." All heard the words, even Gwynet high on her stair. The drummers punctuated them with a beat that rolled off the stone walls like a single clap of thunder. The silence after shivered in the air.

Again, Bevol spoke. "We heard the Words of Creation

from the Spirit's own Mouth and we listened and understood."

Again, the drums sounded.

"The Spirit also listened. It heard the desire of its creation and the wants of man and woman, and It gave them their desire."

The drums spat thunder.

"What was their desire?" Bevol asked.

Below him, the crowd answered in one voice. "Knowledge!"

The drums rolled.

"And pleased, the Spirit gave them knowledge, which they used to bring them other things. And knowledge became a spirit to them, and the people asked that spirit for providence."

The drums uttered a single word.

"What did they ask of Knowledge?"

The crowd cried: "Give-us-land. Give-us-commerce. Give-us-power!"

The drums issued a long roll.

"And the people gathered those things and set them up as spirits and asked happiness of them and joy of them and wealth of them. And surrounded by these, their made spirits, they could no longer hear the Voice of the Spirit of All."

The drums beat a swift measure of staccato notes, while the crowd wailed a high, ululating cry as if singing for the war-dead. Gwynet had not heard that sound before, though she had heard of it from those who had lost loved ones to the sea missions of the Cynes Ciarda and Colfre. It made her shiver all the way to the marrow of her bones and pray for it to stop.

When it did stop, Bevol spoke again. "The Spirit of the Universe looked upon Its silent creation and said, 'My lovers no longer hear My Voice and they no longer call Me Beloved. But I shall be patient. For someday they will call upon Me.'"

The drums spoke their turn.

"And when the people at last tired of praying to their made spirits for things they had no power to give, when they longed, at last, for their God, they cried out to It and listened for reply, but no longer did their hearts speak the same pure tongue they had spoken at Dawn. They could not hear their God, and the Universe was silent to them."

As silent as it was now, Gwynet thought, for not a person in all that vast assemblage stirred, not a mallet fell, not a pipe sang.

"And out of the silence," said Bevol, "was born the Meri — the Spirit of the Spirit of the Universe, Gate between God and Man, Bridge between Heaven and Earth. And God brought Her forth from the Sea to touch man and teach him again to hear the Voice that speaks in the heart of all things."

There was a great celebratory roar then, from throats and drums and pipes alike, and the little old Osraed, Calach (the Sweet, Gwynet called him), came forward to give the Tell of the First Pilgrimage.

Gwynet knew this part — by heart, she was pleased to discover — and followed along, mouthing the words as Calach told the tale of Ochan-a-Coille and the First Weaving. In the swell of light and soft pipe-song, she could see the young boy wandering storm-lost along the rocky cliffs below the mouth of the Halig-tyne, longing for sight of the Castle Mertuile. She felt his terror as he fell into the sea cave, shared his awe when a strange light revealed that the walls of the cave were studded with crystals and that glittering shards lay scattered like unmelting frost upon the rocky floor. Her heart hammered fiercely when the boy took, in his own hands, a blue-white crystal of such clarity and beauty that he was all but blinded by the light that pulsed through it. She cried out aloud with mixed terror and wonder when an Eibhilin Being lifted Itself from the sea pool in the cavern's deep heart and glided to meet Ochan where he stood, crystal in hand, in the star-littered shallows.

Ochan, just fifteen, left the Sea Cave with the Meri's duan singing in his heart and the knowledge of the Runeweave filling his mind to overflowing. Her Kiss glowed upon his brow, Her mission in his soul. He carried his crystal, Osmaer, to the

stronghold of Cyne Malcuim and there gave the first
Pilgrim's Tell.

Osraed Calach's sweet voice rang off on the breeze and
the crowd remained silent. Gwynet felt her cheeks. They
were hot, surely putting out as much light as the myriad
lightbowls on their tall stands. She told herself, secretly, it
was her future she listened to as first Lealbhallain, then
Wyth came forward to give his Tell. The people of Nairne
applauded the wonderful tales with every ounce of
exuberance they possessed. By the time Wyth retired from
the Gallery's balustrade, every man, woman and child was
bubbling over with the spirit of celebration. It only
remained for Ealad-hach to bless them and dismiss them
to the Tell Fest.

He came forward to do so, raised his hands high,
opened his mouth wide and was pressed to silence by a
great commotion at the foot of the Gallery stair. The crowd
there gabbled and milled, the musicians parted, and a
slight figure in a tapestry riot of color scurried up the steps
toward the landing.

"Osraed!" The voice was as strident as the colors its
owner wore. A white hand thrust out of the raucous folds
of fabric and pointed heavenward. "Osraed, hear me!" The
figure tottered to a point just below where an incredulous
Ealad-hach gaped, then turned and addressed the gathering.

"Hearken all, to old Marnie! Hear what I say! These
boys are not the only home-comers here. Ask the Osraed
Bevol and he may tell you of another."

A clutter of murmurs, hisses and guffaws spilled
through the crowd and Osraed Ealad-hach at last lowered
his arms. "What are you saying, old woman? Speak clearly."

"Ah, clearly, is it? I'll tell you clearly what I saw. Me,
Marnie-o-Loom! In the garden at Gled Manor."

Gwynet felt Taminy stiffen and clutch the hand she
held. The older girl made a hissing sound through her
teeth. "Ah," she breathed, "so yours are the curious eyes,
old one. Sharp, they are."

Marnie's audience heckled her now — gently, tolerantly
— and begged her down.

"Leave off, Marnie!" cried Niall Backstere. "Let us get to Fest and I'll give you the fattest cream bonny in my stall."

"Aye, and hot, honeyed cider," added the Spenser.

"I saw the girl, I tell you." Marnie folded her hands before her, smug-meek.

"What girl?" "Aw, she's drunk!" "No, crazy."

"I'm neither drunk nor crazy," Marnie retorted, pose shifting to the defensive. "Nor am I blind. The night Osraed Bevol came in from Meredydd-a-Lagan's Pilgrimage, he had with him a boy, a little girl, and a young woman. The same young woman I saw in his garden not a day past. Meredydd-a-Lagan doesn't lie in the Sea. She *hides* at Gled Manor!"

In the uproar that followed, Marnie-o-Loom fed and flourished; turning her flushed face and glittering eyes upward to the Gallery she devoured her reward.

It was Ealad-hach who turned to Osraed Bevol and asked, "Is there any truth to what she says?" And the citizens of Nairne, catching, one by one, the scent of suspense, quieted to hear the answer.

Bevol smiled. "There is a grain of truth to it." The admission fattened Marnie's grin. "I did," he continued, when the crowd had hushed again, "bring home to Nairne a boy. That was Skeet. You all know Skeet. And I brought home a little girl — Gwynet, whom you also know. And . . . " He gazed around with gleaming eyes until he found Taminy and Gwynet on their stone perch. The smile deepened. "And I brought home with me a young woman."

Again, Marnie reaped her pandemonium, her own gap-tooth smile growing to cover half her face.

"But it was not Meredydd-a-Lagan."

Disappointment. Gwynet felt it the way one feels river rheum or salt tang. It swelled from the crowd like a midnight mist, and she could only wonder at its cause. Had they loved Meredydd-a-Lagan so? Or was it only the sport they missed of scandal close to home? Looking at Marnie, she could almost imagine the Mam of her once-guardian,

Ruhf Airdsgainne, gossip-tongued and mugging — holding out some sinful morsel while the bored dwellers in Blaec-del snapped after it. Could these people from the clean, proud streets of Nairne be at all like those people?

"He lies!" accused Marnie as if the words had been perched on her lips. She let them fly again. "He lies!"

Bevol's expression lost its good humor in a breath. "I do not lie, weaver-woman. The girl at Gled Manor is not my Prentice Meredydd."

"Who then?" asked Ealad-hach and, "Come," said Calach, "stop teasing us and let us meet this young woman."

"Yes," agreed Marnie, nodding vigorously. "If it's not Meredydd, prove it. Show her to us."

Bevol turned to his peers. The Osraed on the Gallery nodded as a man. He returned the nod and looked to where Gwynet and Taminy sat hunkered against the wall. Taminy rose and, drawing Gwynet after her, left the stone steps and crossed to the Gallery. The throng parted before them, eyes probing and curious, eyes hungry and willing to be scandalized. Gwynet glanced up once or twice, then thought better of it.

They passed Marnie on the Great Stair and Taminy paused to greet her eye to eye. "Your sight is sharp, Marnie-o-Loom," Taminy told her, "but your sense of color is failing. Meredydd's eyes are brown."

They continued on then, while the old gossip sputtered like a guttering flame, reaching the end of the climb. There, in the Osraed Gallery, with every wakeful eye of Nairne and the surrounding holt watching, Taminy turned to the Court, dropped her cowl and pulled off her scarf. Wheat-pale hair covered her shoulders in a flood and made banners in the light breeze. But among all the people, only Osraed Ealad-hach and Marnie-o-Loom showed anything more than mild surprise.

It was a deep irony, she thought, that once — dear God, a hundred years ago — she had dreamed of standing upon this great stone platform and of opening her mouth to sing the Meri's duan. But she would give no Tell tonight to ears unwilling and unready to hear it. Osraed Bevol spoke instead, giving a name that rippled quickly across a sea of lips and was gone: Taminy. Only Taminy. Like Gwynet, a refugee found in the course of Meredydd's Pilgrimage.

The crowd, relieved to be able to laugh at Marnie's red-faced discomfiture and eager to be about the business of celebration, accepted it and went about their business.

So, she thought. *So, I'm to be allowed to fade back and away.* But she wasn't, quite. The white-haired old Osraed's eyes bored awl-like and the tall young one's shyly prodded. She glanced from one to the other, then hurried down the steps and into the teeming courtyard where mothers weighed her and sons admired her and daughters feigned indifference. She was dancing before she knew it, marvelling at how little the steps had changed.

It was during a break in the dancing, as she searched for Skeet and Gwynet near a stall selling hot, sweet cider, that she saw the tall young Osraed again, standing gawpishly to one side and trying not to stare too rudely. He moved toward her when their eyes met, his face a patchwork of bemusement and uncertainty. He stopped before her, opened his mouth to speak, then glanced away.

She took pity. "You'd be Wyth," she said and drew his eyes back.

"How do you know me?"

She smiled. "Oh, someone must have mentioned you . . . pointed you out."

A moment passed, filled only with eddies of babble and song from the happy mob. Wyth glanced down at his hands, clasped over his crystal pendant. He let go of the crystal and put his hands behind him. "You're going to think this odd," he said. "But I feel . . . as if I know you . . . or ought to."

"You're Osraed now. There are a good many things you know . . . or ought to. The Meri has surely lifted the bar on your senses. They must thrill to have the doors and windows of your mind thrown open so." *And nothing looks or sounds or feels the same, does it?*

He was shaking his head. "Even the night is different," he said, the words pouring from his mouth as if a bar had been lifted there too. "The darkness, the firelight, the breezes. Darkness has layers, did you know that? Layers of absence. And light" — he paused to glance at the lanterns bobbing about the cider booth — "light peels back the layers and — " The words ended in a blush that spread from his nose to the corners of his eyes. "I'm — I'm sorry. I'm babbling. You'd not care about any of this."

"And the laughter," she said, "has colors. The blues of sorrow, the reds of anger, the gold and silver of true joy."

Gawping again, he shook his head. "How do you know these things?"

"I live with an Osraed. My father . . . was a Cirke-master. I've always been drawn to the Meri's doings."

"You're no mimic." The gangly ogler was gone, replaced by an astute Osraed. "You speak as one who knows. You see the laughter with your own eyes, not Osraed Bevol's."

She shrugged. "I have been accused," she said carefully, "of being fey. Once, some called me Wicke and charged me to prove I was not."

"And did you?"

"I was unable. I tried, but the Meri's will won out. She decided my course. It brought me here."

"You're not Wicke," he said as if his own certitude would make that true for all.

She laughed. "No, I'm not. But you won't convince Marnie-o-Loom of that." Her eyes traveled to the shadowed side of the bright booth where a pinched face trained glitters of jet on them.

Wyth shivered. "And she calls those eyes." He held out his arm. "Will you have a cider, Taminy-a-Gled?"

"Aye. If you will have a dance."

He agreed with minimum awkwardness and she took his arm and let him squire her about before all eyes. They ate, they drank, they danced, they strolled the battlements. And when he looked at her oddly time and again, she knew it was only because he had just realized, time and again, that she was not Meredydd-a-Lagan.

Ah, but a part of you wants me to be that.

"What did you say?"

She glanced up at him. He was a layer of darkness, the

Meri's Kiss glowing from his brow, a silhouette against the gleaming, moonlit peaks of the Gyldan-baenn. She had been watching them, though they had neither moved nor changed for perhaps a million years, and he had been watching her, whose changes were more recent. She had let him watch her, let him see that even under layers of darkness, she was not Meredydd.

"You have sharp ears, Osraed," she told him. "I didn't speak." *And a rare man, it is, who hears words that are not spoken.*

"You tease me. I can't hear your thoughts."

"You feel what others feel. You see the color of their laughter, the shadings of their words."

"Shadings only. But you spoke. There were words."

"There were words. But I thought them."

"Why? Why should I hear *your* thoughts and no others?"

I told you I was fey. She could feel his eyes holding her moonlit face, his other senses straining through layers of darkness the moonlight could not penetrate. He had heard her. He had not seen her lips move.

"Bevol has brought you here for a reason. Why has he brought you here? Who are you? Why do I know you? *How* do I know you?"

"Perhaps," she said aloud. "Perhaps you have seen me in a vision, as I have seen you through someone else's vision."

The Kiss between his brows puckered with thought.

Taminy laughed and laid a hand on his arm. "Don't glower so, Osraed Wyth. You must learn to laugh more and frown less."

Perhaps it was the words or the gentle, laughing voice that delivered them or the moonlight on pale hair. Perhaps it was all those things that set up, in Wyth Arundel's head, a sudden whirlpool of thought and sensation. A second of disorientation was followed by the sharp, clear memory of Master Bevol's aislinn chamber, of a pool of darkness that would not be still, of a Being of Light and a girl on a beach. No, two girls — one entering the water, one leaving it; one familiar and beloved, the other —

"Osraed Bevol," said the moonlit lips, "I have not breathed for a hundred years."

The whirl stopped so suddenly, he was nearly dashed from his feet. Like a man plunged in cold water, he trembled, while just beneath his skin, blood pulsed in fitful heat, scalding him. His face burned. He raised his hands to cover it.

Taminy. Taminy-a-Cuinn. Gifted in the Art, decried as Wicke, condemned to a fugitive Pilgrimage, drowned in the sacred Western Sea. Taminy, whose father returned alone and empty-handed, a seemingly broken man, to give up his duties at Nairne-Cirke and move his household to Ochanshrine at Creiddylad. One hundred years ago. *One hundred years.*

"They spent the rest of their days in worship and service," said the moonlit girl. "They wanted to be as close to me as they could. They wanted to serve the Meri's Cause."

He couldn't reply. He had no words to speak, no mind to invent them. Overwhelmed, he stumbled away into thicker darkness, leaving her behind him — a silky, silver shadow against the Gyldan-baenn and a star-filled sky.

Leaving the barrage of light and life above and behind, Osraed Ealad-hach took refuge in the darkness of his aislinn chamber. Beneath the soft glow of several tiny lightglobes, he sat, pondering the impermeable black core of the room, the crystal that would light it cupped in trembling hands.

He hadn't been here since the dreams began — since Meredydd-a-Lagan had had thrust them into his nights. He had been afraid to come. Afraid to call out the ghosts and the visions he knew were there. Now, his fear had slid headlong into terror. Now, less than ever did he want to call up the visions; now, more than ever, he knew he must.

Because of that girl.

He raised a hand from his lap, cradling the crystal toward the heart of the chamber. The hand shook and his soul shook with it. Whimpering, he pulled the hand back. Already images formed, but in his head, behind his eyes; the girl, dropping her cowl, pulling off her scarf; the girl, dancing on the cobbles, her beautiful, cwenly face alight with pleasure and excitement; the girl, walking the battlements with Osraed Wyth, her hair pale gold in the light of moon and stars.

Ealad-hach moaned sickly, pressing his temples as if his hands could shove the images into retreat. And her name — Taminy! Why *Taminy?* Why that wretched, cursed, *wicked* name?

A flicker of anger insinuated itself into Ealad-hach's fear. Bevol had chosen that name, like as not. Chosen it because of what it implied about that young woman. Well, he was not gullible as all that. The girl was not Taminy-a-Cuinn, that much was certain. Her name was probably not even Taminy, or hadn't been until she met Bevol-a-Gled. Taminy-a-Cuinn she could not be, but she could yet be the creature of his nightmare.

The thought did not let Ealad-hach breathe any more easily. Still, he sat more comfortably in the confines of his private chamber. It was only a matter of knowledge. He would call for the aislinn. That would tell him what to do.

He leaned forward with a will and put the crystal on the raised and tiled platform at the center of the little room. He fed it his energies then, his dreams, the floating images, the contents of his unconscious thought. Verdant light danced over and around the facets, but it was a faded light, fitful and weak. He tried harder, murmuring a duan to give force to his thoughts. The light intensified, steadied. About the crystal, mist that was not mist began to form, spiraling slowly like a twisted wheel of cloud. It grew up, fanned out, gained substance. It separated into earth and sky and sea; a white curl of wave-foam raced up a beach, a moon burned the clouds silver, a wind stirred the air.

Yes, this was the place. Now, show me. Show me the girl.

And there was Meredydd-a-Lagan — clear, sharp, as if alive. She melted, was burned away and, burning, she walked into the waters.

There! There was the girl! Rising from the waves in what seemed a robe of translucent, lucent green. It shed like a skin and she stood, glittering, in the moonlight.

The old Osraed's lips moved more swiftly, his duan grew louder, more rhythmic. Sweat beaded on his brow and his cheeks trembled. Her face — he must see her face!

But he could not see it. No duan, no amount of concentration would show it to him, would make the moonlit phantom any more substantial. After a moment more of struggle, his concentration faltered and the vision collapsed into itself.

Ealad-hach blinked. On its pedestal, the crystal sat, lightless and inert, not even a whisper of aislinn mist clinging to its facets. He felt old. Frail. Worn. He felt barely able to gather up the crystal and return it to its carved and filigreed box, but he did. Then he knelt and prayed that he would be cursed with vivid dreams.

CHAPTER 5

*The wood of the soul can burn and be fire; the Word
of the Spirit is the whirling friction rod above.*

*Prayer is the power that makes the Word turn round.
And when the Word moves, the mystery of God
comes to light.*

— *Prayers and Meditations of Osraed Ochan, Number Five*

❖   ❖   ❖

Wyth found sleep difficult. The merest straying from
consciousness left him literally bewildered, mired in thick
emotion, or reeling on the edge of Ruanaidhe's Leap. In
the chill before dawn, he pulled himself fully awake to sit,
head in hands, trying not to think. His brain felt like a
sodden bath fleece.

He wanted to pray, but wasn't certain he wanted the
enlightenment he knew he should ask for. He wanted to
draw out the visions he could feel pressing like a physical
force behind his eyes, but what he fled in sleep was no
easier to face awake.

The heavy pain in his head at last drove him to draw a
cup of scented water from a carafe by the bed and rifle his
medicament chest for some willow bark. There was none.
Instead, he smudged his temples with a pungent salve and
sat, coil-legged, on his bed to perform a Healweave.

Candle in hand, eyes on the flame, he breathed in and
sang out, letting the duan float away from him, praying it
would take the pain with it. The runesong was only six lines
long; Wyth was halfway though it the second time when
the pain evaporated so suddenly and completely, it
stopped the duan in his throat. The salve's ice-hot touch

penetrated his senses and he imagined, for a moment, that he had felt an actual caress of warm fingers. He took a deep, relaxed breath, letting some gentle force tug him upward out of his tired, awkward frame.

The flame of his candle, steady one moment, guttered and died as if unseen fingers had snuffed it.

In his advanced state of relaxation, he could only stare at the glowing wick with mild bemusement, and wonder why, with the candle out, the room seemed to be growing lighter. He would turn his head and glance at the window, he decided. He would see that the Sun was rising.

But his head would not turn, and at the foot of his bed a soft, golden radiance manifested itself in a way that no sunrise ever had, looking like airborne gold-dust or a galaxy of golden stars. He felt it then, the dawn of a sweet, savory terror. A rapture of quaking awareness. She was here and his desire for Her flowed, pure and shining, toward the gilded whorl that seemed always and never on the verge of taking shape.

She sang in his head, voice crystal-bright. Without words, She communicated perfectly what he must know to take his next several steps down Her Path. He tasted bits of the future, saw it, smelled it, heard it sing and roar and wail. He trembled with a thousand kinds of joy and pain and anger. He laughed and wept and both at once, and woke lying on his face across his coiled legs while the Sun filled his room with solid light.

He blinked at its brightness, feeling at once reassured and barren. The pain and weariness were gone, but so was that warm touch. He schooled himself to patience, knowing he would feel it again.

He was down early for his breakfast, before his sisters could be up — he hoped before his mother. Industrious Fleta, Adken's wife, had already fed her own family and the other servants and hands, releasing them to their play or chores. She was fussing about the spotless tiled kitchen with Wyth wandered in. Adken sipped tea by the broad hearth.

"Master Wyth!" She dropped the skirts of her apron, on which she'd been dusting flour-coated hands, and set to trying to sweep the apron clean. Adken came to his feet, sloshing tea about.

Wyth laughed.

Both servants looked absolutely stunned. Then Adken's face split in a grin. "You sound like a boy again, if I may say it, Master. That laugh of yers has gone long disused."

Fleta's eyes grew big and round. "Is that the way you speak to a Holy One, you daft old boy? Ah, Master Osraed, forgive him; he's wind-kissed. Too many falls from the roof, like as not."

"There's nothing to forgive, Fleta," Wyth told her, loving the kitchen's heat and apothecary smell and the way Fleta's graying hair stuck out about her round, pink face like the wool of a silver ewe. *Was all this here before? Was I senseless and blind?* "I've just come in search of some breakfast —"

"Say no more, Master. I'll have a platterful in a gnat's age. Will you have tea?"

"Oh, yes, please," said Wyth and moved to sit by the huge brick hearth, across from Adken.

Fleta ogled. "Won't you wait in the dining chamber, Master? This place is —"

"This place is warm and bright and happy. And there are people in it. The dining chamber is cold and empty and . . . overwhelming."

Fleta speared her mate with practiced eyes. "Adken, you dimity! Did you not start the fires?"

Adken's dappled-banner brows sailed into a frown. "And when might I've done such a thing? You've had your beadies on me since I quit the sheets. None's ever up at such an hour most days." He cocked a half-contrite, half-reproachful eye at Wyth. "I'll be choring earlier now, it seems."

Wyth shook his head, fighting, for the sake of Adken's dignity, the urge to laugh. "You'll do no such thing. I'd like, if I could, to have my breakfasts here in the kitchen . . . with you and Fleta and the boys. Would that be all right?"

The couple gaped at each other. *As if,* Wyth thought, *I'd just performed some amazing Weave.* He waited, hands folded, eyes hopeful, while a gamut of emotions ran willy-nilly over Fleta's face and her good husband's eyebrows popped up and down like a pair of mottled ferrets. Fleta blushed, then smiled, then shot her husband a most beguiling look. Suddenly, Wyth could see her as a young girl — buxom, winsome and sweet-eyed, wooing the spry lad with the flaming hair.

"Well," she said, smoothing her apron with very real grace. "Well, Master, it would be such an honor. *Such.*" She turned her gaze to him and he knew, with some surprise, that her pleasure was sincere, albeit tinged with anxiety. What would she, after all, have to say to an Osraed?

"You used to call me Wyth . . . long ago," he said, and let his voice be wistful.

"Oh, but you were a *child* then, Master. Now, you're . . . well, you're Eiric of Arundel, first of all and — and *Osraed.*"

"Osraed Wyth, then? I don't really like 'Master.' You're not my hunting dogs or my pupils."

Fleta smiled, broadly this time, and bobbed a self-conscious curtsey. "I'll have your tea in a shake, Osraed Wyth."

Wyth returned the smile and settled back in his chair. Adken crumpled back into his own, shaking amazement from his face.

"Wonders," he murmured. "Wonders, the Meri does."

Wyth met his gaze, making his own as open as possible, willing the older man to confidences.

Adken sighed and shifted his gaze to his tea cup. "When you were a boy, it was like this."

"Before father died."

"Aye." He nodded. "He wasn't a bad man, Wyth. Leastwise, I didn't think he was. But he was surely a *scared* man. At the end . . . at the end, I think fear sat on his shoulder continual." His mouth puckered into a fretful knot.

Wyth caught a niggle of disapproval there. "I think mother frightened him sometimes," he offered. "She's . . . a powerful woman. Strong-willed, confident. I think he loved her strength. I think he also feared it."

Adken looked relieved to hear this confidence. "Aye,"

he said, nodding. "Aye, that rings a true bell, well enough."

Yes, and I see it now. When I was a boy, I saw nothing.
"I don't remember a lot of what happened before that. It's as if father's death . . . wiped it all away."

"No, lad. Not wiped it away. Made you pack it all up with your child-things and lay it aside, is all. Grow up, like. And quick. Too quick. Remember when you used to come down here to play with Cian? Ah, you two boys sure could put terror into the livestock."

Wyth blushed. He did remember. "I was constantly underfoot. Bothering you, hanging on Fleta's apron, begging baking scraps."

"Someone had to pass judgement on Fleta's goods before they left the kitchen," said Adken, chuckling. "Oh, and that old dog, what was his name?"

"Wolf-Cyne."

"Wolf-Cyne, indeed. A very grand name for a burr-bog-gled brindled sheep-cur."

"He was a very grand cur," said Wyth, glowing with the memory.

Adken looked at him a trifle more seriously. "Cian'd be pleased to see you at table. He missed your grand times when you went up to the Fortress."

"I missed him," Wyth admitted. "But this house was a hard place to come home to."

"Aye, has been."

Wyth felt a sudden urge to ask Adken the Question. The Question which had lain in the back of his mind for seven years. He grimaced. No. He didn't really want it answered. What he wanted was to hear someone he could trust say, "No, Wyth. It was not your fault. Nothing you did caused your father to take his own life. And nothing you did could have saved him."

And that was it, he realized, as Fleta, smilingly handed him a cup of steaming tea. What he'd wanted to know, more than anything, was that no power at his command — perhaps none in the Universe — could have saved Rowan Arundel from self-immolation.

"It's like having the years back," murmured Adken, and Wyth nodded, noticing, distantly, that he had burned his hand.

He lingered too long over breakfast, chatting with Adken and Fleta. He spoke, too, to their midmost son Cian, come up to the house to fetch his hat. Spoke and shook his calloused hand and got past the bowing and scraping to a back-slapping embrace.

He would not be late to Halig-liath. He had no classes to prepare for (an odd freedom) and did not really need to be there until the Council session that afternoon. He tried to tell himself his anxiousness to be off had more to do with seeing his private chambers for the first time than with avoiding the Moireach, but the sight of her at the top of the stairs as he fled out the front door destroyed that petty illusion.

Her face was beaming smiles (God, how long since he'd seen that, let alone been the cause of it?), and she descended grandly and gracefully, her hands outstretched toward him, tugging at his heart.

"Wyth! Dear! Off so early? I thought we'd dine together this morning."

"I've eaten, mother. And Osraed Bevol will show me my rooms today." He tried not to gush boyishly, but between the pull of those rooms and the push of the Moireach . . .

She spread her hands, loosing a wave of dismay. "Rooms? Is that so exciting? What about our journey to Creiddylad? We've yet to plan it."

He opened his mouth slowly in his reluctance to disappoint her, but she bowled him over with more enthusiasm than he'd seen her show for anything in a very long time.

"Actually, I've done a little planning on my own, figuring you had enough on your mind." She stroked his cheek. "I assumed you'd rather travel by river — I know *I* would — so I booked us passage on the mid-week packet. It's not much more than a ferry, hardly worthy of Halig-liath's newest Osraed, so we shall just have to pretend it's the Cyne's galley."

"Mother," he said.

"We'll spend a night in Tuine, I think. I was there once when I was a girl. I remember the little altar they put up where Cyne Ciaran died. A tragic spot, it is, and so beautiful, so full of history. Oh, and I thought we might stay a day or two after in Creiddylad, as well. I'd love to take worship at the Cyne's Cirke and visit the Hall and the Playhouse — oh! and Ochanshrine, too, of course — "

"Mother."

Her hands came up to cup his face. "Oh, Wyth! To see you go before the Cyne — "

"Mother!" He raised his hands to cover hers and smiled, as if that might take the sting out of the words he would have to say. "Mother, we may go to Creiddylad, if you wish — although, it will have to be after I've settled into Halig-liath and have some sense of my duties." He plowed on, past the look of bewilderment that cloaked her face. "There will be no Grand Tell at Creiddylad this year."

The Moireach wrenched her hands from beneath his. "What? But that's . . . unthinkable! There has always been a Tell at Creiddylad. Even in Regency years. Is — is the Cyne ill? Is there trouble at court? What's wrong? *Why* can't he see you?"

"He is . . . involved — or so I've been told — with some very important, very *delicate* diplomacy just now."

"With whom? Surely, the Claeg aren't rising again. His Durweard is a Feich, so they can't be the problem. And the Hillwild — "

"It's none of those things, mother. Osraed Bevol mentioned the Sutherlanders."

"The — ?" She raised her hands in a gesture of pure bafflement. "What in the world can they have to say to him that is more important than what *you* have to say to him? What is it to be Osraed, if you cannot command the respect and attention of the Cyne?"

Wyth studied the grain of the entry's polished pine floor. "Commanding the Cyne's respect and attention is not the *purpose* of being Osraed, Mother."

"No? Then what was Ochan-a-Coille sent to do, if not that?"

"He was sent to command the Cyne's attention — "

"Ah!"

"— to certain spiritual matters that were critical to the unity and prosperity of his people and his continuance as their Cyne. The first thing Osraed Ochan did, if you recall, was to alert Cyne Malcuim to a conspiracy against him — to warn him and advise him about the Claeg and the Feich. He performed the Cyne a service."

The Moireach's expression was black and sour as a bird-pecked fruit. "And I suppose Cyne Colfre needs no one at Court to advise him about the Sutherlanders."

"If he needs them, they will be sent. Perhaps that's part of Leal-mac-Mercer's mission."

"And why not yours?" she asked, red-faced. "Why can't *you* go to Creiddylad to advise the Cyne?"

"Because that is not my mission. My mission is here."

She took a step back from him. "But what glory is there in that? To be locked up in that musty old fortress your whole life? It's all over that you've declined a position on the Osraed Council." Her eyes accused him. "I thought that meant you had some greater calling to answer. Am I wrong?"

"No, Mother, you are not wrong. But I am not here for glory. At least, I'm not here for what *you* would call glory. I am here to serve the Meri as She dictates. She dictated that I not hold a position on the Osraed Council."

She made no reply to that, which relieved Wyth immeasurably, so he bid her a polite good morning and left, kissing her cool cheek. He wasn't certain, but he thought she called him a fool. He knew she thought him one.

"A problem with the Sutherlanders?" Osraed Bevol tugged at his beard and glanced at Wyth over one shoulder. "No, I can't say as I've gotten wind of any thing like that. Although, there might arise one if we Caraidin continue to call them that."

His eyes were glancing mirth and Wyth smiled, abashed. "The Deasach, I mean. But they do live beyond our southern reaches."

"And we live live beyond their northern ones. I suppose that makes us Northerlanders, eh? Each man's ground — "

"Is the center of his world," finished Wyth.

"Ah, and speaking of the center of the world . . . "

Osraed Bevol stopped in his subterranean wanderings at a doorway of hewn stone and polished tile. "This is it." He turned to Wyth and indicated the brass latch on the heavy wooden door. "The private chambers of Osraed Wyth. Go on, open."

Heart beating almost audibly, Wyth fumbled his prayer chain and at last grasped its pendant crystal. The crystal, itself, was the key to his rooms. A unique form it had and, pressed into the latchbox, meshed exactly with that mechanism's inner workings. A breath of pressure and the latch slipped, letting Wyth into his suite.

The main study had one great window of thick, mullioned glass that overlooked the southern end of the river bend and the sweep of the Gyldan-baenn running southward into the distance. The large room was filled with books — rows of them on tall shelves along one wall. There was a workbench with drawers and an apothecary table with a medicaments chest above. Furs and braid rugs warmed the floors and a tapestry map of Caraid-land hung on the wall by the door.

"Whose chambers were these before?" Wyth asked, nearly whispering.

Bevol chuckled. "They belonged to Osraed Leodeach the Harper. He taught music. That's one of his favorite intstruments." He indicated a beautifully wrought lap harp that sat canted against the wall in a corner near the window. "It was a gift from Cyne Ciarda, whom he taught to play. Quite a pepper pot, old Leodeach. In his old age, that is. In his youth, he was a lot like you. *Very* serious. *Very* grave."

Wyth blushed under the teasing and Bevol clapped him soundly on the shoulder. "Come. Let me show you the center of your new world."

They by-passed what Wyth took to be the door to the bath chamber and pushed through a darkly carved and filigreed door into the conical aislinn chamber.

Wyth's limbs began to quake. The little room was well-lit now, with sunlight pouring into it like hazy liquid from the canted shafts in the sloping ceiling. The tile gleamed from wall and bench, while the worn ring of flooring glowed with the satiny sheen of aged wood. It had an odd non-pattern, Wyth thought, of small burls like eyes gazing up forever into the vault of the ceiling. He followed the eyelets' gazes without thinking and heard Bevol laugh.

"Yes, you do wonder, don't you, what they're all gawping at. That was Osraed Ochan's doing, of course. It is said this wood is from the Saewode where he lived before the Pilgrimage."

Wyth stared down into the wooden eyes with a thrill of appreciation. "This was Osraed *Ochan's* chamber? Oh, Osraed Bevol, I'm hardly worthy — "

"Nonsense. You are the first Osraed commissioned to Halig-liath in seven seasons and the first after a Cusp. You have been appointed Weard to the Covenant Ochan established and . . . you loved Meredydd." He canted his head to one side, his eyes hazing slightly.

"And still do," said Wyth. "But . . . do the other Osraed feel this is appropriate?"

"I didn't make the decision unilaterally. The Triumvirate appointed you these rooms by unanimous vote."

Wyth sat down on the tiled bench. "I'm grateful. Thank you." *How inadequate words are*, he thought, running fingertips over the bright glazed tiles.

"So." Bevol dropped down across from him, hands on knees, beard and hair turned to hazy flame by the falling shafts of sunlight. "What will your first task be?"

In Wyth's head an aislinn book opened and he read what was plain upon the page. "I'm to study the histories and the Holy Treatises and collect all writings pertaining to the Covenant. Then they shall all be brought together in one place and organized."

"And safe?" Bevol suggested.

Wyth frowned. "And safe, yes. And available to all who would read them."

"Ah, if only all *could* read them. It is a fair portion of our populace, even in this day and age, that cannot or will not read."

"The Cirke-school in Nairne does well."

Bevol made a moué with his lips. "Well enough, yes. But not all villages lie in the shadow of Halig-liath. They have not the resources or the will, often enough, to teach what needs to be taught." He tapped his chest. "*My* commission that, in part. To teach those outside these walls. A sometimes difficult task which all the vigorous cleirachs and Ministers in Caraid-land cannot move forward." He shrugged. "Would you have your sons at school when they ought to be tilling the field or minding the shop? And as to daughters — hoo! — Gwynet's lot is not as unusual as it ought to be. And in Creiddylad, take the problem and multiply it by the stars. Leal will have his young hands full, there, I can tell you. . . . You're wandering, Wyth. Is the old scir-loc boring you?"

"Huh!" Wyth snapped out of his blur-eyed reverie. "I'm sorry, I . . . I was thinking of Meredydd and . . . Taminy."

"Ah. Those two cailin offer much material for thought."

"Is it very strange for you, Osraed Bevol, to have her in your house? To sit with her at table? To — to speak with her face to face? You received your Kiss from her, your knowledge, your duan — and now, here she is — "

Bevol shook his head. "Not the same."

"But Meredydd — "

"Whom you love."

"Whom I love . . . " He glanced up at the older man, feeling as if his soul sat naked in his eyes. "How do you reconcile it? In your mind — in your heart?"

"How do you?"

"I *don't*. That's just it. What I feel for the Meri *must* be pure. It *must* be. But what I felt for Meredydd — forgive me for saying it, Master Bevol — but I can't think *that* was pure. There was so much of my *self* in it. So much of pride and envy and — and other things."

"Possessiveness," said Bevol, then, "Desire?"

Wyth sighed. "In a word."

"And you don't desire the Meri?"

Wyth recalled the night, the gleaming Something that would not be seen, that touched him and spoke to him, unspeaking. "What is the right answer? I . . . yes. I desire the Meri, but — "

"And well you should," said Bevol, all but pouncing on the words. "*Well* you should. I shall be the first to admit that I desire Her. I hunger for Her touch, thirst for every drop of knowledge or wisdom or compassion — every drop of light She cares to bestow on me. Passion, Wyth. In a word. That's the substance of the Covenant you are commissioned to protect. It would shock Ealad to hear me speak of passion and the Meri in one breath, but tell me if that is not what She demands of us. Eh? Am I wrong, Wyth? Is that not what She demanded of you?"

Wyth's face burned and his eyes swam with salt dew. "Yes. Oh, yes, but-but then, when I think of Meredydd — "

Bevol leaned across the circle and laid a hand on his knee. "Meredydd will not exist for another hundred years, Wyth — or more. Not as you knew her. The girl you knew exists only in your heart — in your mind." He sat back and shook his head. "In all truth, she will never exist anywhere else, because when Meredydd-a-Lagan walks out of the Western Sea a century from now, she will be changed. Oh, you would know her, but she might not know herself. Skeet put it very aptly: what must it be like to be dumped back upon the earth after living in the Sea? What must it be like to have to walk, where before you have darted like a silkie?"

Wyth pondered that long after Bevol had gone, his thoughts full of Taminy. It seemed an odd notion to have, and he hoped it was not, in some way, sacrilegious, but it occurred to Osraed Wyth Arundel that after a hundred years of swimming, one would find walking extremely difficult.

"Tell me again why you've no classes this afternoon." Taminy was inspecting the Cirke spire with its gleaming stellate crown and Gwynet could not see her face.

"Because Master Tynedale said he had a Council and trusted no one else with our lessons. So, we were free to do whatever."

Taminy chuckled. "Oh, guileless child! I know every word of that is true, and yet you *still* have such a cloud of guilt about you."

Gwynet scuffled in the dirt of the path and gave the Cirke an apologetic glance. "I come here to study and learn," she said. "I promised Osraed Bevol I'd study hard today."

Taminy bent to look her in the eyes. "But Osraed Tynedale gave you a free afternoon, Gwyn. Take it."

Gwynet drew a dusty circle with her toe. "I never had a free afternoon. It feels guiltful."

Taminy straighted and made a clucking noise with her tongue. "Gwynet, you're a little girl."

"Yes, mistress."

"But you don't even know what that is, do you?"

Gwynet squinted up at Taminy's face, but her expression was lost in the bright sky. She said such odd things at times — like that, about not knowing what a little girl was.

"Look," said Taminy. "If we have a lesson today, will you feel less guiltful?"

Gwynet's heart gave a triple leap. "Oh, *aye*, Taminy. Oh, I would like tha' greatly."

"All right. But first — " She turned her head toward the Cirke. "I'd like to visit the Cirke a bit. Look at the manse."

Gwynet blinked up at the large stone and timber building with its sloping walls and its frosted, stained and crystaled windows. "You lived here," she recalled and wondered at how long ago that was.

"I did. And it seems not to have changed much, but for some new timbers and that window." She pointed. "That window's been replated. And of course, there are more graves now."

Gwynet's heart cringed from the wistfulness in the older girl's voice and quickly took her hand. "Will you show me, mistress?"

Taminy favored her with a wonderful smile and led her on into the Cirke yard, past the Sanctuary and alongside the pretty stone manse with its great, wide porch and, up-tilted eaves and dormer windows. It looked very different from the Sanctuary — newer, Gwynet thought.

"Two hundred years newer," said Taminy from beside her and Gwynet shivered to know that her thoughts had been heard.

There was a breathlessness about Taminy as they walked about the house. She was all over it with her eyes, her lips parted as if to speak, though no words came out. When they'd come round to the front of the house, which was set at a right angle to the Sanctuary, the front door opened and someone stepped out onto the shadowy veranda. Taminy froze at the bottom of the steps and grasped the person with her eyes.

For a moment, Gwynet was sure the older girl would cry out; she had the most anguished expression on her face. *Why*, she thought, *she thinks it's her da*. The thought made her intensely sad.

"Daeges-eage, cailin," said a deep, warm-ember voice. "May I be of service?" The man came out to the top of the steps into dappled sunlight that gleamed, patchwork, in his honey-colored hair.

Gwynet felt Taminy relax, and relaxed herself, gazing up at the man's great height. She smiled.

He returned the smile, shifting his eyes to Taminy. "Ah, wait now! You're the young woman Osraed Bevol introduced at the Tell Fest. Taminy, isn't it?"

She nodded. "Yes, sir. It's Taminy."

"Well, Taminy. I'm Cirkemaster Saxan. Welcome to Nairne."

"Thank you, Osraed, Gwynet and I were just . . . looking about. Is it all right if we enter the Sanctuary?"

"It's always open, dear girl. You may enter it whenever you wish." He studied her for a moment, then chuckled. "Imagine that Marnie, thinking you were Meredydd. You're nothing like her to look at."

"Did you know her well?" Taminy asked.

The Cirkemaster nodded. "Since she was born. My wife attended her birth. Our own daughter is only a few years older."

"Were they friends?"

"When they were younger. But after Meredydd's parents . . . died, after she'd been up at Halig-liath awhile, that all changed. Everything changed for Meredydd then, and I can't help but think . . . " He paused, looking uncomfortable.

"What, sir?" said Taminy gently, almost inaudibly. "What do you think?"

"That perhaps Osraed Bevol shouldn't have disturbed the natural order of things. Should have let Meredydd live a normal girl's life. She wasn't allowed to be as other girls, and they resented that and were suspicious of it. Poor Meredydd was outcast. Not a girl in Nairne would befriend her. Not even, I'm ashamed to say, my own Iseabal. And it wasn't Meredydd's fault. None of it was Meredydd's fault."

"But Osraed, how could she have lived a normal girl's life with her Gift? Surely, that alone would set her apart? Wasn't Osraed Bevol right to teach her how to use it?"

"It might have been more merciful if he had taught her how *not* to use it."

"And would it be merciful to teach a bird how not to fly? Or a child how not to walk and talk? No, sir. It's beyond that, even. It would be as if you tried to teach someone — anyone — not to eat or breathe. It would be impossible."

The Cirkemaster studied Taminy all over again. "You seem to know much about Meredydd's Gift."

"I know she had it. And I know, from what Osraed Bevol has told me, that it was natural as the color of her eyes. How can something given by Nature — which is the hand of God — be against Nature's order? Wouldn't it be truer to say that Meredydd's Gift set her against *man's* order of things?"

The Cirkemaster crossed his arms and shifted his weight against a wooden porch column. "It would," he said. "But look what it availed her. She sought to claim the Sea and the Sea claimed her."

It was not said unkindly, and looking up into his eyes, Gwynet saw wistfulness and wondered at it.

"I can think of worse things," said Taminy, "than to be claimed by the Sea."

They took their leave of the Cirkemaster then, for which Gwynet was grateful. She had felt so much and understood so little of what went on over her head.

"Was that the Cirkemaster's daughter?" she asked as they climbed the steps to the Sanctuary. "The girl in the doorway?"

"Yes, I imagine it was. Iseabal, he called her —

'dedicated to God' — but she won't be. They won't let her be. She'll be dedicated, instead, to her husband and her children and a nice, tidy business or craft. They'll let her weave cloth, but not inyx. Never that."

Gwynet glanced at her friend questioningly. The words were spoken in quiet, measured tones, but another person might have shouted them, they were so unquiet with pain and, yes, anger.

They sat side by side on the first bench.

"Who're you angry with, Taminy?"

"No one. It's no one man or woman's fault. It's the way of things. The way it's always been."

"Perhaps," reasoned Gwynet, "if the Meri had chosen a little girl to carry Her first message — ?"

Taminy shook her head. "There would have been none to listen. Had a girl pounded upon the gates of Mertuile and begged to see the Cyne, the guards would have scoffed at her, or worse. And if she had shown them the great crystal, they would have merely taken it from her and given it to the Cyne themselves to improve their own lot. No, Ochan got to the Cyne because he was the young, strong *son* of the Cyne's Woodweard."

"But in the history it says Cyne Malcuim's cwen, Mairghread, was a great spirit in the Land. Tha' she in— em, influ—"

"Influenced?"

"Aye! How she made great and wonderful things happen for the Land in th' early days. How she studied under Ochan and fed the hungry and helped heal the sick and — and —"

"*Helped*, Gwynet. *Influenced*. You notice it didn't say that she *healed* the sick." There was a hot green light burning in Taminy's eyes. "And let me tell you that she *did* those things. She *did* heal. She *did* make things happen. She, herself. She was as much Osraed as Ochan, but history wouldn't give the Tell of it. Caraid-land in those days, Gwynet, was as much Mairghread's realm as it was Malcuim's and as much Ochan's as either. They ruled together, the three, but history's eyes look over it, and history's mouth talks around it."

She turned her face to the altar and was silent again, with one of those great, heavy silences that drained all the life out of a person. Gwynet leapt to draw her out of it.

"I'd like to heal and Weave great and helpful things, mistress Taminy. And see wisdoms and speak what I see. I do pray you'll teach me."

Taminy looked down at her hands, fingers spread over her knees. "I'm not sure I'm the right person to teach you those things. What I can't do myself —"

"Oh, there's oceans of stuff you can teach me, Taminy! Like herbals and duans and how not to burn down the house."

The older girl chuckled. "All right. Let's go walking and I'll show you where the herbs grow hereabout."

"And teach me more the silent history?"

Taminy smiled all the way to her eyes. "And teach you the silent history."

Gwynet, for her years, was quite knowledgable about herbs. Taminy was able to show her a number of sun-loving plants the dank reaches of Blaec-del had not favored, but she was pleasantly surprised with what the child had learned by eavesdropping and experimentation.

"Well, everyone knows 'bout willow, of course. But I got to think that if willow was good for the head-ague and sassafras for t'other agues and the blood, well then, why not try a bit of both? So the next time I had a bit of pain, I tried tha' and it seemed to work wonderful well. I even tried a cup on Mam Airdsgainne's poor old joints. Worked so well, she forgot to gnaw on Ruhf's customers when they come in."

Taminy smiled fondly at the golden child, watching her dabble pale toes in one of the rare pools in the Bebhinn's swift-flowing stream. Her hair was bright as a newly minted ambre, but not nearly as bright as the mind it crowned.

"This is a fey place, in't it?" she asked.

Taminy made herself more comfortable on her rock beside a gentle waterfall. "What makes you say that?"

"Well . . . " Gwynet swivelled her head all about to take in the dappled cup of greenery that surrounded her. " . . . part of it's the herbals. Look how many of the best ones grow right here — fennel and sassafras and willow and even a little marshie-mallow down there in tha' wee still spot. It's like . . . like a Wicke or an Osraed might've planted it all so they'd only have to come here and not wander all o'er the woods."

"Like we did?"

"Well, aye." Gwynet shot Taminy a roguish glance from beneath her golden curtain of hair. "It did come to me tha' we might've come just here."

"Oh, but we had to come here right at the beginning of even to watch the colors change. You see, it *is* a fey place, as you say."

"I'm right?" squeaked Gwynet. "Are there paeries and — and aelven folk?"

Taminy laughed. *Bless you, Gwynet. Bless you for seeing magic in all things.* "The only aelven folk here are you and me. But once, not that long ago, a little girl named Meredydd came here and met the Gwenwyvar."

Gwynet jumped up, staring back into the pool with wide eyes. Only the rippling wake of her hastily withdrawn toes marked the crystalline surface.

"The Gwenwyvar lives here? But I thought she were in tha' pool above Blaec-del — the one Meredydd dunked me in to heal me."

"The Gwenwyvar lives . . . " How to describe it to the child? "The Gwenwyvar lives wherever she needs to live. She abides in the Water of Life and appears in the aislinn mists to whatever soul the Meri wills."

Gwynet peered hard at the water. Already the shadows were moving — the light, changing — and the aquas, greens and browns of the pool's depths were growing cooler, deeper. "Will I see her again?" she asked, voice wistful. "I only did see her the once, you know, and just for a moment, and I felt so *strange*, like waking from a dream — well, I thought I must've dreamed it, but Skeet and Osraed Bevol both say no."

"You may see her again," Taminy told her. "She's part of every Pilgrim's journey."

"They *all* see her?"

Taminy smiled wryly. "I didn't say all *see* her. I said she's a part of every Pilgrimage."

Gwynet shook her head, settling back on the soft summer grass.

"Not every Prentice at Halig-liath has . . . eyes that will see aislinn visions or Eibhilin beings. Some boys are rushed into the Academy because their parents or their Cirkemaster or the Chief of their House hopes they might have those Eyes . . . or believes they ought to have them."

Gwynet squinted at the water-sparkles rippling away from her in the breeze. "Like Aelder Prentice Brys, you mean? He says he saw *nothing* on his Pilgrimage but some grimy ol' Wicke in a stick shack who gabbled nonsense at him and give him a lump of clay. 'What'm I to do with this,' he says, and she says, 'Boy, it's what you make of it.'" Gwynet nodded emphatically. "It's what you make of it. Sounded wise to me. He thought it was fool-like."

"And what did he make of it? Did he say?"

"Oh, he got a hole in the bottom of his shoe, he says, an' used it to patch tha'. It come out when he crossed the Bebhinn."

Taminy laughed. A clever young man, Aelder Prentice Brys. Clever, but not wise. She sighed soul-deep, then. Year after year they came to the Sea, bright eyed and dreaming. And she would peek into their dreams and hear and see and touch the aislinn spirits they entertained there. Such spirits: Glory and Power and Wealth; Respect and Prestige; Beauty and Knowledge. And once in a long, long while, Love, Passion, Wisdom, a real and urgent Desire for Her.

Taminy shook herself — no, for the Meri, for the Animator. How few and far between those had been in the last hundred years, those earnest, hungering, thirsting souls; souls to whom a full cup was not a chalice overflowing with jewels, but enough Wisdom to be held in the palm of one hand. Jewels. Jewels like Gwynet or Bevol or — bless them — Calach and Tynedale, were rare. So rare.

"He helps out in Osraed Tynedale's class sometimes,"

Gwynet was saying. "Aelder Brys, I mean. An' he knows a powerful lot about — oh, everything. I think he could mouth the herbals in order and not miss a one, but . . . he doesn't seem to care. And Tam-tun, he's another. He says he'd be in Seamaster's school in Eada if he had to pick. But for his mam and da, you know."

Taminy nodded. "I know. It's painful to have to follow someone else's path in life, no matter what the circumstances. . . . What about you, Gwynet? Do you care to be learning the Art?"

Gwyent gazed up at her with the full force of a child's amazement in her eyes. "Oh, Taminy-mistress! I *do* care to learn. And I can't image at all how someone could *not*." She puzzled for a moment then said, very gravely, "It was when Osraed Wyth come home. Prentice Aelbort took me to watch. And in he come with his face all light. And I thought, 'Gwynet, tha's for you. You mun look for tha' light and you mun find it.'" Again that emphatic nod, as if she was making a pact with herself.

Taminy gazed at the child wonderingly, running aislinn fingers through the warm, silken flow of her thoughts — pure, they were, and unvarnished and untrained. *And I am feeling them. And that is the most wonderful thing of all.*

"I only hope," Gwynet went on, "tha' my eyes can see the aislinn things."

Taminy, caught off guard, laughed aloud. "How much proof of your own Gift do you need, Gwynet-a-Gled? You drew fire through a crystal with no tutoring. You found your own way to the use of the herbs and medicaments. And you knew by instinct what I had forgotten." She leaned out from her rock and extended one hand into the gentle tumble of water cascading over its stony ledge. It came back cupped around a tiny pool of water that sparkled in the slanting sunlight like a palmful of jewels. Droplets fell, crystal-bright, from between her curving fingers. "I learned it from the Gwenwyvar, who bid me take a handful of water from her pool and said that if a crystal could not be had, pure water might be used to focus the Weave."

"Water!" marveled Gwynet, scooping of a handful of her

own. "Then when I was praying peace to my dewdrops . . . "

"You were Weaving inyx, even then." Taminy gazed across the glittering liquid in her hand and tried to conjure the sensation, the aura, of the Weave. She watched the tiny points of light dance, out of focus, and emptied her mind of anything else. In a heartbeat she was wrapt in a sparkling veil, shrouded in a teeming world of radiance. The Sun was warmer here and brighter and the gurgle of water became song. Her heart beat faster, buoyed by the ease with which she had come here. Perhaps the sundered pool could someday reunite with the Sea.

"What do they see?" Gwynet's voice floated, disembodied, into Taminy's aislinn state. "People like Prentice Brys, I mean. When the Gwenwyvar comes up from her pool, what do they see?"

"Perhaps they see nothing," said Taminy. "Or perhaps they see only a wisp of cloud or a clot of steam. And when she speaks . . . " She hesitated, feeling something kiss the fringes of her perception. Curiosity. Suspicion. " . . . perhaps they hear only the wind. The Meri gives a call, Gwynet. As you called the fire to your crystal, the Meri breathes a call into the world. It is a whisper, a sweet, still song like a breeze from the Sea. It summons those who hear it. It draws them to the Water of Life and bids them drink."

In a sudden flutter of wings, a blue-black bird dropped from the trees to settle on the rim of Taminy's cupped hand and sip the water there. Indecision — she felt it, sharp and clear, on the periphery of her awareness. Indecision and thirst. "You see, even the creatures feel the summons and, as they have no taught fears, they come." A second bird, this one a bright red, fluttered down to join the first. Wonder washed over the indecision.

Taminy withdrew from her gem-scattered veil and turned her head. Her eyes touched the fringe of brush and fern that ringed the glen Nairne-side and, from the place where her gaze lit, appeared a girl of perhaps seventeen or eighteen — timid, wary, but drawn.

The birds fled Taminy's fingertips and sailed skyward and the girl's eyes followed them out of sight. Finally, she brought her gaze back to Taminy, seated on her rock.

"Are you . . . are you a Wicke?" she asked and Taminy felt as much anticipation as fear in the words.

She smiled. "No. Are you?"

"But you . . . you called me."

"Does that make me a Wicke? You came."

The gray eyes widened. "I'm the Cirkemaster's daughter, Iseabal."

"Yes, I know. I'm Taminy. I'm Gwynet's tutor." She gestured at the little girl, who was regarding Iseabal with open-mouthed astonishment.

The Cirkemaster's girl glanced back and forth between them, picking the leaves from her skirt. "I'm intruding," she said and licked her lips. "I beg pardon."

"Not at all. Please, don't go." Taminy slid down from her perch onto the grass behind Gwynet, then lowered herself to a mossy rock.

Across the pool, Iseabal vacillated. "May I . . . may I stay and listen?"

Well, Iseabal, thought Taminy, *perhaps you are to be dedicated to God, after all.* Aloud she said, "Of course you may stay and listen. Come, Iseabal, and sit with us."

A shy smile preceded the girl from the hedge of brush and trees as she came lightly, with lifted skirts, across the bridge of stone at the head of the pool and over into Taminy's verdant classroom.

The Council session had been relatively sedate. Osraed Wyth had appeared long enough to announce his intention of compiling a Book of the Covenant, and confirmed that he would lead a class on the Covenant for first year Prentices. There was no mention of Meredydd's fate or her guilt or innocence as a Wicke. The subject of formally opening Halig-liath to girls had been broached and a reluctant discussion begun when a dispatch from Creiddly-lad curtailed it.

Bevol was first to read it, his face opaquely denying the other Osraed access to his thoughts.

"Well," asked Ealad-hach. "What is it?"

"The General Assembly has been postponed again due to ongoing diplomatic overtures to the Deasach. Oh, and there is also the matter of a new wing the Cyne is adding to the Castle to house his collection of historical and artistic objects. He's overseeing that project personally, of course."

"This is the third time he has postponed the summer Assembly," observed Faer-wald. "If he waits much longer, we'll be into the harvest. Forecasts indicate a wet, cold autumn is to be expected — with early snows. That could make travel very difficult for the members."

"Well, travel we must," said Bevol, "unless we yield to the idea that this summer's agenda will have to be carried over to the next spring session."

"But we have a full agenda," objected Eadmund who, with Bevol, represented Halig-liath in the Assembly Hall. "After Tell Fest, Ren Catahn Hillwild presented us with an entire list of issues the Hillwild wish to address in the Hall. I assure you, they are not minor ones. Add to that what the villages bring and we could be in session from now until next Solstice. How does Cyne Colfre propose to put these issues off?"

"He does not propose to put them off," said Bevol, eyes still on the dispatch. "He includes a list of items he has gathered for the agenda and proposes to poll the Assembly by post to obtain permission for some of these matters — the 'more mundane among them,' as he puts it — to be fielded by the Privy Council."

"The Privy Council?" repeated Faer-wald. "But that's hardly appropriate. The Privy isn't an elected body; it's not representative. It's purpose is to advise the Cyne in personal diplomacy and the civic affairs of Creiddylad."

"Might we hear the Cyne's agenda?" asked Calach.

Bevol passed the dispatch back to the Chamber Prentice and bid him read it aloud. This he did, while the Osraed scribbled their notes and furrowed their brows and pulled at beards and lips.

When the reading was finished, Bevol shook his head. "He's asking for a blank slate. He's asking us to leave the selection of items for the Privy Council's agenda to their discretion."

"That is unacceptable," murmured Calach. "We must know what issues the Privy Council is to act upon. Most of those items are of regional or even national interest."

"Perhaps we need to remind the Cyne that the Covenant requires the Hall to sit with the Crown on all national issues," suggested Osraed Kynan.

"I say we must go further," said Tynedale. "We should indicate those issues which may not be decided by the Privy Council."

"That," said Bevol, "would be most of them."

Ealad-hach made a sound eloquent with frustration. "The Cyne is no ignoramus. He *knows* what things may be dealt with by his Privy Council and what things must go to the Hall."

"I am sure he knows," said Tynedale. "But if we do not seek to document the limits set on that institution, it may begin to exceed them and assume duties covenanted to the Hall."

"Covenanted. Yes, exactly," said Ealad-hach. "The Covenant stipulates that national and wide regional issues are to be decided by *representative* government. Colfre knows the Covenant. Surely we can trust him to abide by it."

Bevol lifted an eyebrow. "The way we can trust him not to interfere with the celebrations of the Cirke? He has participated, unbidden, in the Waningfeast rite. The Farewelling has not been missed by a Cyne since the last year of the reign of Siolta the Lawgiver, yet Colfre has seen fit to pass it two Seasons running. And the Grand Tell has been waived for the first time in history. Even in the Season of Siolta's murder, Cyneric Thearl and the Cwen Mother saw the newly Chosen at Mertuile despite their grief. Yet this year, with no more reason than a delicate diplomacy, our Osraed remain at home and the Osmaer sits in her place at Ochanshrine." Bevol's voice was gentle, empty of anger, but filled with a passion intended to persuade. "Brothers, if it were one thing or another — *only* the sipping of wine from the Star Chalice, *only* the raising of the Privy Council to handle matters reserved to the Hall — then I would not suggest that perhaps we must offer our Cyne closer guidance."

"He will not like it," said Ealad-hach.

"Hardly germane," countered Tynedale. "I hold with

Bevol. I believe we must reply to this dispatch immediately and seek to define the limits of the Privy Council lest they seek to define their own . . . and ours."

Bevol called for a vote in which only Ealad-hach gave a negative tell. It was decided, then. A response would be drawn and sent to Creiddylad with the new Osraed Lealbhallain on the mid-week packet.

CHAPTER 6

*The Spirit is found in the soul when sought with truth
and self-sacrifice, as fire is found in wood, water in
hidden springs, cream in milk, and oil in the lamp.*

*This Spirit is hidden in all things, as cream is hidden in
milk. It is the source of self-knowledge and self-sacrifice. This is the Spirit of all, which men call God.*

— *Osraed Haefer Hillwild, Commentary and Observations*

His mother and sisters cried and covered him with hugs
and kisses. He returned them with fervor, realizing again
how complete a change he was making in his life. He'd felt
it first while packing — that sense of something slipping
away. When he had closed the door to his room that
morning, he recognized the symbology of that ordinary act.
It was not a happy recognition. The new Osraed, secure in
his faith and purpose, was eager and prepared; the boy,
leaving the security of his home village for an unfamiliar
city, was anxious and sorrowful. And now, standing on the
docks with his family around him, Lealbhallain-mac-Mercer knew what it meant to be torn.

"Well, son." His father's eyes said that he, too, was
caught between gladness and loss, "I guess I need not tell
you how proud I am this day. That a son of mine be found
acceptable to the Meri . . . " He gazed again at the stellate
mark on Leal's forehead and shook his head in wonder.

"Does it matter that I'll not be taking on the trade?"
asked Leal ingenuously.

Giolla Mercer laughed. "Ah, the girls will do fine by the
trade. You've something more important to do with your

years than tending a shop, however fine a shop it might be. You've done well, Leal. But you don't need me to tell you that."

Leal laid a hand on his father's shoulder. "Oh, you're wrong, da. I *do* need you to tell me."

They left him then, amid more tears and smiles and exhortations to be warm and well-fed and happy and to listen well to the Meri. He could promise them that much, at least. He watched them out of sight, his eyes lingering on the corner where sat Iain Spenser's public house, then turned to where the Osraed Bevol and Eadmund awaited him.

Bevol handed him a small leather portfolio, hand-tooled and gilded and fastened with a gold clasp. Leal took it delicately, somewhat in awe of being asked to take a missal to the Cyne.

"Now remember," said Bevol, "that you do not need to wait for an answer to this, but do give it directly into the hands of the Cyne and do tell the Abbod, Osraed Ladhar, what it is you have delivered. And give him this." The elder Osraed produced a second, less ornate envelope and handed that to Leal as well. "This will explain to our Brothers of the Jewel what our message to the Cyne contains."

The message resting in his hand, Leal felt an odd tingling run up his spine and, for a moment, he looked at the other Osraed though a haze of shimmering motes. He opened his mouth and said, "There are Osraed in Creiddylad who will be displeased by this. They have lost the Touch and the breeze of inspiration no longer blows unhindered through their souls."

Bevol, his eyes closed as if he savored the river's perfume, nodded. "Yes. A hard truth, though. We like to believe the connection can never be lost."

"What are you saying? How does Osraed Lealbhallain know of matters involving the Osraed of Creiddylad?"

Leal's eyes returned to focus on Osraed Eadmund's face. The older man was glancing from him to Bevol in startled bemusement. He hadn't felt the Touch, Leal realized, but Bevol had. He was stunned. Despite the evidence of history, it had never really occurred to him that receptivity to the Meri's Eibhilin Light was something that could be lost. Perhaps once, long ago, it might have happened but surely not in this age. . . . He shivered.

Bevol didn't respond to Eadmund's questions. His eyes holding Leal's, he said simply, "We have the lesson of history. Pray the Meri we are not destined to repeat that lesson."

History. That had not been Lealbhallain's strongest subject, but he knew the lesson Bevol referred to. Only once in the history of the Osraed had the Light guttered among the Meri's Chosen. Once, during the reign of Cyne Liusadhe. Once, over two hundred years before.

We like to forget that, Leal reflected, watching the river glide beneath the keel of the westbound barge. *We tell ourselves it cannot happen again. Perhaps we blind ourselves. Perhaps it is happening already.*

He was cold, though the breeze from the water was not particularly chill. The boy in him wanted to protest that he would not allow it to happen. He would go to Creiddylad and wake the Osraed that slumbered there. He, Lealbhallain, would wake the dead if necessary. But the boy gave way quickly to the man who calmly determined to deliver his message and pursue his mission among Creiddylad's poor as the Meri directed, and to never, never lose sight of Her Light.

Standing on Cirkebridge, Taminy let her gaze float upriver toward the quay. Along the broad, slow-moving channel, warm stone took the Sun's light and radiated it into the balmy air. Old stone, new stone; a piebald coat of aging, mellow and new, crisp patchwork. The art of mason and stonecutter reflected dreamily in Halig-tyne's slow, liquid ramble — from the intricately carved balustrade to the rise of brick and beam storefront, the river mirrored all without prejudice.

Taminy's eyes welcomed the watery images. They were more familiar than the sharper, clearer lines of the orderly storefronts. She felt like a child waking from a recurring dream. *Oh, yes. I've had this dream before, of walls that*

*run upright and corners that meet sharply and sunlight
that falls straight down.*

Upstream at Cornerquay, the new Mercer's Bridge cast
its rippling, shadowy twin into the flood. Taminy could just
see a sparse, bobbing forest of masts off to the right where
the river curled lovingly at the feet of the palisades like a
hearth cat. Her eyes made the cliff-climb effortlessly.
Flying, hawk-like up the ageless expanse of rock, they
crested just above the walls of Halig-liath, fluttered with
the banners, came to rest on the gleaming tile roof of the
central rotunda.

How I loved you, she thought, *though I was not
welcome.* Her mouth made a wry twist. *Or perhaps
because I was not welcome.* She still loved Halig-liath. She
loved all of Nairne, pain and joy. *A hundred years has
changed you not at all.*

Ah, not so. All of Caraid-land is changed.

The thought came from close by and far away. Taminy
paused her own contemplations to consider it, not needing
to ask where it came from. It was true, of course. She
could feel it. From the Osraed in their chambers, from the
villagers drifting past her on the bridge, from the
Cirkemaster, from his daughter.

She closed her eyes. Yes, even from the river, crawling
beneath the bridge, vibrating the stone beneath her feet.

"Taminy!"

Eyes open, she turned her head to see Gwynet's bright
head bobbing toward her from Cirkeside, wending her
way around a cluster of chatting women, a pony cart, a puff
of sheep. She paused at the sheep to pat noses and caress
wool, and smiled at the young shepherd as they swept past
her like low-lying clouds.

"Am I late?" she asked, breathless. "I don't mean to be,
but Master Tynedale had a raft of books to carry."

"Hmmm. And a story to tell, too, I'll wager," Taminy
said, tapping the girl's sun-pinked nose. She turned and
began to walk toward Greenside.

Gwynet fell into step beside her — two to her one. "Oh,
and he did! All about how Ruanaidhe's Leap got to be
called tha'."

Taminy's brows ascended in mock dismay. "Oh, well, there's naught like a fine tale of murder and suicide to fill a child's head."

"It was powerful sad," said Gwynet. "Poor Cwen Goscelin — to have to watch her dear husband murdered right afore her eyes. And poor little Riagan Thearl — to lose his da, so."

And what of your da, child, Taminy thought, *whom you never knew? Poor you — but you'd never think it.*

"Cyne Siolta was a very good Cyne wasn't he?"

"Yes, I believe he was."

"Aye. Master Tynedale says so too." Her feet dragged as she spoke. "He says he was one of the very best Cynes ever. . . . Why would Ruanaidhe want to kill him?"

"Now, Osraed Tynedale must surely have told you that."

"Oh, well, yes. For his Uncle Haefer locked up in Halig-liath. But tha's just the scum reason, in't it?"

Taminy glanced at her sharply. "The *scum* reason?"

"Like the scum stuff tha' floats atop a bog puddle. The *real* is underneath, in't it? I figure that were Ruanaidhe's toppermost reason — the one that come out of his head first. But Halig-liath's no kind of prison and his uncle were happy there, which Ruanaidhe must've known, too, for he spoke with him not a sevenday before he went off and murdered Cyne Siolta."

"Then why do *you* think he killed the Cyne?"

Gwynet stopped walking to ponder that. "Not for his uncle. For himself, I think. 'Cause he was grieving."

"Grieving? For what?"

"For the loss of his uncle. He must've known the Hillwild was Prenticed to the Osraed and that he meant to take the Pilgrim Walk. Well, Haefer Hillwild was the Meri's then, sure as could be. Dead to Ruanaidhe, like. He'd no more lead his men into battle with Her Kiss on his soul. Angry, the young Hillwild must've been at tha' and powerful grieved. And so he gave his anger to Cyne Siolta who'd put his uncle away from him. And he passed on his grief to those who loved Siolta as he loved Haefer Hageswode." She paused, nodding, then said, "How raw to know, in the end, that it could nowise stop the hurting. All that grief and he put the biggest burden on himself. He lost all and every. Poor Ruanaidhe."

She put her hand upon the bridgewall and leaned out to peer over into the water running, thick, below. "Do you think he really trans-ported into a river silkie like as they said?"

Poor Ruanaidhe, thought Taminy. "Transformed, you mean," she said aloud. "And in a hundred and forty-five years I doubt five people have bled for Ruanaidhe Hillwild. But you — you bleed for everyone." She put a hand on Gwynet's shoulder and pressed it. "Bless you, Gwynet."

"*Am* blessed, mistress," she murmured, shooting her a sideways glance. "And greatly so." She looked back at the water. "You know these things, mistress Taminy — did Ruanaidhe the Red become a river silkie?"

"What? And ruin a perfectly good legend? *You* must wonder along with everyone else." Taminy grasped Gwynet's shoulders and turned her toward the Greenside shore. "Walk, or we'll never get our errands done."

They visited the Mercer's first, for candles, cook pots and oddiments, then the Tanner's for some shoes and, last of all, they went to the shop of the Webber, Marnie-o-Loom.

The shop had belonged to Marnie's aged grandfather when Taminy had last set foot in it. And here there was change. The cloth that hung on display on wall or rack, that lay folded soft on table and in window, was finer, showed more variety of color and pattern than the old Webber's. Marnie was a wonder at her craft. The shop walls had been covered in places with cloth that was skillfully attached with glue or varnish of some sort. And the floors had the gleam of polished new pine and were covered with a riot of hand-loomed rugs.

A young man behind the cutting table was the only person in the shop, but from an arched doorway at the rear of the room came the clatter-thunk of working looms — like a chorus of arhythmic drums.

"May I help you?" the young man asked and smiled engagingly.

Taminy returned the smile, her hand flitting over a roll of soft, thick twyla wool perched next to the table on a cutting rack. "I'm looking for winter cloth," she said, "for cold weather gear."

"Ah, coat cloth then?"

"Coats and hoods and good, warm blouses."

"That piece you've got your hand on is as fine a bit of wool as you'll ever see. Softest in town and truest of color." He winked. "Granmar's secret."

"It is lovely," Taminy agreed, admiring the vivid green of the fabric. "How much per yard?"

"Seventy-five oonagh. It would look grand on your little sister," he added, smiling at Gwynet, who was inspecting a fleece hood, "and even grander on you."

"Thank you. You're very kind," said Taminy and felt an odd stirring of pleasure at the compliment.

"You're new to Nairne," the youth observed. "I saw you at Tell Fest, didn't I?"

"May have. I'm Taminy. Taminy-a-Gled. Gwynet and I live up at the Manor with Osraed Bevol."

He shifted awkwardly. "Ah, of course! You set my Granmar's tongue wagging, right enough. Like to have fallen off. Leastwise, we'd have *liked* it to at times. So, are you . . . er . . . are you going up to Halig-liath?"

"No."

His open, apple-shiny face gleamed with relief. "Oh, that's fine, then."

Taminy's mouth twitched with the desire to grimace. *Not one of* those *girls, then, eh?* "I tutor Gwynet. She's attending the Academy. And doing quite well, too. Osraed Bevol says she has a natural Gift. . . . You haven't told me your name."

"Oh! Ah. It's Terris. Terris-mac-Webber." He shuffled momentarily behind his long table, then circled it, coming to stand just across from her at the rack of green wool. "My Gram wove this roll. Smooth as velvet for all it's a double weave."

Taminy ran a hand over the thick fabric. It was as vivid to the touch as it was to the eye. That amazed her — not the cloth itself, but the sensation of touch. How different this world was from her world of water and spirit. Amazing, too, was her awareness of this boy — no, of *his* awareness of her. The intensity of his regard prickled her face and made her skin flush.

"Daeges-eage, Terris," said a girl's voice from the doorway of the shop.

Terris jumped like a spooked cat and Taminy realized other eyes than his had tickled her senses. She turned. A trio of girls stood in the doorway. Iseabal-a-Nairnecirke was one of them. The other two, a vivid redhead and a small, darkling cailin with a froth of dark brown hair, Taminy didn't know. It was the redhead who'd spoken, and she now regarded Terris-mac-Webber as if he was a dog she had caught raiding the larder.

"Oh! Daeges-eage, Aine . . . ah, Iseabal, Doireann." He glanced quickly at Taminy, his face reddening. "I . . . was . . . "

Before he could force another word from between his lips, Taminy rescued him from his discomfiture. "Yes, I *will* have some of this fine green twyla. Four yards, please and, ah. . . . " She glanced at a neighboring bolt. "And two yards of the blue. And I'll need some softweave for leggins and sous-shirts."

"Oh. Over there." Terris motioned across the room to a table piled high with goods, then moved to measure Taminy's wool.

Taminy took Gwynet across the shop to inspect the softweave while the other girls, with the exception of Iseabal, moved to linger at Terris's cutting table. Iseabal gave them a glance, then followed Taminy and Gwynet.

She stood silently for a moment, fingering some softweave with careless hands. "I was looking for you, Taminy," she said finally. "I thought maybe you would go to that pool again today." A sideways glance through dark waves checked Taminy's face for welcome.

She put welcome into her smile, and saw it catch fire in Iseabal's eyes.

"Will you, do you think? Go to that place?"

"I thought we might, after our errands. You're welcome to come."

"Am I? Am I really? I didn't get in the way of your

lessons last time? I was afraid I might have. . . . All my questions — "

"They were good questions." Taminy pulled out a length of gray softweave and glanced over at the cutting table where a flash-flushing Terris talked awkwardly with his two companions. "Do your friends fancy a trek to the woods?"

"Them?" Iseabal first seemed shocked at the idea, then admitted, "I suppose I hoped they might, though when I told Aine about your herbals she only wondered if you might have a poultice that would lift off her freckles. And Doireann, well, a trek in the woods would most certainly scuff her shoes and stain her skirts and riot her hair."

Taminy laughed and was immediately aware that the other girls had shifted their attention from blushing Terris to her and Iseabal.

"So," said Aine the Red, crossing the shop's rug-littered floor. "So, you're Taminy. I saw you at Tell Fest — well, the whole *town* did, didn't we? Imagine Terris's Gram thinking *you* were Meri-did-a-Lagan. All that white hair of yours — and, of course, you're so much *thinner* than Meri-did."

"I don't think you should call her that," said Iseabal, blushing. "It's unkind. She's — she's dead, after all."

And Gwynet, who had been watching the overhead exchange, piped, "No, she's not. She's with the Meri. Isn't she, Taminy?"

Taminy only smiled. This was not the time to argue or to shock or to make inveterate enemies. Enemies. Those would come all too easily in days ahead. Gathering up an armful of softweave, she moved past Aine to the cutting table. "She's where she needs to be."

"Oh, like as if you know," said the other girl, following her with appraising hazel eyes.

"Uh, how many yards?" stammered Terris. He caught up the softweave as if desperate to have something to do.

"Six of the grey and four of the heather, please."

"Taminy and I are going to the pool I told you about," said Iseabal. "Over on the Bebhinn, up Lagan way."

"Hunting for weeds?" asked Aine, and Doireann silently wrinkled her nose.

"Not weeds," said Gwynet from the midst of them. "Herbals. Taminy knows bookfuls about herbals."

"Weeds," said Aine. "Common weeds."

"Nothing in creation is common," Taminy said. "Everything has a place and a purpose. A weed can be a wonder in its rightful place."

"And I suppose you've herbals that can cure warts and make eyelashes grow?"

"Well, I know that sassafras purifies the blood and takes away the mooning pain. Skybell, crushed with rosemary and chamomile, makes the skin glow." She thought her own flesh gleamed as she said it; Aine's eyes told her she wasn't wrong.

"Is that true?" Doireann spoke for the first time, her dark gaze raking Taminy's face. "Can your herbs really change someone's complexion? That can't be. . . . Can it?"

"Herbs can help, of course. But it's not just what you put on the outside. It's what you put *inside*, as well. What you eat and drink. What you think and feel." She glanced pointedly at Aine's overly ruddy face.

"Nonsense," Aine said. "What I eat can't possibly affect my skin."

"Of course it can," persisted Taminy gently.

Aine put her fists on her hips. "Oh, *do* tell me it's sugar creams and iced-cakes that'll make my freckles fade. I'll eat them away in a week! Oh, and chocolates to make my hair brown, too, I imagine."

Taminy laughed. Doireann almost smiled.

"I'll get my herbs at the Apothecary, thank you," Aine concluded.

Taminy shrugged. "Where do you think all those fine Apothecary powders and elixirs come from, Aine? Someone must collect them and sort them and process them before they go to the Apothecary."

"Aye!" said Gwynet with much feeling. She glanced down at her green-stained fingertips. "I surely know who *washes* them."

"Hot and cold water," opined Aine. "That's what my Ma says. That's the common healing. Leave the artful stuff and the inyxes to the Osraed. *They* know what they're doing."

"Girls shouldn't go up to Halig-liath," murmured Doireann, sullen eyes on Gwynet. "It's not our domain."

"But you'd go, wouldn't you? If they said it was all right?"

Iseabal glanced from one girl to the other. *"Wouldn't you?"*

"Never," said Aine. "Musty books and histories. Submission and servitude and all that studying. And look at the little one's hands. All green and frog-like from cleaning weeds."

"It's not right," said Doireann.

"I'll tell you what's not right." The voice thrust into the air like a gnarled old tree limb. "What's not right is my grandson wasting precious shop time flirting and fawning with a pack of dandelion brained cailin." Marnie-o-Loom stood in the doorway to the nether room, glaring at the knot of youngsters grouped around her cutting table.

Terris paled, then flushed, then paled again. "Granmar, I —"

Taminy shot the old woman a welcoming smile. "Oh, hardly wasted, Mam Webber. He's mostly been waiting on me." She held up an end of vividly green wool. "This is wonderful fabric, Mam. It feels as if you've woven the warmth of sun on wool right into it."

"Odd you should say that, girl," Marnie said. "For it was told of my Granpar that he could weave the spring and summer into his winter cloth. But then Granpar were a little fey. He wove more than fabrics, if you take my meaning." There was pride in that and a little wistfulness.

"I think you inherited his Gift," Taminy told her.

"God, mighty and merciful! What *are* you on about, cailin? What would an old woman like me be doing messin' about with *Weavin'*?"

"It's not such a difficult inyx," said Taminy, perhaps incautiously.

"Ah! And you'd know it, I s'pose?"

"I do know it." *Yes, indeed, I do. And so suddenly and so clearly, I can feel it in my fingertips.*

Various noises of disbelief rose around her and Marnie said, "Scraps! If you knew such an inyx, you'd use it yourself."

Taminy shrugged, smiling. "But, Mam, I don't know how to weave cloth."

Marnie gave a hoot of laughter. "And me, I don't know how to Weave inyx. And wouldn't, if I could. I've never uttered a duan in my life. Scraps! If I tried, the Eibhilin would just shut up their ears and wail. There's folks as take me for a Wicke already. I'm not like to give 'em more grounds. And neither should you, girlie." She pointed a gnarled finger at Taminy. "You're not Meredydd, but you're like her. Careful you don't go the same way she did. Now, sell 'er the cloth, boy." She glared at Terris, then disappeared into her workshop.

Too late, old woman, Taminy thought. *I've gone Meredydd's way. Now, I am going my own*.

"Uh," said Terris, fumbling the softweave. "That was six?"

She turned back to him. Sweat beaded on his forehead. She nearly laughed, smiled instead, and said, "Six of the grey, four of the heather."

"Marnie's right," said Aine, behind her. "If you knew any Runes you'd Weave them yourself."

"That'll be six ambre, fifty," said Terris.

"Osraed Bevol knows a Rune that will crumble stone," Taminy said. She fetched out her belt pouch and counted out six gold ambres and a sorcha. "I don't think he's ever had reason to use it."

"You don't know any Runes. I'll bet you don't even know the simplest duan."

"Yes, she does," said Iseabal. "I've heard her sing."

"I do know some Runes," murmured Taminy, handing Terris her coins. *Yes, all neatly stacked in my head like books on a shelf. Useless unless read. And my eyes fail me.* "Or I did."

"If you knew the teenicst, tiniest inyx," persisted Aine Red, "then you'd have used it to put some color in that hair of yours."

Taminy took up her package and turned to look at the other girl appraisingly. *Ah, that's the way of it.* "And why would I do that? I *like* the color of *my* hair. Don't you like yours?"

She left the shop then, slipping out onto the street to a pleasant assault of Nairnian sights and sounds and smells. *The Backstere's next.*

The others had followed her, leaving Terris alone to sulk.

"I do like my hair, thank you," said Aine, striking her defensive pose in the middle of the flagstone walk. "I think it's glorious." She tossed it for good effect, making sunlight ripple through it like fire.

Taminy nodded. "You're right. It *is* glorious. If I had hair as bright and beautiful as that, I'd be very glad of it. And very careful about eating too many chocolates."

Doireann giggled and Taminy, ignoring Aine's gawping stare, glanced from Gwynet to Iseabal.

"I think we should go to the Backstere's before we take our packages home, don't you?"

Gwynet's eyes lit up like twin lightbowls. "Oh, *could* we, Taminy? *Could* we go there?"

"We'll still go to the woods, won't we?" asked Iseabal, eying her two friends.

"If you like." She turned to Aine and Doireann. "You're welcome to come along."

Doireann's dark eyes flickered from Taminy's face to Aine's and back. She licked her lips. "Do you really know a poultice for the complexion?"

"Doireann Spenser! You are that gullible!" With a flick of blazing tresses, Aine turned and walked away.

Doireann, blushing rose beneath her olive skin, gave Taminy one last glance before tailing after her friend.

"But she says she *knows*," Doireann's voice came back to them, whining. "What harm is there in calling her out?" Aine said nothing and the two went their way.

Iseabal looked after, her brow furrowed, while Taminy smiled. "Cream cakes!" she said, and led the way to the Backstere's shop.

They didn't go to the pool after all, for the afternoon became cool and dark with blue-gray clouds that threatened rain. Instead, Taminy invited Iseabal to supper and, after a grant of permission from the Cirkemaster and his wife, the three girls started up the road toward Gled

Manor, carrying Marnie's fine cloth and blinking against a lusty breeze.

"Delicious!" exclaimed Taminy. "Oh, delicious breeze!" And she laughed when it kicked up her skirts and flirted with her hair.

Rain began to fall, raising tiny puffs of dust in the roadway. The rhythm of it put a song on Taminy's lips and she sang it:

> *"Tiny, bright, jewelled, light —*
> *Spilling on the ground.*
> *Who has tilt the silver box*
> *And sent the rain gems tumbling down?*
> *Is that you, saucy breeze,*
> *Playing tap-tunes on the leaves?*
> *Does your mistress know you play*
> *And toss her Eibhilin jewels away?"*

"How pretty!" said Iseabal. "You have a wonderful voice. Mama will want you in her chorus, I know. Where did you learn that?"

"I don't — " Taminy began, then hesitated. *I don't remember*, she'd been about to say, but it seemed as if the moist breeze had blown memory back into her head with the tune. "My mama taught it to me. It was our rainy day song. When I was a little girl, we'd sit in the window casement of my room and sing the song to the drops that fell on the Sanctuary roof. I remember how the rain would make the slate of the roof look dark and stormy like the sky."

Iseabal glanced at her, eyes amazed. "Is your father a Cirkemaster, too? Or, I mean, was he? I . . . I'd heard . . . that is, someone said you were orphaned."

Taminy nodded, fighting a sudden sense of vertigo and wondering if it showed. *Time. It's like a corridor. I think I'm at one end and suddenly — whisk! — I'm at the other, looking back at myself and wondering, Who is that girl?*

"I can see the Sanctuary roof from my bedroom window, too," said Iseabal. "When it rains I pretend . . . " She smiled shyly and lowered her eyes to the toes of her shoes. "I pretend the roof is a sea snake's back, long and streaming slick with water, and that I'm riding high up among its great fins, all dry and cozy." She bobbed her head. "I mean, I used to pretend that. Child-ways. I'm too old now, of course."

"Never," said Taminy, tearing her eyes from the other end of the corridor. "Never be too old to ride sea snakes in the rain, Iseabal."

They were running by the time they reached Gled Manor. Running and laughing and soaking wet. They erupted into the hall, swept up the stairs, and collapsed into Taminy's room, dropping packages and scurrying for towels. While Taminy sat on her bed peeling off wet stockings, and Gwynet curled in the window seat, Iseabal dried her hair and wandered. She marveled at the variety of books on Taminy's shelf, admired the hangings of calligraphies, and musical scores, and glass-pressed flowers and feathers, and stopped stone still to stare at a crystal set atop a wooden sconce.

She turned from it to award Taminy a wondering gaze. "Is it yours?" she asked, and when Taminy nodded, "May I . . . may I hold it?"

"Of course."

Iseabal lifted the crystal from the little shelf and turned it in her hands. "It's beautiful! So very beautiful. Pure, like rain and . . . warm!"

Taminy watched the other girl's face bathed in lamp light, her eyes great and pale and very like the crystal. She watched the crystal, too, and wondered if those pale-pure eyes noticed the tiny pulse of light deep down among the converging facets — a pulse that would have been there if every light in the room was extinguished. The crystal knew, if Iseabal did not, what gifts might live in the soul of a Cirkemaster's daughter.

"Look how it glows!" said Iseabal. "Does it have a name? Papa says the Osraed always name theirs. His is Perahta — and, of course, I know about Ochan's Osmaer — everyone does. Does this one have a name?" She turned curious eyes to Taminy.

"Ileane," Taminy said. "Light Bearer."

"And you Runeweave with it?"

"I did . . . once. It's been a long time."

"I suppose I should believe that's wicked. I suppose I should leave."

"Do you want to?"

Iseabal shook her head, dragging rain-heavy hair across her shoulders. "No." She set the crystal back on its sconce and came to perch beside Taminy on the bed. "I did run out on Meredydd. I didn't want to, but I did." She glanced over at the crystal. "Aine thinks it's all so much frivol, or at least she'd like me to believe she thinks that. And to Doireann, it's all impossibly wicked. My father felt sorry for Meredydd. He wanted me to befriend her so I could help save her soul. I didn't want to save her soul — I mean, I didn't think it needed saving — but I couldn't be her friend while Aine and Doireann teased, and Brys-a-Lach threatened that my own soul was at risk, and my father waited for me to steal Meredydd away from her Weaving and visions."

She pulled her knees up and buried her face between them. "It was too much," she said, muffled. "I tried to talk to mother about it, but all she'd say was, 'I imagine your father's right, Isha. The poor cailin's spirit wants saving.'"

"She'd likely say the same of me," said Taminy.

"Aye."

"But you're not running from my house."

"No."

"And why not?"

Iseabal raised her head. "I don't know," she said. She glanced, again, at the crystal, Ileane, then back into Taminy's face. "I don't really know. Maybe I'm a little more wicked now. Or . . . a little less a coward."

Taminy smiled and took the other girl's hands. "I've some dry clothes you can wear," she said.

Below stairs, the front door opened and Osraed Bevol called and the three girls scurried to dress themselves for supper.

Bronwen was the furthest of his colleagues, so the sort to cock up the one wrong smuggle a table. He read the pages, relaxed pages. "I don't suppose anyone has ever laid eyes on such at least. The old books are normally willed in your own way, and the mill couple are much who will be... I don't suppose we... anyone within the... can... retire time...

CHAPTER 7

When the Pilgrim shall have fulfilled the conditions inherent in the name, "Who Seeks Us," that one shall know the blessing inherent in the words, "We shall guide in our Way."

— Osraed Ochan, Book of the Covenant,
compiled by Osraed Wyth

✧   ✧   ✧

Wyth Arundel flexed his cramped hand and stretched. His shoulders felt as if someone had been pummeling them. He closed his eyes, rolled them behind burning lids, then bent to examine his work. The lettering was good, but his hand was cramping horribly. He glanced up as a Prentice laid a set of freshly transcribed pages beside him on the library work table.

"Here, Osraed Wyth. Here are my pages and Fairlea's, too. Ready for proofreading."

Wyth smiled. "Thank you, Peagas. You've done very good work — both of you. Why don't you take a break now?"

The Prentice bobbed respectfully, glowing at having earned the new Osraed's smiles and praise, and hurried away to relieve his companion.

"How goes the work, Wyth?"

Wyth raised his eyes to see Osraed Bevol regarding him from the other side of the table. "Slowly, Osraed Bevol. The Prentices are a great help, but there is so much to get through." He rubbed his stiff fingers. "I don't suppose you know a Weave that will copy these pages without us having to write them out by hand."

Bevol's brows ascended. "I don't know of one. There's a

Runeweave for the printing of books, of course, so the text is clear and the ink won't smudge or fade." He eyed the neatly scripted pages. "I don't suppose anyone has ever had need of such an inyx. The old books are journals, added to year upon year and the only copies are made wholesale. I doubt anyone has ever had a job quite like this one — extracting *pieces* of the text. . . . Why don't you invent your own Weave?"

"I?" Wyth nearly laughed. "I, invent a Runeweave?"

Bevol shrugged. "Why not? You're entitled. Heh! Quite literally. And if you want to be finished anytime soon . . . "

Wyth followed his eyes to the stack of Holy Books and Osraed Treatises waiting to be read. "Yes. And I must be done soon." That was a troubling thought and made him raise his eyes to Bevol's, seeking some reassurance. He got none.

"Yes, I believe you must."

A Prentice scurried to present himself, then, and informed the Osraed Bevol that his presence was requested in the small audience chamber.

"It's the Ren Catahn, Master," said the boy awfully. "The Osraed Eadmund is already with him. I understand it's about the General Assembly of the Cyne's Council."

"Ah, yes. This is no surprise. Tell Eadmund I'll be there immediately." He turned back to Wyth. "Supper tonight, Wyth?"

Heat raced across Wyth's face, followed by an intense chill. *Oh, yes!* he thought. *Oh, no!* "I . . . I don't know if . . . " *If what, you idiot?*

Bevol was smiling at him. "She overwhelms?"

Wyth could only nod. "I don't know what to think of her. I don't know . . . how to behave." He glanced about the library. "Does anyone else know who — ?"

"No. You and I and Pov-Skeet. Gwynet, too, but Gwynet is too young, I think, to understand what that means."

"I empathize," Wyth murmured, then furrowed his brow in puzzlement. No, he was more than puzzled. "You mean *none* of the other Osraed know her?"

Bevol shook his head.

"But . . . how can that be?"

Bevol shrugged. "It simply *is*. Supper?"

Wyth licked his lips. "Thank you . . . yes. I'll come."

When Bevol had gone, Wyth tapped the lightbowl on his work table and watched the glow eddy and pulse. *No one else knew. How could they not when she was a magnet? No, not a magnet — a crystal.*

Someone rustled among the shelves behind him, breaking into his rumination. Flexing his fingers, he bent back to his work.

Osraed Bevol found the Ren Catahn Hillwild in the small annex to the Osraed council chamber, pacing before the tall windows and worrying the beaded sash of his leather shawl. He was a big man, blocking the instreaming sunlight and casting a long, broad shadow across the polished wooden floor. He turned at Bevol's footfall, sunlight glinting from the gold and silver filigree woven into his burgundy-black hair and beard, and flashing from the neat row of cuffs that bound a braided sidelock.

Bevol held out his arms in greeting. "Catahn! Your presence honors the place and cheers its people."

The Hillwild lord awarded him a wide smile, rendered especially brilliant by its dark frame of beard, and moved to smother him in a bear's embrace. "Bevol! God's Eyes, but it's good to see you! Pity we have not more pleasant things to discuss."

Bevol stepped back and glanced to where Osraed Eadmund sat at a small table, grimly shuffling papers. "Perhaps we should sit and discuss these unpleasant things — the quicker to deal with them."

The Osraed seated himself at the table, but Catahn's haunches had no more than grazed the velvet cushion before he was up again, pacing.

"Our Cyne ignores us," he said. "He stoppers his ears and blinkers his eyes and turns from his own mountains to look to someone else's seas and valleys. And if that were not enough, he insults us, slights us." He stopped pacing and faced the two Osraed. "He forgets himself, Chosen Ones. He forgets his duty to the Hillwild." He motioned at the roll of leather among the papers on the table. "We have inquiries, petitions, plaints which have waited months to be taken up in the Hall. Some of these issues have lain since last Assembly. And *there*, they were set aside as if they were of no consequence. The education of our children," he added, "is of *consequence!*"

Bevol pulled the leather scroll about so he could view its contents. He glanced at Eadmund. "Have you copied this?"

Eadmund shook his head. "I thought we should first discuss it. If there are modifications to be made — "

"Yes, yes, of course. Catahn, are you certain about this business with the Caraidin scouts?"

The big man nodded with a jingle of ornamentation. "There are no finer trackers than the Hillwild of Hrofceaster. They know how to read signs. The Cyne's men are scouting our villages, watching our holts."

"But to what end?" asked Eadmund. "Have you confronted them? Asked them what they're about?"

The Ren laughed, teeth flashing white in his dark face. "Oh, aye. Some've been faced off. They pose themselves as vagabonds, oddjobmen. Then off they go. And they dog us, going from village to village, from holt to holt. Watching." He gritted his teeth in a grimace; Bevol thought he even growled. "We do not like being watched."

"What do you suspect them of?" Bevol asked.

The Ren's queer amber eyes narrowed. "If the Cyne was not my own kinsman and covenanted ally, I would say they were assessing the strength of my fortifications, estimating my forces."

Eadmund's face was white. "Why should he — ? Is there a chance they might not be the Cyne's men?"

In answer, Catahn Hillwild reached beneath his shawl and pulled out a pouch. Holding it upside-down, he let a piece of metal the size of an ambre fall to the table with a clatter.

Bevol picked it up and turned it in his hands.

"Sash clip," said Catahn.

"Yes, and bearing the emblem of the House of Malcuim," murmured Bevol. "Caraidin Guard."

"It might have been stolen," conjectured Eadmund. "Or perhaps the man who lost it is an ex-soldier."

"Aye, either thing might be possible," admitted Catahn. "But though they claim to be rough men, they speak a mighty fine tongue in private speech. And of their clothing, only their cloaks and tunics and boots are rough, Master. I have it on good authority that what they wear close to their skin is fairer by far. Then there is the fact of their origins. My men have back-tracked several of their parties. They're coming up from the old outposts in the foothills."

"The outposts? But those have been empty for years," objected Eadmund. "Decades."

"Well, they're empty no longer. They're provisioned and they're populated."

"But flying no banners, I presume."

"No, Osraed Bevol. Not a scrap of cloth on any standard. But the forces are there and they crossed Feich land to get there. Now, as the Feich are a jealous lot, I would expect them to know when pack trains cross their lands and, as the Cyne's Durweard is a Feich, I would expect the Cyne to know what the Feich know."

"Gauging your strength," mused Bevol. "Why, I wonder? To know how many men he may call upon to raise an army?"

"Why would he not come straight about it and ask after our forces?"

Bevol raised his eyebrows. "Perhaps because he wants no one to know he plans to raise a fighting force?"

Catahn considered that. "Aye. He is talking cozy with the Deasach. Perhaps he doesn't trust them. Or perhaps it's the Hillwild he doesn't trust. I want to know the whichever of it, Osraed. My folk are nervous with this cat-footing. And they're angry on other counts, as well."

"Yes," said Bevol, glancing again at the petition. "I see the schools are not being kept up."

"Ah! The schools!" The Hillwild's face reddened. "That's the rawest of it, Osraed." He moved to perch on one corner of the chair opposite Bevol. "Two years have passed in which we have petitioned your Brothers of the Jewel for teachers, for books to fill our wisdom halls. None have come. They seem content to abandon us to ignorance."

"Surely — " began Eadmund, but a look from the Hillwild hushed him.

"Only the Meri remembered us last year, sending several of Her Chosen to us. But it is not enough. Our schoolrooms are crowded beyond their capacity. What teachers we have are unable to take in all the children, and some of the best of those sent to us aforetime have been recalled to schools in Creiddylad and Lin-liath. Our cleirachs have called upon the elder children to teach the younger, but some holts have no teachers at all. None. If their children will be taught, they must travel to a village or holt that has a school. And, to add salt to the wound, the Cyne has raised our Mercer taxes. Our petitions fall on deaf ears."

"A grave matter," Bevol agreed. He took a deep breath. "I think perhaps we, ourselves, must arrange for the cleirachs you need. We have, also, Aelder Prentices who may be assigned as teachers. They are not full cleirachs, but their knowledge should serve you well."

Eadmund uttered a cough of protest. "Osraed Bevol — forgive me, but — without the approval of the Hall and the Cyne — not to mention the Brothers of the Jewel — how can we presume — I mean, it is their responsibility to assign cleirachs to the schools."

"It is a responsibility they have obviously defaulted on. If they are not willing or able to undertake it, then we must. By the Meri's Kiss, we must. We will inform them of what we are doing, of course. And — of course — we must inquire why *they* are not doing it . . . and why it never reached the floor of the Hall."

Eadmund shifted in his seat. "But should we not at least petition — "

"That is precisely what the Ren Catahn is doing, Eadmund — petitioning. But now the Hall will not hold session until only God and the Cyne know when. Our only other recourse is to remand these plaints to the Privy Council."

Eadmund wrinkled his nose and Catahn let out a bark

of humorless laughter. "And have them disappear! That's another issue, Osraed. The Privy Council no longer has Hillwild membership."

"What?" said Eadmund weakly. "Why not?"

"Ren Rhum was our appointee. You recall him, Osraed Bevol — he was from Alt-Reelig. Aye, well, his brother died and he took his family and went up home to bury him and set his affairs in order. At the end of a six-week, he was curried a missal from the Cyne and Council saying he was too long gone and had been replaced by an Eiric of the Saewode."

Bevol frowned. "And his second? Surely he had a hand-picked alternate?"

Catahn watched one huge hand flex and clench on the table top. "Luthai. Dead by drowning a month after Rhum left. Her family was sent home — they were lodged within Mertuile, so they had no recourse."

"Well, of course, they'd have had no reason to stay, would they?" asked Eadmund weakly.

Catahn gave the Osraed a look that drained any remaining color from his cheeks. "Funny thing, that. Her eldest son was love-bound to a daughter of the Eiric Cinge — a new member of the Assembly, as you may recall. The wedding has been cancelled. By order of the Privy Council, according to Luthai's widower. And that's the unseen, Osraed." Catahn poked the leather scroll with a stout finger. "You will not find, in our plaint, mention of all the Hillwild courtiers who have been 'excused' from their posts, nor of all the marriages between Caraidin and Hillwild that have been . . . postponed. How may we petition about that?"

He hauled himself up from the table and paced back to the windows. "It galls me, Osraed. He seems bent to cut our ties, one by one. In the name of the Gwyr, how can he, when his own mother — aye, and his own grandmother — were Hillwild?"

Bevol sighed and sat back in his chair. *Worse and worse.* "We have already sent a message to Cyne Colfre," he told Catahn, "expressing our conviction of the dire need to convene the Hall before Harvest. We can only hope he will respond. Until then, we will send you such teachers and books as we can locate or spare. About the other matters, we can do nothing . . . but pray."

"Is there no Weave you can perform, Osraed, that can unravel these matters?"

"Ah, we may look, Catahn, but we may not touch."

The Hillwild nodded. "Nor can we, without appearing disloyal to the House of Malcuim. Aye, more bite to that beast — I am blood-bound to this Cyne of ours. There are times I wish I was not."

Wyth was preparing to mount his horse when his mother came riding up the estate road and into the front court of Arundel, hair flying, eyes a-light, cheeks flushed to rose. She startled him in more ways than one; just to see her *look* like that was a revelation. His memory provided him no picture of her that contained such life. Not even in his dreams had she ever seemed so vibrant.

He watched her pull up and dismount while, behind her, a second horse and rider galloped into the forecourt. It was the Eiric Iasgair — a widower some years younger than the Moireach. Wyth was startled, again, at the keen interest in the other man's eyes as they followed her . . . and at his own lack of jealousy.

The Moireach approached him, laughing, arms out. She embraced him and gave him a motherly peck on each cheek. "Wyth! You're not just coming in!"

"Just going out. Master Bevol has asked me to dine with him this evening at Gled."

A slight frown curled between her brows. "Then you won't be having supper with us?" She glanced back at her riding companion, now dismounting from a bay mare. "Aidan was so hoping to hear your Tell. He was in Tuine during Tell Fest."

"Some other time, perhaps, Mother. Master Bevol was most insistent."

The Moireach made a dismissive gesture. "Surely, you don't need to call him 'Master' anymore. After all, you're his equal now." She laughed charmingly for the Eiric's benefit, tossing him a winsome smile.

Wyth shuffled uncomfortably. "Mother, I may be an Osraed, but I doubt I shall ever be Bevol's equal."

"Nonsense, Wyth. You're newly chosen. Bevol-a-Gled is an old man. Besides, the Meri called you Her son. She drew you into Her waters. There's glory in that, Wyth," she added, smiling up at him and touching his cheek. "Your light shines so brightly . . ."

He glanced uneasily at Eiric Iasgair, blood flushing his face. "Mother, please, I —"

"You're too humble by far. Everyone says so. Surely you don't have to bow and scrape and curry favor to Bevol-a-Gled."

Wyth tried not to feel the anger coiling in his heart. He pushed her hand gently away from his face. "I have never curried favor to any of the Osraed, but I owe Master Bevol all my respect. Besides, I need to consult with him about my work." He patted the thick portfolio tucked beneath his arm.

His mother glanced at it, new eagerness leaping in her eyes. She laid a hand on the polished leather. "Oh, do stay for supper. You can tell us all about your work."

Wyth felt his face flush yet again and wondered if he could possibly get any redder. "I'm sure the Eiric wouldn't be interested."

"Oh, but I would, Osraed Wyth." The other man assured him. "But please, don't trouble yourself on my account. I'll hear of it some other time — at your convenience, of course." He finished with a courtly bow of his head.

Wyth smiled, relieved. The courtesy was sincere. "Perhaps tomorrow evening, Eiric Iasgair — if that is convenient for you?"

"If the Moireach is amenable." He looked to Brighid Arundel.

She smiled, but beneath the smile seethed fierce frustration. Wyth felt it as heat beating against his face. He stepped back from the furnace.

"Of course," the Moireach said and laughed again, falsely. "And I'd forgotten you might have another reason to frequent Gled Manor." She turned coy eyes to the Eiric.

"There's a girl there. A fair-haired cailin with blue eyes. One of Osraed Bevol's foundlings. I dare say she's the attraction at Gled, not some fusty old Osraed."

Mention of Taminy as if she were no more than a village flirt was enough to stir Wyth's blood to rebellion. "Osraed Bevol is far from fusty, Mother," he said, moving quickly to mount his horse. "And Taminy . . . Taminy's eyes are green."

The Moireach feigned surprise — no, not feigned, Wyth realized. Her surprise was quite real. "By the Kiss! It amazes me you recall their color at all. That tells a deep tale."

Wyth swung his leg over the saddle. "I have to go. I'll be late if I don't." *There must be a Rune for keeping mothers at bay.* "I look forward to our supper with pleasure, Eiric Iasgair. Until then. Good evening, Mother." He swooped to give her cheek a quick peck, then gathered up his horse and rode away.

"And who is this Taminy your son so is enamored of?" he heard the Eiric ask as the two led their horses toward the stable.

"Oh, some marsh bird Osraed Bevol loosed at Tell Fest. The local boys are agog. A great improvement over his last obsession. At least this one's not a Wicke."

Wyth willed his mount to a canter and got swiftly out of earshot.

During supper he alternated between staring at Taminy and trying not to look at her at all. He had to concentrate to keep track of the conversation, made a fool of himself several times (he thought), and spoke in non-sequiturs.

When the meal was over, Gwynet and Skeet cleared the table while Wyth gathered up his portfolio with an eye to soliciting Osraed Bevol's help with his manuscript. But Bevol, begging his indulgence while he helped the youngsters with the dishes, disappeared, leaving Wyth alone in his study with Taminy and the suggestion that he show her his work.

Hugging his portfolio to his ribs, Wyth now hovered awkwardly at Bevol's workbench. A quick glance up into Taminy's sea green eyes spurred him to action with a spasmodic little hop. He flopped the folio onto the table top and unclasped it too quickly, sending a flurry of loose papers over the polished surface. Taminy gathered them up and ordered them while he dithered directionlessly.

"You have a fine hand," she said, returning the pages.

"Thank you. I'm dreadfully slow, though. The Prentices help, but, well, that's really what I was hoping Osraed Bevol could help me with — an inyx that would allow me to copy sections of books onto the fresh pages without having to re-scribe them."

"Oh, like a Printweave, you mean."

He nodded. "Yes, but it's just a paragraph here and a half-page there. And sometimes the originals are so faded or the printing is so cramped . . . " He pulled open a small volume and showed her a finely penned entry. "You see how small this script is? And, of course, it's in a different hand than some of the others. . . . " He patted a second book, more slender, but wider. He peeked at her out of the corner of his eye. "You . . . you wouldn't happen . . . I mean, I'm sure you must . . . Do you know an inyx you could teach me that would help?"

To his utter astonishment, she laughed. It took him a moment to realize there was little humor in it, just a wry sense of resignation.

"No," she said. "I might have aspired to invent such a thing once, but now . . . I think you're best off doing it yourself."

Wyth abandoned work on the puzzle she presented. "Yes, well. that's what Bevol said too, but you see, I've never actually *originated* a Runeweave of my own. Truth to tell, I've never even successfully modified one. Weaving was never my strong suit. I was always better at the Dream Tell. I can only imagine that's why the Meri, well . . . "

A fleeting smile strained the corners of her mouth, but her gaze was disconcertingly direct. "I somehow suspect She looked deeper than that. You're Osraed now. There are powers bestowed with that Kiss, Wyth."

"As I well know. Dear God, I can sense anger through walls and joy across miles. And you . . . " He hesitated, lost in his own impertinence.

"And I?"

He wriggled uncomfortably, wishing he'd better control over his tongue. "I can sense you constantly . . . day and night. I sense something I can't describe. Something I don't understand . . . and — and sorrow. I sense that, too. I don't understand that any better."

She nodded, her eyes on the books and the pages and the open portfolio. "The theory here," she said, tapping the topmost page of text, "should be the same as a Printweave, except, of course, you wish to enlarge the print, yes?"

"Uh." Wyth shook himself. "Uh, yes. Exactly."

"But a Printweave works on direct transference, and this would need to be modified. . . . " Her eyes were sweeping the shelves and cubbies over Bevol's table. "Ah!" She stretched and reached and came down with a flat piece of leaded crystal about a quarter inch thick, edge-bevelled to look like a replacement pane for a mullioned window. She followed that by collecting a couple of wire book stands, which she arranged to form a spindly framework atop the table. On it, she balanced the small pane of glass.

"Yes," she said. "I think that *might* work. Is there something in that little volume you want to copy?"

Wyth nodded. He picked up the book and scrabbled with it for a moment before finding the passage. He held it out to her. "This one — verse three."

"Here." She handed him the glass. "What you need to do, in theory, is to place the glass over the passage and pull the text image into the glass."

Wyth studied the idea for a moment. "Circumscribed, of course; the glass will cover more than one passage."

She nodded. "Circumscribed, of course."

"And then what? I mean, assuming you could pull the image?"

"Then place the glass over the empty page and push the image out onto the paper." She illustrated by slipping a blank sheet under the make-shift frame.

Wyth saw the principle immediately. "And the further from the page the glass sits, the larger the image."

Her mouth twisted wryly. "Theoretically."

"Well . . . " He held the glass out to her.

She actually blushed and took a step back. "I can't. You do it."

He didn't ask, just then, why she was so reluctant, but did as he was told, laying the little pane over the desired passage. After a moment of thought, he brought out his crystal and set it on the table atop its padded purse. Then, eyes on its golden depths, he withdrew into himself, reached above himself and, with one finger, laid a circumscription inyx around the perimeters of the passage.

Taminy watched silently, though her lips moved with the brief duan: "Limits there must be, borders to confine. Boundaries encompass tight within the line."

He paused. Pull the image. How — ?

"Try the water draw," Taminy whispered.

He glanced at her. Even in the tremulously rising globe light, her face was pale — almost casting its own radiance. Her eyes were like dark fires, like the sea before a storm, like deep green jewels that drank light and gave off heat.

"But — but water is liquid."

"Try it," she said.

He did — putting himself into the duan, putting the duan into the inyx, Weaving the two together, drawing the image in his mind: the print rising, bonding to the glass, becoming set in the glass. It was true, there were reserves of power he hadn't known before. He could feel them in a great, deep, wide reservoir behind him, above him. Stretching, like the sea, into infinity, while he stood on the shore and pulled with all his might.

"There," murmured Taminy. "That might do. Try that."

Wyth surfaced from the enveloping aislinn and took the little pane of glass gingerly into his hands. He transferred it to the wire frame, adjusting it carefully over the empty page. He could still just see the golden trace of the circumscription inyx in the transparent panel and aligned it so it allowed a margin. He did not ask himself if this would work. She was demanding it of him. He would simply do it. Perhaps, he would fail.

"Now, push the image through."

He held a hand over the plate and its make-shift cradle —

palm down, fingers straight — and he imagined pushing against its transparent surface, forcing the words out, down, onto the pristine surface beneath. Nothing happened. He concentrated harder. Still nothing.

"I've no duan," he murmured and reached for the crystal.

"No," Taminy said. "You don't need that. Here." She pulled his hand back into position over the glass and laid her own atop it. Then she began to sing.

> *"Page to page, through the window.*
> *"Word by word, through the glass.*
> *"Line by line, let the words flow.*
> *"Through the pane, let them pass."*

He had never heard the duan before and thought she must have just composed it. It worked, too, to order his thoughts, to focus his energies. *Through the window*, he thought, and felt the movement of the Weaving beneath their hands.

On the table, in its bed of velvet, Wyth's crystal caught fire. A golden rectangle glowed momentarily on the page beneath the glass, then words appeared — a paragraph of neat print, nearly a perfect fit for the new page.

Wyth stared at it, hand trembling over the framed plate. "It worked! Dearest Spirit! It worked!" He pulled the glass aside and picked up the loose page with its fresh print. "It's perfect! Well . . . nearly so. It's a little too wide for the page, but if I adjust the height of the frame . . . Look!" He turned and held the paper out to Taminy.

She had withdrawn to the center of the room, hands tucked beneath her arms, tears glittering in her eyes. A fine sheen of perspiration stood out on her cheeks.

Wyth was amazed, apalled. "What, mistress? What's wrong? Have I — ?"

She was shaking her head. "So hard. Such a simple thing. Once I could have *breathed* and woven that Rune. Once I was beyond the Weaving of Runes, beyond the chanting of duans. I *was* a duan. Now, I'm all but deaf to the music."

"But it was your duan that completed the Weave. It was your power. I felt it."

"But weak. So weak. I had thought I would remember more. . . . " She shook her head and grimaced. "No, it's not the memory. I do remember — the feelings, the energies — as a cripple remembers walking, recalls the feel of earth beneath his feet, the freedom of movement. The memory of an act is not the same as the act, Wyth. I *remember* how to walk. My legs will not support my weight."

Wyth let himself down into the chair before the workbench. "I don't understand. You were . . . you were the Meri." He said it. It still seemed impossible, unreal.

"No longer," she said.

"Then . . . what are you?"

She laughed. "An upset balance struggling to right itself. Relearning what it is to be human, while remembering what it is to be Divine. I am dust — "

He opened his mouth to protest.

She raised her hand and smiled, then. "But dust with potential."

"Is it . . . is it that way for all . . . ?"

"Osmaer," she murmured, losing the smile. "Divinely glorious."

Osmaer. The name Ochan had given his great crystal. The Stone for which two wars had been fought, before which Cynes were crowned and wed and plighted treaties. Wyth's reasoning all but drowned in the significance of it. "You . . . you are not the first?"

"Never," she said. "Every hundred years or so — "

"The Cusps! Of course. And always . . . always a girl?"

Taminy nodded. "Thearl was Cyne when I journeyed."

"One hundred and fifteen years ago," marvelled Wyth. The very thought — "And before that?"

She tilted her head and smiled a little. "There was another. A Hillwild girl with silver eyes. Cyne Liusadhe the Bard styled her a Wicke. And before that . . . " She shrugged. "Well, it's a very long Tell, indeed."

Wyth was certain his eyes must fall from his head and his lungs forget how to breathe and his mouth stay eternally open. "But . . . are you all given back from the Sea to wander homeless, forgotten?"

Her eyes sparkled in the muted light. "Oh, not homeless. There is always someone sent to give us a home. And not forgotten. *She* doesn't forget. She's always here, watching, guiding, waiting."

"Waiting?" Wyth repeated.

She didn't explain that but, instead, turned and moved toward the study door. "Osraed Bevol will be with you in a moment," she said, pausing in the archway. "You might want to try that Copyweave again. Do you remember the duans?"

"Yes. Yes, of course." He came to his feet. "But without your help — "

"You will do quite well," she said, and left him alone to try.

He had seen the Castle Mertuile from the Cyne's Way before. As a child he had sat beside his father in an open carriage and driven toward it, awed by the way it perched atop its craggy hill like a great owl hunched on a blackened stump. But his real knowledge of Mertuile ended at its gates. Everything he *believed* of the great heap of stone was founded on history lessons and embroidered by legend and hearsay.

In his childhood imaginings it had been a dark and curious casket full of bearded sages and grizzled warriors, its halls haunted by the wraiths of sorrowful Cwens and treacherous courtiers, its throneroom inhabited by the jewels of Creiddylad and crowned, always, by a wise and just Cyne.

Leal squinted up at the dark walls, trying to see where the ancient foundations and walls met the newer structures added since the reign of Cyne Earwyn — a Cyne so wise and just, his warring had invoked the wrath of the Meri and caused both his castle and his capitol to be ravaged by enemy fire. But the stones of Mertuile offered no clue as to which of them were there as a result of Earwyn's folly, and Leal pulled himself up straight and approached her lower gates.

By tradition, he was clad in ceremonial tunic with stole

and prayer chain, the bag containing his crystal, Bliss, prominently displayed on one hip. The Gate Guards took note of this from their stone and log kiosk, greeting him with respectful smiles. The most senior of them dispatched himself to escort the Osraed Lealbhallain through the massive doubled arches, beneath the sheltering outer walls, into Mertuile's outer ward.

There was much activity here. Jaegers unloaded their wagons in one corner. In another, a Blaec-smythe hammered at a huge horseshoe while his client munched hay. A row of shops marched out of sight along the northern flank of the inner walls. Here, a group of young boys swept the cobbles; there, a bevy of women sat, spinning wool in the sun, their children playing a game nearby with brightly colored wooden balls. Near the broad archway Leal's escort led toward, a knot of soldiers, dressed in the gold and green of the House Malcuim, conversed jovially. They paused to afford him smiles and courtly bows, then took up their dialogue again, loud as before.

It was like Creiddylad in miniature, Leal thought, as they passed beneath an open portcullis into the inner ward — a village unto itself. And of course, there were times in its history when the great Castle of Malcuim the Uniter had been forced to self-sufficiency. Times when the countryside teemed with rebellion or the streets of Creiddylad with betrayal.

Within the inner walls, Mertuile bested Lealbhallain's imagination. The rough stones of the outer ward gave way to carefully laid tiles and brick. And before him, across the narrower inner yard, the facade of the Castle, itself, glistened with native stone, while thick, faceted panes of glass flashed sunlight from every window embrasure. Banners bearing the clasped-hand insignia of the House of Malcuim snapped crisply in the seabreeze, saluting him, he imagined.

The only denizens of this inner circle seemed to be fine-liveried guardsmen, all of whom watched the approach of the young Osraed with apparent interest. Leal's escort took him past these guards and up a broad flight of imposing steps, replete with stone bannisters that mimicked silkies. At the top of these they passed through immensely thick wooden doors into a circular anteroom. Here, Leal's resistance to being overwhelmed faltered and he succumbed to awe, gawping at the chamber like a rural schoolboy — which was really, he thought wryly, what he was, after all.

Fortunately for his Osraed dignity, the guard had also stopped and bid him wait a moment. The man disappeared through the center-most of three doors that opened from the chamber, affording Leal the time to admire the multi-hued tiles, gold leaf and polished stone that graced the walls; the elaborate, pennanted chandelier that hung from a gilded dome whose up-side down bowl spilled sunlight onto the mosaic of the Malcuim crest worked into the tiles beneath his feet.

He was gazing up into the second floor gallery, trying to recognize the motif worked into the bannister, when the guard returned.

"I'm to take you to the Cyne's Durweard," he said and led the way back from whence he'd come.

Through vaulted corridors they moved, up a flight of pale stairs and into a room so full of sunlight, Leal thought it must surely have just replenished itself from that extraordinary vestibule. In several rapid blinks he got his bearings and saw, seated in a throne-like chair near a row of tall windows, a youngish man in splendid dress. The man smiled in greeting and rose to bow deeply before him.

"Good Osraed, I am Daimhin Feich, Cyne's Durweard." Feich gestured to a chair of only slightly less grandeur set at angles to his own. "Pray be seated and tell me of your mission here. The sergeant tells me you bear a message from Halig-liath."

Leal nodded, seated himself, and drew the Durweard's attention to the leather portfolio he carried. "I am the Osraed Lealbhallain," he said. "I have been commissioned this Season by the Meri and sent to Creiddylad."

"Yes, of course," said Feich. "And your message?" He gestured at the folio.

"This missal is for Cyne Colfre from the Osraed of

Halig-liath. It concerns the time of the next General Assembly, and its agenda."

"Ah." The Durweard nodded and extended his hand. "In that case, I shall take it to him immediately."

Leal laid the folio in his lap and folded his hands over it. "I'm sorry, Durweard Feich," he said, and wondered why he was not shaking at his own impertinence, "but I must deliver this to the Cyne with my own hands and witness that he opens it. Those were my instructions. And — " His tongue seemed quite willing and able to continue of its own accord. "And I have messages for the Cyne from another Source as well."

Daimhin Feich raised a jet black brow and speared Leal with uncommonly pale eyes. "Oh? And what source might that be?"

"The Source of Sources."

"The Source of Sources," repeated the Durweard. "Meaning the Meri, I suppose."

"Aye."

"The Cyne is pursuing his muses just now," Feich said. "He dislikes very much being disturbed when he is so involved. I assure you, Osraed, any message from you, I would personally deliver — "

"Durweard, I am newly Chosen. I have been commissioned by the Osraed Bevol and Eadmund and by the Meri, Herself, to deliver these messages to our Cyne. Neither commission can be denied or circumvented. I must see Cyne Colfre — face to face." He amazed himself with that — with the fierceness of his confidence, with the edge that put to his voice, with the certitude of his words. Sweating, because despite that, he knew he looked like a carrot-topped, freckled mouse of a boy, he watched the Durweard Feich and waited for his response.

Eye to eye, they sat — boy and man — measuring each other, until the man finally lowered his eyes and rose. "Of course, you must, Osraed Lealbhallain. I shall endeavor to make my lord understand your imperative."

"Please." Leal inclined his head.

In the Durweard's absence, he quaked and prayed, wondering at the words that had come out of his mouth, marvelling at their Origin. *What message, mistress?* he begged silently — and was swiftly rewarded with a tingling tide of response. He sponged perspiration from his lip with the fine sleeve of his tunic. The Cyne would not be pleased.

Durweard Feich reappeared almost immediately, bowing deeply as he beckoned Leal to follow him. "Please, Osraed. The Cyne will see you at once."

Leal was moved to wry humor at the thought that a Cyne's Durweard (a scion of the House Feich, no less) should bow and scrape to a small town Mercer's teenage son. He then smote himself mentally for the pride in that observation — Feich was bowing to something entirely other than Lealbhallain-mac-Mercer, late of Nairne.

Leal had dared to imagine his first meeting with Cyne Colfre Malcuim. It would take place in the throneroom. The room that had seen weddings and war councils, celebrations and treachery, royal pardons and condemnations. The room that should have seen, for the six hundred fifth consecutive year, the celebration of new Osraed. But the chamber in which Osraed Lealbhallain first met his Cyne was a long, narrow, obviously unfinished room with canvas-draped floor and walls. The Cyne, or so Leal assumed it must be, stood before a multi-hued wall, gazing up at it in rapt concentration. He was wearing a grey smock and carried a paint tray and brush.

As he drew nearer the paint-bedaubed wall, Leal realized he was looking at a mural laid out in lurid hues. He scanned it, eyes picking out familiar shapes, a thread of narration, a flow. When they fell on the section the Cyne now studied, Leal felt a surge of recognition. At the same moment, the Cyne acknowledged his presence.

"Ah! *Dear* Osraed Lealbhallain! You are too kind to visit me while I am in such disarray." Cyne Colfre gestured at the chamber and his own apparel. "But my time is so often occupied with administrative affairs, I quite bury myself in my passion when I get the opportunity."

"I understand, sire," Leal murmured, trying to draw his eyes away from the mural. They clung to the image of a white-shouldered woman clutching a child to her half-naked body as she fled down a dark, tortuous cliffside stair toward a river filled with dangerous-looking water.

"And what do you think of my mural, Osraed Lealbhallain?"

Leal's face felt suddenly cold and clammy. "It's . . . it's the tale of Cwen Goscelin and the kidnap of Cyneric Thearl, isn't it?"

The Cyne laughed. "Well, of course it is, b— Osraed! And more. See there?" He pointed his brush to the upper left corner of the mural. "The uprising of the Hillwild under Haefer Hageswode, his wild appearance at Solstice Fest . . . " The Cyne's brush tip swept across the scene and Leal felt a blush rising from his neck to cover his face. Haefer Hageswode, Ren of the Hillwild during the reign of Cyne Siolta, was depicted not merely wild and half-clad during his legendary meeting with the Cyne at Cyne's Cirke, but was wearing only bright splashes of paint and an ornate necklace.

The brush continued on its way. " . . . his incarceration at Halig-liath, the murder of Cyne Siolta by the Hageswode's nephew, the battle for the Regency. Yes, it's all there. Yet, I must admit you are correct — the courageous acts of my kinswoman, Goscelin, are the capstone of the piece . . . if I dare mix my metaphors freely." The Cyne turned dark, zealot eyes on Leal again. "What do you think of it, Osraed?"

"It overwhelms me, sire," Leal answered in all honesty. "Your sense of history . . . and color . . . is very vivid."

The Cyne, smiling, inclined his head. "Your praise warms me, Master Lealbhallain. But, please, forgive my zealous ramblings. My muses" — he returned his gaze to the mural — "consume me at times." He continued for a moment to gaze at the lurid chain of scenes as if that were literally true, then turned smartly to his Durweard, who still hovered at Leal's elbow. "Refreshment, Daimhin. Have it brought out to the Blue Pavilion."

Feich bowed and left them. Cyne Colfre, laying aside his paints and stripping off his smock, bid Lealbhallain follow him. He led the way to the far end of the chamber and through a pair of incredibly delicate doors with narrow panels of alternating clear and colored glass. They seemed somehow out of place set deep into the thick walls of the ancient Malcuim fortress.

But once through the doors, Leal felt he had been transported to a different realm. A slender bridge of gleaming white stone stretched for several meters across a ground-floor garden, joining the second story chamber to a splendid pavilion with a silver roof.

The Blue Pavilion, indeed, Leal thought, as they moved out onto the bridge. Everything about it that wasn't white or silver was a deep, brilliant azure — pennants, appointments, the pillows and pads on the circle of stone couches. Leal was losing himself in the heady scent of late-blooming flowers and evergreen shrubs when he realized that the Cyne was looking at him, expectant of his commentary.

"*Most* beautiful," he said, inadequately, turning slowly within the pavilion's airy enclosure. Through every sculpted arch was a different view, each remarkable in its own way, whether of courtyard, castle, city rooftops or —

"As you can see, I had the seaward wall lowered and notched so as to obtain an ocean vista. I designed it myself, you know."

Leal glanced at his Cyne, amazed. "Truly? Sire, your talents are remarkable. This pavilion is — is . . . glorious."

"And there are three more just like it. One for each point of the compass. Each decorated in a different color."

Colfre gestured for Leal to be seated, then deposited himself on the most luxurious couch of all — a stone creation in the shape of a recumbent horse. It glistened as if wet. No sooner were they seated than a pair of servants appeared with a silver pitcher and cups, a set of covered dishes, and an ornate folding wooden table.

"I'm designing a high pavilion for the royal suite now," the Cyne continued as the servants laid out a trayful of delicacies and drink. "I'm planning to extend the buttressing away from the side of the western tower and build a little chamber atop it. I've been giving thought to having a suspension bridge connect it to the castle, although I daresay that could be quite off-putting to the Cwen and probably not the safest of conveyances. A drawbridge, now, *that* would be ideal. A Cyne's duties do lend fantasy of splendid isolation a great deal of appeal."

The Cyne dismissed the servants then, while Leal tasted a type of fruit he'd never seen before. It was sweet, but tangy, and had deep red flesh.

"Like that, do you?" Colfre asked.

Leal nodded. "I've seen naught like it."

"Well, no, you wouldn't have. It grows beyond the Suder-Gyldans. In the Southerlands. Aye, but you'll be seeing more of it before long. Now, tell me, Osraed, what service your Cyne might render to you."

Leal held out the folio, its gold clasp and inlay flashing brightly in the Sun. "I bring a message from the Osraed Bevol and Eadmund regarding the holding of the General Assembly. I am told it is in response to your last dispatch."

Cyne Colfre took the folio and turned it over in his hands. He hesitated for a moment, then tripped the clasp, opening the tooled cover to view the contents. Frowning, he leafed through the several pages of dense script, scanned the first page. Finally, he glanced up at Leal. "Are you to wait for a response to this?"

"No, sire. I am not returning to Halig-liath. My mission is here, in Creiddylad."

The Cyne seemed interested in that. "Oh? Doing what, precisely?"

Leal drew himself a little straighter on his couch; he hoped he looked taller. "I am to examine the state of the poor in Creiddylad and to do what may be done to change their lot for the better."

The Cyne's brows rose steeply. "We have already a number of Osraed working under that same charter. I would not presume to question the Meri's wisdom but — "

"Are there yet poor in Creiddylad?"

"Aye. There are always poor in Creiddylad."

"Then the charter is not yet fulfilled. I assume I am to help see that it is."

The Cyne smiled — indulgently, thought Leal. "Quite a great undertaking for so young an Osraed."

"The Osraed Ochan was no older than I, sire. At Cyne Malcuim's side, he helped transform Caraid-land into a nation. I won't be alone. I'll have assistance from the Meri, from the Osraed already here, and from yourself, of course."

The Cyne's smile deepened, his teeth showing white and even, his eyes glinting. They were Hillwild eyes, Leal realized, not brown, as they first appeared, but a peculiar shade of amber.

"Of course." Cyne Colfre tucked the folio under his arm and stood, indicating the interview was at an end.

Leal came swiftly to his feet, shivering with a rush of adrenaline. "I have another message for you, sire."

"Oh? From whom?"

"From the Meri."

A peculiar parade of expressions moved across the Cyne's face: surprise, bemusement, amusement, unease. Unease won out. "From . . . the Meri," he repeated. "For me."

"Aye, sire."

The Cyne let himself back down to his couch. "Pray, deliver your message."

Something in the way he said it. . . . *He doesn't believe!* Leal felt a chill shake his bowels. He wanted to sit, himself, certain his legs must begin to tremble, but he remained standing. *To look less a child*, he thought. *To seem more a man.* A frisson of indescribable warmth welled in Leal's brain, coursing down, spreading throughout his body. He opened his mouth and spoke. "You must first know that the Meri has changed Aspect. The Emerald Meri has given way to the Gold."

Cyne Colfre's face paled visibly beneath his neatly trimmed beard. "Changed Aspect? You . . . you saw this? You're certain of this?"

"The Meri came to me golden. Ask any of the Osraed at court or at Ochanshrine. They will tell you She radiated emerald hues. She has changed, Cyne Colfre. I have seen it and the Osraed Wyth has seen it. Caraid-land enters another Cusp."

The Cyne came to his feet and began to pace the perimeters of his grand pavilion. "A Cusp? Now? What can it mean?" He turned to Leal, his expression wary and fierce. "Explain this to me, Osraed. Tell me what this means."

"The history of Caraid-land gives tell of that, Cyne. Do you recall the last such time?"

The Cyne made a nervous gesture. "I have studied history, of course. It was over a hundred years ago."

His disbelief wavers. "It took place not long after the events you describe in your mural, during the reign of Thearl the Stern. Do you recall the circumstances?"

Relief spread across Colfre's face like a slow stain. "Well, of course. There was an insurrection. The House Claeg and its Hillwild allies moved against the Throne. But we're in no such circumstance now. The Hillwild have long been pacified — by the Kiss, my mother and grandmother were Hillwild. And as to the House Claeg — it is also reconciled to us. . . . You are not suggesting that there is danger to be expected from those quarters?"

"The Meri wishes you to know that She is wounded by disunity and deceit wherever they arise and whatever form they take."

"What! What does that mean? What disunity? What deceit?"

Osraed Lealbhallain gazed into the reddening face of his Cyne, his legs finally giving in to the urge to shake. "I come only to deliver the message, Cyne, as the Meri bids me. Learn the lesson of history and of your ancestors. Guard, Cyne Colfre, against disunity and deceit."

"From what quarter, Osraed? From where will this deceit come? The Claeg? The Feich? The Hillwild? I am opening relations with the Deasach. Will the deceit arise there? And as to disunity . . . "

Lealbhallain could feel the Cyne's concern, now, rippling from him like heat drafts from sun-warmed stone. "I have only to deliver the message, Cyne," he repeated.

"But didn't they tell you *where* these problems would arise?"

"They, Cyne?"

"The ones who gave you this warning to deliver. The Osraed Bevol and Eadmund, surely."

Colfre's disbelief struggled to reassert itself. Leal

quashed it. "I told you, sire. This message is from the
Meri." He raised fingers to the bright mark on his
forehead, drawing the Cyne's unwilling eyes to it. He felt
the other man recoil, sensed his conflicting desire to reach
out and touch the star, to assure himself that it was not
merely painted there.

"It's hot to the touch, sire. Do you wish to test it?"

Colfre took a deep breath, clenching his hands into fists.
"No, I believe you, Osraed."

Yes, he did believe, Leal reflected as he left the Cyne's
company. But it was an uneasy belief, ebbing and flowing;
hot then cool, then hot again. It disturbed the new Osraed
that his Cyne was so ambivalent. He had thought that of all
Caraid-land's citizens, the Cyne must surely be firmly
established in the Meri's Covenant. How, otherwise, could
he effectively uphold it? How, otherwise, could he hope to
hold his realm together?

Disturbing, too, was the message he had delivered. He
returned to his lodgings in the Abbis at Ochanshrine,
striving to banish his misgivings and concentrate on the
task now at hand.

CHAPTER 8

My Children! The prime purpose of the Religion of God is to defend the interests and foster the unity of all people. Make it not a focus of discord.

— Utterances of Osraed Gartain, Verse 1

❖   ❖   ❖

"Where were you yesterday?"

Iseabal stopped, half across the Mercer's Bridge, and glanced back over her shoulder. Aine-mac-Lorimer was hard on her heels. A little further behind, Doireann Spenser hurried to catch up.

"What do you mean?" Iseabal asked and turned toward them, shifting her shopping basket from one arm to the other.

"You didn't go to the Bebhinn," accused Doireann, dark eyes reproachful.

"Well, no, but . . . How do you know that and why should you care? I thought Taminy's doings were all silliness to you two."

"Aye, they are," Aine said. "But we wanted to see what it was she did that made you go all wiggly in the head."

"Aye," breathed Doireann. "What *did* she do?"

Iseabal was suddenly uncomfortable with the conversation. *If I tell them, I've as good as told the whole town.* She glanced away across the bridge. "I have to go. Mother is waiting for these things."

"We'll walk with you," said Aine, and put action to word. "Now, give tell, Isha. Where did you off to, if not the Bebhinn?"

Iseabal pecked at a loose twist of reed on the handle of her basket. "She invited me to supper."

"You went to her house? Did you see her room?" Doireann's eyes were huge. "Were there magical things there?"

Aine snorted volubly. "Doiry, you're such a child sometimes. Of *course* there was nothing 'magical' there."

Iseabal stared hard at the cobbles beneath her feet. "There were wonderful paintings and weavings on the walls — with feathers and flowers."

"What's magical about that?"

"There was a crystal."

That stopped all three of them in their tracks.

"A crystal?" repeated Aine. "A Rune crystal?"

"Oh, Aine, is there any other kind?" Doireann was agog. "Was it *hers*?"

Iseabal nodded. "She called it Ileane, the Light Bearer."

"And did she *Weave* with it?"

"No. Not while I was there, but . . . she let me hold it and . . . " She colored, remembering how the stone had felt in her hands — warm, alive almost.

"And what?" Aine demanded.

"It glowed."

"Glowed?" Aine's expression wavered between amazement and scorn and she spluttered like a dry tap. "You actually picked it up? What an idiot thing to do, Isha! She might've cast an inyx on you while you were touching it."

Iseabal glanced at her askew. "I thought you said Taminy's talk of Weaving was all frivol."

"Yes," agreed Doireann, "you did say that."

"Well, I — "

"What did it feel like?" Doireann asked.

Iseabal shivered a bit, recalling. "Oh, it was warm, Doiry," she said, putting her face close to the other girl's. "And smooth. And deep down inside it, there was this beautiful golden light. Like . . . " She glanced around, making sure no one was eavesdropping from the Tanner's doorway. "It looked like the Osmaer crystal, only smaller."

Aine blurted a rude noise. "You've *never* seen the Osmaer!"

"I have. At Solstice Fest my tenth birthday. Papa took me down to Ochanshrine special to see it."

"Aw, you were a baby, then. How can you even remember?"

"Even *you'd* remember the Osmaer, Aine, if you'd ever seen it. It's that beautiful. And it glows, too, when the Osraed come near it. It glowed for my father when we stood looking at it." She tucked her basket close and began walking again. Doireann hustled to keep up.

Aine lagged behind. "So will you go tomorrow, Iseabal, Cirkemaster's daughter?" she called. "Will you go to your magicky place?"

Iseabal spun about, a finger to her lips. "Hush you, Aine Red!" She took three steps back to the taller girl and met her eye to eye. "You've no call to shout out to the whole town what innocent pastimes I take up."

"Innocent! Silly, you mean."

"And so what, Aine-mac-Lorimer? So what if I've a silly midge in me? Shall I shout on you because you're wiggly over Terris-mac-Webber?" She surprised a giggle out of Doireann and a grunt of dire fear out of Aine. She used that as her walking line, turning on her heel and forging on.

Again, she found Doireann beside her and Aine somewhere just abaft. *I'll never get home*, she thought.

"What do you do there?" Doireann asked. "In the pool glade, I mean?"

"*I* just listen. Watch."

"But . . . ." Doireann glanced over her shoulder at their burnished shadow. "But what does *she* do?"

Iseabal was torn. She savored the secret, anticipated savoring the telling of the the secret. "She . . . called birds down from the trees and they drank water from her hand." She tried to keep her voice nonchalant, but the memory of that, of those enamored birds falling from the safety of their trees, still sent a thrill through her, and the words came out hushed.

"*Called* them?" repeated Doireann, and behind them Aine said, "What? What did you say?"

Feeling suddenly trapped and traitorous, Iseabal shook her head and hurried her step. The two yammered after her, Doireann whining, Aine blustering, until she had made the safety of the Cirkeyard. Before the Sanctuary she stopped and faced them. "If you think this is all so silly, Aine-mac-Lorimer, why are you harping on me? I've no love of your teasing and taunting."

"*I* wouldn't taunt you, Isha," Doireann gushed. "I don't think it's at all silly." She turned her dark-bright gaze to Aine's flushed face. "She says Taminy called *birds* down out of the trees and made them drink from her hand."

Aine scowled. "You're making this up of fool's cloth."

"No, I'm not. I saw it. I was hiding behind a bush and I saw it. But she knew I was there and she called me out."

"Called *you?*" echoed Doireann.

Aine scowled, her face a near match for her hair. "What kind of birds where they? How did she call them?"

Iseabal glanced up to see the Cirkewarden watching them from where he tugged weeds from the ground. Blushing, she herded her two companions up the Sanctuary steps, through the narthex and into the sanctum. There, she sat herself down on a bench before the altar and turned as the others slid in after her, their eyes never leaving her face.

"She was sitting above a pool by a little waterfall," Iseabal said. "She took some water in her hand and held it up and two birds came down and sat on her hand and drank the water."

Aine was still frowning. "But how did she call them? Did she sing to them? Speak to them? Did she Runeweave?"

Iseabal shook her head. "She held up her hand and they came." *So did I*, she didn't say.

"Where they . . . *real* birds?" asked Doireann tentatively. "Or were they Eibhilin birds?"

"*Eibhilin* birds!" snorted Aine incredulously. "And what would you know of Eibhilin anything?"

"Nothing," Doireann returned, voice sharp. "That's why I asked."

"They were physical birds, living birds." *Wouldn't Eibhilin birds be* real *birds?* "There was a black bird and a red one."

They were silent for a moment, then Aine said, "She's a Wicke, Iseabal."

Iseabal felt her face go numb with sudden cold and her heart jump and run. She clutched the basket in her lap. "She's *not* a Wicke. She's just different. Special. She must be or she'd not be in Osraed Bevol's house."

"Meredydd was in Osraed Bevol's house. Look what became of her."

"Oh, Iseabal," breathed Doireann, her voice a hushed breeze in the old stone hall. "Aine's right. Maybe old Marnie isn't such a loon. Maybe, somehow, she *is* Meredydd, back from the dead."

"Doireann, you'd drive an Osraed to tears with that pagan twaddle." Aine's eyes shifted to Iseabal's colorless face. "But if she's got Meredydd's ways, she'll come to no good end. And you know it. Your father would cry Wicke if he knew."

"No, he wouldn't. He never cried Wicke on Meredydd."

"Meredydd didn't do secret magics in the woods."

"How do you know?" asked Doireann. "Maybe she *did* and we never knew."

"Taminy is not a Wicke," repeated Iseabal.

"Oh no, of course not," said Aine. "I imagine the birds just like her very much. What else did she do?"

Wriggling inside, Iseabal shrugged. "She instructed Gwynet about herbs and history."

"Just Gwynet? Or you, too?"

Iseabal came swiftly to her feet. "Taminy is not a Wicke, Aine Red. And if you spread such malicious gossip about Nairne, I shall never speak to you again as long as we both draw breath."

"I *don't* gossip, Iseabal-a-Nairnecirke. I'll not spread any tales about your dear Wicke."

"Don't *call* her that!" whispered Iseabal fiercely, then jumped half out of her skin when the door between the Cirke and the manse squeaked open.

"Iseabal? Well, whatever are you girls doing out here? And where are my eggs and cheese?" Iseabal's mother, Ardis, Mistress of Nairne Cirke, stood in the open doorway to the far right of the broad altar, hands in her

apron pockets, a bemused frown playing between her
brows.

Iseabal leapt to take her the basket of goods. "I'm sorry,
mother. We . . . we just got talking. Here — everything you
asked for. Oh, and mistress Chandler put in some bright
red finger-tapers she made. She wants to know if they
don't burn cleaner than the regular ones. She says they
oughtn't drip either."

"Well, that would be a source of amazement. And very
sweet of her, too." The Cirkemistress searched her
daughter's face. "I'd appreciate your help in the kitchen in
a while. I'm making a special bread for supper this
evening, and the Warden's brought us some lovely
gamebirds to dress."

"Oh." Iseabal glanced aside. "Of course, mama."

"What's wrong, dear?" her mother asked, then glanced
up at the other girls who now stood silently before the
altar. "Did you girls have plans for this afternoon?"

Iseabal stared at the basket in her mother's hands. "I
was . . . I was hoping to visit Taminy. . . . "

"Well, why can't Taminy visit you? She's had you to
supper once; why don't you return the courtesy? Father
and I would like to know her better. I've only met her in
passing, you know. In fact, why don't you invite all the
girls? There's more than enough on those rock hens to
feed us all."

Iseabal's eyes flicked up to her mother's face and found
nothing there but friendly interest. She put a smile to her
own lips. "Thank you, mama."

Her mother gone, Iseabal stared hard at the carved
oaken door as if the pattern might be instructive. It wasn't.
She turned back to her companions.

"I'd *love* to take supper with you, Iseabal," cooed Aine,
her eyes glinting golden in the hazy, glass-filtered sunlight.
"Of course, I'll have to go ask my mam."

"Me too," said Doireann.

Aine smiled and folded her arms across her chest. "You
were going to spend the afternoon in the woods listening
to Wickish tales, weren't you, Isha? Well, maybe we'll hear
some tonight at supper."

Doireann glanced at her friend. "She wouldn't talk Wickish before a Cirkemaster, would she?"

"Don't be daft, Doiry. Of course, she wouldn't. But it could be interesting, anyway. Come on, let's go ask our permissions."

Iseabal watched the two of them leave, consternation roiling in her breast. She wanted to see Taminy. She didn't want an audience for the visit. The thought of all those eyes — the benign eyes of mother and father, the watchful eyes of friends — and quaked at the thought. She could just neglect to ask Taminy, to supper, then tell her mother the other girl had been unable to come. And that would be a lie.

She was ashamed to have thought it. She turned to the altar beneath its tall, light-filled window, begging forgiveness. The shimmering splash of brightness that represented the Meri drew her eyes upward. *Am I to believe that Taminy is wicked? Is Taminy wicked?*

Perhaps it was inspiration, perhaps it was her own impious imagination, but she felt suddenly, certainly, that the answer to that question was "no." She contented herself with that and went to help her mother in the kitchen.

Cirkemaster Saxan slid into his seat in one if the galleries of the Osraed Council Chamber and leaned toward the aging peer sitting to his left. "What has happened, Osraed Parthelan? Why is the Body called to a special assembly?"

The older man glanced at him through rheumy eyes and sniffed audibly. "It's rumored that this is the young one's doing."

"Osraed Wyth?"

"Aye. A Prentice of Faer-wald's let fall that the boy wishes to make significant changes in the running of Halig-liath — though he's not, himself, on the Council. . . . "

"You mean . . . the Meri wants to make changes in policy?"

"So he says. Upstart. Didn't even consult with his elders. Just opens his young yawp and says there're changes to be made."

Saxan straightened, uncomfortable with the tenor of his peer's commentary. "I believe that is his prerogative."

"Aye, well. So they say." The old fellow sneezed, then whipped out a kerchief to mop up. "Damned allergies. Can't isolate the damned pollen can't concoct the right inyx. Heh. Speaking of prerogatives, I've also heard — "

Whatever Parthelan had been about to say was drowned in the sudden wash of sound that accompanied the seven man Osraed Council into the chamber. Osraed Wyth came in behind them to take a seat at the end of the curving table reserved for the Council members. He looked up at the encircling galleries of Osraed drawn here from as far south as Lin-liath and Hrofceaster and as far north as Cuinn Holding, and blinked. His narrow, angular face turned white, then red before he closed his eyes.

"Huh!" muttered Parthelan. "Look at 'im. Sitting there, quivering like a half-set jelly. I tell you, Saxan. The quality of this institution is diminishing every year. No wonder we have arrived at another Cusp. When the only Prentices chosen are an undersized pup and a shivering Eiric — "

"Brother Parthelan, please!" Saxan breathed.

It was pure mercy that Osraed Bevol chose that moment to address the gathering. He struck the crystal summons bell before him on the table and stood to survey the room as the singing tone died away.

"Welcome, Brothers," he greeted them. "As you all know, our Beloved has changed Aspect once again in this, the six hundred and fifth Year of Pilgrimage. She has, in fact, returned to Her original Golden Aspect. In this new . . . manifestation, our mistress has chosen two new Osraed, whom you met at Tell Fest. You have heard the Tell of Osraed Wyth. You know that his entitlement was marked by portentious occurences and that he is commissioned to further the Meri's purpose here at Halig-liath by whatever means the Meri bids him employ. He is further appointed Weard of the Covenant and has already begun his work at collecting and anthologizing all writings pertaining to that critical subject. The aim of this meeting is to acquaint you all with the changes that are to be made here, at Halig-liath. Osraed Wyth will now speak to us."

He gestured at the younger Osraed, then seated himself.

The youth came to his feet with a brushing of hands on robes and a shuffling of feet. He made his way to the center of the Council's crescent table and faced the galleries, looking so ill-at-ease that Saxan couldn't help but feel sorry for him.

"Quivering jelly!" snorted Parthelan beneath his breath.

Saxan hushed him just as Wyth raised his eyes and began to speak.

"For too long," he said, his voice much stronger than the Cirkemaster expected, "we have taught our Prentices the letter of Law, the flesh of Doctrine, the mere clothing of Faith. We have recited to them histories that exist only as a recording of actions. Faithfully recorded, aye, but missing their motive and their meaning. We must change that. The Meri . . . " He paused, scanning the faces in the gallery one by one.

Saxan felt a chill pass over him with the touch of those dark, liquid eyes. It was not unpleasant, in and of itself, that touch, but behind it was an open doorway, and through that doorway, Osraed Saxan-a-Nairnecirke saw darkness. He shivered.

"Huh!" muttered Parthelan from beside him. "The daft boy's gotten all tongue-tied."

Saxan ignored him. *No, old man. He has not. He reads us. He measures us.*

"The Meri," Wyth repeated, "demands of us passion. She desires our devotion, our love. Not our cool respect or our shrewd appreciation of Her teachings. Our passionate devotion is what binds us to Her Covenant. Our love for Her draws Her love to us like a great magnet — like the force that holds our world in its course about the Sun. This will now be taught at Halig-liath: that the essence of the Meri is love, and the essence of our Covenant with Her is love. This must guide everything we do here — from selecting our Prentices to teaching them the Art. This Covenant will be the at heart of our teaching."

He paused again, as if waiting for response. There was silence, though heads were nodded and brows furrowed and arms folded over velvet-covered chests. Saxan found himself among the nodding, and waited eagerly for the new Osraed's next words.

"The second matter is this: Halig-liath will now officially and publicly open its classrooms to female students."

That pronouncement was greeted by a small storm of sound. Osraed Wyth weathered it in silence. Saxan found he couldn't so much as croak, but only stare at the serene center of sibilant storm. He glanced aside, once, to catch Osraed Bevol's face set in a somewhat sardonic smile, then returned his gaze to Osraed Wyth, unable to muster anything more than dumb amazement. Six hundred years. Six centuries Osraed had gone to the Sea boys and returned as men — Divine Counselors. And now . . . and now cailin would go and return — as what?

An Osraed from Lin-liath stood to be recognized. "You can't mean to teach them the Art, Osraed. Surely, they are not capable."

"The success here of Meredydd-a-Lagan would seem to prove otherwise," Wyth told him. "And Osraed Bevol will tell you that the girl, Gwynet, whom he sponsors, is as natural a talent as any boy who's ever studied here."

"But they cannot be Osraed," objected Parthelan, out of turn. "Whatever is the point?"

Osraed Comyn Hillwild, a great, braid-bearded, barrel of a man, interrupted. "Are they to be trained up as teachers for the Hillwild? Ren Catahn has said Halig-liath will send teachers to Hrofceaster."

"Who'd want a woman teaching their children the Arts and Sciences?" asked the Lin-liath Brother. "Women are only suited to teaching the trades, we all know this."

"Then we 'know' a falsehood, Osraed," Wyth observed. "And in answer to your first question: the point of teaching girls is that they become Osraed as we became Osraed — by finding favor in the eyes of the Meri, by following Her path to the Sea."

"When shall this begin?" asked one of the Academy Osraed.

"After Harvest there will be female Prentices at Halig-liath. The Osraed Tynedale and Bevol will oversee the acceptance of applicants. For the purpose of furthering the enrollment of girl children, we will waive the usual age guidelines for first year candidates. We will also publish a call to every village, settlement and holding in Caraid-land asking that their daughters be sent to Nairne as applicants for Prenticeship."

"Absurd!" muttered Parthelan. "Completely absurd!"

"Not if it is the Meri's will." Osraed Wyth was looking right at the old man. "And it *is* the Meri's will."

Parthelan shifted in his seat while, beside him, Saxan wriggled guiltily, realizing he had echoed the old Osraed's thoughts.

"And if you cannot convince the average Caraidin of that?" asked Parthelan.

Osraed Wyth's eyes didn't blink. "The Meri will find Her own candidates."

"Where?" Parthelan persisted.

"She will find them in the Gyldan-baenn," said Osraed Comyn, glowering at the elder Counselor. "We do not question the Meri's will or Her Chosen."

"Our Hillwild Brother is correct." Osraed Bevol rose from his place at the Council table. "It is not appropriate for us to question the Meri's will. When She chooses Her Counselors, we have no right to offer our approval or disapproval. When She gives Her word, we have no right to argue it, alter it, silence it, or ignore it. Not if we are to call ourselves Osraed. Not if we are to be true to the Covenant."

In the ruminative silence that followed, Osraed Saxan felt, with chilling certainty, that a line had been drawn in the ether and that every man in the room would find himself, eventually, upon one side of it or the other.

"Eadmund!"

The Osraed turned to find himself all but surrounded by his Tradist peers. Glancing around at the group of faces, Eadmund was immediately uneasy.

Osraed Ealad-hach spoke again, his voice thin with obvious agitation. "What does this high-handed behavior mean? How do you explain yourself?"

Eadmund frowned, perplexed. "What are you talking

about? What high-handed behavior? I've done no — "

"Sending teachers to the Hillwild — autonomously?" A red stain spread across the bridge of Ealad-hach's nose. "If that is not high-handed, I don't know the meaning of the words!"

"But I — "

"I spoke to Comyn. I know where Catahn got the promise of teachers. You usurp the prerogatives of the Hall."

Eadmund had been going to say he hadn't wanted to make so bold a move — that it was all Bevol's idea — but the attitude of the elder Osraed, the deep censuring frowns on the faces of his companions, made him feel wronged. And feeling wronged, he said instead, "The Hall! The Hall has not met since late last autumn, and it shows no sign of meeting any time soon. The Hillwild have petitioned Cyne Colfre for teachers and he has ignored them. The Brothers of the Jewel have ignored them. Catahn had no recourse but to come to us and we, as Osraed, as members of the Assembly, had no choice but to grant his petition — at least until some other provision can be made. It is within our power as Osraed."

"It is not your responsibility — " began Faer-wald.

"Not our responsibility?" Eadmund echoed. "Not our responsibility to educate our country's children? How can you say such a thing?"

"I can say it with the force of tradition behind the words. The Osraed of Creiddylad educate the people; *we* educate future Osraed."

"The force of tradition is not Law. It's not even inspiration. And you must allow we educate very few Osraed. Most of our students go unchosen. If the Osraed of Creiddylad will not make use of those unchosen souls, then surely we must. Osraed Bevol is inspired to do it."

"Bevol!" spat Ealad-hach. "Always Bevol! Forever Bevol! He will bring Caraid-land to ruin with his meddlesome inspiration. He is inspired to advocate the abandoning of order."

Eadmund was aghast. "Bevol is at Apex, Brother. And he is trying to be of help — "

"Of help, yes!" said Ealad-hach. "But to whom?" He raised a finger before Eadmund's face. "There is power afoot, Eadmund. There is movement beneath and above and around us. There are strange forces at work. We need look no further than the Meri's change of Aspect for proof that. We must be cautious of those forces."

Eadmund's entrails trembled. "What are you saying? What are you suggesting? I wasn't pleased when Bevol first spoke of unilaterally sending teachers to the Gyldan-baenn, but I recognize his right to do it. He is at Apex, he is also a senior of the Hall and, above all of that, the Meri made education his special concern. You cannot be suggesting that Osraed Bevol is motivated by anything other than the love and inspiration of the Meri."

None of them answered him, but only gazed at him silently, their faces closed by suspicion.

"Osraed Bevol has a Tradist ally, then," Ealad-hach said at last.

"Ally? You speak as a warrior, not as a Divine Counselor. The subject is the education of children, Brothers. A subject on which we should not be divided. You speak as if we could be adversaries."

"There is more to this than the education of children, Eadmund," said Faer-wald. "What we speak of is the crumbling of traditions — the decay of order."

"There is no progress without change."

"There is no order without structure. Bevol advocates disorder. We are not happy when our Cyne flouts our traditions. Should we be any more approving when one of our own does it?"

Eadmund shook his head, frustrated. "It's not the same. You *know* it's not the same."

"Perhaps you need to meditate on your beliefs, Ead-mund," said Ealad-hach. "Perhaps you need to ascertain whether you may still call yourself a Traditionalist."

After a moment of pregnant silence the others moved away, leaving Eadmund alone in the Council chamber. Or so he thought. But in picking up his portfolio and turning to the door that led to his chambers, he saw he was not alone. Osraed Tynedale stood, half-concealed by the shadow of one great, open door.

"You heard?" Eadmund asked, feeling a belated dew spring up on his forehead.

Tynedale nodded.

Eadmund shook his head, smiled wanly. "All that fuss about whether to afford the Hillwild some cleirachs and teachers."

One brow glided up Tynedale's smooth, round forehead. "Is that what it was about?"

"Yes. Didn't you hear them?"

"Oh, I heard them. And still I ask you, is that really what it was about?" The portly Osraed bid Eadmund good-eve and left him to rub at the sudden lump in his throat.

"Taminy!" Iseabal squeaked, jumped and nearly dropped the ceramic platter she was holding.

Her mother glanced over at her from before the half-open oven door. "What is it, Isha?"

"Oh, it . . . it's Taminy. She just came into the yard." She pulled her eyes from the kitchen window and hurriedly set down the platter. "I'll go out and meet her."

She did that, scurrying through the vestibule and out onto the wide verandah. Taminy was just mounting the steps as she got there, and smiled up at her. Holding out a basket, she said, "I've brought some fresh herbs and fruit for your supper. We've got apples already ripening."

Iseabal stared stupidly at the basket, then jumped and took it, dropping a half-curtsey. "Oh, thank you. Mama will be delighted. Um . . . can you stay for supper?"

"I'd be pleased to, Iseabal. Thank you."

"It won't be just us." Iseabal couldn't quite keep a frown from her face. "Mama invited Doireann and Aine, too."

Taminy's smile didn't twitch. "Why, that's fine."

Iseabal stood awkwardly for a moment, then glanced over her shoulder. "I'm helping mother just now."

"Perhaps she'll let me help, too," Taminy said, and stepped up onto the verandah.

Iseabal nodded and led into the house where she presented her mother with the basket of herbs and introduced Taminy. The Mistress of Nairne Cirke greeted her daughter's friend with smiling interest. "Taminy, it's good to meet you, at last. Iseabal speaks highly of you." She peeked at the herbs in their net bags. "Ah, fresh rosemary and basil. I can use this tonight."

"I thought they'd do well for rock hens," Taminy said.

"Now, how did you know we were having rock hens for supper?"

"Oh, I must have mentioned it," said Iseabal quickly. "Um, mama, may I — may I . . . show Taminy my room?"

"Come to think of it, when did you have time to run to Gled and invite Taminy down? You've been here all afternoon."

Iseabal glanced at Taminy out of the corner of her eye. She couldn't lie. She just couldn't. And she especially couldn't ask Taminy to lie with her. "I didn't, mama. I was going to go after helping you chop the vegetables."

"Well then, how — ?"

"I just dropped by, mistress," Taminy said.

"Oh, well then, you'll need to let Osraed Bevol know you'll be staying."

"Oh, he knows, mistress." Taminy smiled disarmingly. "He's an Osraed, after all. I reckon there's little I do he doesn't know of in his way."

Iseabal's mother returned the smile, if warily. "Of course."

Aine appeared as the Sun dipped to the treetops, and announced that Doireann had been unable to come. Iseabal thought there was some smugness in that pronouncement. And no wonder — Aine would now be in the powerful position of getting to dispense gossip to the deprived Doireann.

Supper was an amiable enough event, though Iseabal thought her father seemed distracted and a little morose. She watched Aine like a hawk during the meal, afraid that at any moment the other girl would blurt out that Taminy was a Wicke. She didn't, though. She only seemed to be very interested in everything Taminy had to say. Especially the answers she gave to the Cirkemistress's motherly questions — questions Iseabal knew the answers to, but had not revealed, though for what reason, she couldn't have said.

"And how did you come to be in Osraed Bevol's care, child?" The Cirkemaster rallied at last from his thoughtful bog and sought to make conversation. "I'd heard he found you upon his return from Meredydd's . . . journey."

"It may be said he found me," Taminy replied. "Though it may also be said that I found him. On the Sea shore, as it happened."

"Ah, you're from the Seawode, then. Storm, is it — or Mercut?"

"Neither, Osraed. I . . . I'm from Nairne-way by birth, but became displaced."

"Your family moved?"

"Aye, to Creiddylad, eventually. My father served at Ochanshrine."

"Oh, yes. Iseabal mentioned that your father was a Cirkemaster. What was his name? Perhaps I know him."

"Pardon, sir, but that is doubtful. He was not originally from Nairne, you see, but from Cuinn Holding."

The Osraed Saxan frowned. "Cuinn Holding . . . that's well north of here."

Taminy nodded. "Yes, sir. North and east. Above the fork of the Halig and Ead."

"And where are your parents now, child?" asked the Mistress of Nairne Cirke. "Are you orphaned?"

"Yes, mistress. They've both died to this world. So, I came to be with Osraed Bevol, who is my mentor and guardian. I tutor young Gwynet in reading and such. She has a great deal of catch-up to play to come level with the other first years."

The Cirkemistress shook her head and gave her husband a significant look. "Ah, I can't say I agree with the sending of young cailin up to Halig-liath. The child should be in the Cirke School where she can get a good, practical education. Don't you agree, Saxan?"

The Osraed raised his head and gazed down the table at his wife, his eyes glancing off the faces of the three cailin in between. "Well, Ardis . . . this morning I would have agreed, and said that you echoed my sentiments exactly. But what I heard this afternoon foils both our arguments. At today's meeting of the Osraed Body, Osraed Wyth told us that cailin must now be admitted to Halig-liath for full training in the Divine Art."

Iseabal felt as if all the air had been sucked from her lungs and her body given an extra squeeze for good measure.

"*Full* training?" Ardis-a-Nairnecirke's voice was airless, as if she'd suffered a similar fate. "What — whatever for?"

Osraed Saxan spread long, tapered fingers. "Whatever else for? That they may take the Pilgrim's Walk and become Osraed."

Iseabal darted a glance at Aine. The other girl's hazel eyes were as big as sorchas and her mouth was slightly agape. Beside her, Taminy looked on with calm interest.

"But that's absurd! . . . Isn't it? Can he mean that? To train our daughters to Runeweave and cast inyx?"

"He means," Saxan said, "what he says — that our daughters be entitled to the same education we give our sons. And to exercise the same talents."

"But they can't exercise what they don't have."

Saxan studied his fingertips. "Meredydd-a-Lagan would seem to have had the Gift. Taminy tells us Bevol's Gwynet may have it."

Iseabal was fairly holding her breath now, her eyes flickering between her father and Aine and Taminy. Would Aine speak? Would Aine tell all that Taminy could fetch birds from the trees?

"How can you countenance such a change, Saxan? How can the Osraed? In six hundred years — "

"Yes, yes, I know. In six hundred years — and five — there have been no sanctioned female Prentices at Halig-liath. Well, none except Meredydd-a-Lagan, and she was barely tolerated." He shook his head. "Understand, Ardis — we have no choice. Wyth is the Meri's elect. We cannot argue with either Her selection or Her directives." He turned his gaze to the three girls sitting along the sides of the long table. "What do you think?" he asked them. "You, Aine — would you go to Halig-liath?"

Aine's face blazed in sudden color. "Me, sir? Never!"

"And why not?"

"Well, it's not proper, sir. I'm a Lorimer's daughter; I'm

expected to pick up a piece of the trade. My father's not taught me the making of bits and harnesses to have me scrap all and become a Prentice."

"But you've brothers to take the trade, Aine. And neither of them has ever shown a bit of interest in a divine education. What about you?"

"No, sir. I am too old and I've no Gift, thank God. If I did, I'd hide it as deep as I could."

"But I've just told you, Osraed Wyth has brought us the Meri's own word. She has enabled you."

Aine was adamant. "I have a gift for only the Lorimer's art, Master Saxan. I fancy I throw a buck stitch better than either of my brothers."

Saxan pursed his lips, his eyes shifting to the opposite side of the table. "Taminy? What do you say? Would you go to Halig-liath?"

"Well, sir, to be honest, my education has been so complete, I feel as if I have already been. Halig-liath is not for me, now. But I believe it is the highest calling for others. Our Gwynet has a real Gift. It only makes sense that she should learn the handling of it."

Iseabal flinched as her father, nodding, moved his eyes to her. "Isha, would you wish to go to Halig-liath?"

She stared at her lap. "I . . . surely I've no Gift."

Nonsense, someone murmured. Iseabal thought it was Taminy, but no one else seemed to have heard her. It came to her then, as clearly as if she relived it — her hands cupped around the crystal, Ileane, the warmth permeating her palms, the light inspiring her eyes. She blushed a deep rose.

"But what if it was shown that you did have a Gift?" Saxan leaned forward in his chair.

"Saxan, stop this," pleaded his Mistress. "You're asking your daughter to entertain heretical thoughts. Imagine our Iseabal Weaving Runes and — "

"Osraed Wyth has said those thoughts are not heretical." The Osraed's eyes never left his daughter's face. "Come, Isha, tell me. If you could go to Halig-liath . . . ?"

Iseabal raised her eyes and looked down the table at her father. "I would, papa."

"Iseabal!" Her mother was gaping at her, clearly horrified. "How can you say that so calmly? How can you have had such desires and I not know it?"

"I didn't know, either," murmured Iseabal.

"Dear God, child, what inspires you to such a thought — that *you* have a Gift?"

Face blazing, fingers twisting tortuously in her lap, Iseabal shook her head mutely. She saw Aine glance across the table at Taminy. *I know*, her eyes said, and she opened her mouth to say it aloud.

"It's my doing," Iseabal said quickly. "It's my thought — no one put it into my head."

Her father raised his hand to forestall his wife's retort. "What makes you think you may have a Gift, Isha?"

Taminy spoke, then. "She has a Gift, Osraed Saxan. I've seen the evidence of it. Seen it and felt it."

Iseabal's mother uttered a cry of complete disbelief. "*What* evidence? What evidence could you have seen — or understood? These things are for the Osraed, not for children."

Osraed Saxan rose from the table, then, and left the room, leaving his wife and young guests in unanswered turmoil.

"What is it, Saxan?" his wife cried. "Where are you going? What is the girl talking about?" She had risen and trailed her husband as far as the gracefully arched doorway to the central hall when he reappeared from the room opposite, carrying something in his hands. Ardis-a-Nairnecirke glanced at his face as he passed her, then, hand over her mouth, followed him silently back to the table.

Iseabal's eyes were on the thing in his hands — a wooden box carved with runes. She knew it had a green velvet lining, and she knew what nested in that green velvet lining. She had spent hours in childhood staring at it. Now, her father opened the box and held it out to her. The egg-sized crystal in its verdant glen winked and sparkled and played with the light of candle and globe.

"Take it," he said. "Hold it in your hands."

The crystal swam out of focus. Iseabal blinked and

raised her eyes to her father's, trying to read them — to read him. She could not. With trembling hands, she lifted the crystal from its bed and cupped it. She held it before her face, barely aware that the lights in the room were dimming; that her father called them down, hand raised, fingers flexed as if pulling light from the room. She kept her eyes on the crystal, quivering, aware only of it and of a warm presence at her shoulder.

Taminy. Taminy watched her. Smiled on her.

She heard her mother gasp, saw Aine rise slowly from her chair. In her hands the crystal, Perahta, threw forth a sudden pulse of warm light — light that kissed her face and heated her palms. Forgetful of everything but the crystal, blind to everything but its light, deaf to her mother's sobs and her father's murmured prayer, Iseabal smiled.

She stood with her back to the room and wondered at how autumn seemed to be creeping up on them early this year. Already there was a sharpness to evenings, and mornings were reluctant to shed their chill. Saxan had set a fire which now rustled in the grate across the room, but she did not feel warm. Outside their bedroom window, the Cirkeyard was all black and silver-white, there was no warmth in the moonlight that lay, gauzy and snow-like, over gravestone and runepost.

The dead slept or lived elsewhere, unbothered by today's revelations. They had no reason to care that Ardis-a-Nairnecirke's conceptions of right and wrong had been challenged and toppled by the words of an eighteen year old youth.

And her daughter — she'd raised her well, she'd thought, with a sense of propriety. No, it was more than a matter of propriety, this. There were deeper issues. *Iseabal, hankering to Weave! When did it begin? Mustn't it have to do with Bevol and his freakish wards?*

"I've seen the evidence," that strange girl had said. Iseabal had the Gift. Such evidence she could have seen only if she possessed that Gift herself. Only if she new exactly what to look for. Only if she was — Ardis couldn't allow herself to even think the word. Iseabal would have to be kept from her, of course. Then the odd attraction would fade.

"Well, Ardis?"

Her back went up straight at the sound of his voice. She strove to make it relax. "Well, what, Saxan?"

"What do you think of our Iseabal going up to Halig-liath in the fall?"

As if he was discussing her taking a jaunt to Tuine! "I think it shall not happen."

She heard the whisper of cloth as he shrugged or gestured. "And why not? She wants to go."

"There is no reason. It's unwarranted."

"Unwarranted? Ardis, she has the Gift."

"I won't believe it. That girl of Bevol's makes her *think* she has a Gift."

His breath rode out on a sigh. "Ardis, Ardis, dear, you *saw* with your own eyes how the crystal behaved in her hands."

"It was Bevol's girl. I should have known better than to let her befriend someone from that household. I should have known that any child Osraed Bevol brought to Nairne must be dyed to the same hue as Meredydd-a-Lagan. We were foolish enough to think a friendship with Iseabal would bleach *that* stain. I made the same mistake with this one. It's the dark of the dye that spreads, not the whiteness of the pure cloth."

Behind her, Saxan moved further into the room. "Ardis, you haven't listened. There is no stain. It's all right for Taminy to be gifted. It's acceptable for Iseabal, as well."

"How easily you spout the words."

"Well, they are easier spouted than taken to heart. This is not an easy change of season for me, Ardis. But the Meri bids me believe my daughter's Gift is acceptable — "

Ardis wheeled on him, her face chill-hot, her eyes shedding tears. "She has no Gift! Stop saying that she has! Our girl is innocent! Innocent!"

White-faced, he nodded. "Of course, she is innocent. But she also has a Gift. Perahta lit for her. That proves — "

"Nothing! You were there. It might've lit for you. Or Taminy or — "

"If Perahta had lit for me, I would have known it." He came to her then, and took her hands in his. She twisted her neck, looked away, but did not move.

"Listen, Ardis. When Iseabal traveled with me to Ochanshrine, I took her to see the Osmaer. The Sanctum was dimly lit and empty of any but her and I and a few Prentices engaged in prayer. I took Isha's hand and led her up to the altar and, as we drew near, the Stone took fire. She cooed and ah-ed at it, and turned to me and cried, 'Oh, Papa, see how it glows for you!' But it wasn't me, Ardis. It wasn't me the Osmaer reached out to with Her fire. It was Iseabal."

The pain! "No," she said.

"I didn't want to believe it, either. But I had the evidence of my own senses. Somehow, I hoped it would go away. That she would never understand what she had. That she would grow up without having to know. I've always been very careful about keeping Perahta out of her hands, but — " He paused, searching her face. "Do you think it's easy for me to change the beliefs of a lifetime? I have struggled to pretend that Isha is an ordinary girl. I have done so because I believed that if she was not ordinary, she would be condemned. And since I'm her father, the fault could only be mine."

She looked at him then, met his eyes. "And mine," she whispered. "Oh, Saxan, what have we done?"

He put his arms about her and kissed her hair. "We have raised a beautiful daughter who has a Gift granted only to the pure. That is what we have done."

She wept, willing herself to believe. But her will failed her and she wept harder for that.

CHAPTER 9

Everything I unveil to you, every duan I sing to you, is in conformity with your capacity to comprehend, not with My condition or the melody of my Voice.

— *The Book of the Meri, Chapter One, Verse 1*

❖   ❖   ❖

The Library was empty at this hour, early sunlight illuminating untenanted tables and scattering a myriad shadows onto floor and wall and ceiling. On a table near the shelves, the Osraed Wyth's work lay in a curiously rhythmic clutter of sheafs and stacks. It looked as if he had left but a moment ago, but he was nowhere in sight of the door where Osraed Ealad-hach stood peering.

It was not curiosity that had brought him here, nor anticipation of Wyth's progress. It was fear. He was honest enough to admit that, even to himself, but there was enough anger in his fear to make him bold and toothy.

They should never have allowed Wyth to blurt his pronouncements at Council. Never. They should have tested them first — tested *him*. That had never been done before. There was no precedent for it in the annals of Halig-liath. The Kiss of the Meri was its own proof. It could not be falsified — and there had been those who had tried.

No precedent! The old man fumed. There was no precedent for the changes Wyth Arundel demanded in the Meri's name. None. And they were in a Cusp — an auspicious Cusp, if the appearance of a Golden Meri meant aught. Tests came at such times; heinous trials calculated to separate the true from the false, the blessed from the cursed.

He had been Osraed for six decades. Did his word mean nothing? But, no. He would not let himself be personally slighted. It was the time; it was the circumstance. He would never be so roundly ignored by his peers unless Something, Someone, some Power was at work. Sane men would have listened to him when he suggested that Wyth be proved. Faer-wald had listened, and Parthelan and the other Tradists. But even among that brotherhood within the Brotherhood, there were cowards, weaklings, men easily swayed by Wyth's ingenuous sincerity, men who wished to ignore the strangeness of this time, men only too willing to countenance sweeping change when it dressed itself in the trappings of authority. They resisted questioning the Meri's will — and rightly so. They would need proof that Wyth Arundel did not represent that. That he brought them, not new Doctrine, but an old challenge, a test, a touchstone.

"Wish for death if you are men of truth," Ealad-hach murmured, the words a soft sussuration in the empty, cavernous room — a breeze through cobwebs. He shivered slightly and stepped down into the play of light and shadow. Soft soles whispering, eyes darting, he moved to Wyth's tidy work table and hung there, tingling, peering.

Delicately, he lifted a freshly copied page, taken by the cleanliness of it — absolute black on absolute white. His eyes seduced, he read:

You, O God and Lord, have sent down the Book — the Corah — that My Cause may be manifest and My Words glorified. Through this Book, You did enter into a Covenant concerning Me and concerning those created in Your Kingdom. You see, O Divine Beloved, how Your people have made of that Covenant a stronghold for their own desires. Into this place, they have withdrawn from Your Glory; secure, they ignore Your signs. You are the One, O Spirit, who instructed them in Your Book, saying, "Hear the Voice of the Merciful One, O people of the Corah, and deny not She whom I have sent you."

A chill rippled down Ealad-hach's arm, shuddering the page from his fingers. He frowned, rubbing his hands together. No coincidence, his reading those words. They spoke to him — to his very soul — shaking him. A stronghold for their own desires. . . . He had seen that, had he not? The desire of Bevol, of Calach, of Tynedale and others, to admit cailin to the Brotherhood? Had that desire now taken such hold of Wyth Arundel that he became its unwitting instrument? Had it so blinded the young Osraed and his elders that they now failed to perceive the clear signs? This new policy of Wyth's was an assault on the very Covenant he was ordained to protect. And none but this unworthy old man was able to see it. The Meri was allowing another Power to play the field — a Power whose goal was the corruption of the Osraed through the influence of Gifted women. A Power he had seen personified in his dreams.

Ealad-hach wrung his hands, whispering a prayer of thanks that his eyes, at least, were open. That he could see the calamity nearing. Aye, and he could *feel* it, hear its whispered approach. A frisson scurried up his spine. He turned, quickly, expecting to see nothing but the vapors of his imagination. He found himself staring, open-mouthed at Osraed Wyth.

While he struggled to collect himself, the young Osraed smiled at him, disarmingly. He blanched. In abstract terms he could cast Wyth as a traitor to the Covenant, in flesh and blood, he found that conviction difficult to uphold. He had liked the boy, had thought him a young man of staunch principle. And though he had been disappointed when the Meri had passed him over the first time, he had not, then, seen the flaw, the weakness that made Wyth Arundel easy prey for someone like Meredydd-a-Lagan. And after that unfortunate episode, after the young Wicke had tried (aye, and succeeded!) to seduce him, it seemed more than passing strange that he should suddenly find favor with the Meri.

"Hello, Osraed," said Wyth and put a slight bow into his words.

"How goes the work?" Ealad-hach asked, and found his eyes drawn to Wyth's forehead. It could not be falsified, that Kiss. Not falsified, but false, nonetheless. It *must* be false. There was no other possibility.

The younger man stepped down into the room and crossed to the table where Ealad-hach stood and willed himself not to flinch. "Much more quickly since the advent of the Copyweave," Wyth said, and the smile deepened.

"The Copyweave?" inquired Ealad-hach, glad for the introduction of a non-threatening subject.

Wyth lifted an odd little frame of wood and metal from the table and held it out to him. There was a piece of crystal-glass set into the top of the frame and its collapsible, jointed legs sported four wooden feet with leather pads.

"Osraed Saer built it for me," Wyth said. His eyes were bright with boyish enthusiasm. "You see, you place it over the text you wish to copy, then draw a circumscription on the glass, so you only get the part you need. Then, you draw the text into the glass and deposit it on the new page. The frame unfolds" — he demonstrated —"so you can expand or contract the image, as you desire."

Ealad-hach was impressed without intending to be. "A marvelous device, Osraed Wyth. You are a clever young man, to have developed such a Weave."

The boy looked suddenly gawky and uncomfortable. "Well, sir, I must be honest, It wasn't completely my conception."

"Oh? Whose, then?" Was it his imagination, or had the young man tensed? Did the brown eyes dodge his?

"Oh, a — a friend."

"Ah. Bevol, I presume."

Wyth turned the frame in his hands, his expression suddenly opaque. Ealad-hach cursed his lack of Thought Tell ability.

"Actually," Wyth said, raising his eyes a little, "it was Taminy-a-Gled who helped me with the Weave."

Ealad-hach thought his heart would stop and fall to the floor. "Taminy . . . " he repeated, and wondered that he didn't stammer. "The girl Bevol brought to Nairne?"

Wyth nodded, eyes watchful.

"She . . . Weaves?"

"She knew a couple of duans. One, she adapted from a Water Draw, the other, I think she might have composed

. . . although she could have learned it from Bevol." His eyes slid away again. "Perhaps she was only parroting."

"Very likely," Ealad-hach said. He could not quite make himself feel relief. He wanted it; it refused to come. Still, he gave lip service to the safe interpretation, even in his own soul.

"Bevol mentioned," Wyth said, "that you had an aislinn you wanted me to Tell."

Ealad-hach peered at him. *So. You want to read my dreams, do you? Are you being sly, boy? Are you being clever? If I give you my aislinn, what will you do with it? What will you try to make me believe?* He almost said "no." He almost pulled back from the prospect of letting this anomaly into his nightmares. But a sense of duty drove him on. This was a riddle he must solve.

"Yes," he said. "I have dreamed. Let me tell you what I have dreamed."

Oddly, the boy's face seemed to close in on itself. "Are you certain, Osraed, that you wish me to give the Tell?"

Why was he wriggling away? Surely, he would want to interpret the aislinn to the advantage of his cause. "Yes, of course. You were always excellent at the Dream Tell."

Wyth dipped his head. "As you wish."

Ealad-hach told him then, of the Sea and the Shore and the girl upon it. He showed him, too, or tried to, but his Weave was weak and lacked depth and clarity. And when he was finished, he looked at Wyth's face and saw reluctance — no, more than that — distress.

The boy fingered his Copyweave frame and stared at his neat stack of papers and said nothing.

"Well?" prompted Ealad-hach. "Well, what do you say? Give me your Tell."

"I can't, Osraed." Wyth raised his eyes to Ealad-hach's face. "I cannot Tell this aislinn. It — "

"It what? What do you mean, you *can't* Tell it?"

Wyth shook his head. "It's too confused. Too confusing. The images are . . . too thick with personal meaning. It is beyond me."

"Confusing how?" persisted Ealad-hach. "Do you balk at Telling a portent of evil?"

Wyth's eyes met his, sharp and probing. "Is that what you perceive it to be, Osraed? A portent of evil?"

"Whatever else is muddled, that much is clear."

"And if I told you it was not a portent of evil?"

"I would not believe it."

Wyth's shoulders moved in what was almost a shrug. "Then any Tell I might give would be irrelevant."

"Do you say it is a portent of *good*?" *He cannot say that, surely. He won't say it.*

Wyth frowned, his gaze suddenly turned inward. "The same Sun that warms the earth and ripens the crops, burns to ashes the dry grass and blinds the creatures of shadow."

Ealad-hach tried to pry at the boy's narrow face, tried to divine his meaning. The attempt was futile. "Who is the girl?" he asked sharply. "Tell me that much. Who is this Wicke?"

Wyth shook his head. "There is no Wicke in your aislinn, Osraed."

"Then what?"

"I . . . cannot say."

"You mean, you *will* not."

Wyth shook his head again and lowered his eyes to the tidy mess atop the table. "If you'll excuse me, Osraed, I have much work to do."

Ealad-hach withdrew silently, though his spirit was not silent; it roared in ragged frustration. He went away to his chambers, then, to pursue a peace that no longer lived there. Later, he thought, later, when he was calm, he would tell the others what he had gleaned from Wyth.

"And then," panted Aine, "and then, she took the crystal out of the box and it lit up like a lightbowl!"

"No! It *didn't*!" Doireann's eyes all but started from her face. She lifted her skirts higher as they cut through ripening wheat toward the verdant line of the Bebhinn Wood.

Skittering sideways, Aine bobbed her bright head, her voice coming out in short puffs. "And Taminy said . . . Taminy said . . . she'd seen that Isha . . . Isha had the Gift."

"And *then* what?"

"And then the Mistress of Nairnecirke began to wail . . .

and the Master set to praying . . . and Isha just stared at that crystal, smiling like she was bewicked."

"And what did Taminy do?" Doireann gasped, half stumbling over a divot of earth.

"She just smiled — her face all aglow from the stone. Oh, Doiry, it was the stuff of chills. I swear I dreamed of it all night and into morning."

"If only they'd let me come," whined Doireann. "Why did it have to be *my* night to tend the stupid oil pots?"

They'd reached the verge of the wood now, and hushed as if entering the Cirke. Trees formed corridors and leafy branches, vaults. Birds sang in lieu of choirs, and leaves whispered prayers. The girls ignored all in their quiet haste; their skirts swished no louder than the breeze, their footfalls beat no louder than their hearts.

They heard the waterfall before they could make out the murmur of voices. Pace slowed, they crept to within earshot, screened by a puff of greenery, and knelt to watch and listen.

" . . . said naught about it this morning, but I've no illusions my mother will allow it unless father presses." Iseabal sat, cross-legged, upon a rock that lay half-out of the water, shredding flower petals into her lap.

"Do you want to go?" Taminy asked her. She was on a rock by the fall, looking for all the world like a Cwen holding court. Aine thought there ought to be an audience of squirrels and rabbits sitting in attendance.

Iseabal was slow in answering. Her brow furrowed, she abandoned her task and rubbed her palms together. "I want to learn the use of my . . . my Gift. If I must go to Halig-liath to do that, then I shall, but . . ."

"But?"

"But I'd rather learn from you."

"Would you?"

Iseabal nodded. "Oh, yes. And so would Gwynet, I wager. Am I right, Gwyn?"

Aine noticed, then; that the woodland Cwen had other courtiers. Gwynet and a second young girl sat sprawled on the grassy streambank between the older cailin with books and whiteboards.

"Oh, aye!" said the blonde gamin at once, and her companion looked up with wide eyes and cried, "Oh, me too, Taminy! Me too!"

Why, that was Niall Backstere's youngest girl, Cluanie, Aine realized, gawping at the mouse-hued mop of hair. Could her da have any idea — ?

"It could be slow learning," Taminy said. "You can't learn what I can't teach."

"But I've learnt bushels already," protested Cluanie. "My mam's all but sung over the perfumes I made her and she was mighty glad of that moonwort physic you taught me. She's been raw sick with this baby and all."

"Herbals are only a small part of the Art," Taminy said. "The Osraed have the knowledge — "

"Not the way you have it," said Iseabal. "I know. Prentices study for years and all they learn is how to make a dog chase his tail till he drops or how to interpret a dream. But look . . . " She put a hand in the water beside her rock and gently moved her fingers.

Aine frowned and looked at Doireann, who merely shrugged and dug her hands deeper into the pockets of her skirt. It was when she glanced back at the pool that she saw it — the guicksilver flash and dart of tiny, water-borne bodies as they rushed to gather about Iseabal's rock. Aine swallowed a gasp. Doireann clapped one hand over her own mouth and brought the other one to her breast in a tight fist.

The two little girls on the bank jumped up and tumbled to the water's edge, squealing with delight. Taminy laughed too. "A useful trick for a fisherman, Isha, but hardly earth-shattering."

"But it is for *me*," enthused Iseabal. "It's *all* earth-shattering. All of it. The world looks different to me today. The whole, entire world!" She raised her hands, flinging them wide as if to embrace that world and, suddenly, the air was full of birds, full of their songs, full of the rhythm of their wings.

It was Iseabal they flocked to, Iseabal they circled and wheeled about and chittered to. And the little girls danced and Iseabal laughed and Aine's heart beat so hot and so fast she thought she would swoon. Beside her, Doireann trembled and cowered and clutched her hands to her breast.

Then, Taminy, Cwen of the Bebhinn Glade, stood up on her rock and raised her hands, palms outward. The birds were gone faster than Aine could blink an eye. Back to their trees they went, in a hush so profound, Aine was sure no Cirke had ever known it.

"The Gift is not for the drawing of birds," Taminy said, and Aine felt a sudden prickling at the back of her neck. "Nor is it for the gathering of fish."

Gwynet and Cluanie giggled and Taminy turned her face to the puff of greenery Aine and Doireann had thought concealed them.

"The Gift is for the drawing of spirits and the gathering of souls . . . Come out, Aine. Come out, Doireann. Come sit with us and sing duans."

Both girls started up, bumping painfully in their haste and tumbling from their sanctum. Finding Taminy's eyes right on her, Doireann shrieked loudly enough to wake the dead and hurled whatever she had been crushing to her heart in Taminy's direction. It was a good throw, and the lumpy wad landed nearly at Taminy's feet. As the girl lifted her skirts and bent to pick it up, Doireann shrieked a second time and dashed back into the woods.

Heart tripping over itself, Aine followed. She caught Doireann up at the edge of the fields where she had crumpled into a forlorn heap, arms and face patterned with pale scratches, tears streaking her face.

"She's a Wicke! She's a Wicke! And she's made poor Isha into a Wicke! Oh, I knew it! I knew it!"

"Stop babbling, Doiry!" Aine told her crossly. Her own body threatened to quiver itself right into the ground, but she would never let the other girl see that, or even suspect it. "Stop babbling and tell me what that was you threw at her."

Doireann hiccuped loudly and grasped Aine's wrist, all but toppling her. "It was a runebag."

"A what?"

Doireann merely nodded frenetically, spilling hair into

her eyes. "Daffodilly and marigold, vervain and a piece of chalcedony scratched by emery."

Aine shook her head dumbly. "What good — ?"

"To drive away the wicked! To expose and expel them. Daffodilly and vervain and chalcedony cut by emery *all* do that, so I thought why not put them together?" She hiccuped again.

"Oh," said Aine, not knowing what else she could say. "And the marigold?"

Doireann pulled herself to her feet, using Aine's arm for support. "Repels Wicke. Did you see how she tried to get away from it?"

Aine sighed. "I think she picked it up."

"No, she didn't! She lifted her skirts clear and bent to inyx it away. I saw her."

"Doireann, you're wind-kissed. Besides, if what Osraed Saxan said is true, Iseabal and Taminy may gather all the fish and fowl they want."

Doireann peered at her from beneath a jumble of dark curls. "Do *you* believe it?"

"Well, it was brought from Pilgrimage by an Osraed."

"Huh. Osraed Wyth Arundel. You know Wyth. Were sweet on him, *I* recall. Are you ready to believe he's the voice of God?"

Aine could only stand blinking. Wyth as the Voice of God, was rather a difficult concept to grasp.

"And she didn't just speak of gathering fish and fowl, Aine-mac-Lorimer," Doireann continued, her eyes growing huge and dark. "She spoke of gathering *souls*. Of collecting *spirits*. It's *our* spirits she's after, Aine. *Our* souls. You heard her. Come out, she says. Come out and — and sing duans." Her hand, clutching Aine's arm, shook as if palsied.

Aine met her friend's eyes and couldn't help but shiver, herself, at the abject fear in them. She opened her mouth to utter quashingly brave words, but a loud shaking of shrubbery within the wood robbed her of them. Doireann set off, wailing, across the fields, with Aine hard on her heels.

    ❖ ❖ ❖

Aine-mac-Lorimer and Doireann Spenser might not welcome her, Taminy reflected, but there were others who did. The pleasure of the Apothecary would have been hard to miss, even for one utterly without the Gift. Her eyes on the basket of herbs and confections in Taminy's hands, she sailed from behind her counter like a galley under full sail, skirts and sleeves and aprons bilowing about her ample bow. One arm swung wide to embrace, the other went straight for the basket.

"God love you, child! Look at that wealth of riches! Wyvis! Rennie! Taminy's here!"

Taminy smiled as the embrace landed around her shoulders. Already she could hear the scuffle of feet on upstairs floorboards; the Apothecary's two youngsters presented themselves in their mother's shop before that lady had retreated behind her counter again to admire her new goods.

At fourteen, Wyvis was showing every sign of being a winning young woman. The gamin smile she now bestowed on Taminy would someday cause male hearts to quiver. Her brother, Rennie, three years her senior, was a big-boned lad who tended to favor his mother's plumpness. He was, as his mother would say, "a boisterer" at most times — a little loud, a little undisciplined — but in Taminy's presence, he seemed most tame; Nairne's Mistress of Medicaments threw the two of them together at every opportunity.

"Oh, look what she's brought us! Catamint, isn't it? Ah, but the Beekeep will be glad of this. He's afraid his new queen will take her tribe elsewhere. But not with a potion of *this*. Wherever did you find it? Catamint's been so rare in these parts of late."

"Oh, I've a place," Taminy said, noncommittally.

"Well, you shall have to take Rennie with you next time you go so you can bring back more."

"Me too," said Wyvis quickly. "I've heard it's a truly fey place. That's what Cluanie said, anyway."

"Cluanie's just a babe," protested Rennie, peeking into the basket with veiled interest. "She thinks there're paeries in every tree and silkies in every puddle."

"Well, good for her, I say," said the Apothecary. "Too few see paeries anywhere at all. There's good herbs and such in fey places — which you'd know if you'd listen to Taminy, here. By the way, Mistress Liathach says thank you *very* kindly for the Five-leaf plaster. I told her it was your recipe. She says her tooth is much better and she'll see Osraed Torridon about it on your advice. It scared her to think of anyone touching it when it pained her so. She wanted me to ask if you knew of a cure for the catarrh. She has weak lungs, you know."

"You wouldn't think so if you'd heard her bray at her husband," offered Rennie.

"Shush, you! Such manners. What will Taminy think of you?"

But Taminy was laughing. She fingered a leafy packet on the counter. "Tell her vervain boiled with honey. Oh and, of course, one of your good herb steams."

"Vervain? Well, now, I've used that for a salve — heals up cuts and what-not quick as you please — but, boiled with honey . . . hm." She pulled a box of paper and a scribe from beneath the counter. "What's the dimensions?"

"Four parts vervain elixir to one part honey. Mix two spoonfuls in boiled water." The basket empty, Taminy, picked it up and settled it on her arm. "Well, I'm off to the Webber's now."

Wyvis and Rennie leapt at her in perfect unison.

"We *will* go to the fey place soon, won't we?" asked Wyvis.

"To gather Mam's herbs," Rennie qualified the utterance, giving his younger sister a sideways glance.

"Cirke-dag, after worship?" Taminy suggested and garnered two eager nods and a wide smile from the watching shopkeep.

Out on the street moments later, Taminy closed her eyes and took a deep sip of the late summer morning. It flew her to the far end of her time corridor again, depositing her in a place that only looked the same. It came to her in a rush so vivid she almost believed she could open her eyes and walk to the Cirke manse and find in it the familiar, the lovely, the secure — her father, her mother, her own room, the room where Iseabal now slept.

Oh, if she could only do that . . . well, what, then? Would she live things any differently, given another chance? Would she lock herself in her room and close her ears to the call of the Meri? Would she bid Iseabal deny that call? Or Gwynet or any of the receptive spirits that now graced Nairne?

"Daeges-eage, Taminy."

Dragged forward through time, Taminy opened her eyes to the here-and-now Nairne and a trio of interested male faces. "Daeges-eage, Brys," she murmured and nodded to the other boys, Scandy and Phelan. Odd, she thought, the impression that had struck her when her eyes first touched them. They had felt like stones: Brys, coldly metallic; Scandy, chalky and pale; Phelan, malleable as clay. She shook the impression, waiting for them to speak. But the self-assured Brys seemed ill-at-ease, hovering there before her with his coterie. At once eager and reluctant, he shuffled and blinked and thrust bold-coy glances at her.

"Em," he said finally. "Em, will you be in Sanctuary this Cirke-dag, Taminy?"

"Yes, of course."

"Oh, good, then . . . " He glanced at the others. "That is, I mean, I was hoping perhaps you'd join me at the Backstere's after for tea and cakes."

Ice hot, his voice, full of passionless want. She beheld him, there — so handsome and golden, so like iron — and shivered in spite of the warmth of the day.

"Well, I'll tell you, Brys-a-Lach," she said lightly, "that if you'd asked me that ten minutes ago I'd've had no reason to say 'no' to it. But I've made my promises for Cirke-dag already."

Brys's mouth twitched, but his expression, otherwise, didn't alter. Scandy, on the other hand, looked almost smug, Phelan, merely stunned that a mere cailin could refuse his awesome companion.

"Ah, well then . . . " murmured Brys and shuffled more.

"But you will ask me again?" Taminy suggested, making her voice bright.

"Oh, *aye!*" He smiled. "I will." He muttered of errands for Osraed Faer-wald and led his devotees away. Out of earshot, they dug elbows into each other's ribs and laughed, while Taminy made haste to the shop of Marnie-o-Loom.

Terris was there — alone, this time. His Gram and Da were out to Arundel, he said, looking over some wool.

Taminy pulled from her pocket a little jar of ointment and a bit of carved and polished wood. "These are for your Gram," she told him. "I noticed her hands were a bit knotted and I thought she might try this salve on them."

"And this?" Terris asked, holding up the misshapen dowel.

"That's a sort of amulet. After putting the ointment on her hand, she should take up the wood and rub it until the tingle from the ointment wears off. Then she should salve the other hand and rub the wood with it."

Terris was more than doubtful of this, he was clearly discomfitted and, when she turned to leave, he stopped her, coming from behind his cutting table to put himself between her and the door. "I've words to say to you, Taminy-a-Gled," he told her dramatically. "And I'd be pleased if you'd listen."

She paused and gazed at him. *What form shall the speech take today? Will you warn me off Wicke Craft or warn me off your Gram or warn me off myself?*

"It worries me," he said, waving the amulet at her, "to see someone like you flirting, mad-hearted, with these Wickish things."

"Wickish things?" she repeated. "An herbal balm and a rubbing stick?"

"That's just the toenail of the beast, Taminy. I know. I've heard my Gram's tales. And while I'd be mostly inclined to give them air, I've heard tell from others, too, about your paerie pool and your ways with animals and the things you're teaching Gwynet."

"Gwynet is a Prentice. She's supposed to learn those things — "

"From her Osraed. You're no Osraed."

Taminy lowered her eyes, her face flushing for reasons

Terris could never appreciate. "That is certainly true."

"Then you've no business teaching her the Art."

"And is it your business to tell me so?"

Terris put out his hands then, and took her shoulders and met her eye for eye. "You're a fine cailin, Taminy-a-Gled. As lovely and fair and fine a cailin as I've ever seen in Nairne or beyond — and I've been as far abroad as Lin-liath," he added, begging her to be impressed. "And you've a temper of matching fairness from what I've seen. It worries me sick to think of you dabbling in unseemly matters."

So, he would protect her from herself — a noble gesture. She smiled. "You're sweet, Terris," she said. "And I'm flattered you're so concerned, but there's naught unseemly about my matters or my ways or the things I'm teaching Gwynet. You worry yourself needlessly. Now, *please* give your Gram that ointment. Her fingers are paining her more than she lets show."

She tried to disengage herself, but Terris wasn't finished. He clung to her tenaciously, bent, she realized, on making himself understood.

"Don't think me a nosy-body, Taminy. Or a meddler. It's just that . . . well, I — I've been all but smitten since you first came in here — with *you*, I mean — smitten with *you*. If I wasn't, I'm sure I'd've kept my mouth shut."

Seized by a sudden frisson of tension, Taminy jerked her head toward the front of the shop. Aine and Doireann stood framed in the open doorway, one with hands on hips and fire in her eyes, the other with hands clutched, squirrel-like, upon her breast.

"Well, I should think," snapped Aine, "that one of these days, you'll learn to keep your mouth shut. At least in places you might be overheard."

Doireann's mouth, open, added nothing to that as Aine backed out of the store, reaching out at the last moment to grasp her elbow and drag her into the street.

"Not all truths were meant for utterance," Taminy murmured, paraphrasing the Corah.

"Aye," Terris agreed, "but that one was. I don't care that they heard it. It won't change how I feel.

"Terris, you hardly know me — "

"I know you're different," he said earnestly. "I know you're like no cailin I've ever known."

"Aye, and so what do you want me to do, the first time you've serious words for me? You want me to change. You want me to behave another way. Think another way. Ponder that, Terris. You like me being different, but you want to take the things that make me different away. Now, I thank you for your kind concern, but it will not change me or the things I do."

She left him standing, stunned, in the middle of his family's shop, and prayed only that he'd not withhold her medicines from his grandmother.

Osraed Lealbhallain swept a grimy wrist across his forehead and succeeded in doing nothing more than grinding filthy sweat into his skin. His face and forehead itched abominably, but there was little he could do just now but scratch it. The huge kitchen of the Creiddlylad Care House was too hot, kept that way by an eternally roaring fire. There was only one other usable fireplace on this level. It was at the other end of the long children's ward and it, too, burned night and day in an attempt to keep the sea-damp chill from the bones of the ward's inmates.

Leal scratched at his forehead and looked doubtfully at the last bundle of herbs he had extracted from the larger bale beside him on the floor. "How is it these supplies come to you in this condition?" he asked the dour Aelder Prentice working across the table from him.

The young man shrugged and flung a limp, beetle-infested flower head into the refuse bin. "What other condition might they be in . . . Osraed Lealbhallain?" he added.

"Well, the herbs and roots might be washed, the buds might be healthy, instead of diseased and dried out. The foodstuffs might not be half-rotted or dessicated or worm-eaten or" — he held up an apple with a very distinct bite removed — "sampled."

The Aelder Prentice's mouth twitched. "Osraed, these

aren't so much foodstuffs as they are refuse. If it falls off the cart, or gets crushed at the bottom of the wagon, it comes to us. Merchants aren't likely to give their best to them." He jerked his head toward the ward. The gesture was timed perfectly to coincide with a wild bleat of pain and fear from that dismal place.

Lealbhallain cringed, feeling as if someone had dug a fork into his ribs. He tried to concentrate on the herbs. "How long has it been like this?"

The Aelder Prentice looked at him strangely. "Always. As long as I've been here, anyway. You'd have to ask Osraed Fhada about before that."

"How long have you been here?"

"Three Solstices past." The youth's eyes shifted aside, glancing off the crystal hanging from Leal's prayer chain.

Leal felt sudden recognition. Of course, he should have made the connection; Aelder Buach had been Prentice Buach-an-Ochmer three Seasons ago at Halig-liath. A most promising student, according to all accounts, yet the Meri had twice passed him over. *And now, he is here — a weary drudge, up to his armpits in grime and unhappiness.* "Well, three years is plainly too long for this to continue. I must be intended to remedy the situation." He realized how arrogant that sounded as the words left his mouth. "There was a time," he went on, quickly, "when the Merchants cut their best from the very top to send to the Care House."

Buach's brow knit. "Why ever would they do that?"

Leal was at a loss to know how to answer. He was framing a set of words when another shriek of agony from the ward tore through his head. He clutched his side.

"It would be a hardship for them, after all," Aelder Buach said, as if he'd heard nothing. "Market tariffs being what they are."

"Market tariffs?" Leal glanced uneasily toward the ward's crumbling archway. Torchlight flickered eerily across the floors, making him imagine that ghostly snakes crawled there.

Buach nodded, reaching down from his stool to toss another bale of weedy-looking dried flowers onto the table. "To sell their wares in the Cyne's Market."

"They have to pay to bring their wares to market? Why?"

Buach shrugged. "Cyne Colfre needs the revenue for the work going on at Mertuile. For the Cirke, too."

"The Cirke?"

"Cyne's Cirke. He's adding to the Sanctuary and rebuilding the altar. And there's to be statues."

"Statues?" repeated Lealbhallain, beginning to feel like a parrot-bird.

Buach's lips twisted wryly. "A fine artist is our Cyne," he said, "as you've seen."

Leal nodded and reached out to grab a handful of stems. His ribs erupted with sudden pain, forcing a cry from his lips and all but toppling him from his rickety stool. Buach stared, his mouth open, but before he could say anything, the lanky silhouette of Osraed Fhada appeared in the kitchen archway. His leonine head tilted toward Lealbhallain, firelight haloing the shock of gold-red hair.

"Pardon, Osraed," he said, tugging at his prayer chain, "but are you well-practiced at the Healweave?"

Leal blinked and straightened, rubbing his rib cage. "Yes, sir."

"Could I presume upon you to assist us?" Fhada made an uncertain gesture in the direction of the ward.

Leal's agreement was immediate. He followed Fhada from the kitchen, through the pitiful, over-full ward into a cluster of chambers that served as a clinic. In one of these rooms, attended by an Aelder Prentice and an aging Osraed, a small boy lay atop a table, surrounded by blood-soaked rags.

"What happened to him?" Leal asked, feeling, again, the gouging in his side.

"We think he was in a fight," said Fhada. "He came in with the wagon of provisions. The jaeger found him on the edge of the Marketplace."

Leal didn't comment that the Osraed was charitable to call what they had received from that wagon "provisions," though he thought it. He moved to the table and shifted aside the wads of rag. The wound was horrid. Rag-edged and oozing, it looked as though a powerful set of jaws had taken a bite out of the boy's flesh.

Leal's bowels trembled in a fit of weakness and his own flesh took fire. Swallowing bile, he glanced up at the child's face. It was pale, and dark, frantic eyes stood out in it like red-rimmed coals.

"You've cleaned the wound thoroughly?" Leal asked, and the attending Osraed nodded. "I'll need to wash my hands — could you bring hot water?" He looked to the Aelder Prentice. The boy hesitated. Leal lowered his voice, attempting to sound less like a squeaky adolescent. "In the kitchen, over the fire, there's a pot — " He added a mental shove.

The youth nodded and scrambled through the door. While he was gone, Leal tried to survey the wound without touching it, holding, on a tight rein, the anger that had begun to roil in his breast. "Osraed Fhada," he said finally, because he found silence impossible, "conditions here are wretched. No, worse than that, they're unbearable. This clinic is ill-provisioned and filthy, you can't afford hot tap water — and the pipes are too pitted, if you could — you can't afford proper medicines, what passes for food here, is barely that, you're understaffed, and the staff you've got, if I may say so, sir, is uninspired."

Fhada's angular face reddened. "Yes, you may say so. It's only true. No one wants to serve here."

"But the lack of funds — how is it this Care House is so poor when Ochanshrine is so near by?"

The Aelder Prentice reentered the room, then, with the pot of water and some fresh rags, and Fhada's eyes followed him momentarily before he answered.

"It is precisely because Ochanshrine is so near by that we find ourselves in these circumstances, Osread Lealbhallain, or at least partially so. The Cyne has determined, along with his Privy Council, that the Shrine and Abbis need repair and redesign. They are, in his words, 'relics.' They do not 'show well.' That is where the preponderance of the Osraed monies go these days — to the refitting of the Shrine and the Abbis."

Leal finished scrubbing his hands and dried them before he moved back to the table. The child, watching him, whimpered.

"Who makes these decsisions — about the funding?"

Fhada shrugged. "I know I don't. The Cyne, the Council, the Chancellor. He has signatory authority."

"Over Osraed funds? Why? How? Why are you not in charge of your own monies?"

"Some years ago, the Osraed committee in charge of our financial matters was accused of mismanagement." Fhada glanced at the elder Osraed, who merely grunted. "Much was being spent here, then."

There was a wealth of sad irony in those words. Leal knew he must pursue the subject further with Fhada. Now, however . . . He laid gentle hands on the little boy's forehead and closed his mind to the others. "What's your name?" he asked the child.

"Leny." The answer was a raw whisper.

"Leny, I'm Osraed Leal. I'm going to take the pain away and help your wound heal."

"Please," said Leny. He shivered convulsively in his own sweat.

Leal didn't ask himself if he really could perform the Weave. He simply decided he _must_ perform it. Meredydd had told him once that he had a Healer's hands. He chose, now, to believe her. He chose, also, to believe that the Meri would aid him, whatever he had to do.

He withdrew his rune crystal from its pouch and cupped it in his hands. Before his eyes it glowed gently, but enough. He could feel it through his palms, through his fingertips. Holding the crystal in one hand, he laid the other, once again, on Leny's head and began a painblock inyx. Beneath the fingers of his left hand he felt the boy's frenetic energy calm, his trembling subside. When the small body had completely relaxed, he moved his free hand to the wound.

In his right hand, the crystal burned amber, pulsing with his heartbeat. He reached upward, then, with fingers of thought, feeling for the stream of energies he knew was there. Fishing, he'd called it in school, and had joked that he'd be lucky to catch a minnow. There were more than minnows in the stream today. There were energies he swore he'd only just realized existed in more than theory. He caught them, channeled them, and flooded Leny's wound with them. He heard the old Osraed murmur, the Aelder Prentice draw a sharp breath. Fhada was silent.

He ignored them all, singing out his duan, calling for the cohesion and healing of the boy's torn flesh. The energies answered, danced to his music and wove together the torn edges into a new, pink, tender cloth.

Later, Leal walked the dismal halls of the Care House with Osraed Fhada, trying to frame questions.

"You have a remarkable Gift, Osraed Lealbhallain," Fhada told him. "We've not seen its like here for some time."

"Why? Have you no one who can perform a Heal-weave?"

Fhada's mouth twitched. "We have you. At least for the time being."

"And no one else?"

"Yes, there are the Osraed Dhui and Piobair, but they're on mercy rounds just now, tending those too sick to be moved. I was once able to perform a Healweave — though never so efficiently as you did. Now, I can deal with cuts and bruises. There are a few others — again, none of them as accomplished as you. The Meri has not blessed Creiddylad with many Osraed of late — your arrival was quite a surprise. And the ones that are sent eventually take up work in the Abbis or in Mertuile, at the Cyne's . . . request. The Eiric hereabouts appreciate having their children educated by select Osraed and cleirachs."

"But what about the children here? They must be educated, too; they need healing. Does the Cyne offer these Osraed no choice?"

Fhada glanced at him askew. "Would you decline an offer to work in the Cyne's Clinic or the Eiric's schools to work here?"

"Yes."

Fhada stopped walking and gave him a long look. "I believe you would. But why?"

"Because this is what the Meri has commissioned me to do."

"To squander your talents among the ruins?"

"To improve the lot of those I am sent to serve. My talents are hardly squandered if I can do that." He peered into Fhada's face, trying to read his expression. He was able to read more than that. "Why are you here, Osraed Fhada?"

The older man raised his eyes to the shadow-pocked ceiling of the corridor. "Because I once felt as you do. That this was my place. That I had a . . . mission, I suppose. As I said, I once could perform a Healweave. But over the years, it seems I've lost my ability to concentrate, to feel the Touch . . . Her Touch."

Leal felt the bitterness of that — the loneliness. Impulsively, he reached out his hand and laid it on Fhada's arm. "She is nearer than your own soul, Osraed. Reach for Her and She *will* answer."

Fhada shook his head, "I've reached for Her in desperation for ten years. I'm exhausted with the effort. Once in a while I think I've recaptured something — a spark, a warmth — then things conspire to snuff it out. She no longer speaks to me."

"Perhaps She is speaking to you now," said Leal, and was stunned by his own audacity.

Fhada's brows ascended. "And what does She say to me?"

"That this is wrong." Leal's gesture took in the crumbling building around them.

"That I see, already, Osraed Lealbhallain. My question has always been — what can I do about it? Except for a few tough-minded souls, like our Hillwild Dhui, I have had the best talent siphoned away to the schools of the wealthy, to the halls of Mertuile."

"You could have spoken to the Brothers at Ochanshrine."

"Why do you assume I haven't?"

Leal blushed. "I'm sorry. I shouldn't have assumed that. Did you go to them?"

"Yes, and they spoke to the Cyne and the Cyne pledged

his support. But then came the rebuilding of the Abbis and the changes to the Cyne's Cirke — surely more important than feeding and educating a handful of orphans or the sons and daughters of un-landed commoners."

"There are more than a handful of orphans here, Osraed Fhada."

The older man turned his face into the shadows. "That is pathetically true."

"The Cyne must know."

Fhada uttered a bark of laughter. "He knows. He doesn't care."

"Then, Osraed Fhada, he must be *made* to care."

CHAPTER 10

The Shrine of your heart opens to your enemy and closes in the face of your Friend, for you have taken the love of another into your heart. Listen to the True Friend Who loves you for your own sake and not for your possessions. Will you show disloyalty to such a Friend?

— *Utterances of Osraed Aodaghan, Verse 24*

❖   ❖   ❖

Alone in the sunny classroom, Ealad-hach forced himself to relax. He was almost happy here among scattered books and papers, with light from the tall windows flooding every corner. He came here now to think and plan, and told himself it was because of the sunlight. He had not been inside his aislinn chamber for three days.

With his students gone, he found his mind revolving, again, toward what he now believed was a dark conspiracy. He knew not who, among the conspirators, were culpable and who were ignorant puppets, but he knew that at the core must be a powerfully gifted Wicke who wanted her prodigies at Halig-liath, who surely had designs on Halig-liath itself. He must find her, expose her.

Again, he murmured a prayer to the Meri to open a door in the wall of uncertainty he pressed against. Sighing, he rose to erase the white-wall; the names of Cynes, of great Osraed, the history of Caraid-land, disappeared under the powdered fleece. Malcuim, who first heard the Meri's chosen; Bearach Spearman, who, with the great Osraed Gartain, protected the Osmaer crystal from Claeg usurpers; Liusadhe the Purifier, who checked the influence of the Wicke in his time.

There had always been heroic Cynes to be found at previous Cusps. He erased the name of Colfre and wondered if this Cyne would be equal to the task.

He moved to the shelves near the door next, replacing text books, gathering written assignments. It put him in precisely the right spot to hear the conversation in the hallway. Later, he would think it the answer to his fevered prayers.

"Will you tell none, then?" Scandy-a-Caol's Northern accent was unmistakable.

"Who am I to tell?" That was Brys-a-Lach. "She's an Osraed's pet. He no doubt taught her everything she knows."

"In the time she's been here?" Phelan's reedy whine ended in a pronounced squeak. "I don't believe it."

"Why not? She didn't do aught that were so grand."

"She mended a broken tree branch," said Brys dryly. "That's more than you or I could do."

"Mended it and put it back on!" snorted Phelan.

"Aye," said Scandy, "and I heard Cluanie Backstere say she healed a sheep's broken fetlock."

"That's not all Cluanie said. Did you catch that twaddle about the Meri regenerating?" Brys uttered a sharp laugh. "Osraed Ealad-hach would have a fit if he heard her version of history."

The volume of their voices was falling; they were moving off down the hall. Ealad-hach hurried to the door and peeked through. They were headed away from him toward the main corridor.

"Look Brys," Scandy was objecting, "shouldn't we tell someone?"

"It wouldn't do any good. Especially since Wyth's grand announcement. We're to have female Prentices. Next thing you know we'll have female Osraed."

The three boys disappeared around the corner. Ealad-hach, shamefaced, scurried to keep within earshot.

"But this in't the same thing, Brys. She's saying and doing stuff I never learnt, and you saw the way of things there, in tha' damn glen o' hers. There was a gatherin' a' tha' pool, Brys. I'd swear't. Tha' Taminy's calling up a

coven. And on Cirke-dag, more's the sin. God-the-Spirit,
I'm wishin' we ne'er went poking after 'em."

Ealad-hach all but choked on the air he breathed. He
heard the boys' steps cease and Phelan ask, "Did you hear
something?"

Afraid they might turn back and find him cowering
there, Ealad-hach slipped into an empty classroom. His
shame at hiding from a trio of mere boys was quickly
eclipsed by a dreadful rapture. It was certain now;
Taminy-a-Gled was a Wicke. But was she _the_ Wicke? Was
she the power source he sought, or merely a gifted
minion? Either way, his course was clear. He must find a
reason to call the girl out and expose her.

"My Lord, the Osraed Lealbhallain to see you."

Durweard Feich's voice and face were both devoid of
expression as he addressed his Cyne. They were in the
throneroom this morning, receiving visitors and petition-
ers. Leal counted himself as just one more of those, or
would have if Cyne Colfre had not, upon seeing him, leapt
to his feet exclaiming, "My _dear_ Osraed Lealbhallain! How
good of you to visit me! Come, sit . . . Refreshment," he
ordered the ether, and servants scattered.

Visiting courtiers, Eiric by the cut of their clothing,
muttered and looked annoyed at the intrusion. Colfre
waved them away from the throne. Leal sat where he was
bidden, in a chair on the Cyne's dais recently vacated by a
rotund gentleman with a beet-red face.

"How may I serve you?" Colfre asked, dipping his head.

Leal was taken aback. He was certain he had offended
the Cyne at their first meeting — offended and disturbed
him. He had expected nothing more than cool indifference. He chose his words carefully. "Sire, the Care House
is in great need of supplies, staff and renovation. I have
observed how fond you are of such projects and as Care
House has always been associated with Mertuile and lies in
her shadow, I thought you should know that it stands in
need of your loving attention."

Watching the Cyne's face, Leal caught his sideways
glance at the hovering Durweard. He also caught, as one

catches a distant tune, a shift in the interest of the courtiers, who stood in a knot just within earshot. His spine tingled.

The Cyne smiled, amber eyes exuding warmth. "You read me well, young Osraed. But I regret that I am already over-extended in the area of renovations. No doubt Osraed Fhada has informed you that I am overseeing the renovation of the Abbis at Ochanshrine as well as the alterations to the Cyne's Cirke."

Leal nodded. "And the work here at Mertuile, which is a wonder to behold."

The Cyne inclined his head, accepting the compliment.

"Which is why," Leal continued, "I suggest that the funds to mend the Care House and its inmates be placed directly in the hands of Osraed Fhada. He's a competent man and knows, better than anyone, what needs to be done there."

"Did Fhada ask you to make this request?"

"No, sire. This is my recommendation." He stressed the last word.

The Cyne made a rueful noise and shook his head. "I regret, Osraed, that, with the improvements being made to the Abbis and the Cirke, the funds are also rather over-extended."

Leal glanced down at his folded hands. His prayer crystal rested between them. "Sire, may I then recommend that you disengage some funds from these other projects and allot them to the Care House? There are lives involved there — the lives of children, largely. Surely, those lives are more important than ornamentation."

Again, Leal felt a subtle shift of energies in the room; the courtiers and servants laid their eyes upon the Cyne and waited for his reply. Colfre glanced again at Feich and bowed his head. "In the life of every Cyne, Osraed Lealbhallain, comes a time when he needs the wise counsel of the Chosen in order to make a decision. Apparently, my time has come. I have been remiss. Rest assured that a remedy is forthcoming. If you will tender a list of your needs to Daimhin Feich, he will see to them."

Leal did not recall having asked the Cyne to fill a

shopping list. He did not say this, but instead asked, "And the Osraed funds?"

"Have been managed well by our Chancellor. We see no compelling reason to change. Surely, Osraed Fhada could do without having to juggle finances along with his other, more important duties. After all, he will soon have renovations to oversee."

Lealbhallain regarded his Cyne's smiling face for a moment, then inclined his head slightly. It was not the time for a shoving match. Not the time to over-reach himself. "You have exceeded my expectations, sire. I'll inform Osraed Fhada of your generous response."

He rose and left, then, and did not miss the look Colfre exchanged with Daimhin Feich, though he didn't see it.

"I dreamed last night, Bevol," she said, and the dark circles beneath her eyes gave mute testimony that the dreams had not been pleasant. Her breakfast sat, half-un-eaten, on her plate.

"What did you dream?"

"Flashes of fire and a great tumult. I dreamed of a collision of paths, a confusion of lives. I dreamed of our future, fast approaching."

Bevol nodded, his eyes seeming to focus on something outside the dining nook window, but she knew he saw nothing external. "To be expected, I suppose. It worries you?"

Taminy slipped a loose strand of hair behind her ear. "May I tell you what really worries me?"

"Of course, anwyl."

She smiled at the endearment. It comforted. "I am distressed by my own feelings." She pressed interlaced hands to her breast. "People look at me strangely and whisper. I hear my name on the lips of people I don't even know. People who smiled at me two days ago, now frown and look away. Brys-a-Lach . . . " She paused, dropping her hands to her lap. Her head tilted, sending a curtain of flax to cover her eyes. "He asked me to have tea with him last Cirke-dag. All this week, he's avoided speaking to me, though he's watched me like a sheep dog. And Terris-mac-Webber won't even acknowledge me when I enter his Grandmother's shop. And neither Doiry nor Aine will even so much as glance at me." Her words ran out, leaving her feeling stranded. She put back her hair again.

"It's true, y'know, Maister," said Skeet, looking up from his meal. "There's more gossip in th'air than dust these days, an' more gossips than birds."

"And what are these gossips saying?"

Skeet made a face. "That this cailin of Bevol's is just like the last one — fey and dangerous."

Bevol's eyes touched Taminy's in a caress. "And is this so unexpected?"

"No, of course not," she said.

"I'm sorry you must endure this again."

"It's not the enduring that pains me. It's that I'm so hurt by it. When I'm alone sometimes, I feel . . . so very human. So unwanted by the people around me."

"You *are* human, anwyl. Your experience in the Meri's Sea did not change that. But, make no mistake, you are wanted desperately." Bevol clasped his hands around his mug. "Do you doubt that Iseabal wants you? Or Gwynet or Wyvis or Rennie or Skeet or Wyth or myself? But most of all, Taminy, the Meri wants you."

"Yes. And because of that, I cannot afford to be human and frail and hurt. I try to pretend I'm not bothered by it, but I am. And I feel weak. I feel unworthy."

Bevol reached across the table and took her hand. "What you have described to me, anwyl, is a strength, as well as a weakness."

"But it's so *selfish*, this fear of mine. This hurt."

"Is it? Look at your fear, Taminy. Ask it its name. When those souls reject you, scorn you, shun you, what are they *really* rejecting, hmm? You know the answer to that. So ask this: is it your own loneliness you dread, or the loneliness of those souls who will not suffer themselves to embrace you — to embrace *Her*?"

She pondered that. He was right, in part, she realized. She could not lay claim to being lonely or unloved. Not in any real sense. And on the deepest level of her being she could feel the Meri's breath fan her soul. A breeze. A

Touch. More and more often she felt connected to the Source of her fitful Gift, but the connection was capricious, uncertain — and in those gaps of uncertainty, yawned a gulf of loneliness. And now, a fiery collision approached. Was she ready for it? Could she withstand it?

Watching her pensive face, Bevol said, "You don't have to go to worship Cirke-dag if it will distress you."

"Aye," said Skeet. "The gossip-mongery will gather there in all force with their sharp eyes and sharp tongues."

Taminy shook her head. "I have no reason to hide from them. I will *not* hide from them. And I *can't* hide from what my dreams reveal."

Bevol patted her hand. "Collisions can take many forms."

She managed a smile. "Oh, aye. That I know."

She tried not to think of collisions as the week moved by. Eyes still poked at her, tongues still wagged. Twice she walked into the Backstere's only to have silence fall among the animated patrons. Once a young woman carried her child from the place, shielding its eyes from her. Niall Backstere, himself, clucked and shook his head and confided to her in quiet tones, as he wrapped her a loaf of bread, that he didn't understand what made some folk so gullible as to believe every tale they heard. Somehow she knew that the moment the door closed behind her, he would be in the midst of it all, absorbing every rumor. Still, he did nothing to keep Cluanie from her company, so it seemed he did not believe the gossip he help spread.

Mistress Lusach, the Apothecary, pooh-poohed the whole situation, saying it was the natural thing to happen in a small town when one member, especially a new member, stood out from the ordinary folk so startlingly.

"It's jealousy, Tam, dear," she said. "You do what they can't or won't or don't dare and it sets them off. And for all that the Osraed have given their cailin permission to Weave, well, you can't put aside six hundred and some years of 'we know what's right an' we know what's wrong' with the flick of a tongue — even a holy one."

That much was true, Taminy knew. Terris-mac-Webber still wouldn't speak to her when she entered the shop, but his Grandmother would, and bluntly too.

"You know what's gnawing at 'im?" she asked, when Taminy's appearance to purchase some thread sent Terris scuttering for the back room. "It's the stories they're telling of you."

"Who? Who's telling stories?"

"Oh, all the young cailin. Terris is a catch, don't you know, and I doubt they want someone doing the catching who hasn't lived here all her life."

Taminy nodded and said nothing.

"They're saying you've strange powers. Well, I could've told 'em that, couldn't I?" Her thin lips cracked into a smile. "Some has it you're a Hillwild Renic in disguise. Legend says they're all fey, every one of 'em. I wouldn't know, never having met one. Their men are rare beauties, though." The smile deepened.

"Are they saying I'm Wicke?" Taminy asked.

Marnie-o-Loom screwed her wizened face into a map with a thousand tiny canyons. "No one's used the dread word, to my knowledge — least, not in any seriousness. Though Cluanie Backstere has it you're half paerie." She tilted an eyebrow at Taminy. "But what is a Wicke if girls be going to the Fortress?"

She had turned to leave when the old woman spoke again. "I owe you thanks, cailin. For the medicaments. My hands" — she held them up, fingers straight — "My hands thank you."

When Taminy smiled at her, she sobered. "Be careful, cailin. When the old meaning of Wicke fails us, we'll be quick and sure to come up with a new one."

But she could not be careful. She could only be what she was bidden to be.

By the end of the week, she was becoming accustomed to the ambivalent behavior of her neighbors. Besides which, in the furor over Wyth's call for female Prentices, a young woman who dabbled in the Art and taught undisciplined children how to make themselves useful was often eclipsed by debate over that mystery. Already, the Hillwild had produced a handful of candidates, and Nairnian parents fretted over what effect those half-wild females would have on their boys.

Taminy found she was still welcome at Cirke-manse, though the Mistress there was disinclined to inhabit the same room. She and Iseabal wove closer bonds along with their inyx, while Osraed Saxan looked on, alternately pleased and fretful. She hadn't seen Aine or Doireann face to face since that day at the pool, so it was a great surprise when the two of them followed her into the Apothecary's one afternoon to inquire if she'd be going out to the pool that Cirke-dag as had become her custom.

She looked at Doireann, who had asked the question in a sweet voice, and reached out questing tendrils of sense, guiltily seeking cleverness or dissimulation. All she felt from the other girl was a shimmer of anticipation. Glancing at Aine, she met a glowering mental roadblock.

She nodded slowly, not quite sure what to make of the question. "Most likely, I'll go," she said.

"Well, Aine and I" — here Doireann glanced at the other girl for support — "Aine and I would very much like to come along. After all, we may all be at Halig-liath soon and we've got to start somewhere." She smiled. "And some of our friends are going. It would be a raw shame to miss out on all the fun and let them get ahead of us."

"You're certainly welcome to come. But, Aine" — she tilted her eyes at the red-head — "I thought you'd no desire to go to Halig-liath."

Aine's jaw set. "A person can change her mind." She toyed with the laces of her vest. "What do you think you'll be doing? I mean, what are you teaching?"

"Oh, yes!" breathed Doireann. "Do tell us! Shall we learn to cast inyx?"

Taminy recoiled slightly from the sheer intensity of their energies. She offered a shy smile. "I thought we'd try some simple Wardweaves. They're not difficult and they teach discipline. Besides, they often come in good use for protection."

Aine nodded, lifting her chin. "Fine, then. We'll see you Cirke-dag. Come on, now, Doiry."

Doireann pouted. "I wanted to hear more about Wardweaves."

"You'll hear more than enough on Cirke-dag, I imagine.

Now, come *on*." She grasped the smaller girl's arm and pulled her from the shop.

Taminy glanced across the Apothecary counter at the shop-mistress and her son. They gazed back, brows in matching furrows.

Mistress Lusach shook her head. "Odd pair, that. Like sunrise and shadow."

Taminy had to agree. They were an odd pair and an ambivalent one.

The birds were strangely silent this morning. Osraed Ealad-hach construed that as a sign. Outside his chamber window, the air hung still and damp with sun-hazed river rheum. He had spent the night in his aislinn chamber in meditation and prayer. No visions had come, save one of a piercing white light that had all but blinded him. Still, he knew what he must do.

Before him on the table he had the things he needed: a mirror and a crystal. The mirror was for the Weave he would perform to record the Wicke's doings by the pool. The crystal was protection. It had belonged to the Osraed Lin-a-Ruminea — one hundred years ago, the courageous advisor of Cyne Thearl, who had been on the Throne during the last Cusp. There was a rightness to that that brought comfort to him. Of comfort, too, was the thought that he had, among the youth of Nairne, spies and allies. He had lost Wyth Arundel, but there was still Brys-a-Lach, a young man who fulfilled where Wyth had disappointed. And when next Solstice came, he had no doubt Brys's Pilgrimage would end in his acceptance by the Meri.

Ealad-hach breakfasted in the Refectory at Halig-liath, his appetite better than it had been for months, then he took a carriage down into Nairne to the Cirke. He rarely attended worship at Nairne Cirke, preferring, instead, the less crowded, more intimate atmosphere of the small sanctum at Halig-liath. So it was that his presence caused a stir among the worshippers. It was unavoidable that the object of his presence should see him and send him an unreadable glance from those great green eyes. He shivered at the sudden familiarity of that look, of those eyes. He met them and felt a pang of pure sadness engulf him. He blinked and it vanished and the girl looked aside.

He sat along the wall of the Sanctuary where he could see her face in profile. Brys-a-Lach sat beside him. Taminy did not look at them from her place facing the altar. In the company of Bevol, Gwynet and the boy Skeet, with Iseabal-a-Nairnecirke tight at her side, she was well-guarded. That was all very well. She could flank herself with daemons if she would — it would not stop him from pursuing his duty.

Osraed Saxan had selected Scriptural passages that spoke of callings and duties. This, he said, in light of the recent mandate from the Meri (here, a nod to Osraed Wyth, seated in the midst of the worshippers) to bring girls to Halig-liath. He had selected several Prentices to read or recite from the Holy Books, but a mild furor arose when the final reader stood, for Saxan had given to his daughter, Iseabal, the task of reading a dissertation on Occupation revealed by the Meri through the Osraed Gartain.

Iseabal, black hair curried to the gleam of hard coal, waited out the murmurs that her journey to the altar caused and, when the congregation had quieted, she read in a clear, unwavering voice: "That one who puts forth his best effort in the line of duty, then gives his work to the Spirit of All, attains perfection in service. This service is the great sacrifice of life which each soul must offer to the Source of Life. It is better by far for one to perform his duty in the world, no matter how lowly or faulty, than to perform the duty of another. That one who does the work indicated by his own nature errs not, but follows the guidance of the Spirit. Natural inclination toward a calling when yoked to the ability for its performance is worthy to be performed and, indeed, becomes duty. Let all remember that . . . " Iseabal blinked and cleared her throat, glancing across at Taminy. "That every calling, every duty, every life, has its pain and its joy, its hindrances and its helps, its sorrow and its triumphs."

Iseabal returned to her seat and her father assumed, again, his position at the altar stone. "Osraed Wyth . . . " He picked the younger man out of the rows of upturned faces. "If you would be so kind as to share with us a bit of the Meri's wisdom from your own Pilgrimage, we would be grateful. I fear my secondhand comments could hardly be adequate."

Wyth rose, tentatively, it seemed, and Ealad-hach's spirit roiled. He wanted to cry out, "Blasphemy!" He wanted to shake the Sanctuary with the thunder of reason — shake it until he'd toppled every stone and awakened them all to what was being played out in Nairne. But a calmer voice prevailed. Soon, it said, soon they would see. There were still Wicke in the world and they had now been given permission to masquerade as something else. He glanced down his row and caught the Osraed Faerwald's eye. He was not alone.

"The Meri," Wyth was saying with some diffidence, "the Meri has given me this about the calling of our young men and women."

He paused and, in that pause, a visible change overcame him. His entire frame, his expression, his eyes, shed all hint of timorousness. Light from the windows played through the strands of his dark hair and made his angular face appear, almost, to glow. His prayer crystal, on its long, complex chain, followed suit, causing all who saw it to draw admiring and awful breaths.

Ealad-hach's jaw tightened against his will and he wondered if he oughtn't listen, if instead he should recite a duan to keep the words from affecting him. In the end, he listened.

"True faith, O People of the Corah," said Wyth in a voice that rang with music, "is for each soul to pursue its calling in the world as dictated by the gifts bestowed by its Creator. Hold fast to the Spirit of the Universe, treasure His gifts among you and use them in accordance with His desire, not with your own. Seek His grace, which is My grace, for in Our hands lies the destiny of the world."

There was a silence, like the silence of the morning's birds, in which no adult spoke and no child shuffled its feet. Then Wyth sat and the congregation murmured in complex harmonies until Osraed Saxan recaptured their attention. He spoke then, of the things the Scriptural passages alluded to and announced, to the surprise of many, that his own child, Iseabal, had a Gift for the Art and that he had decided to offer her the opportunity to attend Halig-liath.

It was during this disturbing revelation that Osraed Ealad-hach first noticed the peculiar odor in the room. At length, he began to think that it, and not Wyth's "revelation" was the cause of the continued undercurrent of unease in the room. It came to him especially strongly when they rose to sing the lays. He glanced at Brys, intending to ask if he smelled anything odd, but the expression on his face made the question unecessary. He tried to cull the scents as he sang. He made out bay laurel, he thought, and perhaps garlic, but beneath that was a fetid, almost putrid odor that grew stronger and more unbearable with each moment.

The relief in the room when Saxan intoned the homeward blessing was palpable; worshippers streamed toward the door the moment they were free to do so. Ealad-hach, hampered by his location and age, was one of the last to reach the door and was puzzled to find that here, near a knot of young people, the horrid stench was concentrated. Phelan was there and Terris-mac-Webber and Scandy-a-Caol and two girls he barely knew — the Spenser's daughter and a taller girl with stridently red hair which, coupled with that odor, annoyed him almost beyond patience.

As he approached along the back wall of the Cirke, he saw the youngsters' eyes move in unison to the central aisle where Iseabal and Taminy walked, engaged in conversation. He paused, thinking perhaps he could glean something from their interaction.

He was rewarded but surprised. The youngsters by the door purposefully blocked the girls' exit and encircled them in sly smiles and confrontational glares.

"So, Taminy," said the boy, Scandy, "tell us, are ye off to your Wickie glen today?"

"Please, say you aren't," insisted mac-Webber.

But the Spenser's girl said, "Tell us you *are*." She pouted her lower lip and added, "You promised us, didn't she, Aine?"

The red-haired cailin nodded, frowning. "Aye. I suppose she did."

"Oh, might we come?" Scandy asked. "Can we see you cast a love inyx? We know you must've tossed one a' poor Terris, here." He clapped the other boy on the back, making him shrug away.

"Wheez!" said Phelan, screwing up his face. "Whatever's that *smell*?"

"You just noticed it?" asked Scandy. "Maybe it's the foul odor o' Wicke." He looked straight at Taminy.

Iseabal-a-Nairnecirke went white, then red. "Taminy's no Wicke. She's just Gifted. Tell them, Taminy. Tell them you're not Wicke."

"No, I'm not Wicke."

"It's sinful to lie in a Cirke," said Scandy.

Again Phelan whined, "What's that smell?"

The Spenser's girl left the redhead's side to glide between Taminy and Iseabal. "Well, it's not Taminy or Iseabal, so there's that idea put to rest." She gave Scandy a supercilious glance then turned her eyes back to the girl, Aine. Her nose wrinkled and she thrust out her arm, pointing at the other girl. "Aine-mac-Lorimer, whatever is that on your skirt?"

All eyes were drawn to the redhead then, as she stared down, herself, at the horrid-looking stain spreading from the large, square pocket in the apron of her skirt. She reached a hand in, face covered with dread. Her expression altered swiftly to a wide-eyed grimace and she jerked the hand out again with a wild croak. A dark egg-sized object flew from her hand to land with a grotesquely wet plop at Taminy's feet.

The Spenser's girl screamed and leapt back. "What is it? Oh, Aine, what *is* it?"

The other girl just shook her head mutely, her eyes on the sodden lump at their feet. Scandy picked it up.

"It's furry!" he said. "Gah! An' it stinks rotten!"

"Why, it's a runebag, isn't it?" asked the Spenser's girl. "Aine, what are you doing with it?"

Ealad-hach stepped forward as swiftly as his aging bones and muscles allowed and snatched the wretched wad from Scandy's hand. It was, indeed, the source of the rancid smell. He held it up to the light from the nearby window.

"It's an animal skin," murmured Brys, at his shoulder.

It was a mole skin, to be exact and, seeing it, Ealad-hach suspected he knew what it contained. He peeled back enough of the putrifying skin to see what lay beneath. "Bay leaves," he murmured, "soaked in garlic, it would seem. And would there be a snake's head wrapped inside?" he asked Aine.

The girl merely gawped at him, her mouth open.

"A snake's head?" asked Brys, and the other boys made sick faces.

"A snake's head wrapped in garlic-soaked bay leaves and a fresh mole skin. If I am not mistaken, this runebag is intended to keep any Wicke present in this Cirke from leaving it." Ealad-hach turned his gaze to Taminy, who stood with Iseabal clinging to her arm. "Are there Wicke in this Cirke, cailin?"

She met his eyes, then, and a chasm seemed to open up beneath his feet, leaving him teetering on the edge of vertigo.

"There may be Wicke here, Osraed," she said, "but I am not among them."

"No?" Ealad-hach looked around at the group of youth. His eyes found Aine again. "Do you think this girl is Wicke, cailin?"

In answer, the girl screwed up her face and bolted out through the half-open sanctuary door.

Ealad-hach turned back to Taminy, holding up the horrid fetish. "Someone is accusing you of practicing the Wicke Craft, Taminy-a-Gled. Do you deny the accusation?"

"I have studied the Art, Osraed, both under my father and Osraed Bevol. It is the Art I practice, in my small way, not Wicke Craft."

"You do claim a Gift, then?"

Taminy nodded. "A small Gift, Osraed. I understand herbs and healing. Is there something harmful in that?"

"You cast no love inyx on young Terris, as this lad suggested?"

Terris-mac-Webber blushed profusely. "That was a tease, is all, Master. He meant nothing by it, but to twit me."

"Are you certain?"

"I cast no such inyx, Osraed," Taminy said. "That would be an abuse of the Art."

"Will you suffer yourself to be tested, cailin? Before witnesses?"

The girl didn't blink. "If it's your wish, Osraed."

"Do you want the Osraed Bevol here?"

"He's no doubt returned home. There's no need to call him back."

"You don't want your champion present? I find that odd."

"If my actions have brought this accusation upon me, it's my responsibility to face it, not Osraed Bevol's."

How calm she was. How composed. Any normal teenaged girl would be in tears now . . . if she was innocent. He glanced at the Cirkemaster's daughter. Already her eyes were filling with fearful tears and her hands, clasped over her companion's arm, shook.

"Will you witness this?" he asked the group of young people. They nodded — eagerly, he thought. Good. Let them see this creature reveal herself. He raised his eyes, looking down the aisle over the head of the Spenser's girl. "And you, Osraed Saxan, will you witness the test of this cailin?"

Iseabal turned to her father, her eyes spilling tears. "Please, father, make him stop this. He wants to hurt Taminy."

"If Taminy is innocent," Ealad-hach observed, "then she need have no fear of hurt."

The Cirkemaster clenched his fists and thrust them into the pockets of his robe. "I can't see what you hope to prove, Osraed Ealad-hach. Osraed Wyth has given us news that makes the Art a noble pursuit for our cailin."

"This is true — the *Art* is noble. But there are dark inyx that are not part of the Art; there are dark Runes that are not to be woven."

"And how shall you prove that Taminy has woven such dark Runes?"

Ealad-hach allowed himself a grim smile. He dropped
the runebag to the floor before the Sanctuary door and
gestured toward the front of the Sanctuary. "Come to the
altar and we shall see."

Once at the altar, he had Brys place Taminy, seated,
upon the great, carved stone, while the witnesses fanned
out below her. Then he reached into his belt pouch and
brought forth the crystal there. He held it so that light
struck it, shattering in its perfect facets.

"This is the crystal given to the Osraed Lin-a-Ruminea
upon his Farewelling. Have you heard of this Osraed,
cailin?"

She surprised him. "Yes," she said. "It was the Osraed
Lin who advised Cyne Thearl in the time the histories call
the Emerald Cusp."

Ealad-hach did not let his surprise show. "Lin-a-Ruminea was a man of surpassing wisdom and absolute
purity. This is the crystal he wove with. It's name is Gwyr
— pure — and it is said to be one of the purest stones in
existence. A pure stone, as you may know, will not suffer
itself to be used for the impure Weavings of the wicked.
Which is why," he added, "the sinful have never been able
to raise the power enjoyed by the innocent."

He thrust the crystal nearly into Taminy's face. "Take
this crystal, cailin. Let us see what it tells us about you."

She reached up her hands without hesitation and took
the stone, holding it before her eyes. For a moment,
nothing happened, causing feet to shuffle and eyes to trade
secret glances, then the core of the crystal caught fire.
Light erupted from it in a blinding cascade — streamers of
flame like the fire shows of Farewelling reached up and
out, harmlessly passing the stunned watchers, arcing to the
limit imposed by the stone walls. The walls, themselves,
began to glow then, as if the light, liquid, poured over
them, coating the cold stone. The Eibhilin beams moved
as if alive, weaving themselves into an intricate awning that
wheeled over the awed and stupefied. The awning
contracted slowly into a blazing web that held Taminy and
the crystal within.

Osraed Ealad-hach clutched at his racing heart, barely

able to take in what he was seeing, able only to cry mutely that it could not be. That *this* woman could not manipulate the Eibhilin energies through a pure stone. What did it mean? His mind flailed for an answer and found none.

He panicked. He must have time to think. He must wrench the crystal from her hands. Yes, it would at least make him seem to be in control of this trial. He willed his hands to move, but they would not. It was an ordeal of will just to press his lungs and throat into service. He shrieked. "Stop!"

The web of light dissolved into a billion tiny points of incandescence, a glittering powder that settled to the Sanctuary floor, pulsed, and melted like snow before sun. Ealad-hach's heart and bowels trembled. He did not want to lift his eyes again, to see her mocking him, but he must. Control was necessary. He looked up quickly to catch her expression. So far from mocking, was it, he could almost imagine he saw wide-eyed, open-mouthed amazement there.

The girl shook herself, then, blinked as if waking, and proferred him the crystal. He took it gingerly, speechless. It scalded his fingers and he nearly dropped it before juggling it into a fold of his robe. While he fumbled, Taminy slipped from the altar stone, bid the watchers daeges-eage and left the Sanctuary, stepping lightly over the discarded runebag. Ealad-hach turned to watch her, by now unsurprised that it did not cause her to hesitate.

There was a hush in his soul. A cold, dark silence. The stone was pure. He knew it was. He knew the impure could not handle it, could not use it. His startled mind reached into the quivering shadows and thrust forward the thought that the girl might be innocent. Perhaps he was looking for his Cwen Wicke in the wrong place, or perhaps there was no Cwen Wicke and his aislinn was, as Wyth had suggested, a portent of good rather than evil. What then? What if Taminy-a-Gled possessed nothing but a strong natural Gift?

From a place where time had stopped, Ealad-hach confronted the idea of Taminy's innocence. He closed his eyes and beheld her again, bathed in radiance, dripping it,

shedding it like . . . like the woman in his aislinn, the
woman who rose from the Sea, laughing. He fought the
mad desire to swoon under the sudden weight of his
certitude — Taminy and that woman were one and the
same; the Cwen Wicke of his nightmares had put on flesh.

The Osraed Lealbhallain let himself be awestruck,
again, at the grand beauty of the Cyne's Cirke. The long
nave, with its vaulted ceiling, looked to him like the rib
cage of some giant, ossified Eibhilin beast who had lain
down here and slept the ages away that men and women
might have a place to worship. Light from windows set
high on the flanks of the peaked roof poured down the
walls in a myriad hues and tumbled across the floor. He
could almost hear the bubbling froth of light.

The appointments, too, were magnificent — the huge,
carved and polished doors with their copper, silver and
brass trims and fittings; the raised dais of dark wood,
polished by the feet and knees of Osraed, royalty and other
penitent worshippers; the altar stone, a-glitter with crystalline fragments from Ochan's Cave; behind it, a standard
bearing a great star of gold and crystal — symbol of the
Meri's presence.

Of all things here, that altar stone was the constant. It
had not been renewed or refurbished since its placement
there by Cyne Kieran, called the Dark, in response to a
prophecy that made him fearful of wedding at Halig-liath
or Ochanshrine. It was Cyne Saeward who enlarged the
Cirke from those original, relatively humble beginnings,
and who retiled the floors, replaced the paneling and
added the largest of the windows. Since then, no major
changes had been made.

Colfre's alterations, Fhada had told him, lay concealed
behind a great tapestry that hung just beyond the altar.
Leal couldn't imagine what changes the Cyne believed
justified the tariffs he was levying against local merchants.
Surely nothing, Lealbhallain thought, could increase the
grandeur of the place or enhance its sense of history.

He heard the wind-bells, then, from their aerie above
the altar, and realized the Sanctuary had all but filled with

worshippers. Beside him, Osraed Fhada, who had been lost in his own meditations, stirred and glanced around.

"Ah," he said, "the Cyne."

Leal turned to glance up the broad central aisle. It was, indeed, the Cyne and, with him, an entire entourage. Before him a pair of boys carried the standards of the House Malcuim and Colfre's personal crest — a dove bearing in its beak a wild sea-rose. Thereafter came the Cyne's Durweard, Daimhin Feich, followed by the Cyne himself and the Cwen Toireasa, both borne on thrones of gilt wood. Behind them, on a smaller throne, was the young Riagan, Airleas.

Leal ogled. He had worshipped at Ochanshrine these weeks past in the small seaside chapel called Wyncirke. Only this Cirke-dag had an invitation from Mertuile brought him and Fhada to Cyne's Cirke. He had never imagined this pageantry; down the broad central aisle the Royal Family was borne, followed by a troupe of court Eiric, Ministers and Osraed. The less impressive members of the congregation merely watched.

Osraed Fhada leaned close to Lealbhallain. "The first alteration our Cyne made here was to have the great aisle made greater that he and his Cwen might travel it enthroned."

Leal watched, as he was intended to, while the courtiers found themselves seats in the front row — cordoned off for them, Fhada said. The thrones continued on, to be set upon the altar itself, flanking the great stone. The standards, too, were placed there, one to each side of the golden staff which held the Meri's effigy.

Leal glanced sideways at Fhada. The older Osraed's face was flushed and his jaw set. He shook his head. "Sacrilege," he murmured. "Placing himself on the same altar as the Meri's Star."

Leal faced front again as the Cyne's Cirkemaster took his place at the altar stone and began the devotions. The worship was traditional; there were readings from the Corah and the Book of the Meri interspersed with congregational lays and stunning chants from the Cirke chorus, accompanied by fine musicians on feidhle, pipe and badron. It was, in all, a glorious worship, and Leal lost himself in the Weave of sunlight, incense and song until the final prayers had been offered. Then, when traditionally the Cirkemaster would offer a blessing or commend some thought for the personal meditation of the worshippers, he instead placed an ornate wooden box upon the altar stone.

Leal recognized the motif upon its carved panels and a chill coursed up his spine. The Cyne rose then, to place himself, kneeling, before the altar stone. Whereupon, the Cirkemaster opened the box and removed from it a chalice. Water lapped gently at the sides of the cut crystal bowl while skillfully channeled sunlight leapt from the facets and raced like wildfire along the curves of the graceful stem.

The Star Chalice. A relic beneath which a war had once been fought. A ceremonial goblet created for the ascension of Cynes and Osraed. A vessel which Osraed Lealbhallain's lips had touched but once, upon his arrival at Ochanshrine. That sacred vessel was now lifted up before the crowd while the Osraed of Cyne's Cirke intoned the words usually reserved for coronations, "Behold, Caraid-land. Behold your Cyne — Colfre, son of Ciarda of the House of Malcuim."

He gave the Chalice into the Cyne's hands and watched expressionlessly as Colfre raised it to his lips and sipped from it a draught of water taken from the place were the Halig-tyne and the Sea comingled.

Lealbhallain's senses halted. His lungs recalled on their own how to breathe, but he could no longer feel them. The Universe lay between his eyes and the Chalice and the beatific expression on Cyne Colfre's face.

Colfre opened his mouth and cried, "Ecstasy, O Meri! Your Voice is ecstasy! How beautiful to the ears is Your Song. I am moved! I am moved to tell of troubled and uncertain times. There are changes upon us, people of Caraid-land. Great and puzzling changes. The order of things is challenged!"

In the swell of murmurs that surrounded this pronouncement, Lealbhallain shook his head. Of course there were changes. They were in a Cusp. There were always changes in a Cusp. Why was the Cyne putting on the pretence of prophesying?

Rise.

Leal heard the word as clearly as if it had been shouted in his ear. No, he more than heard it — he felt it vibrate his frame.

Rise.

He rose.

To the altar.

He left his seat and slid out into the central aisle. Answering a prompting only he could hear, he moved toward the Cyne, amazed at his own audacity. He felt men leap to approach him, but none touched him or impeded his progress in any way. In a heartbeat he was face to face with the Cyne.

As Colfre, his eyes rolled blissfully back into his head, opened his mouth to speak again, Lealbhallain took the Chalice from his hands and held it aloft. In some fiery confluence of sun and crystal, a shaft of light caught the stone set in the heart of the Meri's Star and leapt from there to the Chalice. The bowl filled with glory, exciting in the congregation cries of astonishment.

Over the flurry of reaction, Lealbhallain heard himself say, "The Meri speaks through the mouths of Her Chosen. The Meri is known through the Counsel of the Divine. No man among you knows the changes I have wrought. These are the words of the Meri."

He lowered the Chalice then, and, looking his Cyne squarely in the eye, took a sip of its contents. Salt and sweet. The warm wash of flavor embraced his tongue — the meeting place of the Halig-tyne and the Sea. He rolled the liquid in his mouth before swallowing it. Then, he handed the Chalice to the Cirkemaster.

"Return it to its place, Osraed," he said, then turned and left the Sanctuary.

Fhada met him at the doors. The older Osraed said nothing at first, preferring to watch him from the corner of one eye as they strode the Cirke's broad plaza toward the Cyne's Way. When his eyes touched the spires of Mertuile rising above the Way's nether end, Fhada's silence broke.

"What have you done, Osraed? And what, in the Meri's fair Name, prompted you to do it?"

"*She* prompted me." Leal's limbs shook with a sudden trembling realization of what he had just done. Adrenaline washed through his core, freezing him.

"She? The Meri, you mean?" Fhada's eyes seized his. "She spoke to you? You heard Her? There — in the Cirke?"

"She bid me rise, then She — She simply moved me."

"And the words?"

And the words. Leal grasped the links of his prayer chain, his eyes on Mertuile's massive landward flank. "Were not mine."

"Cyne Colfre won't know that. He will lay blame on you. Dear God, how will he interpret this?"

"To his advantage."

Fhada stopped and stared at him. "Those were not your words, either, I think."

"No, I suppose not. These are. What difference does it make how the Cyne interprets my actions? If my words are from the Meri, She has already taken his interpretation into account. And his reaction." Leal took a deep breath. "Yes. The Meri's will cannot be thwarted. Regardless of what may happen to me, Her will is served."

Fhada shook his head. "You shame me, Leal."

Leal was aghast. "What? No, Osraed Fhada. Don't say that."

Fhada laid a hand on his shoulder. "Let me speak. You shame me by being what I should be — what I should have been. Perhaps, even *could* have been. Cirke-dag after Cirke-dag I have sat in that Sanctuary watching the Cyne mold the worship to his own will. First the aisle and the thrones — they were set below the altar at first, you know, creeping closer with time until finally they appeared upon the altar itself. And the standards preceded them, growing taller by degrees until, as you saw, they fall just short of the Meri's standard. And to watch him drink from the Chalice — !" He shook his head. "He was to drink from that cup *once* in his life.

Once, only, as he stood before the Stone to receive the Circlet of his office. And I, Fhada, sat and watched those things and did nothing."

"The Meri did not expect — "

"She *did* expect, Lealbhallain. Once, I could feel Her. Then. Now, there is only a guilty niggle. But even then — damn me! — even *then*, I resisted. And do you know why?"

"No, sir."

"Because men I respected told me to. Oh, I am not excusing myself, no. I merely want you to understand how I let myself be led astray — how I rationalized my inaction." He made a disgusted face. "The Osraed Ladhar said it. The Abbod, himself. 'Question these promptings, boy. They test you.' If you cannot trust the Abbod, I reasoned, who can you trust?"

Leal licked his lips, stunned to sweat by the implications of Fhada's words. "Osraed Ladhar is still Abbod."

"Indeed. He's aged now, certainly, but powerful."

Powerful. And Fhada did not mean that, Leal knew, as once he had naively defined power. "What did he tell you?"

Fhada began walking again, slowly now, into the shadow of Mertuile. "When I went to him with my first great tremulous dilemma, he told me I was being tested. He instructed me to question the Voice I heard, to resist it, to seek to understand its dark origins. He said there were portents of great calamity in the future of Caraid-land. He said my testing was surely a part of that."

"Did he know — ?"

Fhada shrugged. "How can I know what he knew?"

"What did *you* feel?"

"That he had the means to be certain of the Voice I heard and Its message, but did not use it. I told myself that was because he did not need to use it. He had seen portents; that was enough. I wanted to believe he was certain of what he told me. I couldn't contemplate anything else then."

"And now?"

"Now, I accept that we were both wrong — Osraed Ladhar for dissuading me and I for letting him."

Leal's body wanted to fold in on itself. A vacuum existed where his heart had been. "Perhaps . . . perhaps you were not wrong. Perhaps I am being tested too."

"Perhaps you are, but you are passing your test, where I failed mine."

Leal laid a desperate hand on the other man's arm. "No! You're too young a man to give yourself up. The Meri still speaks to you, I know She does."

Fhada disengaged himself, gently. "Don't trust me, Leal. Don't see in me what is no longer there. What was, perhaps, *never* there to begin with."

"It's there, Fhada," Leal said, as they took the turn away from Mertuile toward the Care House. "And I'm not the only one who sees it."

CHAPTER 11

Do you imagine that the secrets of your souls are hidden? Know with certainty that what you have concealed in your hearts is as clear as day to the Spirit. That it remains hidden is pure mercy.

— Utterances of Osraed Wyth, Verse 13

❖   ❖   ❖

The sky did not fall. Ealad-hach did not pursue her with chains and fetishes, though she knew from the talk passed by Brys to Scandy and Phelan and, thence, to all of Nairne, that he had constructed any number of Wardweaves. She knew from Bevol that Ealad-hach had also closeted himself immediately after the Cirke incident with some of his Tradist comrades.

"He will not," Bevol told her, "let it lie. He's just regrouping."

"But I held the stone," Taminy observed. "I stepped right over that horrid runebag."

"And you are not so naive as to believe that means aught to Ealad-hach. His judgement has been impugned, anwyl. He said a Wicke could not hold Lin's crystal or Weave through it or exit a Cirke when confronted by a moleskin-covered, marinated snake's head." His mouth twitched into a grin. "It appears he was wrong. Wicke *can* do those things."

"I'm not," said Taminy, "a Wicke."

"I think it would be harder for Ealad-hach to believe that — to believe himself wrong about that — than it would be for him to believe he merely underestimated a Wicke's powers." He paused and cocked an eye at her.

"You put on, to all descriptions, an amazing display. He can't doubt that he underestimated *you*."

Taminy tilted back her head and peered up into the high-beamed ceiling of their parlor. *Ah, yes, as even I did*! A smile intruded when her lips would be serious. "I meant for nothing to happen, really. A simple schoolroom Weaving, I said to myself. A spark of light in a bit of stone. Gwynet might have done as much. But instead, a shower, a fountain — nay, a — a downpour!" She was laughing now, remembering their faces — startled, perplexed, awful, astonished — gleaming in the Eibhilin light of Taminy-a-Cuinn.

"They say you were a rare wonder with crystals, when you used them."

A rare wonder. Had she been? The laughter stilled and she lowered her eyes. "I couldn't control it, Bevol. I took that stone in my hands and completely lost control. It was like a — an Eibhilin *sneeze*. Forgive me," she added when Bevol began to chuckle. "I don't mean to make light of it."

He laughed outright at that, and she heard, somewhere out of sight, Skeet's boyish bray. Raw emotion flared in her heart — anger, self-pity, hilarity, sorrow, all rode the crest of an ill-defined wave that swelled, tumbled and broke in tearful laughter. And when it broke, every lightglobe in the house flared full on, dazzling the occupants. She heard Skeet yawp squeakishly and Gwynet's footsteps, rabbit-rapid on the stairs, her high voice piping, "What is it? What is it?"

She wanted to laugh, but it wasn't funny; she wanted to weep, but the situation provoked her to laughter. In the end, she let Bevol take her in his arms while she laughed and wept in turns.

"Let me see," said Osraed Faer-wald, "if I understand you." He was seated in a low sack chair in Ealad-hach's chambers in the company of the Osraed Parthelan, Eadmund, Ladman and Ealad-hach himself. Just now he gazed at the ceiling of the room as if collecting his thoughts from it, his fingers steepled on the grand curve of his stomach like a little pink Cirke on a massive hill. "You tested the girl — "

"As I said," interjected Ealad-hach irritably. He did not like Faer-wald when he was in a mood to be interrogatory — setting himself up as grand inquisitor. It fairly curled Ealad-hach's eyelashes to be so carefully grilled.

"As you said last Cirke-dag. You gave her the Gwyr crystal, supposing her to be a Wicke and expecting that it would go dull or burn her or some such, I assume."

Ealad-hach felt angry heat blaze up his neck to scorch his ears. "You know very well what I expected. We've been through this. I *told* you what I expected."

"So you did, but the plan failed, correct?"

"My original plan failed — to catch her teaching dark runes at that glen. If it hadn't been for that idiot Lorimer girl, I might have done that. I had a mirror. I could have caught her in it without her knowledge."

"Pardon," said Ladman, "but according to your young spies, catching her unawares at that pool has yet to be done."

"Not so!" Ealad-hach raised his hand, a dull fire lighting behind his eyes. "Aelder Prentice Brys and his cronies caught her unawares the Cirke-dag previous and brought my attention to her doings."

"They beheld her Weaving dark runes?"

"They beheld her doing things they did not understand."

"Well," said Ladman, in that word summing up what he thought of Ealad-hach's Aelder Prentices.

Parthelan raised white brows. "She can't sense men, is that your thought?"

"Or can sense only those who carry darkness in their souls."

"Irrelevant," said Faer-wald, "since the plan never came to fruition. You did not catch her Weaving dark runes. You improvised a test and she . . . well, failed to meet your expectations." He tilted his head and gave Ealad-hach a long look. "When you reported this, I took it to mean that she failed to prove to be Wicke."

Ealad-hach shook his head emphatically. "No! No! You miss the point!" He sat forward in his chair. "She did not prove pure. She proved *powerful*. My misjudgement was in applying so simple a test to her."

"Simple?" asked Osraed Eadmund. "What more telling a test could you have given? Outside of the Osmaer, the Gwyr crystal has no equal in purity."

"Gartain's Giddian," murmured Parthelan.

"Well, yes. With the exception of Gartain's crystal, Giddian. Are you suggesting we've encountered a Wicke whose power approaches the Meri's?"

"Nonsense!" exclaimed Parthelan, and Ladman clutched his prayer chain.

Ealad-hach was shaking his head. "No. I'd never suggest that. What I . . . What I see happening is what Eadmund suggested to us some time ago. A test. A test of such importance that the Meri has allowed — *allowed*, mind you — Her laws to be bent and Her truths to be circumvented."

"By this cailin, Taminy-a-Gled," said Faer-wald.

"By this Wicke — " Ealad-hach hesitated. He could not say what his dreams had led him to suspect, perhaps because he could not bring himself to believe what those dreams implied. As he turned the name in his mind — Taminy-a-Cuinn — he rejected the absurdity of it. Wicke she must be — hundred year old Wicke, she could not be. Bevol simply wanted him to believe that to heighten his fear. He pursed his lips. "She is simply more powerful than I expected."

"But the crystal," objected Eadmund. "The runebag . . . "

Ealad-hach dismissed that with a wave of his hand. "Ah, that runebag was Wickery in and of itself. I used it merely because I thought *she* might believe in its power. She didn't. She's no fool."

There was a moment of thoughtful silence. Faer-wald broke it. "And no Wicke, either, it would seem."

"I told you — " Ealad-hach began, cold fury raising his voice.

"She *failed* your test."

"Damn you, Faer-wald! Why will you not see? We are in a Cusp. A dangerous Cusp. We've all sensed that much. New Osraed bring us insupportable doctrinal changes and impossible accounts of that girl Meredydd's so-called transformation, the Cyne tugs at the reins of our governing power, and this *girl* appears to — to juggle the Art before our faces as if it was a carnival toy."

"So she has a Gift. Enroll her in Halig-liath and discipline it."

"She has no intention of attending Halig-liath. Her education, according to Bevol, is complete."

"We oughtn't sanction that," interjected Parthelan. "No one should make careless with the Art outside Halig-liath."

"Only within, eh?" asked Faer-wald, winking.

"You joke," accused Ealad-hach, "about what is not a joking matter. She does her little miracles every day now. People afflicted with odd ailments go to Taminy for a confection and when next Osraed Torridon sees them, they are cured. Have you seen Marnie-o-Loom's hands? She was severely arthritic. Torridon could do nothing for her but ease the pain. I say *was* arthritic, Osraed, because Taminy gave her a salve and a bit of wood. Do you care to guess at the results?"

Faer-wald sat forward, sending the pink Cirke crashing to his lap. "Look," he said, "what do you want from us? Why are you bringing this up again? What is your intention?"

"I want you to join me in recommending that Taminy be called before the Osraed Body. I will devise a more thorough test and publicly try her. I want to trap her, Osraed. And destroy her."

Four pairs of eyes met in the center of the chamber, leaving Ealad-hach entirely out of their deliberations.

Eadmund cleared his throat. "We *are* in a Cusp."

Parthelan shook his head. Faer-wald and Ladman echoed the movement.

"We cannot recommend that, Osraed," Faer-wald told Ealad-hach. "There is too little evidence to support you."

"*Too little evidence?* What of my dreams? My aislinn?"

Again, glances were traded at the center of the room. "You said you couldn't see the face of the woman who came out of the Sea."

"I have seen it. Late the night before last. It was *her* face. The face of Taminy-a-Gled." He glared at the silent ring of faces. "Do you doubt my vision?"

"Perhaps 'doubt' is too strong a word." Faer-wald now attempted to soothe him. "If you would take us to your aislinn chamber, show us this woman — "

"I cannot." Ealad-hach curled back into his seat, wrapping his arms about himself. "My ability to draw on aislinn vision has been severely impaired by my health. I haven't slept well since I made the discovery — the stress . . . I have been unable to bring the aislinn back."

"Well, what can we do, then?" Faer-wald glanced about at his cronies and shrugged his bovine shoulders. "If you could show us, perhaps we would be convinced to back your recommendation, but without that evidence . . . " He shrugged again. "You have tested her and failed to prove her to be anything but a young woman with a strong Gift, which Bevol has no doubt nurtured. I agree with Parthelan about the questionable wisdom of allowing the Art to be taught outside the Academy. But even at that, she is under the tutelage of one of the greatest masters Halig-liath has produced — come, Ealad, you must agree with that, regardless of what you think of his theology."

Ealad-hach was silent.

Osraed Parthelan rose and shook out his long tunic. "I agree. Understand, Ealad, I am with you in your desire to keep cailin out of Halig-liath. I cannot believe this change will be beneficial to the Brotherhood. But calling this child a Wicke, blaming her for our troubles — "

Ealad-hach pounced on the admission implicit in that. "Then you don't believe Wyth Arundel's Tell?"

Parthelan's eyes widened. "Not believe? Have I a choice? He wears the Kiss — gaudily. I suppose I must believe. He is the Meri's Chosen, Her emissary. That doesn't mean I *agree* with what he says or must like it."

"But if you will go that far — "

"I will go no further." Parthelan excused himself and left, taking Ladman with him.

Faer-wald took that opportunity to make his own excuses. "As I said, Ealad, if you could show us this aislinn, if we could see this woman's face and be convinced . . . Perhaps when your health improves, your concentration will improve with it."

"I *will* show you," murmured Ealad-hach. "By the Kiss, I will show you." If Faer-wald heard him, he did not show it, and Ealad-hach found himself alone with Eadmund and a black mood. He vented the darkness at the younger Osraed. "Well, what about you? Are you going to mock an old man?"

Brow furrowed, Eadmund shook his head. "No, Osraed. I would never mock you. I . . . I understand your respect of this Cusp, of the unique danger it poses, the unique challenges it brings."

"Then you do believe me — about the girl?"

Eadmund's eyes traced the pattern in the thick carpet. "It's hard to . . . to accept that such a young, seemingly innocent cailin should be the repository of such wickedness, such power."

Ealad-hach allowed himself a grim smile. "And that, Eadmund, is her advantage. Her youth, her sweet appearance. But she Weaves. She Weaves darkness, constantly. She Weaves disagreement and dissension and if we are not astute, if we are not prepared, she will Weave our destruction. . . . Yes, yes, I know," he added, seeing the expression on the younger man's face. "Hard to accept. But we have seen much lately that is hard to accept, have we not?"

"You mean Osraed Wyth's Tell?"

"Aye. That's hard to accept, yet it seems we are bound to its acceptance."

"You strive to connect the two — the girl's Gift and Wyth's Tell. That, I think, is what I cannot accept."

"She sought him out at Tell Fest. They conversed privately for some time. They, who supposedly didn't know each other."

Eadmund ghosted a smile. "Well, he is a young man and she is a lovely cailin."

"Loveliness," said Ealad-hach, "is like the crust on a snow. It glitters brilliantly and seems temptingly solid, but a man would be a fool to set foot upon it and trust it with his weight."

Eadmund nodded. "But the snow isn't evil, Osraed. It is cold by nature — a nature decreed by the First Being."

"Your point?"

Eadmund gazed at him a moment, then shrugged. "None that is worth elucidating. Pardon, Osraed, but I must go over the Academy accounts with Aelder Marschal."

He was gone, then, and Ealad-hach had only his black mood for company.

The sky did not fall. The Cyne did not send soldiers after him, did not censure him, did not stop the newly established flow of goods to the Care House in the shadow of Mertuile. Leal had feared that, in the dark hours, staring at the ceiling of his new room at Care House. Had been terrified that, for his brash acts, Fhada would suffer — worse yet, that those who depended on the Care House for subsistence and healing would suffer.

But that didn't happen. The goods — fresh goods, now — arrived from the Cyne's Market by the cartful and Leal relaxed a little, thinking perhaps the Cyne had taken the Meri's words to heart and would cease to imagine himself Her spokesman.

By the second day after the incident, he was convinced nothing would come of it and allowed himself to be pleased with the results of his brief tenure in Creiddylad. That was the day the Abbod of Ochanshrine visited Care House and called Leal aside in the presence of Osraed Fhada.

The Osraed Ladhar was an imposing man despite his advanced age. He was not as tall as the conifer-like Fhada, but what he lacked in height, he made up in girth and presence. Balding at the crown, he had a froth of silver hair that lay densely upon his collar and framed heavy jaws. In his broad, ruddy face, his eyes stood out like diamonds pressed into red clay. They were that colorless, that chill, that piercing. *Indestructible*, Leal thought. Cynes had come and gone but Osraed Ladhar was still here and the Kiss on his forehead was still here, though Leal had to face him head on to see it — a stellate mark the color of peridot.

"Well, young Lealbhallain!" The Abbod's smile was a

fatherly embrace and his voice exuded joviality. "You've made yourself a bit of a celebrity in Creiddylad."

The eyes didn't change and Lealbhallain knew that either they lied or the voice did. "I'm sorry, Abbod. I didn't mean to do that."

The old man chuckled, warm tones rolling deep in his barrel chest. "No? What did you mean to do?"

Splinters of glass could not have cut more sharply than those eyes. Leal struggled to believe he had done nothing wrong and groped for an answer. "I wasn't trying to do anything, Abbod. Except, of course, the Meri's will."

"The Meri's will? Why, I believe we all strive to do that. It's not always easy to divine." Ladhar flicked a glance at Fhada, who stood in his office's one window embrasure, watchful. "How did you become convinced it was the Meri's will that moved you?"

"I heard Her Voice."

"Ah! That sweet Voice. How did She sound?"

"Determined," said Leal, without thinking.

"Determined? How so?"

Leal shook his head. "She simply did. And it wasn't *sound*, exactly. She bid me rise and go forward and was determined that I do so."

The Abbod nodded, leaning back in his chair till Leal feared he would become wedged there. He chastized himself for the impious thought.

"Did it occur to you, for even a moment, to question this determined instruction?"

"No, Abbod, it did not."

"Really, Osraed? Not for one moment?" He smiled as an old man might smile at the antics of his grandchild.

"No, sir."

"Ah, but what if it had not been the Meri's voice?"

"It was. I've never heard another like it."

"Never?"

Leal shook his head.

"Nothing else has ever whispered in your heart? Not fear or zeal or anger, perhaps?"

"Yes. Of course they have. But not like this."

Osraed Ladhar considered that for a moment, his eyes

taking slices out of the stone floor instead of Leal's face. "Some time ago," he said at length, "this young man here" — he gestured at Fhada — "came to me with some concerns raised by an experience similar to yours. He heard a voice — a beautiful, determined voice — that prodded him to act rashly. He, too, was certain the voice was that of his Beloved. But we advised him to be cautious, to question the voice, to hold out against it until he was certain of it. This, he did, and finally the voice subsided, ceased to plague him with its . . . determined demands. As we advised him, we advise you."

Leal glanced at Fhada. The man's face had no more color than the dust-caked, light-washed glass behind him and his eyes were as bleak. *Ladhar is wringing out his soul.* Anger whispered to Leal, then; he had no trouble recognizing the voice. He silenced it and returned his attention to the Abbod. "I don't want the Voice to subside. I have no doubt that it's the Meri's. No one has ever spoken to me as She does. I did what She desired."

"She expressed no such desire to me, or to Fhada, who was with you."

Osraed Fhada turned to gaze out the window. Ladhar's eyes followed him, falcon quick, then returned to Leal.

"Abbod," Leal said, "when you came here after your Pilgrimage, did you have a mission — a calling?"

"Of course. I was called to Ochanshrine. To take part in its administration and to serve the Abbod."

"Then, you made no changes in its running?"

The Abbod's brows crested. "Of course, I made changes. I oversaw the addition of the High Reliquary and re-instituted the Registry of Stones. I brought fine artists and craftsmen to Ochanshrine to be trained up as cleirachs. A regular program, mind you, not haphazard like before, when most of our cleirachs were failed Prentices who didn't want to return to the family stead."

"Those are fine accomplishments," Leal complimented him. "Wonderful ideas. Were they yours or, perhaps, Cyne Ciarda's?"

A red flush crept over the Abbod's face. "They were given me by the Meri."

"And not to your Abbod? Not to one of the more experienced Osraed?"

"No." Ladhar fingered the links of his prayer chain. "I was fresh from Pilgrimage. It was part of my mission — to improve the Abbis as a repository of spiritual artifacts and a retreat for the Osraed, to increase its ability to produce well-taught cleirachs for the schools."

Lealbhallain nodded. "As my mission is to see to the welfare of the citizens of Creiddylad — most especially, its children."

"A broad purpose, but one which has nothing to do with what the Cyne does in his Cirke."

"Osraed Ladhar, it's not his Cirke. It's God's Cirke, the Meri's Cirke. And what the Cyne does before the citizens of Creiddylad, what he says to them about his relationship with their God affects their welfare at its most elemental level — the spiritual."

Ladhar's eyes moved to Fhada's back. The younger man stiffened, as if sensing that touch. "Still, none of the changes *I* made at the Meri's behest publicly embarrassed my Cyne."

"Might they not have embarrassed your Abbod, who would have expected such insights to come to him?"

The fatty wattles beneath the Abbod's ample jowels shivered. "Do you deliberately misunderstand me, young man? You have embarrassed the Cyne of Caraid-land."

"Is that what he thinks?"

"He's not sure what to think."

He had spoken to the Cyne, then. Leal inclined his head, trying not to shake. "If I have embarrassed the Cyne, I will apologize to him. I didn't mean to embarrass him. Not at all. But he was implying a relationship with the Meri — "

"That you couldn't abide?" suggested Ladhar.

"That *She* couldn't abide."

Abbod Ladhar studied Lealbhallain through diamond-bright eyes. Studied him until he felt all the flesh had been flayed from his face. Then the old man gathered himself and rose, slipping easily out of the chair and back into his fatherly smile. "Well, I must go, young firebrand.

Come, both of you, and walk me to my coach."

They did as bidden, passing through the corridors of the
Care House in relative silence. They passed by newly
repaired fireplaces with freshly cleaned chimneys; Ladhar
remarked on them and on the well-lit halls and clean
floors. When they reached the outer courtyard, the Abbod
paused to regard a dray that had pulled up before the
kitchen entrance to offload goods from the Cyne's Market.

"Well, Osraed Lealbhallain," he said. "You have made a
good beginning to the fulfillment of your mission here. It
seems you have reminded Cyne Colfre of his duty to the
poor and cautioned him to kindness. What a rain of bounty
you've precipitated! What a pity if it should cease and all
this be lost."

Fhada spoke for the first time. "You caution him to fear
the Cyne? To bend to the Cyne's whims?"

Ladhar shot him a slivered glance. "I would not so caution him. It is the Meri's wrath we must fear — God's
approval we must obtain. I am concerned only that all the
good you have wrought here in the Meri's name might be
lost. If the Cyne's whims, as you call them, are foiled,
they may suffer most who have the least." His gaze
strayed back to the dray, dragging Fhada's and Lealbhallain's with it. There, several older orphans and a man with
one arm helped the jaeger unload goods. All were smiling
over the Cyne's largesse, dreaming, no doubt, of the
meals to come.

The Abbod turned then, clambered aboard his coach
and was borne away. Fhada and Leal watched him through
the gates.

"Damn him," said Fhada. "Damn him."

Shivering, Leal returned to the Care House. He spent
the rest of the day thinking about Ladhar's visit without
thinking about it. It sat in his conscience where his soul
could see it. Sat there without moving, captured in that last
tableau: the three of them there in the court, watching the
delivery of the Cyne's bounty.

Wrong, though, Leal thought. Wrong. The food and
goods arriving by royal dray were not gifts, they were duty.
It was the joint occupation of Cyne and Osraed to care for

the Caraidin, and in the long history of Caraid-land, it had been the Cyne who supplied the means while the Osraed provided the way. Leal knew, as Abbod Ladhar implicitly suggested he forget, that Cyne Colfre of the House Malcuim would not be on his throne today were it not for the Meri and Her chosen representatives. It was the first Osraed, Ochan, who gave Malcuim the wisdom necessary to establish his House as the House from which Caraidin Cynes arose. Another history there might have been if Ochan-a-Coille had not staggered to the Cyne's threshhold six centuries ago and warned him that the Houses Claeg and Feich were engaged in covert rebellion.

Still, there was a point to what the Abbod said. Leal's mission here was to see to the welfare of the citizenry of Creiddylad — especially the poor. The Meri had impressed that upon him, that and the need for change. He had made a good start, coercing Colfre to be more open-handed. True, he hadn't convinced the Cyne to give control of the Osraed funds back into their own hands, but that could come if . . . *if* he didn't lose the ground he had won.

In the Meri's name, Ladhar had said. *The good you have wrought in the Meri's name. Lost. Because you could not abide . . .*

Had the voice in the Sanctuary been his own? Had he been motivated by simple jealousy, unable to tolerate the Cyne's communion with his Beloved?

Feeling wretched and confused, Leal secluded himself in his chambers. He meditated himself to calm, then took out his crystal and slipped into his aislinn chamber. The chamber, like all those at Care House, was make-shift, little more than a cylindrical closet built up with screens of wood. Leal sat cross-legged on the floor of his, while the crystal, Bliss, lay at center atop a carved wooden stand. Incense burned, home incense that carried scents of Nairne — the pines, the river, the wildflowers and spices. He breathed deeply and let his mind flow to the crystal.

He did not ask to see visions — he wanted only certitude — it was visions he got. The crystal lit and spoke. In the ancient aislinn tongue, it poured pictures into the darkened place, pictures that passed like storm-driven clouds. There was a huge room — the Assembly Hall at Mertuile — filled with people and anger and fear and tense silence. There were flashes of fire that became torches and light globes carried high in the hands of people who laughed and cried and reached out in joyous celebration to a figure standing high above them upon a gleaming dais. The people gazed up at the dais and its occupants. Leal tried to see them, to determine who they were, but the image eluded him, subtly altering itself. The people still chanted, but their laughter shattered into barks of rage, fingers curled into fists, faces twisted, hideous. The Hall trembled with their rage. They became a sea of faces, a teeming ocean of souls, their emotions like a myriad waves in a crossing sea. There was thunder.

No, Leal realized, there was someone pounding on his door.

"Coming!" he managed to croak, and withdrew himself from the aislinn realm. The crystal sucked in its light and its darkness and his visions, folding them up again into silent facets.

The young girl at the door bobbed an awful curtsey her eyes on Leal's face. "All pardon, Osraed Leal," she said in a loud whisper, "but you bid me tell you when Aelder Buach returned from the docks. He's in Refectory, Osraed."

"Of course, Fris. Thank you." He smiled at her and she returned the smile before dropping another curtsey and scurrying away.

Buach was indeed in the Refectory, tucking away an impressive amount of vegetable stew. He nodded at Leal as the younger boy slid onto the stool opposite him, a bowl of stew and a spoon in hand.

"How are things along the riverfront?" asked Leal after downing several bites of stew.

Buach gave him a watery smile. "Is there mail, do you mean? As it happens, Osraed, there is." He reached inside his tunic and pulled out a small folio of hide and cloth packets. "Here." He held one out to Leal, who took it eagerly.

The packet was from his family and contained letters from

each of them, the longest appearing to be from his sister, Orna. Grateful, Leal thanked Buach and laid the letters on the table. "You did some care calls today, did you?"

"Aye. A few. It was a clothing run, mostly. To the families down under Farbridge. Autumn comes early down there."

"And did you visit your family while you were there?"

Buach's father owned a shop just above Farbridge and his entire family had been in the Cyne's Cirke last Cirke-dag. He often paid them a visit when out on care calls in the area, but his wary expression said he wasn't sure why the Osraed had brought it up. "Only after I'd done my dues," he said.

"Did you talk to them at all about the happenings Cirke-dag?"

Buach tried to hide his grin behind a chunk of bread. "You mean when you came head on into Cyne Colfre's ceremony?"

Leal swallowed. "Yes. I couldn't help but wonder what people are saying about it. I knew your family was there. . . ."

Buach studied his stew-sodden bread. "Tongues are flapping, Osraed. I can tell you that. No one I've spoken to can agree altogether on what it meant, though. Now my Gran'da says you busted the Cyne pure and simple — showed him who's charged by the Spirit in Caraid-land. My elder brother, on the other hand, says you were doing no such thing; that you were confirming the Cyne's right to speak for the Meri."

"How does he figure that?"

Buach shrugged. "You said only the Meri's Chosen spoke for Her. Since the Cyne claimed to speak for Her, he must be Chosen."

Had he said that? The words came back to him. *The Meri speaks through Her Chosen. The Meri is known through the counsel of the divine. No man among you knows the changes I have wrought.* "I believe I said no man could know what the Cyne claimed to know."

"Oh, aye. Which, in my brother's frail brain means that since the Cyne claimed to know it, he's no mere man."

"You don't agree."

Buach made a rude noise. "If the Cyne's divine, I'm the

Gwenwyvar. I say with my Gran'da. You busted him."

While Buach's new admiration was preferable to
his sullen disinterest, his words did little to reassure
Leal. He didn't know which extreme was worse — to
have it thought he'd humiliated the Cyne, or to have it
thought he'd accorded him divinity. He prayed those
were just extremes and turned to the reading of his
letters.

The letters were full of the chatter of Nairne, telling him
what his family thought he'd want to know about the furor
Osraed Wyth's announcement had caused, about the
Cirkemaster's daughter having the Gift and being a candidate
for Prenticeship, about how the Hillwild Ren, Catahn, had
come up with an entire classroom full of candidates, which
included his own daughter, the Renic Desary. It was the longest
letter, the one from Orna, that brought him the most disturbing
tale. Osraed Bevol's choice of wards had once again plunged
Halig-liath into controversy. Orna described in detail the gossip
resulting from Ealad-hach's attempted test of Taminy-a-Gled,
adding her own opinion that the old man must be daft to
suspect such a brave and obviously gifted cailin of being Wicke.
He was not to tell Ma or Da, she confided, but she had sought
Taminy's company herself and heard and seen some truly
wonderful things. She enumerated.

Leal must have groaned or gasped for he felt Buach's
eyes suddenly on him.

"Trouble at home, Osraed?"

"Oh . . . you could say. One of the Osraed has accused a
local girl of being Wicke."

"Oh, aye!" The Aelder's sallow face lit with enthusiasm.
"That's the news come in on the galleys, too. All over the
    waterfront, that. It's true then, it's in one of your
letters?"

Leal nodded and Buach grinned. "There was an official
packet for the Abbod, too, and one for the Cyne. The
boatman thought they must be about the acceptance of
girls at Halig-liath. Did your letters mention that, too?"

"The Ren Catahn's daughter is a candidate, according to
my father."

"God-the-Spirit, a Hillwild Renic at the Academy!

These are interesting times. . . . " He glanced coyly into Leal's face. "So what do you think, Osraed . . . of girls at the Holy Fortress?"

"I think it's a great thing." He thought of Meredydd, then. Meredydd, who had wanted, above all else, to be Osraed; who had wanted, failing that, to come heal the wounds of Creiddylad's poor. He supposed, in some way, he was here in her stead. "A great thing," he repeated and cleared his plate from the table.

Cyne Colfre sat in his favorite place, breeze rippling his dark hair and teasing the corners of the paper spread before him on the stone table. His eyes caressed the inked lines of the sketches lovingly; they were his, he had put them there himself with an architect's delicate skill. The design was his own and he fancied it carried such distinction that, generations hence, architects and students of art would look at it and say, "Ah, now *that* was Colfrian. Classic Golden Cusp. A fine work." They would see the power and grace in those lines and marvel that such a thing, such an aerie, could stand. . . . *When it ought to soar*. He smiled, not looking up even when he heard the footfall on the pavilion's stone walkway. He knew the stride. "So," he said, without glancing up, "how is our Abbod today?"

"Our Abbod is in quite a state." Daimhin Feich gave a cursory bow and seated himself on one of the stone benches.

"Our Abbod is always in a state, what with one thing and another. What's the excuse of the day?"

"You won't like it."

The Cyne glanced up from his drawings. "The boy again?"

" 'The boy' has sent a letter to the Apex at Halig-liath. An *urgent* letter."

Colfre's expression was wary. "Not a progress report, I gather."

"The Abbod thinks not. It was sent out with a special seal rune — something even the Abbod was loathe to tinker with. The letter was directed to the eyes of the Apex Osraed only."

"I thought the Abbod spoke to the boy."

"He did, but I gathered from his report that the conversation was far from satisfactory."

"He said he rattled him."

"He said what he thought you wanted to hear. He also said the boy seemed ambivalent. On further prodding, I got him to admit that our littlest Osraed has gotten Fhada inflamed again. According to Ladhar, he was openly hostile during that last visit."

"Damned Osraed pups! Every time we're sent a new one we must go through the same nonsense. Every one of them comes to Creiddylad full of ideas and voices and impertinences. Every one of them wants to dabble in government."

"Well, the Cyne has traditionally had an Osraed as close advisor. Malcuim well-established it, and every Cyne since has upheld the practice . . . because the Meri desires Her emissaries and institutions to have a voice in governing Caraid-land. You've been somewhat remiss in that area . . . at least, where Halig-liath is concerned."

"Damn Halig-liath. I need no advisor. And I will not beg permission for every move from some . . . bedazzled schoolboy."

Feich seemed amused. "May I remind you that this bedazzled schoolboy has the Meri's Kiss planted indelibly on his brow?"

Colfre shook a finger at him. "Not indelibly, Daimhin. Not at all indelibly. When I was a boy, Osraed Ladhar's Kiss was as bright as the moon. The years have dimmed it. They will dim this Osraed Lealbhallain's as well."

"May be, but he could raise a lot of dust in those years, my lord."

"Ungrateful wretch. I'm feeding his orphans — can he begrudge me the right to determine what ceremonies are played out in my own Cirke?"

"Ah, now that seems to be the point of contention, sire. The orphans are more particularly *yours*, while the Cirke, for all it was built by your ancestor, is still God's. Osraed Lealbhallain thinks you've got it backwards."

"And what would he do if I cut Care House off again? I'm sure I could find some excuse to leave them to their own devices."

Feich shook his head. "A bad idea, sire. Passion is not something we want to arouse in our Osraed."

Colfre stood abruptly. "I'm sick of dealing with them, Daimhin. Sick of cat-footing around them, avoiding them, placating them, trying to ease them out of government . . ."

"Well, that's the problem, isn't it? You're trying to ease them out of their covenanted and traditional role in the Court of the Caraidin Cynes. I don't doubt they drag their feet. The Chiefs, Eiric and Ministers of your General Assembly haven't been terribly pleased with the scarcity of meetings, either."

"They're represented on the Privy Council — they can be mollified."

Feich brushed some lint from his leggins. "Some of them can. I'm not too certain about the Claeg."

"Hang the Claeg. Heh! That would've been done centuries ago, but for the Osraed's merciful intervention. The Claeg are passive now, at any rate. Surely you can't expect any trouble from them? They've got a man on the Privy, anyway."

"Who only attends to nag about how often the Assembly is *not* meeting. Besides, the Osraed have men on the Privy, as you so colorfully put it. Osraed Ladhar, for one."

"You think they'll be satisfied with that? No. But they will have to be. This Cusp is a sign, Daimhin. A sign that their power is waning and the power of the Cyne is waxing. I will be rid of them. Those damn burn-brows will not tell me what my Privy Council may or may not adjudicate on, or dare to assign top cleirachs to some verminous tribe of Hillwild. Let them sit in their fortress and mutter inyx and gaze at the stars. Let *me* rule Caraid-land as I was destined to."

"What will you do? You will no doubt be embroiled with the Osraed Body shortly."

"The Cusp, Daimhin, will do it for me. I know what this Cusp means — better than they do, I sometimes think. They'll be at their weakest now, chasing Wicke, seeing signs and portents in everything. An opportunity will present itself, Daimhin. *My* opportunity. And when it comes, I shall take it."

CHAPTER 12

Men shall be hindered from loving Me and spirits shall be shaken when they utter My Name, for minds cannot comprehend Me, nor hearts hold Me.

— *The Corah, Book I, Verse 50*

✧ ✧ ✧

The gossip had not stopped, though now it took on a different tone — a variety of tones, in fact, as the citizens of Nairne struggled to make sense of the reported results of Ealad-hach's test of Taminy-a-Gled. There was not a soul who didn't know about it, who hadn't compared their version of the tell with their neighbor's, swapping details until no one could recall what they had from whom.

Several embellished versions were carried quayside and given into the keeping of the galley crews. They could take their pick of the litter and did, carrying, each his favorite version — or a combination of versions — down river to Tuine and Creiddylad.

Taminy heard the various embellishments with chagrin and wry bemusement; the unadorned truth seemed startling enough without bringing in Eibhilin voices and lightnings and thunders. Most bemusing of all was the windfall effect of Ealad-hach's attentions. Taminy was suddenly the cynosure of Nairne's youth, especially her young females, while mothers who had previously suspected her now seemed to think her a fine and fit tutor for their girls.

She mused on that now, feeling the slant rays of late summer's afternoon sun on her skin, hearing the chatter of her companions and the passage of their bodies through the wild wheat that grew between Nairne and the Bebhinn

Wood. In the eyes of that village, Ealad-hach's attempt to condemn her had, instead, removed the shadow of suspicion. Whatever the differences in the accounts of the Cirke-dag incident, there was one overwhelming agreement: Taminy had woven with Lin-a-Ruminea's crystal, seated on the Cirke altar stone. And she had done it before credible witnesses. If that did not prove her to be other than a Wicke, nothing could.

Acceptance was not universal. Iseabal's mother still was cool toward her and Terris wouldn't look her in the eye. But today, incredibly, her entourage included Doireann Spenser and Phelan Backstere. There were other new faces, as well; Wyvis and Rennie had brought friends and Orna-mac-Mercer now found the woodland more interesting than the business that would someday be hers.

As to the parents, if they knew where their young spent some long afternoons, they expressed no great distress. All knew that if Taminy's methods were unorthodox, her teaching must be straight from the Books — Osraed Bevol said so, and that was nowadays acceptable.

"My little brother is Osraed," Orna had said. "My da said he'd not be surprised if we shared a talent. And, well, if I've got a midge of the Gift, I'd like to know."

She had a midge of the Gift, as it happened. It hadn't the the refinement of her brother's, nor native strength of Iseabal's, but then she'd never been encouraged to develop it. She would be good at the Heal Tell, Taminy thought, and might show a talent for natural divination. The farmers hereabouts wouldn't fault that.

Phelan, now . . . well, what he had was an eyeful of curiosity. If Taminy-a-Gled was not Wicke, then what was she? He devoured everything she did and said, partly, she realized, because he was spying for Ealad-hach. Doireann, too, was a kettle bubbling with anticipation — and something else. Something quick and nervous Taminy could not quite put a name to.

She could see the Cirke spire now, just peeking above the top of the next grassy hill. The mellow sun washed the high cupola with rose-gold, staining the blue slate roof purple. In a matter of minutes, the Divine Artist would dip

His brush again and mute the vivid hues even further.

"I think the light of your Weave must have shot right up through the tower."

Taminy glanced away from the Cirke to meet Doireann's shy smile. "Oh, I doubt that."

The other girl fell into step with her as they drew toward the crest of the long, low rise, her hands clasped behind her back, her eyes bright and cheeks rosy from the uphill walk. "Whatever was Osraed Ealad-hach thinking to confront you in the Cirke? Could he really have thought you a Wicke?"

"Quite a few people thought me a Wicke, Doiry."

"Aye. Like Aine." Doireann swished her skirts back and forth. "I still can't believe she brought that *horrible* runebag in to the Sanctuary . . . Did you know she had it?"

Taminy laughed. "I knew *somebody* had *something*! That smell was enough to curl up my hair."

"Or straighten mine," Doireann agreed, grimacing. "But did you know Ealad-hach meant to test you?"

Taminy recalled a dream — the fiery collision of wills, heart-stopping and unavoidable. "I knew something was coming. Some confrontation. I thought it would be Ealad-hach simply because he seems to hate me so."

"Oh, you *terrify* him! I mean, *I* think you do. And that snouty Brys-a-Lach and" — she smiled — "that silly Terris. But *I'm* not afraid."

Taminy studied the shining face. *Not quite true*, she thought but said, "I'm glad of that."

"Tell me, Taminy . . . " Doireann hovered closer to her side. " . . . can you read a body's mind?"

The thought pulled a shroud over Taminy's head. *Fog. Or woolen wadding. That's what I live in, here*. Once all minds, all hearts, all souls had been open to her gaze and she would read them and rejoice or lament — mostly lament. Hearts held lamentable things in these days when Her Kiss faded from a man's brow like a bad dye, or tarnished like silver in sea air. Days when men turned their minds to how the Divine might profit them and the Cyne stretched his standard out over the Cirke. It should be a relief not to know the thoughts behind the words and the smiles and the psalms of praise — not to fully sense the machinations behind the manner. But it was not a relief.

Can I read minds? About as well as I can read a book through a wad of fleece. She opened her mouth to say it when there was a shout up ahead at the top of the hill. Iseabal stood there, and Rennie and Wyvis, pointing down the opposite slope. She could hear the dull thunder of a horse at full gallop before she crested the hill. She waited there, at the top, till the flame-haired rider met them, pulling her mount to a hurried stop.

"Hello, Aine," Taminy said and offered a smile.

Aine glanced about at the group of curious faces and reddened. Her eyes fastened on Taminy. "I'd speak with you," she said. "Alone."

Taminy looked up at her, reading, sensing . . . or trying to. Confusion, she got. Anger. Fear, yes, that too. "Of course, Aine," she answered, and looked to the others. "Why don't you all go ahead home? We'll come along after."

There was hesitation. "Are you sure, Taminy?" Phelan asked, while Doireann fixed Aine with a dour stare and the others scuffled in the wheat.

"Aine hasn't been your friend," observed Iseabal. "Shall I stay?"

"No, it's all right. It is."

"Aye, well," muttered Phelan, "she might have another of those runebags about her."

Aine's face flamed, a near match for her hair and the sunset. She dismounted, turning her face away as the others drew off, sending back suspicious, darting looks. She was alone with Taminy then, eyes cast down, fingers toying with her reins, flapping them against the leg of her riding breeches. Taminy waited for the welter of hot emotions to settle; they teased through her woolly wadding veil like the scent of spices through the steam of cooking.

Aine raised her eyes. "I wanted you to know . . . " She struggled. "That runebag. It wasn't me. I didn't bring it into the Cirke. I didn't put it in my pocket. I'd never touch such a hideous thing, let alone *make* it." The reins slapped her boot-top. "Besides, if *I'd* cured it, it would've been done right. . . . *I'm telling the truth.*"

Was she? Taminy sifted again through the rush of emotion the other girl had released into the words — face-singeing indignity, gut-curling fear, humiliation and anger, anger, anger. Was it directed at her? If so, why this painful apology?

"If not you," she said, "then who? Who'd put such a horrid thing in your pocket? And why?"

Aine's face knotted in anguished frustration. "I don't know! It could've been any of them — Scandy or Phelan or Terris. They were all in arm's reach."

"Not Terris," Taminy said, half-smiling. "He'd die before he'd touch anything that smelled of Wickery. Although . . . I'd have thought, so would you."

"I *would.* I didn't make the runebag. I can't say I like the thought of my friends getting themselves sucked into these mystical doings of yours, but I'd never do something so foolish and — and *sneaky.* It's not my way. I *hate* sneaks."

"And what about Terris?" Taminy asked, recalling, vividly, Aine's over-hearing his protestations of nascent affection. "Would you do it for him?"

The other girl shook her head emphatically, sending fragments of sunset tumbling about her shoulders. "I'm not all that sweet on Terris and I'm not that daft *and* I don't know how to put together such a noxious mess."

But someone did. "Who threw the runebag at the pool that day?"

"Well, Doiry did, but — " Aine's face paled. "No, it couldn't be Doiry. I mean, she's such a mouse and all and . . . Oh, no, Taminy, she'd've had to kill the mole and the snake and" — she shuddered — "it's too grotesque. There's a big difference between that little flower sachet she took to the pool and that horrid . . . fetish."

"Who then?"

"Phelan?"

Phelan. That made sense, Taminy had to allow. She knew he was Ealad-hach's ally — or at least Brys-a-Lach's, which amounted to the same thing. He was an Aelder Prentice only by the skin of his teeth, and would most likely end up being Backstere after his father, but he had the training and access to the lore.

Aine was watching her, waiting for a pronouncement. She sighed. Dear God, how fine a thing was certitude. If only she had it. "Take my hand." She held one out to the other girl.

"W-why? Why must I take your hand?"

"I want to *know* you're telling the truth, Aine. I must at least try to know."

Face twisting, Aine stared at the proffered hand.

"I'm not evil, Aine-mac-Lorimer."

Aine gasped. "I'm sorry. I — " She snatched the hand and held it in a quaking grip.

For Taminy, it was as if shadows had suddenly become solid, real, colorful. The fear was for her, the anger was not. Humiliation burned and stung. *How dare they? How* dare *they?* Yes, the indignity, the sense of betrayal, was real. And so was the confusion. Aine-mac-Lorimer was not the maker of the runebag.

There was something else there, too, though. Something that tickled up Taminy's spine and tingled behind her eyes. She recognized it immediately and, in the moment of recognition, she reached up her free hand and pressed the palm against Aine's forehead.

What? Aine had been going to say, but the word came out in a stunned gasp.

"You've got a Gift in you, Aine. A Gift of Sight. Your thoughts trouble you and your dreams wander ahead of you. You hide them. Why do you hide them, Aine?"

Aine cried out, though weakly. The sound of her own voice was enough to break her free. Tearing from Taminy's gentle hold, she stumbled backward against her horse, arm flung across her face, brandishing fear like a weapon. She mounted, scrabbling into the saddle without once taking her eyes from Taminy's unmoving form, then pivoted her mount and sent it into a wild gallop down the meadow toward where Nairne lay in long shadows.

Taminy stood for a moment, silent, aching, pressing her

hands together. To live with such dread, to cachet such dreams. She could see Aine, vividly then, taking the dreams apart on long, dark mornings, wondering what they meant and why they were hers. Not knowing whether to interpret them or how, because no one had ever taught her. Did she think everyone had these dreams?

Taminy began her walk down the long shallow hill, her eyes on the shadows of Nairne. She was on the Nairne road when she heard someone running toward her and made out two forms. It was Iseabal, with Gwynet close on her heels. She felt Iseabal's tears before she saw them, knew Gwynet was stunned and frightened.

"Taminy!" gasped Iseabal and fell to silent sobbing.

"Oh, come mistress!" Gwynet caught her arm and pulled her. "It's awful, it is! Poor Aine's fallen from her horse by the Cirkeyard an' she don't move!"

Taminy ran. Gwynet, gasping, told her the Cirkemaster had come down and Osraed Torridon had been sent for but he was up at the Fortress this time of day and mightn't come in time. The others were scurrying for any other Osraed they could.

They reached the spot and already there was a gathering by the low wall that ran round the Cirkeyard. Rennie and Wyvis had brought their mother and others came to where Osraed Saxan had set lightglobes out upon the wall and ground. They illuminated the spot where Aine lay on her back, her arms flung over her head, her bright hair fanned out like a billow of red mist.

There was a different red splashed wetly across her temple, but that did not alarm Taminy so much as the angle at which her head lay. She came to her knees beside the other girl's body, stretching out her hands. Already she could feel the life ebbing away. "What happened, Osraed?"

"I don't know. She was thrown. . . . " Saxan's face was pale and sweat sodden. His fear vibrated on the breeze, sharp and tangy like sea brine. "Her neck is broken, I think," he murmured and chewed his knuckle. "Dear God, where is Torridon? This is more than I am capable of."

Taminy's hands framed the place where Aine's neck twisted so absurdly. Eyes on the spot, she strained for a power that had once been autonomic — like the drawing of breath that was becoming increasingly difficult for Aine.

Please, dear God, dear Mistress, Beloved — let me see! To feel vaguely is not enough. Let me see!

It was like the clearing of mist from the valley, details coming clear as light burned through the layers. *There are layers of darkness*, Wyth had said. They pulled away now, and let her see the bone and the break and the torn tissue around it, lit as if by the globes of golden light that sat about them.

Despair clutched at her heart. Aine was dying beneath her hands, while she sat in this puny human frame, *despairing*. A scream of sheer frustration rose in her throat. It issued out as a whimper — like so much else. But, no. She must try. Osraed Saxan had admitted his failing and no one else here could hope to do anything. The Meri had graced her with the Healing Sight, perhaps —

Hands gripped her shoulders and lifted her away. Stunned, she could only acquiesce, and found herself sprawled in the grass, staring at the stooped shoulders of the slight, middle-aged man bending over Aine in her stead. Torridon — she heard his name spoken.

She picked herself up and wiped her hands on the fabric of her skirt. Voices and torches began to mill and, with them, questions. She glanced around hoping to see someone who might have answers.

"Her horse bolted." Rennie stood beside her, his lower lip raw from the chewing he'd been giving it. "Threw her right into the wall. Didn't even see how it happened."

"She was riding so fast," Wyvis said. "And she pulled up just there." She pointed toward the Cirkeyard's open gateway. "Just level with us. I thought she was stopping to talk to us. She came up beside Phelan with this funny look on her face — "

"Like she was trying not to cry," added Rennie. "And then the horse — " He gestured with his hand.

"It almost fell on her," said Wyvis.

The noise seemed to escalate suddenly and Taminy could hear a high keening from behind her. She turned to see Doireann Spenser leading an older woman through the crowd. As they came into the light of torch and globe, there was no doubt that this was Aine's mother. A man followed, and three tall, red-haired boys.

The woman saw Aine's still body lying between the kneeling Osraed and shrieked. "What's happened to my girl? Oh, dear God, what's happened to Aine?"

Doireann saw Taminy then, and blanched. Sensing that her guide had become an anchor, the Mistress Lorimer stopped and followed Doireann's gaze.

"What is it? What?"

"N-nothing," said Doiry. "It's just that . . . Aine was talking to Taminy just before. She'd ridden out to see her. She was on her way back when — "

Anything more she might have said was cut off by a raw cry of anguish from the place where Aine lay. One of the Lorimer's red-haired boys rose from the ground and cried, "Mama, she's gone! Aine's gone!"

No, Taminy thought. *It can't be. It mustn't be. Not Aine.* She was drawn to the spot against her will. To see vibrant Aine, dead. *Mustn't be.* She watched the mother all but swoon over the girl's body; watched Torridon age and wither; watched Saxan sweat and shake while he held his own daughter in his arms.

The Lorimer lifted his wife away and cocooned her. Torridon sat and shook his head. She moved forward without them seeing her and knelt opposite the Healer. She put her hands out — one over Aine's heart, the other over her throat.

If I never Weave again, let me Weave now. If I never know the Gift of Healing again, let me know it now. All else will I sacrifice to this moment. Only let me give this life back!

There was a rustling of leaves no one else could hear, moved by a breeze no one else would feel. Something stirred among the people gathered at the Cirkeyard. Something rose out of the earth and descended from the sky and radiated from the stones and the trees and the tiny particles they all breathed. Blue Healing gathered itself in Taminy's soul, collected from the stirring Thing. The prayer was answered.

"What's she doing? What are you doing?"

Hands pushed at her, reached for her. She willed them away.

"I can't — ! What has she done?"

"Get her away from my daughter!"

"What's she doing?"

"What's happened here?"

Ealad-hach. She knew that voice now. It was part of her dreams. He was close to her. She gave him a corner of her mind; she could spare no more. The Healing was gathering in her, she must concentrate. She could feel it like an ice-hot liquid crown upon her head.

"By the Kiss, that glow — !"

"No, no! Leave her be!" That was Saxan.

Hands again. Ealad-hach's hands. She raised one of her own, reflexively, heard him give a shocked cough as he met a sudden, invisible resistance that sat him back on his heels.

"She's woven a Shield! I can't touch her. Damn! Your stone, Torridon — give me your stone!"

The bone. The bone. The bone, cracked, must mend. The sinews, taut, must bend. The crushed breath, flow; the heartbeat, follow. The bone. The bone.

She found her rhythm, began a duan, praying the corner of her mind given to the Shieldweave would continue to support it.

Across Aine's body from her, Ealad-hach held out Torridon's crystal and tried to Weave against her. He had little strength, caught as he was in the grip of fear, but his voice, loud and sharp, distracted her. She gave a thought to the weakly glowing crystal he held in trembling hands. It flared with sudden blue light and winked out. Ealad-hach shrieked and Taminy's duan faltered.

No! I can't! Beloved, it's too much! These people, the Shield — I can't. Not alone.

She thought of Saxan and Iseabal and nearly reached for them when she felt him at her back, calm, though quivering with her need. She reached up a hand and Wyth took it in a firm grip. And there was another. She dared glance up. Bevol stood across from her near the gate, his eyes shining.

She returned her own to Aine. Yes! The bones! She could see them. Twisted, so. Time slipped by; she must hurry. First the Healweave, then the Infusion. She sang. No one had heard the duan before — only the Meri knew it. It pulled at the bones and tissue in Aine's broken neck. It molded them as a sculptor molds clay, with fingers of Blue Healing — Divine Fingers, forever unseen.

Taminy's fingers, poised over Aine's throat, flexed, there was a sound like a stick being pulled from mud and a breeze sprang up, cool, from the river. Within it, the Stirring Thing moved and breathed over Aine-mac-Lorimer's spirit, all but drained away. In Taminy's hand, a ball of light formed, blossoming like a little flame rose, petals opening in her hand, glorious. She placed the full flower on Aine's breast and watched it explode into filaments of molten light before sinking like ground mist into the girl's flesh. The breeze gusted and Aine-mac-Lorimer gasped for air, throwing herself into a ragged fit of coughing.

Taminy's Shieldweave shattered into a million motes. Spent, she sagged back against Wyth's legs. He lifted her out of the way of the pandemonium that engulfed the waking Aine and helped her to the wall, letting her down against it. From there, she watched Aine's family, Torridon and Saxan all but crush the poor girl in their concern.

"Thank you, Wyth," she murmured. "How did you know to come?"

"You called me . . . or She did."

"Yes, I suppose I did — *we* did." She smiled wanly and shifted to move a rock from under her hip. But what her groping hand found was not a rock.

"How did this happen?" Ealad-hach's voice came from nearly atop her. "How did *she* come to be here, in the thick of it?"

It was a runebag. It was hard and damp and smelled sharply of camphor and valerian. She looked up, puzzled, to see the old Osraed glaring down at her, clutching Doireann with one hand and Phelan with the other.

Doireann's eyes, horror stricken, lit upon the runebag and would not let go. She pointed. "*She* did it, Osraed. She had private words with Aine and then made her horse go crazy and — and dash her into the wall. She was getting even for that happening Cirke-dag. See, she's got a runebag in her hand, now."

Taminy turned her eyes to Ealad-hach, ready to protest, however weakly. His smile stopped the words in her throat.

"A reckoning, cailin. Now we shall have a reckoning."

She was at the center of a whirlwind, then — a whirlwind made of torchlight and darkness, of faces with harrowed eyes, of guiding hands and demanding voices. It reminded her of another such whirlwind, long ago. A wind that was part of her memory, if not her experience. Where that cyclone had blown itself out in the throne room of a Cyne, this one spent itself in the courtyard at Halig-liath, leaving Taminy surrounded by people who understood little more of what was happening than she did.

Ealad-hach, his face flushed and shining, was speaking loudly and authoritatively about her use of the Wicke Craft to cause Aine's horse to bolt. He spoke of revenge and jealousy. Questions were asked and voices raised and over the rush and murmur came Doireann Spenser's trembling testimony that Taminy must have maddened Aine's mount with the runebag she was holding, must have made the horse throw her.

She started to protest, but realized no one would hear her — no one but Bevol and Wyth and Gwynet, who didn't believe a word of Ealad-hach's harangue anyway. They were close to her; Bevol's hand was on her arm. She was safe.

Ealad-hach called for the Osraed Council to meet. Aine's father added his voice to the demand and Doireann's mother, and Iseabal's. Prentices scurried into the dark and, in what seemed like only minutes, Taminy was led from the cool, starlit courtyard into the confines of the Academy. Through the ancient stone hallways she was brought, at last, to the large chamber in which the Council of the Osraed met. There, Bevol left her side and took his seat at the long, crescent table, prepared to act as Apex.

"One moment, brother." Ealad-hach raised his hand in

protest. "Is it appropriate for you to be part of the Council when you are so obviously prejudiced in favor of this girl? You would not find against her if the world depended on it."

"And you would not find for her," said Bevol.

"This is absurd, Ealad," objected Osraed Calach. "And unprecedented. The Apex has never been asked to step down for any reason."

Bevol raised his hand. "Stay, brothers, I will not be the center of needless argument. I will step down. I accord the duties and privileges of Apex pro-tem to Osraed Calach." He retreated then, returning to Taminy's side.

"Very well." Calach glanced at Ealad-hach. "You too will step down, Osraed Ealad-hach. It isn't appropriate for you to act as inquisitor and adjudicator . . . I can only assume you are leveling some charge at the cailin."

"A very specific charge, Osraed. I charge that she is a very clever and powerful Wicke."

The chamber erupted into chaos then, as if the spoken words had invoked a human storm. The Osraed were forced to clear the room of all but their own number and such people as they hastily agreed were to be called as witnesses. The curious townsfolk settled for a long wait in the broad outer corridor, where Prentices were posted to keep them from leaning too heavily on the doors.

Taminy watched all from a high state of trembling detachment. Watched as Ealad-hach called upon Iseabal and the other youth to relate what had happened earlier. Watched as he advanced his pet theory — that she had struck out at Aine-mac-Lorimer in revenge for the paltry effrontery of an amateurish runebag and caused the girl's death, then, realizing she had gone too far, been forced to resuscitate her.

"The girl was dead?" asked Calach.

Ealad-hach was momentarily discomfitted. "She was . . . brought back by an Infusion Weave."

Calach turned his eyes to Taminy. "Your Weaving, child?"

Taminy nodded. "My Weaving, sir. With the help of the Osraed Wyth and Bevol. Osraed Ealad-hach tried to remove me . . . it was very difficult."

Calach looked to Ealad-hach. "You tried to remove her? Whatever for?"

"I was afraid she meant the girl further harm."

"She was dead, Osraed. What further harm could be done?"

Taminy heard Bevol chuckle. The sound soothed her somewhat. It had a somewhat different effect on Ealad-hach.

"She had already caused the girl bodily harm. I was concerned for her spirit. And it was Torridon's province, not the girl's, to remedy the situation."

"Torridon? Was the girl interrupting your ministrations?"

Torridon shook his head. "The damage was too severe. It was beyond me. I had given up . . . I am ashamed to say," he added.

"Then you are all in agreement that Taminy-a-Gled performed a successful Infusion, saving Aine-mac-Lorimer's life. *Is* that agreed?" Calach glanced around at the witnesses. All nodded or murmured their accord. "Are you also in agreement that Taminy caused the girl's accident?"

This question elicited no such positive response.

"If I may," said Osraed Saxan and was recognized. "Taminy didn't even arrive on the scene until I had gone out to see what had happened. I heard the children screaming and shouting. Taminy wasn't there."

"Taminy didn't need to be there. Taminy did her work from afar." Ealad-hach held up the pungent little runebag Taminy had found by the wall. "She had this in her hand. Camphor, valerian, peppermint. This concoction is known for the fear its smell inspires in certain animals. According to Doireann Spenser, Aine sought Taminy out to speak with her. Their relationship was strained, hostile. When the Lorimer girl remounted her horse, Taminy produced this bag and used it to madden the beast. It plunged down the hill and threw Aine-mac-Lorimer into the wall by the Cirke."

"That concoction," said Bevol quietly, "is also thought by some to ward off evil and keep Wicke from working their Craft."

"It seems," said Calach, "that we are more certain

Taminy saved Aine's life than we are that she took it. I would like to hear from Taminy, now. Come forward, child, and give us your Tell."

She did as bidden, finding that her legs would still carry her from here to there. She stood in the center of the great room with all eyes on her and said, "Aine rode out to see me as we were coming home over the hill. She told me she wasn't the one who brought the runebag into the Sanctuary last Cirke-dag."

"Did she tell you who did?"

"She didn't know. I accepted her at her word and she left me."

"She rode like daemons hunted her," objected Ealad-hach. "Do you claim not to know why?"

Taminy turned her head to look at him. *I could blow on him and he would fold up and fly away.* It was a chilling thought. She was further chilled by having had it. "I do know why, sir. When I held her hand to read the truth in her, I sensed that she had a Gift. I knew she had been having troubling dreams and had seen portents, but hid them from everyone. I told her what I felt. My words frightened her. Then, too, she felt betrayed. If she hadn't made that runebag and put it in her pocket, then someone else did. Someone who wanted her to be blamed. Aine was much troubled by that. Troubled and hurt." She let her eyes wander toward Doireann, whose olive complexion had taken on the look of fresh, pale cream.

"And do *you* know who was responsible for the runebag last Cirke-dag?"

"The same person who was responsible for the one I found tonight on the ground by the Cirke wall. The one Ealad-hach saw in my hand."

"And who is this person — this secret maker of fetishes?"

Taminy felt the dark eyes burring into the side of her head. "I cannot say, Osraed. I believe they must come forward of their own will."

"She's dissembling!" argued Ealad-hach. "*She* brought the runebag. She cast the inyx that toppled Aine-mac-Lorimer from her horse."

"Who originated the idea," Calach asked, "that Taminy was responsible for the fall?"

Ealad-hach moved to catch Doireann's shoulder and push her forward next to Taminy where she quivered under a room full of eyes. "This girl — Doireann Spenser."

"What put this idea into your head, child?" asked Calach gently.

Doireann cleared her throat. "They didn't get on well. Aine was sweet on Terris-mac-Webber and-and she saw them together in his shop one day. Heard him . . . heard him plead his great fondness for Taminy." She fairly spat the name, then quailed again, her eyes darting about the floor.

Like a wild little mouse, Taminy thought. *Straining to keep just ahead of the falcon.*

"That was when she thought about making the rune-bag," Doireann continued, her teeth near chattering. "I *think* that's when, I mean — she certainly said naught of it to me. She must've wanted to fight Taminy on her own ground. She must've thought she could prove to Terris that Taminy really was a Wicke. Or — or perhaps she meant to scare her into staying away from him. But they had words up on the hill — harsh words, I think. Aine was angry and afraid."

"Might she have made that runebag herself, thinking it would protect her from Taminy?" That was the Osraed Eadmund. Taminy looked at him. A pale young man, awash in uncertainty. "It was, after all, a wearding fetish similar to one she . . . or someone else . . . brought to Cirke."

"I — I suppose so, Osraed." Doireann glanced at Taminy, then aside, as their eyes nearly collided.

"May I speak?" asked Wyth. Calach acknowledged him and he came to stand between Taminy and Doireann. "Last Cirke-dag, Taminy is reported, by credible witnesses, to have poured more Eibhilin Light through a crystal than most of us have ever seen. This evening we experienced her handling of an Infusion Weave, which she performed while shielding herself against the attempts of Ealad-hach and others to physically remove her. Can you believe someone with that kind of ability would resort to a pungent fetish to accomplish anything?"

The men of the Council nodded their heads sagely.

"He's right, you know," said Faer-wald. "Runebags have traditionally been the refuge of people who have no inherent Gift, but who are trying to protect themselves from those who do. The fetish that turned up on Cirke-dag had a recipe intended to ward off Wicke; this second bag may have been created with the same intention."

Ealad-hach all but exploded. "The damned runebag is irrelevant! What is relevant is this young woman's power."

"Which does not," injected Bevol gently, "make her Wicke. Taminy is a young woman of extraordinary ability. I am well aware of that. But she is not evil. She is not a Wicke. You have built your accusations on sand, Ealad."

"There was enmity between the two girls — "

"No," said Taminy, "there was not. I like Aine, very much. I would never do anything to harm her."

Calach looked around at the other members of the Council. They gazed back as if at a loss to know what to say or do next. One by one, they shrugged, passing the decision back to him.

"Has she got you all so completely dazzled?" Ealad-hach cried.

Calach leaned forward, his bony elbows propped upon the gleaming crescent table. "Osraed, what is to be gained from this exercise? No one has been harmed. If there was any mischief done, it does not seem to have been done by Taminy. Indeed, it appears that Taminy has thwarted any such mischief. Unless you can offer some more substantial proof — "

Ealad-hach ground his teeth. "Would you accept an aislinn?"

Calach sat up straight in his chair. "To prove that Taminy used the Craft to harm Aine?"

"No. To prove that she is not what she seems. To prove that she is not merely a Wicke, but a Cwen Wicke, a supremely powerful Wicke, and that she is a chief architect of this Cusp we are now in."

Silence was the only possible answer to that. The five

Osraed at their curving table glanced at each other with unreadable expressions and found invisible threads on the cuffs of their chamber robes and flaws in the table top.

"Really, Ealad," said Faer-wald at last. "Are you certain you wish to pursue this?"

"I *must* pursue it. I have no choice."

"She is not Wicke," said Bevol.

"You are too close to her to — "

Wyth interrupted. "She is absolutely not Wicke."

Ealad-hach ignored him. "I told you of my aislinn weeks ago, when Wyth was on his Pilgrimage. I saw the rising of this woman from the Sea."

"You saw the rising of *a* woman from the Sea," corrected Calach. "She was faceless."

"She had flaxen hair."

"Many women have flaxen hair."

"I will show you her face!"

Calach gazed around the room. Taminy followed his eyes. It was in the face of every Osraed there: this had gotten suddenly beyond a mere dabbling in the Craft by a village cailin. Aine had become incidental; Doireann's accusations were forgotten; the mumblings of frightened parents were as the buzzing of bees, mildly jarring, vaguely threatening.

Calach dismissed everyone but the Council members and Osraed Wyth, who insisted upon staying. The loiterers in the outer corridor would no doubt repair to the Backstere's or the Quayside Road House to get their ears filled with the evening's Tell, but Osraed Saxan made certain they did not fill them in the hall. Taminy could hear his voice as the great doors closed behind him, exhorting everyone to leave. Then the doors shut, cutting the grumbling like a pair of blades.

That Calach was at a loss was evident; he polled the other Osraed visually again, then made a gesture that opened the floor for their input. "What shall we do, Osraed?" he asked them, and Faer-wald provided an immediate answer.

"Why don't we hear him out? At the very least, it should settle this matter in his mind. If he can show us a

convincing aislinn, fine. If not, we can then request that
the matter be *dropped*." He looked to Ealad-hach then, his
gaze punctuating his remarks with little subtlety.

Calach nodded. "A sound idea . . . Osraed?"

They agreed to a man. Better, they all thought, to get
this over with. Better to placate their elder brother. Better
that he be at last forced to lay these accusations to rest.

Seated again between Wyth and Osraed Bevol, Taminy
watched as Ealad-hach took his place at the center of the
chamber. Watched him in the dimming light as he brought
out his crystal and prepared himself for the Weave,
murmuring duans that sent frissons of anticipation up and
down her spine. She glanced aside at Bevol. His face was
impassive, his eyelids half-closed, his mouth drawn into
almost a smile.

Ealad-hach began his Weave, walking his circle, circum-
scribing its limits. He set his crystal down in the center of
it. A spark appeared at its core and light trembled there,
uncertain. He sang and the light strengthened, though it
still behaved like a candle wick in a capricious wind. He
chanted louder, straining to steady the light, and Taminy
felt a response from Bevol — a soft pulse in his attention.
She glanced at him again, found that his eyes were locked
on the crystal. The light in it steadied.

A smile brushed Ealad-hach's lips; his duan changed as
he called upon the Eibhilin world to intrude into his own.
Within the circle he described with his steps, a fitful image
swelled — a dark, turbid phantasm that struggled to
resolve itself into something recognizable — tried and
failed. Ealad-hach's smile stretched and grimmed.

Beside Taminy, Bevol exhaled a long, whispered breath;
a shiver of sound, accompanied by a shiver of something
else. Ealad-hach's aislinn gelled, becoming surf and sand
and dark, bright sky. Taminy was certain, then, that Bevol
was aiding the weakened old Osraed in his Weaving. She
was not certain why, but understood that the result was
likely to be another fiery collision. *Am I ready for that?* she
wondered, and trembled at the answer. Yet, she must trust
Bevol; she had no choice.

She held her breath and watched the surf writhe,

shimmering, onto the glitter of aislinn sand. Each wave was more luminescent than the last, infused with a shade of gold-green that Nature used so sparingly most human eyes had never seen it. In a breath, gold and green seemed to bleed away from each other, drawing into separate pools within the greater pool of the Sea. The green deepened to emerald — a verdant, crystalline color that pulsed momentarily with light before muting.

In the midst of the aislinn depiction, out of the rippling water, appeared a pale form. Ealad-hach's eyes seized on it, his words came more quickly, his steps quickened on their circular path. A sizzle of Eibhilin vigor shot from Bevol, tingling up the back of Taminy's neck and raising the hair on her arms. The form tightened, became a woman's head and shoulders, glittering with Sea jewels and irradiated with light.

She waded to shore, dripping radiance and salt water, stepping, at last, onto the beach, gleaming, naked except for a gown of sea tears. Hair the color of moonlit wheat cascaded down her back and over her shoulders, chastely mantling her breasts. She looked up, her eyes focused on someone the aislinn did not show, and laughed. "Ah, Osraed Bevol! I have not breathed for a hundred years!"

Taminy heard and felt the collective gasp that circled the room. She was looking into her own face, blushing at the sight of her own body, naked before all these eyes. She felt Wyth, sitting to her left, coil defensively. To her right, Bevol relaxed, nodding.

"There!" Ealad-hach's voice issued out on a hiss of breath. He ceased his pacing of the circle and turned to appraise what he thought to be his own handiwork. "You can now see it with your own eyes."

Indeed, they could. And he let them see it long enough that there could be no doubt whose face that was — no doubt whatever who was receiving a warm robe from unseen hands. And yet, he asked her, his voice trembling with effort, "Taminy-a-Gled, are you that cailin?"

She thought her voice might fail her, but it did not. "I am that cailin," she answered.

Ealad-hach took his attention from the aislinn and

focused it on Calach. The supporting aura from Bevol faded, and with it, the Woven vision. Taminy all but held her breath as the globes in the room shed more light, revealing the stunned and very sober expressions of the Osraed.

Ealad-hach struck a pose, hand outstretched toward her, palm up. "Have you any doubts now?" he asked, holding her in that palm, offering her up to the Council. "Have you any doubts that she is the Cwen Wicke I have dreamed? Have you any doubt that Osraed Bevol is involved in her deception?"

Osraed Calach, his face pale as the whites of his eyes, looked to Bevol. "Bevol, what is this? What have we been shown? Is this young woman the Wicke of Ealad's aislinn?"

Bevol stood and moved from Taminy's side to share the floor with Ealad-hach. "She is obviously the young woman of his aislinn, but she is not a Wicke."

"Then what? Surely we have never seen this before . . . did this cailin arise from the Sea as the vision suggests?"

"The vision mirrors reality, Osraed. She arose, just as you saw. What you did not see is what happened just before. You did *not* see Meredydd-a-Lagan go *into* the water."

Calach shook his head. "I don't understand."

"Isn't it obvious?" asked Ealad-hach. "Meredydd-a-Lagan was also a Wicke."

Bevol shook his head.

"Then where is she now?" asked Osraed Kynan.

"She is in the Sea," said Ealad-hach. "Drowned. Dead."

Again, Bevol shook his head. "She is in the Sea, but she did not drown and she is not dead. That is the truth."

Ealad-hach pointed a shaking finger at his colleague. "You! You dare speak to this Council? You presume to speak about what is true when you have been consorting with evil?"

"I have not consorted with evil, Ealad. Could I wear this and do so?" He pointed to the vivid star upon his forehead, then turned to the Council. "Will you hear me out? Will you let me tell you what you have seen here this evening?"

There was a moment of indecision, then the Council gave their consent, man by man.

"Why do you listen to him?" asked Ealad-hach. "He will tell you nothing but nonsense calculated to confuse."

"We are already confused, Ealad," said Faer-wald. "Nothing you have shown us makes sense, either. Why should this Wicke come up out of the Sea? The Sea is the province of the Meri."

"She competes with the Meri."

"She does not," said Bevol. "Osraed, may I speak before you condemn me for my part in what you've witnessed? All will be made clear, if not acceptable."

Calach gestured for him to begin.

"What you saw, Osraed, was a ritual. A ritual that results, as Ealad-hach believes, in what we have come to refer to as a Cusp. A young woman who possesses both Gift and devotion goes to the shore of the Sea and there, she is transformed. In her new state, she enters the ocean, there she meets and exchanges places with the one who came before her. And that one is also transformed and arises from the Sea, as you have witnessed through Ealad-hach's aislinn. Meredydd went to the Sea and was transformed, exchanging places with this young woman." Bevol paused.

"But . . . " Eadmund gazed about at his fellows before asking, "who *is* this young woman?"

"Hers is a name I think you will recognize, if only from legend. This, Osraed, is Taminy-a-Cuinn."

Their astonishment could not have been more profound. Taminy felt it rock her, as if their sudden regard possessed a physical weight and force.

Ealad-hach's mouth moved soundlessly before words finally formed. "Taminy-a-Cuinn died over one hundred years ago."

"No, Ealad. She stands before you. Not dead. No more dead than Meredydd. And you know it, too. You've suspected it."

"You have only wanted me to suspect it."

"Come, old friend, you've had other aislinn, other dreams. You've seen other cailin perform this ritual, have you not? Have you not dreamed of the time of Liusadhe the Bard? Liusadhe, whose condemnation of women he supposed to be Wicke earned him the title of the Purifier?

An unwarranted title, as he understood in later life."

Ealad-hach paled. "How do you know my dreams?"

Bevol ignored his question, turning instead to Osraed Calach. "What will convince you?"

Calach's eyes had not left Taminy's face. "Speak, cailin. Is what Bevol says true? Are you Taminy-a-Cuinn?"

She rose and all eyes followed her. "I am. What Osraed Bevol says is true."

The Osraed Ladman smote the table and Kynan expressed his disbelief loudly. "This is absurd! No — it is obscene!"

Calach raised his hands, clapping them together to restore order. "Let her speak! Let her speak!" He gestured at Taminy. "Go on, cailin. Give us your Tell."

Taminy gathered herself, ignoring the dagger glares of Ealad-hach and the disbelieving Osraed. "In the Year of Pilgrimage four hundred ninety, I went to the Sea on a forbidden Pilgrimage with my father acting as my Weard. The Meri came to me on the second day of my waiting, wearing the silver of the clouds. She called me into the water, into Her Sea. She breathed Her knowledge into my soul. She changed my very nature. She passed on to me all that She was. We embraced and we parted. And when we parted, it was I that remained behind in the Sea and she that returned to the land on the same two legs that carried her in nearly one hundred years before."

"What do you mean?" Calach's voice was a raw whisper. He turned stricken eyes to Bevol. "What is she saying? What did we witness?"

Bevol smiled. "Isn't it obvious? You have witnessed the regeneration of the Meri."

CHAPTER 13

A STUDY OF THE BLUE CUSP
— Cusp to Cusp, by Osraed Tynedale

*By the twenty-fifth year of the reign of Cyne Liusadhe,
Creiddylad was host to a number of women who possessed the Gift of Runeweaving. Though the Osraed
tried to raise the Cyne's suspicions against these
women, he remained, at first, uncondemning of
them. It was not until he discovered a connection
between one of the accused young women and his
unscrupulous ex-Chancellor (a man who had abused
his position sorely) that he became agitated and
brought the women to trial.*

*This resulted in a dozen or so women, including Lufu
Hageswode, fourteen-year-old daughter of the Renic
Bana-Meg, being banished into a hard, biting winter.
Also among the exiles were several members of the
ex-Chancellor's immediate family, one of whom died
of exposure during the ordeal.*

*It was directly after the accused Wicke left Creiddylad
that the Meri changed Aspect. This was the Silver
Manifestation, which we now know to be linked to
the person of the girl, Lufu Hageswode (called "Mam
Lufu"). It is of note that this Cusp took place out of
Season, in the early spring of YP 396.*

❖   ❖   ❖

The darkness was complete. Suspended within it,
Lealbhallain attempted to read its limits. It was not a silent
darkness. Hollow, it echoed with tiny, bright noises like the

whispered notes of a harp. It was not a still darkness. Alive, it rippled with breathings and sighs.

He was no longer in his room at Care House, he knew. He was in the sea cave below Ochanshrine. The realization brought light into the place — a tiny pip of light, a seed that grew and blossomed before his eyes, unwavering. In a gold-traced pattern of glory, the gleaming petals of a crystalline rose unfolded before him in the dark, reflecting off the pool below and the glittering walls around. Drippings from the ceiling shook the reflection and shivered it into countless tiny wriggles of light.

He breathed in his awe. The Osmaer crystal. He knew it was that, though the shape was wrong; the Osmaer was not shaped like a rose. But this was the Osmaer, nonetheless. He reached out a tentative hand.

The darkness turned inside out, whirled away and regathered itself in a different form. Leal shook and shivered, blinking his eyes and struggling to make sense of his surroundings. He was standing on a tall place — a hill, a tower — and looking toward Nairne. Halig-liath sat upon its clifftop like a great, squat beast, dark and waiting. But as he watched, a light sprang up, radiant, from the ramparts — a brilliant, piercing light that appeared, at once, in the shape of a crystal and a rose.

Leal flew from his hill, sucked toward the crystal-rose as if by a silent whirlwind — a wind composed of his own passion. He turned as he ascended, his eyes finding all of Caraid-land laid out below him as if upon a gigantic, living map. And beyond Caraid-land, the Sea.

He paused in his flight. The Sea was changing its color, roiling from blue-green to gold-amber, frothing in all the hues of the Sun's journey across the sky. Like molten gold it beat upon the shores of Caraid-land and rose up in boiling waves and over-ran the dry land. Leal watched, horrified, as Mertuile and Creiddylad disappeared beneath the swell; as every village and settlement, every estate and manor, every farm and stead, every hill and valley and mountain was inundated, swallowed up.

Over the place where Caraid-land had been, the water boiled as if with great heat, as if a battle of giants raged beneath the golden tide. And then the water began to subside and the tops of the Gyldan-baenn thrust above the waves, gleaming, golden, as if the molten Sea had coated them. But in the valleys . . .

Leal looked away. There would be death. Corpses would lie in the low places of Caraid-land and ruins would litter her slopes. Most especially, he could not bring himself to look at Nairne, at Halig-liath, at the place where the crystal-rose had been. He screwed his eyes tightly shut, hearing the beginnings of Caraid-land's mourning — a high keen that lay, weeping, upon the wind, that swelled into a great, grieving wail.

Leal came upright in his bed, hands clamped over his mouth. His own throat had been the source of that horrible sound. He sweated, chill, and wondered if anyone had heard him.

Ealad-hach rubbed his arms briskly. Chill this morning . . . or was it just him, reacting, again, to the events of the past days? He smiled — lips parting, tight, over fierce teeth. Victory. He had her now. It was a matter of time. Couriers had gone already, birds had been dispatched to the northlands, a Summonsweave had been performed for those who could sense such things. The Osraed Body would decide her fate and, by the time it convened, he would be strong and well-able to repeat the Weave that had unmasked her.

Taminy-a-Cuinn.

His smile spasmed and folded down at the corners. He shivered, rubbing his arms harder. Hunted. He was hunted now. He could feel eyes on him, constantly. The eyes of her minions, he was certain. He had revealed her and she had spread her dark mantle over him — a mantle full of the eyes of daemons. They snatched at him. They would try to prick him, hole his Wardweaves and suck out his soul. His eyes moved furtively about the sunny room. In the corners . . . yes, you had to be careful of corners.

A tiny noise at the door brought his eyes up sharply.

Osraed Wyth stood there, gazing at him through his great, sad eyes. Ealad-hach pressed his lips tight together. "Yes? What is it?"

"The Ren Catahn is here."

"Catahn? Whatever for? I thought he'd gone back up to Hrofceaster."

"He wants an audience with the Council."

"Oh?" Ealad-hach felt suspicion curl in his breast. "And why are you the messenger, Osraed? Could not a Prentice have carried this Tell?"

"Yes. But I wanted to bring it. Catahn says he's had a . . . a vision."

"Catahn?" Ealad-hach uttered a rude, barking laugh. "So now we're to be plagued with Hillwild sorceries, too, eh?"

Wyth shifted from one foot to the other. "Catahn wouldn't be Ren if he wasn't Gifted, Osraed. The Hillwild prize prescience just as we do."

"Prescience! *Pretence*, is more like. So . . . the Ren wants me to hear of this *vision* of his, does he?"

"He wants the Council . . . and Bevol."

"Bevol is suspended — as you would be, if I had my way."

Wyth pulled himself fully upright. "I am Chosen, Osraed."

"Yes . . . but by what, I wonder?"

"The Kiss cannot be falsified."

"*Anything* can be falsified if the right powers are applied . . . or the wrong ones."

"The Meri gave me this." He pointed to his brow.

Ealad-hach shook his head. "Perhaps you believe that. I am almost persuaded that you do. But, *if* you do, you have been misled. Betrayed, as we are all being betrayed."

"No."

"Your mistress is strong, *Osraed* Wyth, but she is not invincible. The Meri will out."

"Yes, She will."

"I pity you."

"And I, you."

Ealad-hach shivered, but covered the twitching movement by coming to his feet and pushing his stool back beneath his workbench. "Where is Catahn?"

"In the small audience chamber."

"Very well, I'll go to him. Have the others been informed?"

"They will have been."

Ealad-hach approached the door, but was loath to pass near Wyth. He paused, quailing a little beneath the younger man's dark gaze.

"You're wrong," said Wyth. "You're wrong about Taminy, about Bevol, about me. Caraid-land is in danger — we are *all* in danger — but not from her. She may be Something we don't understand, but she is not evil."

"You're blocking my path, Osraed Wyth." Ealad-hach raised pale eyes, trying, with every ounce of himself to pierce Wyth Arundel's poise. He felt a thrill of victory when the young man dropped his gaze and stepped silently aside.

Wyth returned to the chambers in which Taminy had spent the last several days. He could think of nothing else he should do. She spent her time reading, meditating, praying, and studying the courtyard from the window embrasure. She was there when he entered, with a book she was not reading, staring through the small panes at the rain-blurred sky without.

Thunder trampled through the clouds, rumbling like hunger in their grey bellies. The air was late-summer balmy and full of the tingle of electricity. There was something else in the air, too, but Wyth could not name it. He wriggled within his clothing and watched Taminy and marveled at how calm she was.

"I wish I knew what they were going to do," he said. "I wish I could do something to prepare."

Taminy turned her face away from the window. "And what would you do? How could you prepare, regardless of what they do? If they find me Wicke, which they might, how would you prepare for it? And if they find me innocent, is preparation needed? Even if they were to accept what I am and have been, what then?"

"But . . . isn't there a *plan*? I mean, doesn't *She* have a plan?"

Taminy smiled. "Of course She does."

"And are you part of it?"

She nodded.

"Then . . . ?" He made a futile gesture, wanting her to interpret it and reassure him that everything was under the control of Someone much more powerful than he was.

"What they do is contingent upon their will. What we do is contingent both upon what they do and what the Spirit and the Meri will us to do. The future must be built moment by moment, Wyth."

"But you have the Sight — "

"I see turmoil."

"I see it too, but surely the will of God — "

"The will of God is known only to the Meri. That will is victorious, always, but how and when devolves upon us . . . and them." She nodded toward the thick, carved door of her makeshift prison.

"But if the Meri won't let us know what to do — "

"We'll know. Whether we do it or not is a matter of choice, for that is what we are, Wyth, creatures of choice. Creatures of will. When our will aligns with Hers, there is peace, there is wisdom and unity, there is the possibility of joy. When it doesn't . . . " She shrugged.

Turmoil. "What do you suppose they will do? There hasn't been a serious charge of Wickery brought against anyone since the time of Liusadhe. What . . . what would they do with a Wicke?"

Taminy chuckled. "Odd, isn't it — Ealad-hach is convinced I am some powerfully evil creature and yet he expects me to be contained by four stone walls."

Wyth glanced at her sharply. She was smiling a girlish smile of pure humor. And she was right; it was a ludicrous idea. He laughed for the first time in days. "There isn't even a decent lock on the door," he said. "Anyone with a midge of the Art and a crystal can get in — "

As if to prove his words, the door opened, admitting Skeet and Gwynet. They had food and drink and gossip with them and used all three to nurture the levity Taminy had released into the sombre place. As they ate, Skeet talked, his words punctuated by peals of laughter, rain and thunder. It was all over town, of course — Ealad-hach's accusation before the Council — and the opinions about it were as various as those carrying them. Marnie-o-Loom had it that Ealad-hach was a senile old wind-bag and really ought to be ignored. The Spensers insisted that he was right, as they'd always known. To hear them talk, they'd sensed something wrong about Taminy from the beginning. Niall Backstere, meanwhile, blythely passed gossip both ways, while the Lorimer family was irritatingly silent.

"How is Aine?" asked Taminy. "Has anyone said?"

"Closed up in her room, seeing none. Not a peep out of her. Maybe not a peep into her, either, for what her ma and da seem bent on protecting her." Skeet leaned across the table toward her as if someone who oughtn't might overhear. "I've heard she's to have an audience with the Council before the Body meets."

"I tried to see her," said Gwynet. "Her ma was kindly enough, but she wouldn't let me."

"Ah, now, *here's* a noodle you'll be interested in!" Skeet fairly bounced in his chair. "Seems Brys-a-Lach and young Phelan have had a falling out and Phelan's place has been usurped by Scandy-a-Caol."

Wyth blinked. That was an interesting piece of gossip, if for no other reason than that Phelan and Brys had been inseparable since he had known them. He'd had to separate them in class several times for behaving as if no one else existed. "That *is* odd," he murmured and glanced at Taminy. "Do you think Phelan was sincere in his attachment to you?"

She didn't answer him, in fact, he thought she might not have heard him. She was gazing at a point in mid-air, her brows drawn into a slight frown, her eyes bemused.

"Taminy?"

She shook herself. "Sorry, I . . . There's something . . . "

He nodded, some inner sense coming to sudden life. "I feel it, too. That is, I feel something. A sort of — of quivering in the air."

She came to her feet, glanced at him oddly, then moved to the window, peering down through the panes. Before he could guess her intent, she pulled the window open, admitting rain and a clammy breeze, and leaned out, eyes on the narrow stone walk that ran beneath the window one long story down. For an instant, Wyth was taken with the absurd conviction that she meant to jump or fly from the window. He hurried to her side, looked where she looked.

There was someone standing below them on the walk — a girl with a wild mass of black hair and eyes like jet. He could see those eyes because she was staring up at them, her face glistening with rain, her riding breeches and jacket water stained. She made no gesture, spoke no words, only gazed upward while her eyes filled with water that may or may not have come from the sky. The air around her seemed to shimmer, to pulse. Distrusting his eyes, Wyth blinked, but the shimmer persisted.

"Who is she?" Taminy asked, finally, her voice barely louder than the breeze or the soft whisper of rain.

"Her name is Desary," Wyth told her. "She's the Ren Catahn's daughter."

"Hillwild, then," said Taminy and smiled. "Of course." She held out her hand, then, beyond the window frame. Held it out palm downward as if bestowing a blessing.

The Hillwild girl's lips parted soundlessly and she ran, disappearing into the fortress where the walkway met the wall. A moment later, she reappeared with a man the size of a small mountain. A man whose hair sparkled with interwoven jewels and whose broad shoulders were mantled by a leather cape. The Ren Catahn.

He joined his daughter on the walk below Taminy's window — joined her in staring upward, while she, holding up her clasped hands, fell to her knees.

"My Lady," she said in a clear voice. "My Lady of the Crystal-Rose!"

It was just one more proof — as if he needed any more proof — that the Osraed were inept. In a week's time the entire Osraed Body would sit in judgement at a Wicke trial. A *Wicke* trial. How antiquarian. There hadn't been any real Wicke trials since the heady days of Liusadhe. There had been mutterings — there were always mutterings — but no trials had taken place.

"Interesting tidings, aren't they?" Daimhin Feich

watched his Cyne's face with amusement spread across his own. "One lonely little heretic — and a girl, at that."

"According to this," — Colfre waved the letter brought to them that morning by Abbod Ladhar — "she was aided and abetted by Osraed Bevol."

Feich's brows twitched. "Does that distress you?"

"Why should it? He was my father's advisor, not mine. Although, he tried to advise me once upon a time. I believe he gave it up as a bad job and scurried off to Halig-liath to sit at Apex." Colfre shook his head. "It's the Cusp, you know. It makes them see heretics and Wicke everywhere. It makes them jump at their own shadows."

"I wonder what she really did."

"According to this, she performed secret and dangerous acts that may have resulted in injury to another and made claims that — ah, how do they put it? — threaten the foundations of religious faith."

"Quite an accomplishment for one small village girl." Feich leaned back in his splendid chair. "Rumor off the galleys says this Wicke of theirs is quite a popular young lady. By all accounts, Taminy-a-Gled has turned Nairne and its environs into a divided camp. And now, it seems, the fracas will move to a national battlefield. Imagine it, sire, one lone, defenseless girl against a hundred powerful men. It fairly tears at the heart."

Colfre laughed at that. Envisioning his Durweard's heart being torn by anything required more imagination than he had. But the thought of that girl — Taminy — standing to be judged by the illustrious Osraed . . . well, he could imagine that. It was the stuff of an heroic painting. His mind provided the scene — all those closed Osraed faces turned toward the lone, brave figure. His mind rendered her beautiful, of course; heroic, lone female figures were always beautiful. He rose and wandered the sunny breakfast room, pausing now and again to stand in a bright patch of light, noting how the soft radiance of it diffused through the nap of his velvet tunic. He would have to find a brush technique that could emulate that with more truth —

"Do you see an advantage in this, sire?" Feich asked him.

Advantage? He paused, roughing the velvet with his

fingertips. He turned and met his Durweard's eyes. "What advantage — " he began to say, when it came to him with the clarity of the morning sky. He smiled. "What I see, Daimhin, is that this potentially explosive and divisive situation has been building without my direct knowledge and that the Osraed have been deporting themselves in a most high-handed way. They may, for all I know, be persecuting a completely innocent girl. I should take an interest."

"For the sake of the people of Caraid-land," said Feich, "I believe you must. What would they think if what you say is true — if this girl is an innocent victim of . . . Osraed scapegoating."

"Indeed, what would they think?" Colfre turned in his shower of sunlight. "I believe we must be a presence at that great assemblage, Daihmin. See to it."

Feich rose and bowed. "With pleasure, sire."

The rain beat hard upon the second floor window of the Lormimer's house. It did not wake his daughter, Aine, but it invaded her dreams. The droplets marched across the window; an army marched through the land. Driven by the thunder of war drums, they advanced up the Halig-Tyne from Mertuile, inexorable, light flashing from their helms, water streaming from their armor. They marched, not on the river road, but in the river itself, or upon it, and as they gathered momentum, they melded, as the drops of the sea, becoming a wave that rode upstream on its own force, tumbling, rising, growing. From her window, Aine could see it, bearing down on Nairne, advancing on the great bend that wove around the cliffs. Higher it grew, stronger, rolling onward to where it would crest.

Mute. She was mute. And her legs would not carry her with a warning to Halig-liath. She would be trapped here in this room when that wave broke and, trapped, she feared she would watch it breach the great stone walls and sweep Halig-liath away.

The army marched all through the night, never reaching the Holy Fortress. Time after time, Aine would shut her dreaming eyes to the final cataclysm and, time after time, the army would would renew its march upriver. She woke gratefully, cheered by the sight of Halig-liath, massive, on its clifftop, but cheer faded quickly during her morning ablutions; the dream hung behind her eyes like a dread curtain, reminding her of Taminy's words to her on that evening of chaos, reminding her of Taminy's touch. Her palm tingled, still, a feeling that did not pass with the application of warm water and soap.

Funny . . . She rubbed a towel across the faint discoloration there. An odd place for a bruise, and it didn't hurt. She stared at the mark without seeing it. She should go to Halig-liath. She should beg to see the Osraed. She should tell them about her dream.

And what, Aine-mac-Lorimer, should persuade them to listen?

She shook her head and picked up her hair brush, sitting down before her mirror to pull it through her thick cinnamon mane. The face that gazed back at her from the silvered glass was pale. So pale, every freckle stood out in relief. She stared, hypnotized by the movement of her brush sweep-sweeping through the hair, burnishing it. It seemed to her, for a moment, that she faced someone else in the mirror. Someone with flaxen hair and eyes like the leaves of spring.

She blinked and the illusion passed. The freckled face stared back at her, its hazel eyes wide and haunted, the bruises and lacerations from the fall all but faded.

She saved your life. Could you make some effort to save hers?

Oh, but that was arrogant thinking. How could she, the daughter of a Lorimer, hope to impress the Osraed of Halig-liath with her testimony? Would they even care that Taminy had had nothing to do with her fall? Had only to do with bringing her back from death?

She shivered, her whole body convulsing with chill. Death. She dropped the hairbrush to the little dressing table and went downstairs, rubbing her tingling hand against the fabric of her breeches.

Her mother was downstairs alone; her father and brothers had already gone to the shop. She ate a small breakfast — too small for her mother's liking.

"Are you feeling ill, Aine? You look right enough, but

you've eaten barely enough to fill a nut shell these last days." She smoothed her daughter's hair, lifting it away from her eyes, so she could peer into them. "Maybe you should see Osraed Torridon."

Aine lowered her eyes. "I do want to see the Osraed, mother. I . . . I need to tell them what I remember about the fall. I need to tell them Taminy didn't have anything to do with it."

Her mother nodded. "I was wondering when you'd come to that. Are you sure, Aine? Are you sure she had nothing to do with it"

"I'm sure, mam. I wish da would believe me."

"He thinks you may be inyxed."

"No. Taminy didn't do anything to harm me. She only saved me from harm. I have to tell the Osraed that."

Her mother nodded. "They said they were going to call you before the Body meets."

"I want to go now — today. I . . . need to — to . . . " How to say it: *Mother, I dream. Mother, I see visions. Mother, Taminy says I have the Gift of divination.*

The Mistress Lorimer caught her daughter's face between her hands and captured her eyes. "What is it, Aine? Something is troubling you, and you might as well tell me now, what it is, as tell me later. For I *will* find out."

Aine hesitated.

"Please, Aine, things have happened I don't understand. And I'm worried for you, and for that girl up there at Halig-liath."

That decided her. "Mam, I've been dreaming. Clear dreams and awful dreams. They've come to me for some time now, and I've been silent about all of them. But now, I know something is wrong and I've got to go to the Osraed and try to warn them of it."

"Wrong? What is it? What have you dreamed?"

She described the dream army then, and its watery march upriver. And she told of other dreams as well. She did not say that Taminy had told her she was Gifted — she hadn't the courage for that. But when she was done, her mother let her go and said, "If you feel you must try to warn the Osraed, then you must. But go quietly and don't ride past the shop — your father would stop you if he knew what you were set off to do. He still believes Taminy-a-Gled is your enemy."

"But you don't, do you, mother?"

Her mother sat down at the kitchen table and gazed at her, looking wearier and older than she had only a week past. "I don't know what to believe, Aine, except that Torridon took you from my arms dead, and Taminy put you back into them alive. And that, I suppose, is all I need to believe. Go tell your dreams to the Osraed, daughter. I will pray that they listen to you."

"This letter is most disturbing, Ealad." The Osraed Calach smoothed the pages upon the table, as if by doing so he might also smooth out the situation at Creiddylad. "Osraed Lealbhallain has confirmed what we have chosen to regard as rumor. We shall have to bring this before the Body —"

"We shall do nothing of the sort. Not now. Not in the midst of all this other business." Ealad-hach paced the Council chamber, empty but for the three Osraed who made up the current Triumvirate.

Faer-wald, senior of the remaining Council Osraed, sat in Bevol's chair. "Are you sure that's wise?" he asked. "Surely we can't let the Cyne blythely rewrite the rituals of the Cirke to suit his own whims. Nor can we afford to have men like Abbod Ladhar turning a blind eye to it."

"I'm not suggesting we do that. Only that we table this matter until we've dealt with Taminy-a-Cuinn."

Faer-wald's face flushed. "You believe her, then. You believe she *is* Taminy-a-Cuinn."

"Don't you?"

"I don't know what to believe. That a cailin could walk into the Sea and walk out again over one hundred years later, that she was, during that century, transformed into what we know as the Meri —"

"I *don't* believe *that*!" said Ealad-hach pointing a rigid finger at Faer-wald's broad nose. "Not now, not ever, will I believe it."

"There is power in the Meri's Sea," observed Calach quietly. "There is power all about us. You saw the evidence of your own eyes, Osraed — a girl died, then lived again.

In all my years, I have seen two men perform Infusions —
Torridon and Bevol. But even they could not mend the
sort of damage that killed Aine-mac-Lorimer's body."

"You exaggerate."

Faer-wald shook his head. "No, he doesn't. It's true.
Dear God, what *is* she?"

"She's a Wicke, a daemon. What else could call the
damned Hillwild down from their aerie?"

"Perhaps what she claims to be."

Ealad-hach speared Calach with gimlet eyes. "An
ex-regeneration of the Meri? Do you want to believe that?
Do you want to believe that those arrogant young females
who've marched to the Sea and wreaked havoc in
Caraid-land are the vessels of That?"

"It makes very little difference whether I *want* to
believe it or not, Ealad. If it is so, it is so."

Ealad-hach rounded on him, placing his gnarled hands
flat upon the crescent table. "Do you realize the implications
of that? I have dreamed, Calach, of the Wicke of Liusadhe. I
have seen one of them — a girl with eyes like the belly of a
cloud and hair like the night wind — stand up by the Sea
with arrogant smile, waiting for the touch of God. Waiting
for the embrace of perfection and power. If what Bevol
claims is true, then how do you explain the tragedy that
followed? How do you explain the Purge? The Meri
eschewed every Osraed connected with those Wicke."

"Connected?" Calach's colorless eyebrows crept beneath his fringe of matching hair. "Aye, they were
connected. They tried to have the Wicke executed instead
of merely exiled. The Purge touched nearly every Osraed
in Caraid-land, Ealad."

"Because they *failed* to convince Liusadhe to act with
conviction."

"Or because they tried to have innocent women murdered and, failing that consented to having them tortured
and banished from all they held dear."

Ealad-hach covered his ears. "I won't hear this, it is
blasphemy!"

"Oh, stop it, both of you!" Faer-wald pounded one
hammy fist on the table. "What about this other thing? What

about Colfre? We cannot let him continue on in this —
starving the poor in his charge, twisting the Holy Rites as if
they were so much cheap rope, letting the affairs of
Caraid-land fall into the hands of a select committee. We
must act."

"You have no conception, have you," said Ealad-hach,
"of the gravity of this situation with the girl. We can let
nothing else distract us from it. Nothing!"

The silence held only the labored breathing of three
men struggling with their particular passions. Finally,
Faer-wald said, "I say we put it before the Council."

"*After* the convening of the Body."

"No, *before*. It makes no sense to call everyone back a
second time if the Council decides the Body must consult
over this business in Creiddylad."

"You stubborn old —"

Scowling, Faer-wald pointed at Calach. "Tie-breaker."

Calach folded his arms across his narrow chest. "I agree
with Faer-wald. When the Council meets to interview
witnesses tomorrow, they can consider Lealbhallain's
report as well."

Ealad-hach all but ground his teeth. "Very well."

A chime interrupted them and a pale-faced Prentice
peeped his head gingerly around the half-open door.
"Osraed? I — I beg your pardon, but there's a young cailin
to see you. It's Aine-mac-Lorimer, masters," he added and
his eyes added awe to his timorousness. "She's mighty
distraught."

"We'll see her tomorrow —" began Ealad-hach, but the
Apex pro-tem interrupted him.

"Send her in please, Luc."

Ealad-hach shut his mouth and returned to his seat. A
moment later, the girl entered the room. Whatever passion
had propelled her through the doorway faded as she came
further into the room. She had not reached the table when
it gave out altogether and left her trembling in the middle
of the polished floor.

Realizing how imposing they must look, seated, scowling behind the gleaming expanse of wood, Calach rose and
moved about the table to meet her, a smile creeping to his

lips. "Aine! How do you feel today? Are you sure you're quite ready to be out and about?"

The girl's eyes bounced frenetically between Calach and his companions — still seated, still scowling. "I — I'm feeling f-fine, Master Calach. In body, at least. It's my spirit that's encumbered and I must speak to you about it."

"Ah!" Ealad-hach produced a smile. "I was right, then. The Wicke *did* do some foul craft to you."

"The — the Wicke? Oh, no, sir! She's *not*. I mean, she *didn't*. It's not like that, at all." She grasped Calach's hands and wrung them. "Please, Master Calach. I need to tell you —"

Calach disengaged his hands and brought a chair for Aine to sit on, placing it on the inside curve of the table, opposite his fellow Osraed. He seated her in it, then perched near her on the table. "There now. Speak to us at will. Say whatever is on your mind." He ignored the rolling of Faer-wald's eyes and the twist of Ealad-hach's lips.

"I've come with a warning, masters."

"A warning?" Ealad-hach was suddenly interested.

"Aye, sir. I dreamed last night — all night — of a great army that marched inland from the Sea, from Creiddylad. It marched in the river itself and appeared to me as a wave, sweeping aside everything in its path. It was bound for Halig-liath, masters, growing with every mile. Higher than the clifftops, it grew. Mightier than the stone in these walls. It put me in dire fear and I knew I must come and warn you."

Calach rubbed at his arms where the hair had risen. "Have you had this dream before, Aine?"

"No, sir. Not this same one, but . . . others. Dark dreams, all of them — or, well, most of them."

"Only now, these dreams have come to you?" asked Ealad-hach. "Since the Cusp?"

"*This* dream, Master Ealad-hach. The one about the river-army. But I've had these sorts of dreams since I can remember. I just never knew what to make of them. And — and they frightened me."

"Well, my dear child, why *should* you make anything of them? Indeed, why should we?"

"Because, sir, they always come true. One way or another, they always come true."

✧   ✧   ✧

They hadn't listened to her. She didn't know what could have inspired her to think they would. Ealad-hach had tried for a while to convince her the great wave had something to say about Taminy, but she knew it didn't. It had to do with something else, she just wasn't sure what. And when she told them Taminy had said she had an aislinn Gift, she thought Osraed Ealad-hach would have her thrown from the room.

Calach had calmed him and had listened to her account of the accident. Someone had thrown something at her horse, she'd said, and had spooked it. She wasn't sure who; she could only rule out Phelan because she'd been looking at him when it happened. But it hadn't been Taminy — she was sure it hadn't been Taminy and she said so.

They had little use for her after that. Calach saw her to the door, ushered her out and closed it behind her, leaving her to stand awkwardly in the hall outside the chamber, listening to their voices rise and fall. Mostly rise.

She turned away at last and made her way down the concourse to the main rotunda. She was nearly across it when the patter of quick footsteps made her pause and turn. A young Prentice slid to a stop on the worn tiles and bobbed his head at her.

"Pardon, young mistress, but I've come with a message from the Osraed Calach. He says you must tell Osraed Bevol what you told him. All of it, he said."

"But, I don't know where Osraed Bevol is."

"Oh, it's all right. I'm to take you to him. Look." The boy held up a small crystal set onto a golden ring. "He gave me this. It's from his own prayer chain. Can you imagine an Osraed handing off his prayer crystal like that? This must be a very important mission he's given me."

Heart hammering in her breast, Aine smiled, encouraging the boy's self-congratulation. "Aye, it must be, at that."

CHAPTER 14

Material eyes perceive only material beauty; lifeless hearts take pleasure only in the withered rose. Like seeks like and delights in the fellowship of its own kind.

— *Utterances of Osraed Gartain, Number 128*

❖   ❖   ❖

Ealad-hach had spent the night in preparation for the inquiry. His witnesses were convincingly fearful, his line of questions carefully thought out. That was especially critical now, when he knew he could no longer rely upon his knowledge of the Art to tip the scales against Taminy. The hours spent in his aislinn chamber had been fruitless; he could not recreate the vision, and prayed he would not be called upon to do so.

Cursing his fickle Gift, he made his way down from his private rooms to the Council Chamber. The other members of the Council were already waiting in the small audience chamber adjacent to it. All, except for Bevol, who was excluded, and Calach, who was probably wherever Bevol was.

Ealad-hach wrinkled his nose, indignant, and made his way across the chamber. Though the thick, weighted curtains that gave onto the larger hall were drawn, he could guess the attendance at today's event by the sheer volume of noise. He sidled up to Ladman, who was peeking through the brocaded folds.

"Quite a crowd," observed the younger Osraed. "We will be much loved by the end of this day . . . or much hated."

"Hated? How can you mean? Who should hate us, beside the evil in the land?"

"Has it escaped your attention, Osraed, that the lady we seek to try is vastly popular?"

Ealad-hach shook his head. "You are misled, Ladman. Mark where their fickle loyalties fall when all is revealed."

Ladman merely let the curtain fall and moved away. Ealad-hach shuffled to take his place, peeping through the heavy fabric to scan the chamber. Over the top of the crescent table, which was directly before the door, he had a cross-room view of the public galleries. Three tiers high with five rows per tier, they marched up the western wall of the chamber. Above them, a triad of stained-glass windows shed muted splendor. Along the northern and southern walls of the long hall, between the crescent table and the great doors, lay the galleries reserved for the Osraed Body. They were of a clever construct; each gallery could be divided in twain and the section furthest from the Council table swung in so that it sat at right angles to its stationary twin. It gave the members of the Body seated there nearer access to the Council in a closed session. But today's session was open to the public and the Osraed boxes lay against their respective walls so the audience in the public gallery could view the proceedings.

It was to that audience that Ealad-hach's eyes moved, trying to pick out faces down the length of the hall. He saw the Lorimers and their daughter, Aine, in the first tier, waiting for her turn in the witness box. She was no longer a good witness, but she would be offset by Doireann Spenser and Brys-a-Lach. Phelan Backstere had proved a disappointment; claiming a bad throat, he declined to testify. Ealad-hach contemplated Aine-mac-Lorimer's flushed face. The girl was obviously unstable — her peculiar dreams were ample testimony to that. Perhaps he could lay those at Taminy's door, as well.

He saw Saxan, then, speaking over the balustrade to his wife and daughter. Iseabal . . . yes, he might call her out — show how Taminy had seduced her — but only if it was necessary. He had plans to make his key point deftly. Two important and unimpeachable witnesses were all he needed to do that.

He was annoyed to note that the Hillwild Ren and his

daughter were present. He considered having them sent away, but realized such a move would hardly conduce to his popularity. It would suffice to prevent their testimony. He could not have them spouting off about their dreams and visions here.

He had just let the curtain slip from his fingers when he glimpsed a face that sent daggers of chill all the way to his soul. Eyes like the cold, silver sky of twilight peered at him out of a face the sun had darkened to maple, a face framed by hair of light-drinking black. It was the smile that wounded him deepest — the knowing, watchful smile. It held every mystery he had ever encountered and divulged nothing.

It was a striking face, and one he knew, for he had dreamed it, just as he had dreamed Taminy's. It was the face of a nightmare, the face of another Wicke from another time. He struggled for a name; it eluded him, lost in the rolls of a history that was nearly two centuries old.

No. He gathered himself, closed his eyes, licked his lips. It wasn't possible. No more than Taminy-a-Cuinn possible.

Hand shaking, he pulled back the curtain a second time and peered across the room. He relaxed. No, of course it wasn't the same girl. This was no cailin; this was a mature woman — not aged, but much older than the Wicke of his dream. The skin was sun-browned and wrinkling, the hair iron grey, not black. Still, the eyes were that fierce, the smile that unreadable.

A hand clamped on his shoulder, making him jump and choke. Osraed Eadmund blinked at him apologetically. "I'm sorry, Osraed, but Calach is here; we can begin."

Ealad-hach nodded, patting his portfolio, adjusting his prayer chain, and cursing whatever foul daemon had tricked his eyes into seeing some long-dead Wicke girl.

Walking to the little wooden stand she would inhabit during the inquiry, Taminy had felt the hush in the chamber as a physical presence. She knew the feeling well. On more than one occasion her appearance in a room had caused all conversations to cease, breaths to be drawn, eyes to be narrowed balefully, suspiciously, speculatively.

When the hair on her neck rose and her spine tingled and her knees threatened treason, she remembered that not all of those eyes were hostile.

Seated now, alone in her box, with Wyth and Bevol at floor-level below her, she dared to glance down the room into the public gallery. She saw Iseabal and Aine and, above them in the second tier, Catahn and Desary Hillwild. She could close her eyes and still see the Hillwild there, see them with a sense clearer and sharper than sight. Aidan, the Hillwild called it — "little fire" — and it made flames of both the Ren and his daughter. But, above them, in the third tier, was a Sun. She was older, her hair shot through with grey, but Taminy knew her, would have known her if two hundred years had passed since their last meeting instead of a century. They exchanged a long look and Taminy recalled another Exchange — a seaside Exchange of flesh for Eibhilin glory.

She was still lost in that gaze when Osraed Calach began to read the charges. There were three: promoting Wicke Craft, perversion of the Divine Art, and heresy. The charge that she had willfully harmed Aine-mac-Lorimer had fallen by the wayside.

Witnesses came forward then, to point fingers and make claims. People she barely knew swore they had seen her walking upon the air or conversing with strange animals in the wood. Some she did know claimed she was misleading their children, teaching them strange home magics and stranger philosophies, suggesting that the Meri might visit other shores or the Gwenwyvar appear in the pools of the Gyldan-baenn as the Gwyr. Taminy listened attentively to all, trying not to react to the shrill accusations, trying not to cry out against the lies or beg to correct the half-truths. Presumably, she would have a turn, a time when Bevol and Wyth would produce those who would speak kindly of her.

Ealad-hach, oddly, did not pursue the stories his witnesses told. He merely let them pass, one after the other, until their tales were exhausted. It was then that he called down Osraed Saxan and bid him describe Aine-mac-Lorimer's accident and Taminy's subsequent appearance and performance of the Infusion Weave. Just that, nothing more; he asked no questions. And so, Osraed Torridon followed the Cirkemaster to the witness box amid speculative murmurs.

"Osraed," Ealad-hach said, his voice smooth as the velvet of his chamber robes, "does our brother Saxan do this episode justice?"

Torridon nodded, lank, just-greying locks brushing his shoulders. "Yes. It happened, incredibly, just as he said."

"The girl, Taminy, re-animated Aine-mac-Lorimer with an Infusion Weave you had neither heard nor seen before."

"Yes."

"Tell me, Osraed, why did you not perform such an Infusion on the girl?"

Torridon blushed. "I . . . couldn't do it."

"You *couldn't* do it?"

"No. The damage to the girl's neck and throat was severe — the Heal Tell revealed that. I tried a Healweave. It simply didn't work."

"Yet this girl not only repaired the damage you say was so severe, she restored life to the body?"

"Yes."

"She did something, then, that was beyond your Gift as an Osraed."

"Again, yes."

"And what sort of being could accomplish that?"

Torridon wriggled in his robes, glancing aslant at Taminy. "I couldn't say. . . . We are told the Gwenwyvar has such powers."

"*The Gwenwyvar?*" Ealad-hach had clearly not expected such a reply, but recovered himself immediately. "The Gwenwyvar, brother, is seen only on Pilgrimage by especially perceptive Prentices. Are you suggesting that she has abandoned her woodland environs and put on flesh?"

Torridon blanched. "I said, I don't know what sort of being she is. I know only that she possesses a Gift I do not."

"Thank you, Osraed Torridon, for you bring up a most critical point. I will now inform you, and the Body, what this cailin claims, for it is more strange, more outrageous, than even you suggest."

"I do not suggest — " Torridon began, but Ealad-hach, rising from his place at the Council table, waved him a dismissal. The old Tradist came to stand before Taminy, putting her even more on display, while she, feeling a strange awakening at the core, ever aware of the tingling web of support that touched her from a handful of souls, watched in silence.

"This girl you see before you, esteemed Osraed, claims to be none other than — " He paused, rubbing his fingers together as if he held her soul between them. "Well . . . " — he looked from one of the twin Osraed galleries to the other — "let us hear it from her own lips." He turned on her, eyes hawk keen. "Who are you, girl? What is your name?"

"Taminy, sir."

"Just Taminy? Oh, surely not. What is your *family* name, cailin?"

"Cuinn."

"Ah, and your father's name was — ?"

"Coluim-a-Cuinn." She had to admire the way he dragged it out, the way he prolonged the moment so that the realization would gather like a storm swell. Already she could see the slow dawn of recognition in the eyes of those Osraed who knew Nairne's history well; Osraed Saxan's face was near pale as the whites of his eyes.

"And what was his profession?"

"He was Osraed."

"And?" He cycled one hand as if to hurry her along.

"And Cirkemaster — "

"Of?"

"Of Nairnecirke, sir. He was Cirkemaster of Nairne."

Confusion tumbled through the room. Saxan was Cirkemaster of Nairne, and before him had been Osraed Bonar. What was this strange child intimating?

"And in what year did he last hold that position?"

How you relish this, she thought. *How you enjoy this moment of revelation.* "He retired to Ochanshrine . . . " — she swept the galleries with her eyes and found she

relished the moment almost as much as Ealad-hach did —
" . . . in the Year of Pilgrimage four hundred ninety."

The tide of amazement in the room crested on a unified
gasp. Taminy could scent the various forms of incredulity
that rode that crest. Ealad-hach rode it, too, throwing out
his next words while the surge of astonishment was at its
peak.

"Then, are you that Taminy-a-Cuinn, daughter of
Osraed Coluim-a-Cuinn, who took an unlawful Pilgrimage
to the Sea in that same year?"

"Yes, I am." She thrilled to say those words before all
these witnesses. They were vindication and challenge.

"But it was supposed," continued Ealad-hach over the
swell of noise in the room, "that Taminy-a-Cuinn drowned
one hundred fifteen years ago. You don't appear to have
drowned."

"I didn't drown, Osraed."

"Then what did happen to you?"

"The Meri did not want me as a Teacher of Her Lord's
word. She wanted me as a vessel for Her own spirit. I
entered the Sea and was transformed, absorbed, infused.
The Emerald Meri was manifest in me."

A hurricane might have been gentler than the storm
those words loosed. Taminy rode out the human gale in
silence, feeling momentarily small and alien. But within
the small, the alien, lay a tiny seed of Eibhilin light,
burning surely. The hurricane would not touch that.

When order was restored, Osraed Parthelan spoke out
in evident disgust. "This inquiry is absurd. Could not the
Council see what is perfectly obvious? This child is mad."

Ealad-hach smiled at his brother Osraed. It was a smile
that Taminy had come to mistrust. "That simple, is it? The
child is mad? Explain to me, Osraed Parthelan, how
madness gives one power to restore the dead to life."

Parthelan blanched, glanced at Taminy and reseated
himself anonymously amidst the Body.

"Well, Osraed?" asked Ealad-hach, parading between
the galleries. "What say you?"

Saxan rose, now, his face pallid. "You are asking us to
condemn this child as a Wicke?"

"Child?" repeated Ealad-hach. "By her own testimony, she is something in the order of one hundred thirty-two years old. That same testimony condemns her as something considerably more potent and evil than a mere Wicke."

"No!" Saxan protested. "I have never known her to do evil. Nor can I believe evil of her. She is strong in the Art — Gifted. She's counseled my daughter in the use of her own Gift, and counseled her wisely. I've never heard her utter a word that was counter to Scripture."

"What?" That was Parthelan again. "What of the words we've heard her utter at this inquiry? She claims identification with the Meri, Herself. She claims divinity!"

A roar went up from every corner of the room. It was beyond Taminy not to flinch. Wyth rose from his floor-level seat and edged toward her. She allowed herself a brief smile for that unnecessary and futile bit of protectiveness. Whatever dire thing might befall her would not happen in this room, before all these eyes.

"Proof!" shouted Parthelan. "Let her prove herself!"

"Proof! Proof!" The cry was picked up, one throat at a time, until the chamber rocked with it. "Proof! Proof!"

The Council pounded for order and Ealad-hach turned to Taminy with a self-congratulatory smile. Her witnesses were now useless. There would be no pretence of attack and defense. Her position was indefensible. "You hear them, cailin. They demand proof. Proof that you are divine and not the embodiment of evil."

The moment. Taminy came to her feet and gazed about the hall, affording each Osraed face a glance. She could see now, into each mind, could plumb each heart — this one fretted after what the girls in his parish would do once wind of this reached them; that one wondered why this must happen now, when things seemed so secure; another secretly blamed the Cusp and the Cyne and his rumored excess; others' thoughts turned to banishment or, trembling, to something much more final. Yet, a handful of hearts held neither punishment nor blame, but a willingness, however slight, to consider the possibility that she might be telling the truth. She could count them on the fingers of her hands.

"Have I claimed divinity?" she asked.

"Can you say you have not claimed it?" asked Osraed Faer-wald from his place amid the Council. "You claimed to be the Meri. If that is not a claim of divinity — "

"I said, the Emerald Meri was manifest in me. I was the vessel of that Manifestation, but not in this human form. She transformed me and, transformed, I became the channel by which She could communicate with all men. When my time ran its course, She released me and took another in my stead. Osraed Bevol brought me home."

"To what purpose?"

"To a purpose I may not reveal, because I cannot."

"You *cannot?*"

She smiled. "I am not granted all vision, Osraed."

"Do not try to win me with that imp smile, Wicke. Do you say you are *not* divine?"

"No," she said, "I'm not saying that, either. I am . . . Osmaer — Divinely Glorious. That is my station."

"But the Osmaer," objected Parthelan, "is our most holy relic. It was given to Ochan by the Meri, Herself, as a talisman — as a symbol of her purity and power."

She looked directly at him, feeling him wither beneath her gaze. "Yes."

Another ripple of outrage and astonishment circled the room and Parthelan sucked in a noisy breath. "Proof," he said.

"Aye, proof!" said his left-hand neighbor.

"A miracle, Taminy!" shouted someone from the public boxes. "Give them a miracle!"

The cry repeated itself until Calach brought it to a ragged halt. Feet shuffled, seats creaked, lips whispered the words they had been shouting: "Miracle — give us a miracle."

"Yes," said Osraed Tynedale, "let us see the dark Weaving this girl is accused of performing." He turned his eyes to Calach, who nodded. Tynedale raised his hand above his head. "Vote."

The vote was not unanimous, but enough of the Body raised their hands to carry Tynedale's demand. Wordlessly, Ealad-hach opened his belt pouch and dug about in it. A moment later, he produced a small, dried out flower head. He held it up to the light radiating from window and lightglobe.

"I have had this rose bud in my medicinal pouch for over a year. It is dessicated." He handed it into Taminy's palm. "Make it produce a bloom."

She looked at the bud. It was, indeed, dessicated — dry and lifeless. "Aine-mac-Lorimer's body was this lifeless, or nearly so, when I began my Infusion Weave. Do you imagine reviving this flower could prove more difficult?"

Heads nodded and a hum of agreement filled the room.

Ealad-hach's lips drew back in a snarl. "You are afraid to accept this challenge, cailin?"

Taminy's sigh was spirit deep. "No, Osraed. I am not afraid." She held the wrinkled thing out on the flat of her hand — low, so everyone in the room might see. There was a great shuffling and creaking as necks craned and bodies shifted forward in chairs. Before the eyes of all, a faint glow embraced the bud and, wrapped in that glow, it went from mucky brown to vivid green. Without water or soil, the thing grew and put forth a stem and leaves; it branched, produced a second bud. And the first bud, finally fat and full, gave birth to a flower of delicate white with deep gold in the velvet folds of its petals. The room gave up a long, slow sigh, drawn from hundreds of throats; the scent of that rose was as delicate and beautiful as the rose itself.

Ealad-hach's throat was silent and his face as pale as Taminy's bloom. She held it out to him. "Shall I cause the second bud to blossom, as well?"

He struck the rose from her hand. "Fraud!" he called her. "Wicke!"

"Am I both?"

The old Osraed threw himself at her, hands grasping the rail of her box and shaking it. "*Yes*, damn you, *both*! You prove nothing by this display!"

Wyth was there in an instant, defending her. "*You* demanded it of her, Osraed Ealad-hach! You gave her the test, you can hardly blame her for completing it. If she had refused, you would have called her a fraud for that!"

Ealad-hach shrugged away from the younger man, striding between the galleries toward the public tiers. "This is a mere parlor trick! No Weaving is at work here, only cheap sleight of hand."

Wyth bent to pick up the flower where it had fallen to the stone floor. Holding it aloft, he followed Ealad-hach into the center of the chamber. "Look! Is this a fraud? This rose is *real*! And it came from the dry, dead bud Osraed Ealad-hach placed in Taminy's hand!" He held the flower out to Osraed Saxan. "Is this not a real flower? Is this not, as Ealad-hach said, a rose?"

Saxan took the thing into his cupped hands and beheld it, his face paling. "Yes," he said, loudly so as to be heard above the babble of sound. "It is quite real. More than that, it drips with Eibhilin energies — see, it still glows from her touch. There is no fraud here." He turned to Ealad-hach. "Give up this charade, Osraed, and let us concern ourselves with this girl's claim . . . which you now struggle not to address."

Osraed Parthelan reached over and snatched the flower from Saxan's hands. He dropped it just as quickly. "By God, Saxan's right! This girl's plainly Wicke. Meredydd-a-Lagan might have performed such a trick as that."

"And why not?" Taminy asked, drawing all eyes back to herself. She leaned forward on the box rail, quiet in her passion, her hands outstretched and imploring. "Why not, when we are Sisters? She is as I was. A supplicant at the Shore of the Meri, she was called into the Sea of Life, embraced in the arms of glory. It was she who replaced me as the Meri's mantle. It was she whom your Prentices this Season sought, she whom only Wyth Arundel and Leal-mac-Mercer found. She who visits you with aislinn and allows you to Weave. She is my Golden Sister. And when her time is complete, she will come forth again as another takes her place. It has been this way since the beginning. Yet, those the Meri calls to embody Her spirit, you deny even the right to seek Her presence!"

The crowd howled.

"Drown her!" someone cried.

"No, *burn* her!"

"No! *Listen* to her!" The voice that roared from the public boxes belonged to the Ren Catahn. He stood, dwarfing those around him. "Night after night I have dreamed, and my daughter, also. We have seen this lady in those dreams. She is evil's blight. She is the fruit of this time, of this age, of this Cusp. She is Osmaer. Our *aidan* — our Gift — tells us this in a pure, clear voice. Don't listen to this dried up old Osraed. Listen to Taminy-Osmaer."

"But we must have proof!" cried Osraed Faer-wald, when Ealad-hach could only stand in mute, blushing rage.

Time. Taminy felt of the room and knew it was time. There was a balance here, of terror and fury and distrust and struggling belief. "I will give," she said, "whatever Sign is asked of me. Only ask it."

Ealad-hach approached her again, drawing Wyth back across the hall in his wake. "What Sign?"

"Any you choose." She gazed down into the dew dappled face; its eyes gleamed, feverish, its lips twitched. Repulsed, she raised her head and, once again, let her gaze address the Osraed Body. "Hear me, Divine Counselors. If you can agree upon a Sign that will prove I am what I claim, I will give it."

The Osraed murmured among themselves. What would constitute a Sign of proof? For what should they ask?

"But," she continued, slicing through the murmurs, "if I give the agreed upon Sign, you must *believe in me*."

"Believe? Believe . . . what?" asked Faer-wald.

Bevol, long silent, finally rose from his seat and came forward to speak, moving to the very center of the vast room. "Believe that she is none other than Taminy-a-Cuinn; Prentice one hundred years past, Emerald Meri for the last century, now returned to human form, but still in possession of the Eibhilin Light — a Light we must look to to guide us through this Cusp. In a word, brothers, Osmaer. Not divine, but divinely glorious. That is what you must accept. And your acceptance will become the foundation of a New Covenant."

Taminy had witnessed many storms at Sea, but this battered her as no physical storm could. The room unleashed a rage that hammered at her spirit and threatened to engulf her soul. Violence trembled in thoughts and tumbled from lips. The Osraed were engulfed in it, as well, some demanding her punishment, others shrilly and fearfully counseling agreement with her terms. Taminy glanced about the room; brother railed against brother, shaking fists at Ealad-hach, shaking fists at her and her two defenders.

At one end of the hall their audience watched, bright-eyed and eager for the climax; at the other, Osraed Calach began to pound upon the crescent table, trying to restore order, while beside him, the Osraed Kynan and Tynedale threatened to come to blows.

"Silence! Silence!" Calach cried, but his words were lost — swept up in the squall of human voices and tossed aside. He signaled a Council Prentice and the boy moved swiftly to man the chimes behind the Council table. The sharp tones clove the storm and humbled it, at last, to a pool of trembling eddies.

"Order!" Calach's voice could finally be heard. "We must have order!"

"Indeed we must," agreed Ealad-hach. "But we will *not* have it until we are rid of *her*." His out-thrust finger found Taminy, calm within her box.

"Then allow her to prove herself," said Bevol. "Settle this once and for all."

Ealad-hach reddened. "It would prove nothing. You said the same of Meredydd-a-Lagan. Let her take Pilgrimage, you said. Let the Meri decide her fate. Let it be decided, once and for all. That proved nothing, just as this will prove nothing but a forum for her wicked deceptions."

"She ain't wicked!" Marnie-o-Loom's voice cut shrilly through the rumble and hiss of her fellow Nairnians.

"Aye!" the Apothecary agreed.

"Aw, what do you old hags know of it?" asked someone else. "You're both half-Wicke yourselves!"

"I say we accept the challenge," said Saxan, ignoring the outburst. "How else will we know? Surely, we can devise a proof — "

"Useless," argued Parthelan. "Entirely useless. She's obviously powerful, be she Wicke or otherwise."

"Is there no difference, then?" Saxan turned to look imploringly at his fellow Osraed. "Brothers, if we fail to accept this challenge, are we not admitting we *can't tell the difference* between good and evil?"

"Saxan's right," said Osraed Tynedale. "We must surely be able to draw a distinction between darkness and Eibhilin light. And what reason have we to suspect this young woman save a handful of inconclusive rumors given us by witnesses we would normally pay no heed to? Our experience with Taminy-a-Gled is that she has used her Gift to give life, not take it. She has enemies here. Powerful though she may be, she has not harmed even one of them."

"She tried to kill a girl who was her enemy," protested Osraed Kynan.

"That's a lie!" Aine-mac-Lorimer was on her feet, hands pounding on the bannister of the public gallery. "It's a lie! She did nothing to me!" Her father grasped her wrist and reseated her roughly.

Ealad-hach turned to his brothers on the Council. "You saw my aislinn. You know this is the girl."

Tynedale shook his head. "She doesn't deny being the woman of your vision. She disputes your interpretation of it. I say we must consider the challenge or admit our own lack of discernment and wisdom."

The sound that came from Ealad-hach's throat made Taminy's heart all but melt with pity. Face sweating, pale and red in turns, eyes glittering with tears, he hop-hobbled toward the Council table. A comic figure, were he not so dangerous, so full of hate.

"We must consider nothing," he said, "but how to be eternally rid of this creature. The aislinn that revealed her was mine — MINE! And I interpret it as a sign of her complete evil. No one else may interpret it for me. *No one!* Especially not those who are bewitched and besotted by her. Not those her evil has touched!" He turned feral eyes on Bevol and Wyth, then, spittle running along his lower lip. He licked it quickly away.

"I vote with Ealad-hach," said Osraed Kynan. "We will not be manipulated by this Wicke."

"I did not ask for a vote," Calach snapped.

"Vote!" shouted someone among the Body. "I vote with Ealad-hach!"

Osraed Comyn, Hillwild, rose and pounded a beefy fist on the gallery rail. "And I vote with Tynedale and Saxan!"

More voices were raised while Calach pounded for order. In the midst of it all, Aine-mac-Lorimer came to her feet again and began a cry of "Cowards! Cowards!" Marnie and the Apothecary joined her, standing in place and shaking fists at the Osraed.

"Aye! Cowards! They daren't face her!"

"Cowards! They're afraid! Afraid of a little girl!"

The jeers mounted and did battle with warring cries of "Wicke!" and demands that Taminy be drowned or burned or banished. The battle moved to envelop the Osraed in their galleries and rose to such a pitch that even the shrill ringing of the chimes could not halt its progress.

Calach stood, helpless, amid the fury, his eyes turned to Bevol, pleading. Taminy looked up into the public boxes. There was movement there as a number of people made their way down to the floor. Her eyes scanned the top row, finding, again, the face of an elder Sister. The silver-eyed, iron-haired woman nodded once and faded away into the clamoring crowd.

On the floor, Taminy could see the Ren Catahn making his way toward her, Desary at his side. But there were others who would reach her first; two tall men in cowled robes the color of periwinkles. Taminy knew them, though she had met neither. She awaited them with curious eyes and a calm heart, her hands crossed on the bannister of her box, her ears closed to the pandemonium around her.

The men reached the box and gazed up at her through the folds of their cowls, while Wyth eyed them suspiciously in turn. Two fox faces peered up at her, enough alike to be brothers; but she knew it was a brotherhood of spirit, not of blood. Both were fair-skinned and dark-haired, one with eyes piercing pale, the other sunlit gold. She revised her assessment — fox and falcon.

The fox eyed her with open appraisal, the falcon smiled. Then he mounted her box, holding to the rail with one hand, reaching to drop his cowl with the other. The cowl fell away and a roomful of light gathered to dance on the skillfully carved facets of the Circlet upon his head.

Wyth gasped. "The Cyne!" Then, more loudly. "*The Cyne!*"

Soon half the people on the floor were bawling the words. The cry circled the room but once, reaching up into its recesses and dragging all throats to silence.

Cyne Colfre, royal falcon, gazed around the chamber, fixing all with a stern, raptor eye. "If Malcuim and Ochan, together, came before me and described this scene," he said, his voice ringing well on the tense hush, "I would not have believed it."

Taminy, her own eyes fixed on the royal profile, knew the consternation to be false. Beneath Colfre Malcuim's Circlet, gears spun intricately; beneath his periwinkle robes, a boyish eagerness gamboled and rubbed gleeful hands.

"I would not have believed it," he repeated, shaking his head. "Have you all gone mad?"

It was better than he had hoped, *dreamed*. Far better. The Osraed of Halig-liath, in their inept wisdom, had already done half his work for him. Those who had looked upon them with awe and honor now heckled and turned away with disgust. And the Osraed themselves were divided — hopelessly, passionately and impotently, divided. And all because of a seventeen year old girl.

Colfre looked on her where she stood on the deck of his galley. Looked on her with a strange, quaking mixture of anticipation and dread. She was beautiful — every bit as beautiful as he had imagined in his mind's eye. And she was gallant — ah, and heroic — standing up to the bluster and the cries for her blood. More than that, he knew, she had the Gift. She dazzled him with it; the very atmosphere around her was charged with a soft, warm lightning. A breath of the aidan, his Hillwild mother would have said. Nay, more than a breath, a storm. And he was bringing the storm to Creiddylad.

Shivering, he pushed dread aside, unread, and surveyed

the party that would accompany him down river to his capitol. She, of course, was foremost, but there was Bevol, renegade Osraed, and his boy-servant — an underfoot rascal named Skeet.

Osraed Calach had tapped the young Osraed Wyth to take Bevol's place on the Council and Triumvirate. It had infuriated the old fool, Ealad-hach and his crony, Faer-wald, but pleased the Cyne. A young man was an inexperienced man, a man who would vascillate and hesitate. And the young Osraed, like Calach, seemed quite timorous.

Colfre smiled, recalling the expression on Ealad-hach's wizened face when that appointment had been made and confirmed by the Cyne, himself. He could not despise the old man, though, for he owed him much. He, more than any other, had forced the situation with Taminy into a shape pleasing to his Cyne.

"Everyone's aboard, sire." Daimhim Feich stood beside him, now, at the galley's oaken rail. Enigmatic, his eyes moved among the crowd still roiling upon the dock.

Colfre glanced aside at him. "Are we not right to be pleased, Daimhin? Have we not taken a great stride forward today?"

Feich smiled. "We have, indeed, my lord."

"I could never have *dreamed* such a windfall. Never . . . " The Cyne let his eyes drift back along the dock, beholding faces filled with perplexity, disgust, fear, anger, even grief. One thing was certain, the eyes of the people of Nairne would never again see their Osraed as they once had. "Never," he repeated. "One might almost think . . . it was ordained."

Feich's smile rippled, assuming a slightly different shape. "One might, indeed, my lord."

The Council Chamber was empty now. Bright sunlight cascaded through the stained-glass windows above the public gallery, blazing a trail of glory across the polished agate of the floor. Ealad-hach, still seated in his place behind the crescent table, was blind to its beauty. To him, all was dark; the sun was an intrusion in the black world he inhabited.

He tried, but could not comprehend how everything had come so completely apart in his hands. No, not in his hands, for in the end, it had been ripped from them. By whom, he wasn't certain. He had laid the blame at Colfre's door initially, but when the crowd and clamor had cleared from his mind, he acknowledged the possibility that the Cyne was doing a will other than his own.

The thought terrified him. But more terrifying, still, was his own trembling impotency. He was a pile of pebbles, waiting to be scattered by the next wave — no cement to bind, annihilation its only possibility. He could do nothing against Something so strong, so ancient. That face he had seen in the crowd haunted him. One of Liusadhe's Wicke, still alive; Taminy-a-Cuinn, still alive. And able to manipulate even the Osraed — even the Meri's elect.

He had thought himself alone and was jolted by the soft sounds of feet upon the floor — encroaching, intruding, as the sunlight did, inexorably. He shifted uncomfortably and glanced toward the doors, blinking against the Sun's glare. Someone stood there in the blaze of colorful light, haloed like the Eibhilin, but obviously and solidly human. Though unable to see his face, Ealad-hach knew Wyth Arundel by his stature.

He turned his eyes away. "Come to scoff at the old fool, Osraed Wyth? Come to lay blame?"

"No, sir. Neither. I merely came to see if you were all right. This day's events have posed a great strain on all of us . . . "

Ealad-hach glanced at Wyth sharply, but his expression was lost in a warp of light and shadow. "The Council met just now, did it?"

Wyth nodded. "Just long enough to plan a meeting. Tomorrow morning, if that's agreeable to you."

"I hardly care. It's out of our hands now, isn't it?"

"There are other things to be discussed," Wyth reminded him.

Ealad-hach ignored him. "What are the others saying? Do they blame me? Is it my fault the Osraed have been censured and called into doubt?" He hadn't meant it to come out like that, so pleading, so desperate. It *wasn't* his fault, of course, but that the others might think it was . . .

"Some of them . . . blame you for . . . for pursuing Taminy so relentlessly."

Ealad-hach curled his lip. "As I suppose you do."

"Blame is too strong a word, Osraed. I suppose I . . . understand that you must do what you feel is right."

"What are they saying about me?"

"Some of them believe you were . . . over zealous. That bringing Taminy to trial was a mistake. They feel it would have been better if you had allowed time to reveal her."

"Time! There *is* no time! They're fools not to understand that! Do they think the Cyne came here of his own accord? A man who has avoided Nairne as if it was plague-ridden? He wouldn't come for Farewelling; he wouldn't receive you and Lealbhallain for the Grand Tell. Why should he come here now? Do they believe that a coincidence? Do they believe it is *he* who has taken Taminy out of our hands?"

Wyth's silhouette stiffened. "But, that's what happened, isn't it?"

Ealad-hach smiled bitterly. "Fool. You're all fools to believe that. There are powerful and awful forces at work here. Forces we dimly perceive. It is those forces that will decide the outcome, not the Cyne and not the Assembly."

"Yes," Wyth said, "that much is true."

Ealad-hach stood, quaking. "This is the Most Holy Fortress, Osraed Wyth. *This* is the most holy spot on the face of this world." He jabbed a finger at a point on the glossy table top to which the sunlight had laboriously crawled to meet shadow. "If we could not control those forces here, where and how and when shall we ever control them?"

Wyth shook his head. "The evil is not what you imagine it to be, Osraed. You imagine a friend your enemy and prepare to take an enemy to your bosom. But you are right, I think, in one thing — Taminy is not for us to control, or perhaps even to understand."

"Taminy!" He spat the name from his lips. "Such colossal arrogance! To call herself Osmaer — to name herself after the most sacred relic — !" Ealad-hach paused, his hand in mid-gesture. He could see it, as clear as he could see the Sun in the sky over Nairne — the thing that must surely, *in the right hands,* become the Wicke Cwen's nemesis.

He lowered his arm; calm descended with it. He smoothed his chamber robes with careful fingers. "Have I any allies, Osraed Wyth?"

"You have."

"You don't lie to me. Why not?"

"Lying dishonors both the liar and the one lied to. I have no wish to dishonor myself or you."

"Is Eadmund among them?"

"You would have to ask Eadmund, sir. He is a quiet man."

Ealad-hach curled his lip. "He is a weak man. Has he left yet for the Assembly in Creiddylad?"

"He's in his chambers packing. Shall I have him called?"

Ealad-hach peered up at Wyth through the brilliant rainbow haze of sunlit dust motes that surrounded him. "Such a strange lad, you are, even now . . . *especially* now."

"Shall I — ?"

"No. I will find him myself." He pushed back his chair then, with a difficulty he refused to show, and left the scene of his humiliation behind.

Wyth put his feet up on the hearth fender and listened to the complete quiet of the house. He imagined that on most evenings it was full of laughter and life and duans. Taminy singing and Gwynet Weaving and Bevol telling tales and Skeet . . . doing whatever it was Skeet did. Playing tricks, Wyth thought. He surely played tricks upon the girls and his Master, making laughter bubble from their lips and souls. But now . . .

He stretched in Bevol's chair and found it fit his lanky frame quite well. Bevol and Skeet and Taminy were miles down river floating toward the Jewel, while poor Gwynet cried herself to sleep upstairs, alone. They were alone together. Gwynet had no family and Wyth's had all but disowned him after he'd come home and announced he'd be taking up Bevol's residence and guardianship of Gwynet until the older Osraed's return.

His mother had begged him to bring Gwynet and stay under her roof at first and, flattered, he considered it . . . until it became clear that she intended to treat Gwynet like a unwanted pet and himself like a trophy. On Osraed Council, now, by God; member pro-tem of the Triumvirate; nominally in charge of Halig-liath. She wanted to invite the entire province to come gawk at him.

But she'd tried to send Gwynet to the kitchen for dinner, making asides about the taint of "that Wicke girl," and Wyth, more furious than he thought he could ever be, took the little girl and went to Gled Manor.

And here I will stay. He gazed around at the high ceiling, cob-webbed and spattered with firelight. *And wait.*

CHAPTER 15

Excerpt from *A History of the Royal House*, by Osraed Tynedale

Cyne Siolta was dead. At the age of nine, Riagan Thearl was made Cyneric and set before the Stone. His Regents were three — his mother, Cwen Goscelin; her dead husband's Durweard, Harac; and the Chancellor, Diomasach Claeg. This arrangement caused some perplexity of government since the Cwen's co-partners were given to overstepping the bounds of their respective stations. . . .

The subtle battle between Harac and Diomasach grew more earnest until, finally, the Claeg contrived to separate the Cyneric from his mother. . . . It took a time of pretending to bow to the Chancellor's will before Goscelin was even allowed to speak to her boy. She made no attempt to subvert him, but instead bided her time. Then, under the guise of taking a pilgrimage to Ochanshrine, the Cwen left Castle Mertuile with her son concealed in a clothing chest. But, instead of heading for the Shrine, she made-upriver for Halig-liath.

❖   ❖   ❖

Leal awoke from troubling dreams to a troubling reality. Before breakfast, Buach had spread the tell throughout Care House: the Cyne was bringing the Nairnian Wicke to Creiddylad.

Lealbhallain was astonished, not because of the news, but because he'd already known, bone deep, that Taminy-a-Gled was on her way here and that Osraed Bevol was with her. He was disturbed by the news, disturbed that it came by way of popular rumor. The streets literally buzzed, according to Buach, despite the fact that the Cyne had left Nairne only the evening before, despite the fact that he and his party would not arrive in Creiddylad until the day after next.

It was as if the entire city of Creiddylad had been made party to Leal's aislinn — a vision thrust on him in some way by Wyth Arundel, and which seemed to invade his thoughts further, moment by moment. That was impossible, of course, and Leal couldn't help but wonder: where had the rumors arisen? According to Buach's testimony, they were all over the Cyne's Market.

Duty drew Leal there in the late morning, where he shopped for medicinal herbs and where he heard the same tell repeated ad infinitum with various permutations: the Wicke had been near death at the hands of the Nairnian villagers when the Cyne had rescued her — he'd saved her right from the Cirke chime tower where they'd planned to hang her; or he'd saved her from the Council Chamber where the Osraed were planning to burn her; or he'd come across her abandoned in a wooded glen and been bewicked by her beauty; or . . .

Curious, Leal asked a vegetable-pinching merchant where he'd heard the story, and was pointed toward a fish vendor. That was it, then, Leal thought. The story must have floated down river on the weeklies from Nairne. He asked the fish vendor, anyway, and got an unexpected reply.

"Ah, that! Why the Gatekeep told me when I came in this morning. 'Have you heard,' he says, 'about the doings in Nairne?' Well, I'd heard plenty of Nairne these last weeks, I'd say, with all this about cailin taking the Kiss — Lord! what a stew! But you'd know about all that, young Osraed."

"The Wicke?" prompted Leal.

"Oh, aye, that. Saucy bit of news, isn't it? Gatekeep had it the poor girl was headed for the gallows when the Cyne stepped in and took her out of Osraed hands." He paused, looking suddenly uncomfortable. "No offense, Osraed, but that's the tell. They'll be here day after tomorrow. It's going to the Hall, or so I've heard."

"The Gatekeep told you?" asked Leal and the vendor nodded.

He didn't talk to the Gatekeep himself, but dispatched one of the Care House orphans to it. He wasn't sure the man would be quite so open with an Osraed, and he was more than open with the ragged little urchin who asked him, wide-eyed, all about the Wicke-lady coming from the east.

"Pigeons," said the child, dark eyes like saucers in her pale face. "They got the tell by pigeons late last night."

Leal frowned, puzzled. "The gatekeepers?"

"No, no! In the castle. At Mertuile. Gatekeep said the Cyne's Steward told him before he opened up the Market grounds this morning. Pigeons!" she repeated, awfully impressed. "Be they magical pigeons d'you think, Osraed Leal?"

He shook his head absently. "I don't suppose so . . . " The child's face rippled with obvious disappointment. "Then, again, I suppose they could be magical pigeons."

The little girl brightened. "Well, at least they be *royal* ones. That's almost magical."

She went off to play among the bright market stalls then, leaving Leal surrounded with his own uneasy thoughts. Royal courier pigeons, magical or not, had brought the rumor of Nairne's Wicke to Creiddylad — a rumor it seemed Cyne Colfre had some interest in spreading.

She stood in the galley's prow looking as if she had been carved there — a living, breathing figurehead. That was appropriate, he thought, for a figurehead she would become. He shook the cynical thoughts aside and settled himself near her along the starboard rail, where he could see her in full profile. He took out a graphus and, balancing his drawing pad on one knee, he began to sketch her.

She was wearing green for her entry into Creiddylad; he had made certain of it. The dress was simple — sinfully so, when one considered who wore it — but of the most vivid green he could imagine. It was a color he could not capture, for his oilsticks were in his studio at Mertuile and he had only graphus and smudges. Against that green, her yard or so of pale gold hair was a banner of precious metal silk and her eyes, if she would only look at him, would be emeralds.

His graphus stilled. She *was* looking at him. His thumb moved reflexively to rub the chalcedony set into the gold band on his middle finger — proof against Wicke. He resisted the reflex and nearly dropped the graphus. "Good morning," he said and smiled. He had a dazzling smile and knew it; many women had told him. "Please don't move. I wanted to capture you just as you were."

She responded with an almost courtly bowing of her head (although it was hardly deep enough to be awarded a Cyne), and turned her face down river again, not quite hiding her smile.

Tease, he thought, and continued his sketch. "What were you thinking before I interrupted you?"

"I was listening to the duans the river sings."

That raised an eyebrow. "Duans? So, the mighty Halig-tyne is a Weaver of inyx, is it?"

"Of course. Listen. You can hear it."

He did listen and heard the rush of the water beneath the keel, the lapping of wavelets as they curled away from the galley's bluff prow, the soft, silken sound of wind in the trees along the shore, the flutter of the loose sails on their spars.

"Duans, eh? And what do they Weave?"

"Peace. Contentment. Solace. Whatever inyx is needed."

"Perhaps I think they are just the inarticulate yammerings of nature. Saying nothing; meaning nothing."

She didn't rise to his bait. "Your ancestors would disagree with you, Cyne Colfre."

"My ancestors?"

"Aye. Cyne Paeccs, for example. Where would he have been without the yammerings of the river? Imagine him, the brave young man, leading his little family out of besieged Mertuile, down the steep cliff path, out to his galley on the Halig-tyne. What chance would he have had to glide unseen past his enemies if Ochan and the river hadn't sung to each other? Dorchaidhe Feich was a mighty warrior and peerlessly cunning. What else but a Weaving could cause those sharp eyes to miss such a thing as the Malcuim's royal galley creeping through his blockade?"

"Legend," said Colfre. "Myth. It was a fog. A simple river mist."

"Quite a fog. And was it a simple river mist that concealed Cwen Goscelin the Just when she spirited little Thearl away from his kidnappers?"

"A simple river mist," he repeated, smiling.

"To muffle the sound of oars in their locks? To quiet the cry of a babe in a box?"

Colfre chuckled. "I know the old lay. And you obviously know your legends. But they *are* only legends." She didn't answer, so he continued, applying a smudge to the penciled lines of her dress. "And you believe in them, don't you?"

"Aye."

"Aren't you afraid your Cyne will think you a simpleton?"

"Do you fear me thinking you a jade?"

He did fear it. "Do you think me a jade?" She didn't answer, so he asked, "Do you also believe in your own mythology, Taminy-a-Cuinn?" He watched her face closely, but it gave up nothing.

"My mythology," she repeated.

"Do you believe you are one hundred thirty-some-odd-years-old?"

"I have little choice."

"And that you spent one hundred fifteen of those years . . . beneath the Sea?"

"*In* the Sea," she said. "In the Sea of Life. The spiritual fact underlies the physical one."

"You were a silkie."

"I was not."

"Ah, no. You were the *Meri*."

"I was."

"And what is that? Explain it to me."

"When I cannot explain it to myself?"

"You perplex me."

"I perplex myself," she said. "In that Form I contained all things and comprehended all things. In this form, I am merely aware that I once comprehended them. I am memories and yearnings and bright flashes of meaning. But I know what I was and why. I was Caraid-land's Beloved. . . . I was *your* Beloved, Colfre Malcuim. Why did you not return My love?"

He stopped sketching and stared at the beautiful profile, sudden desire struggling with that niggling sense of dread. He laughed, falsely. "I should have you thrown oversides for that heretical outburst, young woman, but I've not finished my sketch." He returned to it, then, but the graphus refused to behave.

"Will you make a mural of me, Cyne Colfre?" she asked. "Will I share a wall with your kinswoman, Goscelin, and little Thearl in his clothes chest? Will you paint me as a legend, also?"

The dread doubled. "How do you know I have painted the Flight of Thearl?"

In answer she merely turned her face to him and smiled. It was a girl's smile, innocent and perverse and enigmatic.

He closed the drawing pad. "We'll arrive soon. I must go below and prepare."

"Cyne Colfre." She stopped him before he reached the forward cabin. "Why do you bring me to Creiddylad?"

"You don't know?"

"Why?"

His smile did not fit his lips well. "To make a mural of you, perhaps. Or perhaps, a legend."

He went below then, only to half-collide with Osraed Bevol, whose insolent smile and barely appropriate greeting set his teeth on edge. *Damn the man*, he thought, for he knew that to his late father's spiritual advisor, he would forever be "Ciarda's little boy." He ground his teeth and swore again, consoling himself that to Creiddylad, he would soon be Cyne Colfre Malcuim, Peacemaker, Savior of the Innocent, by the grace of God, Divine Ruler of Caraid-land.

"Osric." He whispered the word lovingly. Divine Ruler. He would be that. All eyes would see him as that. All hearts would love him as that. Only one obstacle remained between him and that blessed title — the Osraed of Halig-liath. And Taminy, whoever or whatever she was, would help him remove it.

The shore, the docks, the riverside promenades, all teemed with agitated bits of color. Skeet made a deft little sign over his heart. "All the *people!*" He glanced up at Taminy. "You've an audience again today, mistress."

She quivered inside — quivered like that thrumming mass of curiosity onshore. Osraed Bevol's hand tightened on hers; she squeezed it back, anchoring upon it. They debarked under the scrutiny of countless eyes. Necks craned, fingers pointed, mouths babbled. The "Wicke of Nairne" was now "the Cyne's Wicke," and Colfre let his stewardship be known by personally escorting her ashore and to the open carriages awaiting them on the dock. He seated her on the high rear seat of the first carriage and took up a place beside her. The Durweard Feich took the second carriage with Bevol and Skeet, while guards kept the crowds at bay.

From her high perch, Taminy looked down into a sea of faces, curiosity eddying around her in rising waves, threatening to overwhelm. She pulled her senses away and glanced aside at Cyne Colfre. Without, he was the essence of calm dignity, regal savior of the maligned village girl, upholder of Caraidin justice. Within, the gleeful boy paraded, waving, growing drunk on the inquisitive stares. His eyes burned with a fire so hot Taminy could not bear to look at it. She turned her head away and sought the spires of Mertuile. She found them, held them with her eyes until the carriage hove onto the Cyne's Way. Its cobbled miles were lined with more citizens from every level of society. Beggars rubbed shoulders with Eiric and forgot to beg; merchants pressed close to paupers and neglected to disapprove.

Taminy scanned the faces in wonder, then turned her eyes to her destination.

Ahead, high up on its jag of rock, Mertuile sat enthroned, awaiting her arrival. Towers soared above their protective walls, wearing sheaths of pale marble and crowns of precious metals, beaten smooth and gleaming by craftsmen's skill. Gold, silver, copper shone in a diadem of blinding splendor beneath the green Malcuim banners.

Colfre looked down at her and murmured, "Welcome to my Jewel, Taminy."

The staring crowds did not dwindle until the entourage was secure within the castle's inner ward. Only then, when the inner portcullis fell to behind them, were they without hordes of onlookers. But there were watchers, still; servants peered from their doorways and children from their corners; soldiers threw sly glances from a pretence of disinterest. And somewhere, high up, a pair of eyes — no, two — looked down in curiosity and suspicion, respectively.

Taminy raised her eyes to the facade of the great edifice. There, in that window. . . . The watchers withdrew — suspicion, then curiosity — and Durweard Feich came to hand her down from the carriage.

They placed her in rooms off a broad, muraled corridor far removed from the chambers Osraed Bevol shared with Skeet. It was the royal wing, the Durweard assured her, and left her alone in a bedroom the size of the entire upper floor of the manse at Nairnecirke. There was a long balcony on which to stroll, but Taminy quickly discovered it was open to the view of a large portion of both the inner and outer wards of the castle. She sat — in the window seat, because the couches and bed would have swallowed her — and waited for Mertuile to make a move.

"I wouldn't blame you if you didn't believe me," Leal said, willing his feet to move faster up the cobbled way.

"I *believe* you, Osraed Leal!" Fhada panted and glanced up at Mertuile's towering flank. "God bless me, I think *I* even knew he was here. I dreamed last night for the first time in years."

"Oh, you've dreamed, Osraed Fhada, but last night you let yourself *remember*."

Fhada graced his young companion with a sharp glance. "It wiggles my insides when you say things like that, Leal."

Leal blushed, realizing he had spoken without thinking. "I'm sorry, sir."

"No. Don't apologize. It's good for me."

They had puffed their way up to the outer gatehouse by this time and presented themselves to the Gatekeep. Leal spoke, being less winded than his companion. "The Osraed Lealbhallain and Fhada to see the Osraed Bevol."

"Osraed Bevol?" repeated the Gatekeep.

"He arrived this morning from Nairne with Cyne Colfre and Taminy — the — the girl . . . ?"

The man nodded. "Oh, aye. Well, Osraed, all due respects, but I've had no orders about visitors for the Osraed."

"Well then, be so good as to ask, would you?" Fhada smiled affably. "This is very important."

The Gatekeep nodded again and called to one of his men to run courier for him. Meanwhile, he escorted Leal and Fhada into the outer ward and bid them sit in a small garden area along the wall.

"Is it my imagination," asked Fhada, "or are we drawing more attention than we usually would?"

Leal swept the broad outer area of the castle, eyes sharp. Fhada was right; around and about Mertuile's little warren of shops, eyes fixed on the two Osraed and mouths fluttered.

"What's happened?" Fhada asked. "Can the rumors about the Wicke be true? Or . . . "

Leal glanced at the elder Osraed. "Or is it a smoke screen?"

"He would like us to take less notice of his doings in the Cirke, I'm sure. You know this girl, Leal. Do you think she's Wicke?"

Leal shook his head. "I know her hardly at all. But if Osraed Bevol is her champion, then she's no Wicke."

"Good enough," said Fhada, and leaned back against the slats of the bench they shared.

"The courier," Leal murmured as that gentleman hastened toward them cross-court.

"Begging pardon, Osraed," — the man bowed deeply from the waist, his eyes darting nervously back over his shoulder — "but the Cyne's Durweard bids me tell you Osraed Bevol may receive no visitors. At least, that is, until after the General Assembly meets."

"The General Assembly?" Fhada repeated. "To try an alleged Wicke?"

"To try them that tried her in Nairne's my guess, Osraed." The man reddened. "But that's only a guess of mine. Based on hearsay . . . I'm sure the Cyne will make an announcement. But until then, his guests are receiving no visitors."

Guests, not prisoners. Leal rose.

Fhada echoed the movement. "When's the Hall scheduled to convene? . . . A guess will suffice, sir," he added, when the guard hesitated.

"A week from today, Osraed Fhada. Giving the members time to arrive."

"What about the time it takes to give the Call?"

"Call's been given, Osraed. Two days ago."

"Two days," Fhada repeated as he and Leal wandered back to Care House. "Colfre was in Nairne two days ago."

Leal nodded. "Pigeons," he said. "Magic pigeons."

"Do we go to Ladhar?"

"Would it do any good?"

Fhada sighed. "How impotent I feel. Is there nothing we can do?"

"We are Osraed," Leal said, and felt it in his gut for perhaps the first time. "There is always something we can do. If they will not let us see Bevol face to face, then we will see him aislinn to aislinn."

As if by silent consensus, the two walked faster.

Taminy felt the approach long before the door opened, sensed the war between curiosity and courtesy and a peculiar bristling resentment. Several times resolve wavered, but at last it won out and there was a tentative knock at her chamber door. The door opened before she could respond, though, and she turned her head to see a boy standing there, regarding her with an expression that was at once eager and sullen. He was about eleven, she guessed, and had thick, dark hair and tawny eyes that appraised her boldly. Resentment smoldered in those eyes. She rose to meet it, coming to stand demurely in the center of the chamber.

"You must be Airleas," she said.

"*Riagan* Airleas . . . And you must be Colfre's Wicke."

"I'm no one's Wicke."

"You're pretty," he said, and did not mean it as a compliment.

"You're angry. Can you tell me why? I haven't done anything."

He smiled — or rather smirked — his mouth curling wryly. "You don't have to do anything. Colfre will do it all."

"You don't call him 'father.'"

"Why should I? He's less a father to me than Daimhin is."

"I see."

"I doubt it." He stepped into the room. "Are you a Wicke?"

"I already told you — no."

"You said you weren't *anyone's* Wicke. There's a difference. So, you aren't a Wicke. You can't do inyx?"

His disappointment was so obvious, Taminy couldn't repress a smile. "I didn't say that. I can Weave."

"But that makes you — "

"No. There's a difference."

"Show me." He folded his arms across his chest, eyes narrowed.

Taminy laughed, delighted by his audacity.

The boy lifted one foot, then lowered it, unwilling to give in to a display of temper. "Why is that funny?"

Taminy sobered with an effort. "Sorry, Riagan Airleas. What would you like me to do?"

His arms unfolded into an uncertain gesture. "I don't know. What *can* you do?" Then: "Make a — a catamount appear . . . there." He pointed at the carpet between them.

"A catamount? Oh, I think that would be dangerous."

"Oh, well . . . a buck deer, then."

"On this lovely carpet?"

"You can send it away again, right after."

"I've never Woven a buck deer. I don't usually use the Art that way."

"Then how do you use it?"

"For healing, for seeing the unseeable, for warding against ill."

He considered that. "Can you show me what my father's doing?"

"That could be almost as dangerous as the catamount."

He glared at her, mouth open to retort, but she stilled him with a gesture. "Look," she said and stepped onto the carpet, her toes just touching the outer edge of a great, round medallion pattern woven into its center. She held her hand out, palm down, and closed her eyes. Colfre. She sought him. Found him one floor below. Her eyes opened and she began to sing, using words from a tongue more ancient than most Caraidin knew. "Chi mi . . . Chi mi . . . Chi mi na Colfre. Chi mi, clares, nam Malcuim Cyne."

Beneath her palm, motes of light rose and fell as if the dust were illumined, moving in sourceless sunlight. The boy's golden eyes seemed to reflect those motes, following their slow coils in fascination. The motes took on color, solidity, form. In three breaths, no more, they could both see the white-clad figure gamboling in a haze of light, surrounded by a riot of color — face, sweat polished, eyes gleaming.

"The murals." Airleas stepped back from the aislinn, his fascination collapsing into feigned boredom. "You can make it go away now."

"Airleas, what are you doing in here? Make what go away?" The woman in the doorway was beautiful. Petite, she had hair the color of honey and eyes of liquid blue. Those eyes were now focused on the image suspended between Taminy's palm and the carpet. "So, you *are* Gifted. I hadn't believed it."

Taminy withdrew her hand, dissolving the aislinn, and bowed her head respectfully, but the Cwen Toireasa took no notice. "You shouldn't be here, Airleas," she told the boy. "Please go down to dinner now."

"It won't be ready, yet."

"Please, Airleas."

"Yes, mother." The Riagan gave Taminy one last glance, then obeyed, slipping out past the Cwen, who continued to regard her with a cool, blue gaze. "My husband tells me you were falsely accused of being Wicke."

"Yes, mistress."

"Yet, you perform this . . . display before my son." She gestured at the empty air above the carpet.

"I am, as you said, Gifted. That does not make me Wicke."

The Cwen smiled tightly. "That would disappoint my husband. He's half Hillwild, you know. He quite fancies Wicke. More than that, I believe he sometimes fancies he *is* one." She turned to go, but paused just outside the door. "It doesn't do to disappoint Colfre Malcuim. But perhaps you already know that."

"I don't understand you, mistress."

The Cwen laughed. The sound was humorless and flat. "Please, girl, don't pretend with me. You insult both of us." She disappeared down the corridor, leaving Taminy to puzzle over her antipathy.

The midday meal was a tense experience and Colfre was glad to at last be able to lead Taminy away from the table and show her his domain. She was interested, he thought, but not as impressed as a young village girl should have been.

He showed her the Goscelin mural; she behaved as if she'd seen it before. He supposed he should have expected that. He took her to the Blue Pavilion; she said only, "It's very beautiful." He told her the design was his; she complimented him on his cleverness and artistry. That pleased him, but throughout their tour, he felt as if a barrier existed around her — a shroud of cool light that held her aloof. At last, he took her for a walk along the top of the inner curtain and began to speak to her of the future.

"In a week's time," he said, "the General Assembly will meet. Do you understand why?"

"You want them to find me innocent of heresy."

"*I* want? Is that what this is about, do you think?"

"Isn't it?" She stopped walking and leaned against the parapet, gazing down into the outer ward.

He wasn't certain whether he should find her insolent or disturbing. "What I want is to see justice done. The Assembly will decide whether the Osraed over-stepped their bounds. If it were up to me, alone, I would proclaim your innocence from the Throne and that would be that. But I think you understand that this is something that must be decided by the Hall and the Throne together."

"Oh, I do understand. But what of the Osraed?" She was looking at him now, green eyes opaque.

"They're represented in the Hall. . . . Does that worry you? They make up only a fourth of its membership."

"*That* doesn't worry me, no."

He didn't miss the inflection. "But something does." *Which means you are not all-powerful.* She declined to answer, so he continued, "Your claim is . . . startling, to say the least. I guarantee it will shock the Assembly."

"It doesn't seem to shock you."

He opened his mouth to admit it bemused him considerably, then thought better of it. "No. It doesn't shock me. But then, we are in a Cusp. In these times, one must expect the unexpected. The Osraed were caught unprepared. They refused to see you for what you are — to their detriment. Perhaps they now realize their mistake. But recognizing their own error in judgement doesn't mean they will accept you. Chances are, they'll now martial their forces against you, attempt to try you again in the Hall. That is why strategy is important."

She looked at him aslant, then began strolling the parapet again, moving toward the suspended walkway that linked the inner and out walls of the castle. "Strategy," she repeated.

"Indeed." He fell into step beside her. "And I believe your strategy should be silence. Say nothing. Let the Osraed accuse if they will. Let my testimony and Daimhin Feich's pass without comment, and say nothing."

"And how will that exonerate me?"

"The Hall is a representative body, Taminy. It is expressive of popular sentiment. Especially where the Eiric and Ministers are concerned. By the time the Hall convenes, the people of Creiddylad and its environs will know you on sight and by deed. Beyond Creiddylad, you will be known by reputation. And you will need to utter no words of defense, because the members of the Hall will read your defense in the faces of their people. And their Cyne."

They had crossed over the outer ward now, and stood on the broad walk near the gatehouse that overlooked the Cyne's Market.

"All that," Taminy said, "in a week."

Colfre smiled at her. How sweet she was, how little she understood the dynamics of statesmanship. He directed her gaze over the parapet to the Market grounds below. There, people had seen them and stopped to stare and point. A small crowd began to cluster in the shadow of Mertuile.

"Look, Taminy. Already, people are drawn to gaze at you. Where you go, they will gather, because of what they've seen and heard. Your story has been spread far and wide, my dear. The people know of you. Soon they will come to care about you." *I have seen to it*, he wanted to add, but did not, preferring his own manipulations to be at least a little obscured.

Taminy leaned out over the wall, her long hair a streaming white-gold banner in the Sea breeze, her cheeks flushed to rose by its briskness. She raised a hand and waved to the people below. They, in turn, waved back, some removing hats and fanning them overhead.

Colfre stood back and watched, pleased, thinking that she began to understand his intention. "Tomorrow," he told her, "you will meet a rather important local Osraed. His name is Ladhar and he is the Abbod of Ochanshrine. More than that, he represents the Osraed in the Hall and on my Privy Council. He would be a formidable ally."

Taminy turned to look at him. "He will be shocked by me, Cyne Colfre."

He smiled, taken, again, by her beauty. "Not if you do nothing to shock him."

Eadmund reached Ochanshrine in the early evening. For the first time in his life, he crossed that sacred threshold and did not feel refreshed. The letter he carried weighed upon him, making his steps unsteady. He wanted to be rid of it more, almost, than he wanted anything else, but there was a ritual he must keep before he handed his burden over to Abbod Ladhar.

The Shrine was nearly empty at this time of day; the cleirachs and Osraed were at their evening meal. One lone Aelder Prentice sat in the last row of low, padded benches in the circular amphitheater, staring soulfully down at the room's centerpiece. Eadmund smiled in a wash of empathy, turning his own eyes to the Thing around which Ochanshrine was built.

It sat upon a pedestal of fine, hard, dark wood. Gold filigree and sea shell was inlaid among cleverly carved sea motifs, suggesting an ocean treasure trove. If a paean could be sung in wood, that pedestal was it. If a benediction could be said in solid stone, the Osmaer Crystal was that benediction. Twice as large as a man's fist, it glittered beneath an evening shower of lightglobe radiance, its perfect facets presenting their flawless planes to the glow of manmade light and returning a rainbow to the unadorned beams. Colorless it was, clear and pure, waiting for some atuned soul to call forth its Eibhilin colors.

Eadmund approached it hopefully, full of need, full of desire. He thought he heard someone call his name, but ignored them and gave the Osmaer his all. He was trembling by the time his feet trod upon the thick, verdant carpet that underlaid the pedestal.

It had been a decade since he had seen the Meri — since She had pressed burning lips to his brow and branded him to his very soul. This relic was as close as he could come, now, to meeting Her face to Face. He relived his Pilgrimage every time he came here, relived it and savored it and wished, with all his heart, that he had been

assigned to Ochanshrine instead of Halig-liath. For Osraed
Eadmund, in his own soul, valued devotion above justice,
contemplation above administration. He did what he did at
Halig-liath, served as he did both Council and Hall,
because he had to, not because he desired it. He would
gladly relinquish all temporal power to Ealad-hach or
Faer-wald or Kynan, who seemed to delight in it. He
would gladly have given the letter he carried into some
zealot's hands or told Ealad-hach to deliver it himself. But
he had been asked to carry it by an elder, by a member of
the Triumvirate, by a Brother. It had become duty.
Eadmund took duty seriously.

He turned to the Crystal for release, now. He suppli-
cated the Force behind it for wisdom and steadfastness.
He looked to the Stone of Ochan and the Stone answered.

A light. A very tiny light, at first, that blossomed to
bathe the supplicant's face with warmth and radiance.
Eadmund's eyes, wide, reflected that radiance in awe. He
had not excited that response in the Crystal since the year
of his Grand Tell. Tears started and the Crystal swam in
them, warm, aglow.

"Osraed Eadmund!"

Startled, he straightened and glanced about. Across the
circular Shrine, at the top of the shallow bowl formed by
its terraced floors, Osraed Ladhar stood just inside the
western doors, accompanied by a cleirach of Eadmund's
acquaintance.

While Eadmund stared stupidly, still in the thrall of the
Stone, Ladhar dismissed his companion and trundled
down the sloping aisle. "My God, Eadmund! What are you
doing? You should have come to me immediately. What in
the name of all things holy is happening in Nairne? I have
heard nothing but wild rumor since the Body was called.
Who is this girl Colfre has brought to Creiddylad? Is she
really Wicke?"

Eadmund's eyes moved only momentarily to the
Abbod's flushed face before going back to the Osmaer.
Then he gasped in dismay; the Crystal's Eibhilin glow was
fading. He puzzled, reaching out a hand as if to steady the
light, but it did no good. By the time Ladhar reached him,

Ochan's fantastic Crystal was no more than a beautiful rock, lit only from without.

The Abbod dropped a meaty hand to his shoulder and shook him. "Come, Eadmund! Are you ill?"

Eadmund managed to control his tongue. "No, merely weary. I . . . I have a letter for you . . . from Osraed Ealad-hach."

"Come, then — to my chambers. We can talk there." The elder Osraed prodded him into motion, leading him to his private chambers on the first floor of the Abbis.

"Tell me about Nairne," Ladhar said before Eadmund had even settled into a seat by the hearth. "What's happening at Halig-liath?"

Eadmund allowed his body to slump into the chair's padded depths. He wanted sleep suddenly, hungrily, but must be content to sit beside this fitful little fire and entertain questions he had no answers to. "What is happening at Halig-liath?" he repeated. "I can't begin to tell you . . . There is a fork in our path, Abbod. A fork caused, I assume, by this Cusp. And somehow, this girl, Taminy, is forcing us to confront it."

"This girl . . . the one the Cyne has brought to Creiddylad?"

Eadmund nodded. "And Bevol with her, since he was her sponsor and defender." He felt the letter, again, as a guilty weight, but was loathe to produce it. "The Cyne arrived at Halig-liath as the Osraed Body questioned her regarding a charge of heresy — "

"Yes, yes. I know that. Or at least I knew there was an inquiry. I thought it . . . a local matter, easily handled by those closer at hand — "

"You've no need to defend your absence, Abbod. Your duties here are important. It was not, after all, a universal call."

"I was defending nothing," said Ladhar with some vinegar.

Eadmund blushed. "I meant no disrespect, Osraed. However, it is now more than a local matter. The Cyne felt . . . *feels* . . . that the Osraed Body over-stepped its bounds and that the girl was being unjustly accused and unfairly treated."

"That decision hardly rests with him."

"Of course not. Which is why he has brought her to Creiddylad to stand before the Hall."

Ladhar frowned, his broad brow becoming a field thick with furrows. "To what end, I wonder? To what purpose does he import Nairne's problems to Creiddylad when she has so many of her own?" His eyes moved sharply to Eadmund's face. "You said you had a letter."

"Ah, yes. I . . . I do." He took it out reluctantly and gave it into Ladhar's hands. "Understand," he said, "that Ealad-hach is, himself, the girl's main accuser." A weak thing to say, he reflected, as he watched the Abbod's eyes devour the epistle. Ealad-hach's attack on Taminy-a-Cuinn had been nearly single-handed . . . in the beginning. But Eadmund could not bring himself to speak ill of his elder and, in truth, he understood little of what was happening. Perhaps Ealad-hach possessed insights denied the rest of them.

He glanced at Ladhar. The Abbod's face was mottled red, his expression, fierce enough to terrify. Eadmund decided the struggling fire was a preferable subject for his gaze and watched it play restlessly among the perfumed coals.

"You know the contents of this letter?" Ladhar had finished reading and raised his eyes to spear Eadmund to the back of his chair.

The younger man cleared his throat. "I do."

"And you are in agreement with it?"

Ladhar's scrutiny was more than he could stand. Eadmund got up and paced away across the room, trying to look ruminative while sweating inside. "I . . . I am unable to arouse in myself the hatred our brother obviously feels toward this girl."

"Hatred or lack of it is not the issue, Osraed. The issue is the danger the girl poses to Caraid-land."

"I find it difficult to believe she is dangerous. She's a girl. A seventeen-year-old girl —"

"Who claims to be inextricably linked to the Meri. Who spouts unheard of doctrine; who performs acts of Craft —"

Eadmund's arms moved in a convulsive gesture of desperation. "Perhaps she is merely confused."

"Then she has done none of these things Ealad-hach writes of?"

"Yes. Yes, she has done those things. And, yes, she has made those claims, but — "

"But? Osraed Eadmund, this girl is obviously a heretic. The proof of that seems to have come unforced from her own mouth. Moreover, she is a heretic who apparently has a mastery of the Wickish Craft. A heretic who has drawn the attention — no, more than that, the support — of our Cyne. Ealad-hach suggests it was her will that brought Colfre to her defense at Halig-liath. If that is true, then she cannot fail to be a danger . . . to all of Caraid-land."

"What if she tells the truth?"

"*What?*"

Eadmund stopped to watch the fire's unsteady crawl across the curved ceiling. "I said, what if she tells the truth?"

"That the Meri regenerates in this . . . unimaginable fashion? Unthinkable!"

"So Osraed Ealad-hach found it."

Ladhar was silent. Eadmund's ears picked up the soft crackle of flame — like muted applause, far distant. It was a silly thought; there was nothing to applaud here.

"And you," the Abbod asked, "do not?"

"I am at a loss to know what to think. But what Ealad-hach proposes we should do — "

"May be entirely necessary. Osraed Eadmund . . . " Ladhar's voice lost its sharp edge entirely. He leaned forward in this chair. "Eadmund, I recognize that you are a compassionate man. That is a quality we dare not belittle or undervalue. But you must realize what is at stake, here. The souls of untold thousands of people, of our Cyne, of — "

"I understand what is at stake," Eadmund murmured. "*We* are at stake. We Osraed."

"Precisely." Ladhar shuffled the pages of the letter and folded them back into their leather packet. "I am to hold an audience with this girl. Tomorrow morning. At the Cyne's request. I will decide, then, what is to be done."

Eadmund nodded. "I'm exhausted, Osraed Ladhar. Will there be a room for me in the Abbis?"

The Abbod rose, his gaze steady and solemn. "Dear Brother, there is always a room for you here."

It was a quiet room. She could hear no owls, no nightbirds, no chittering bats. But if she stood in the open doorway to the balcony, she could hear the pounding of the Sea far below Mertuile's perch. That comforted.

The night breeze carried laughter and song up from the outer ward. They arrived on Taminy's balcony as if thrown by the handful, like rose petals — sweet, unreachable. She could smell the roses, too; their perfume lifted from the Cyne's gardens and mingled with the scents of Sea and city.

She shivered because the breeze carried the chill of the Sea and because she was alone — cut off from Bevol and Skeet. She could sense them, below and away, separated from her by Mertuile's stony bulk. The distant laughter seasoned the aloneness, made its taste sharper, more pungent. Taminy left the balcony and closed the glass-paned doors. The laughter was gone, but she could still feel the rhythm of the Sea.

She went to the little trunk she had brought up from Halig-liath and took from it a carved and inlaid box. It was a small box, just big enough for Ileane to nestle in its velvet nest. Taminy took the crystal out and gazed at it, while it, like a pet intent on pleasing its mistress, displayed its Eibhilin finery and played with the light. Ileane was all she had of her past. All that was physical. Oh, well, there was this body, too, but the soul that animated it had changed considerably since it last walked and talked and felt.

The crystal shimmered, bathing her face in its glow, warming her palm with its vibration — a little stone dog, wagging its tail.

You don't need that, you know.

Joy. Sudden and complete, it washed over her. She was flooded with it, drowned in it. "I know," she said and took her eyes from the crystal. A cloud of golden light roiled in the center of the huge bedchamber. Formless, ever-moving, never-ending mist. A Mist like the Sun.

You were lonely.

"No longer."

And will be again.

"I know."

But there's much you don't know and would like to. Questions you want to ask, but won't.

Taminy smiled. "A conceit, I suppose, to say I am content with the Will of God . . . and Yours."

Even the content may be curious.

"Yes . . . What happens now?"

The Mist curled about itself in silence, shedding little bits of its splendor over the rich carpet, leaving gleaming trails to fade against the pale ceiling. *They speak of Cusps — the Cyne, the Osraed. Yet, so few understand the nature of a Cusp. In this time, as in no other, the entire Creation stands at a crossroads. Every soul has been called. Some have heard a Voice, others an inarticulate cry, others only an annoying whisper. They have been called to a peak, a forking of paths, a choosing.*

Some of these souls understand that, but even they may fail to see the nature of the choice, or who must make it. If it were My choice, it would be one thing. If it were yours, perhaps only a slight variation. But it is not My choice, or yours, Sister. Nor is it strictly the Cyne's nor his Durweard's nor his Cwen's. It lies not with the Council, or the Body, or the Hall. The Abbod Ladhar cannot make it, nor can the Osraed Bevol, nor any other single human being. For the Cusp is choices upon choices, woven through and into and over each other until a pattern emerges and a new fabric is created.

I am the Weaver. And all these souls provide the thread. I add My own thread to the Weaving, now, and I guide the shuttle, ever mindful of the patterns.

Taminy nodded. Patterns. She saw them and knew that the dominant pattern was Colfre's. At this moment.

Colfre will not succeed . . . in the end. But I cannot promise he will not succeed in the beginning. The destiny of Caraid-land lies in a handful of threads. I will Weave Mine, also. We will Weave it, ever mindful of the Pattern.

The bright cloud faded then, leaving behind its after-image like an echo of sweet music. Taminy curled up upon the great bed, knees to chin, arms hugging her legs, and rocked to a Duan only she could hear. The pattern of Caraid-land was uncertain, but she was not. The Cyne's castle was a place devoid of contentment, but she was content. She was more than content; wrapped in the ghost-fragrance of the Meri's presence, she was happy.

She slept then, and in her dreams she stood before a great, world-filling Tapestry and in her hand she held a golden shuttle which she plied with a Weaver's care, ever mindful of the Pattern.

CHAPTER 16

*Light the lamp of affection in every gathering; delight
every heart; cheer every soul. Care for the outlander
as for your own and show the stranger the same compassion and tenderness you give to your beloved
companions. If someone cause you pain, give him
healing medicine. If he give you thorns, shower him
with sweet herbs and roses.*

— *Utterances of Osraed Lealbhallain*

❖   ❖   ❖

Haesel the Sweep worked the Merchants' Rows most
mornings, coming out just at sunrise to make her rounds
and collect her pocketful of coins. This morning she had
plied her broom and brushes along the Cyne's Way
because she had heard that, this morning, the Cyne's
Wicke would go to Ochanshrine. The Cyne's Way merchants had heard it too, and wanted their shops gleaming
and sootless for the Passing.

Haesel could see the outer gates of Mertuile clearly
from here, and would know the moment they opened. The
royal entourage would pass this way, would turn at this
corner to go north to the crossing of the Halig-tyne at
Saltbridge. It would slow here and turn, and then . . .

Haesel glanced over at the front stoop of the shop
which walkway she now swept. Huddled against it was
what might be taken as a pile of discarded clothing; it was
not that, it was Losgann, her son. He was six years of age
and had neither walked nor stood fully upright for half that
time. But today the Cyne's Wicke would be abroad and
Haesel would see to it that she stopped here. The Sweep
would beg, she would grovel, she would throw herself

before the carriage if she had to, but the Wicke would stop and the Wicke would see Losgann.

"Mama?" His voice was transparent as the dawn sky.

"Yes, Losgann?"

"Mama, I'm awful thirsty. Is there water?"

"I'll ask it of the shopkeep," she said and did, though the man docked her payment for it. She gave Losgann the whole cup, though she was thirsty herself, and went back to sweeping and waiting.

It was mid-morning, and Haesel was scrubbing the cobbled steps of another shop, when the gates of Mertuile opened and the Cyne's retinue exited. She straightened, muscles complaining, and stretched, watching the gleaming carriage with its hedge of mounted soldiers make its way through the Cyne's Market to the Cyne's Way. It was a sparse hedge today — only four men — and they rode behind the carriage as a rearguard. Even at this distance, Haesel could distinguish the Wicke; she was a spot of sunlight, golden amid the more sedate greens of royalty.

The Sweep returned to her work, one eye on Losgann, sitting, now, in the shadow of the steps where early patrons would not see him. He was wondering, she knew, why he was not in his classroom at Care House. She had tried to make it seem a grand outing. "Oh, but you don't want to miss the passing of the Wicke!" she had told him when he pouted and said he would miss his friends. "Why, there'll be a festival on the Cyne's Way this morning — vendors and tricksters and musicians — you'll see."

And there were musicians. She could hear them now, and her street corner was beginning to fill with people; a couple wheeled out a cider trolley, a man had set up a brazier and laid out chunks of skewered meat on its blazing coals.

Losgann lifted his head, sniffing after the cooking meat, and Haesel felt in her pocket, counting the coins there. She palmed a pair of claefers and held them out to her son. "Here, Losgann, Go buy yourself a nice bit of meat."

He snatched the coins, then paused, looking up at her with dark eyes. "Are you sure, mama?"

She whisked her hand at him. "Go. *Go!* Can't let a nice

festival pass by without we join in." She smiled, but the smile slipped from her lips as she watched his painful, stooped and rolling hobble away from her toward the brazier-man.

She could close her eyes and see a morning three years ago — a morning not unlike this one, with its burnished sky and fresh sea breeze. She had had a flower cart then, a brightly painted little trolley decorated with hearts and dancing couples and pictures of young men giving gay posies to their favorite cailin. She had felt almost in control of her life then, for the first time since Losgann's father — another woman's husband, she learned too late — had abandoned them finally.

That morning, with her beautiful cart full of even more beautiful blooms, with Losgann playing at her skirts with a little flying bird-toy she had bought him, she had felt whole and happy. Gentlemen bought her flowers for their ladies and ladies bought them to pretend they were from gentlemen.

Haesel hadn't heard the commotion in the street, hadn't sensed the odd confluence of wind and wildness that sent Losgann's toy bird into the street and a jaeger's dray into a frenzy — she was helping a young lady choose a bouquet to match her fine new dress — but she heard the shrill scream of a child and the raw cursing of a man. That was when she had turned and seen Losgann lying in the street with the great, wild horse prancing too near his head, fighting the man who struggled to hold it.

The jaeger brought the boy to her, crumpled and torn, like the little bird she had held in her hands during the endless drive to the doctor. The jaeger was kind, but there was little he could do once he had delivered them there. As it happened, there was equally little the doctor could do.

Haesel turned her head, glancing through a blur of tears up the Cyne's Way where the royal retinue had disappeared behind street-hugging buildings. The flower cart was gone; she couldn't work and care for Losgann. Yet, money was needed to pay for the doctor — the doctor whose skills could not mend the shattered bones in the boy's leg and pelvis.

"Mama?"

She turned at the tug on her skirts. Losgann smiled up at her, panting a little and holding out a wooden skewer with a fist-sized chunk of meat on it. He clutched a second one in his other hand.

"Look! He gave me two! One for me and one for you."

It was an unexpected and welcome kindness. Haesel was famished. She glanced over at the vendor, who touched the brim of his hat and smiled. "Did you — ?"

"I *said* thank you, mama." Losgann rolled his eyes and bit into his chunk of seared meat.

The corner was becoming more and more populous. Before the crowd grew too thick, Haesel tucked her bucket, broom and brushes under the steps of the shop she'd been cleaning and called Losgann to her. She wiped his hands and face with her apron, telling him, when he complained, that the Cyne musn't see her son with charcoal smeared across his face. Her heart beat faster now. She could sense the crowd's anticipation turning uphill. When she could hear the sound of horse hooves on the cobbles, she wended her way to the edge of the crowd.

"Oh, lift me, mama!" begged Losgann. "Lift me so I can see!"

She did lift him, high up in her arms so his head was above hers. "Do you see her, Losgann? Do you see the Wicke Lady?"

"Yes! Oh, mama, she's *pretty* . . . and very young."

Haesel's eyes followed his and she bit at her lip. The girl in the carriage *was* young. Too young, one would have thought, to be a powerful Wicke. Her resolve trembled. But no, she *must* take this chance.

The carriage drew close; the Cyne on his high seat waved and smiled while, beside him, the young Wicke sat and gazed at the crowd. They were in the intersection now, and the driver turned the horses northward.

Haesel moved swiftly. She was in the road squarely before the horses before Losgann could utter a surprised squeak.

"Stop, please! Stop, please! I beg you! Lady Taminy — my son. Look at my son!"

The Cyne stood up in the carriage and gestured for her to move aside.

"Mama!" Losgann wailed.

"No, sire. Please! Let the Lady see my son."

Men on horses attempted to surround her and drive her back. Desperate, she squeezed herself between the lead horses of the Cyne's team. Losgann shrilled again as Haesel twisted, trying to see the Wicke. The girl was looking at her and she had her hand on the Cyne's arm and her lips were moving, though Haesel couldn't hear what she said because of the crowd noise and the hammering of her own heart. She felt someone grasp her arm and found herself staring up into the face of a Cyne's-man.

"Please!" she begged, but was wrenched from between the horses. Losgann began to sob.

"Here!" a man's voice shouted. "Bring her here."

Wonder. She was brought round the carriage to stand with the Cyne and his Wicke gazing down at her. She dared not look into the Cyne's face, but the Lady Taminy's welcomed her to look. Her heart stumbled madly over itself.

"What is it, woman?" the Cyne asked. "What do you want?"

"It's my son, lord. Losgann." She shifted the crying child higher on her shoulder. "Three years back, he was run down by a dray and his leg crushed. Twist it is, mam." She turned her plea to Taminy. "So twist, he can scarcely walk and he's never free of the pain. If you could but try — if you could but snatch the pain away . . ."

The girl turned her great green eyes on the Cyne. "I'd like to help him, sire."

Cyne Colfre hesitated, eying up the crowd — hushed now, and intent. Then a smile broke across his face; it seemed to Haesel the most beautiful smile she had ever seen and it made her heart pound all the harder. He nodded, and the Lady Taminy reached out her arms for Losgann. Haesel released him, her mouth open to comfort his fear at being given up into the care of a stranger, but it seemed he had no fear. His tears had evaporated and his eyes smiled at the beautiful lady who took him up into her lap.

Haesel held her breath and prayed and watched as the Wicke girl felt along her son's twisted leg from hip to ankle. Her pretty brow furrowed and Haesel all but swallowed the hope that clogged her throat. But the girl's expression cleared and she laid her hands firmly on Losgann's leg and began to sing in a clear, loud voice, words that Haesel didn't understand, but trembled at. They were icy words, hot words, words that chilled and comforted. They made Haesel's heart trip over itself and stagger and freeze in her breast.

Then, a billow of blue light, like nothing Haesel had ever seen, rolled down out of nowhere and crowned the Wicke girl's head and tumbled down her arms and washed all over and around Losgann, whose mouth and eyes were wide open, carp-like. So were the Cyne's, Haesel noticed, and if it had occurred to her, she might have laughed. But she could only stare at the Wicke and her son bathed in azure light and pray harder and remember to breathe.

Haesel wasn't certain how much time had passed before the light faded. She still stared, along with the silent crowd until she heard her son's voice. "Oh!" he said. "Oh! Oh, mama! Mama, my leg!" He kissed the Lady Taminy and gave her a tremendous hug before scrambling down from the carriage and into his mother's arms. Then, he walked all around her, his body upright, limping only the tiniest bit. His left leg was straight. *Straight!*

"He'll need to exercise it," the Lady Taminy said, her voice like balm. "Some of the muscles have grown weak."

Haesel turned to her with every ounce of her joy and gratitude pouring from her eyes. "Oh, mam. Oh, mistress! How may I thank you? How may I repay you?"

The girl reached out her hand and Haesel took it, squeezing it between her palms. "You are thanking me now. And your joy repays me a hundred-fold." She released Haesel's hand and straightened, and the crowd roared with approval.

And it was done. While Losgann capered for the crowd, Haesel watched the Cyne's carriage pull off down toward the Saltbridge Crossing, feeling as if a part of herself trailed after it. She didn't try to stop the tears that covered her cheeks, but merely thanked God silently and wondered at the Wicke's touch, still tingling in her palm. They called Wicke "Dark Sisters" in most places, but Haesel knew that the Cyne's Wicke was full of light.

Lealbhallain sat uneasily on the padded bench and tried to concentrate on his devotions. It was difficult and, in the end, he had to beg the Meri's forgiveness for his inattention. He glanced sideways at Osraed Fhada, wondering if he was similarly troubled. Leal's mind slipped, unbidden, back to yesterday's session in Fhada's aislinn chamber when they had seen, not Bevol, but something Bevol surely wanted them to see. That something had been the Cyne's walk with Taminy atop the battlements of Mertuile.

Leal could see her now, flaxen hair in breeze-blown banners, waving at the people far below the great walls. Smiling. He had been struck by a sense of familiarity. A familiarity which had nothing to do with their brief meeting at Tell Fest. Both he and Fhada had been overwhelmed by a frenzied need to meet Taminy-a-Cuinn face to face. They were here now, at Ochanshrine, shifting restlessly on their benches, because they knew *she* would be here and knew, also, that Osraed Bevol must have some reason for giving them that knowledge.

Leal tensed and felt an answering awareness in Fhada; Osraed Ladhar had entered the Shrine in the company of a pair of cleirachs and now lumbered down one sloping aisle. They were speaking in murmurs and Leal knew a guilty desire to eavesdrop. Ears sharp, he groped in his mind for an inyx he might Weave, but before he could recall one, the Shrine's solitude was shattered. The pounding of feet in the outer corridor was accompanied by a hubbub of voices, the loudest of which cried hoarsely for Abbod Ladhar.

Before the Abbod could do more than turn and glower up the aisle, a middle-aged Osraed appeared in the doorway at the receiving end of that dark gaze. His face was bright red, save for the pinched brackets of white around his nostrils, and shone with a heavy dew of sweat.

"Abbod! Dear God — ! Abbod!" He rushed down the aisle toward the elder Osraed, oblivious to the commotion he caused in this sacred Place. "I've seen — oh, dear God, what I've seen! The Cyne — the girl — !"

Abbod Ladhar was a bulwark of stone. "Calm, Tarsuinn," he said. "Calm! Tell us what you've seen."

"The Cyne is coming," stammered Osraed Tarsuinn, "and the girl is with him."

"Yes, Tarsuinn, I know this. I am to meet with them. The girl, as I'm sure you've heard, is suspected of Wicke Craft by some members of the Osraed Council."

Osraed Tarsuinn let out a wild moan. "Oh, she's more than suspect, Abbod! I've *seen* it!"

Ladhar's face flamed. "You've seen what?"

"A healing! Oh, dear Meri — such a healing! In the middle of the street a sweep-woman stopped the Cyne's carriage and thrust her crippled child at him, begging healing of — of that girl! And she took the boy into her arms, at the Cyne's say-so — "

"The girl did — this Taminy?"

Tarsuinn nodded vigorously. "And she put her hands on him and pulled Blue Healing out of the Beyond like it was in full flood. Oh, *blinding*, she was, *blinding!*"

"And the boy?" asked Ladhar. "The cripple?"

"Whole and fit and straight."

"A trick?"

"Oh, I think not, Abbod. I fear not. I've seen the child before, in the streets, at Care House. He was run down by a jaeger's dray, his left hip and leg mangled."

Ladhar scowled. "And no Osraed could help him?"

The flustered Tarsuinn shrugged and dithered. "His mother took him to a physician first, I'm told. By the time he went to Care House, he was beyond even Osraed effort."

Ladhar's pale eyes seemed to turn inward, then. "And this girl from Nairne heals him at a touch. . . . " The icy marbles snapped back to Tarsuinn's face. "Using what Runeweave?"

"Using none *I've* ever heard. She spoke the old tongue — words I know only from long hours in the library."

Abbod Ladhar's broad face was set in inscrutable lines Leal couldn't begin to penetrate. "We must be sure," he said. "We must know she is a Wicke. If she is a Wicke she may be destroyed, or at least rendered harmless."

"How, Osraed?" asked the cleirach nearest him. "How may she be neutralized?"

"The greatest evil is neutralized by the greatest good." Ladhar glanced back over his shoulder at the Osmaer Crystal.

Following his gaze, the cleirach's eyes lit with the radiance of pure zeal. A hard radiance, it glittered like the points of false glory reflected from the Osmaer's dark facets. Fever-hot, it shivered like Sun on baked cobbles. Leal was amazed to feel all that in one glance at a man he'd only just noticed. The cleirach was nodding now, his eyes narrowed to slits. "Please, Holy One, may we observe your audience with this Wicke?"

Ladhar merely inclined his head and indicated the cleirach and his companion should seat themselves. This they did, while all others within earshot, politely, or fearfully, removed themselves from the chamber. Leal, for his part, scrambled to remember an invisibility Weave and began to run the duan through his mind. Out of the corner of his eye, he could see that Fhada's lips were also moving silently. And none too soon. With the air of someone announcing the dawn of doom, an Aelder Prentice entered the Shrine and proclaimed the arrival of the Cyne.

He appeared with all the dignity befitting a Malcuim and, if he was smaller in stature than his father or his father's father, his silhouette, starkly filling the doorway, didn't show it. Then, a female figure appeared next to the Cyne. Both stepped down into the artificial light of the Shrine and Leal held his breath.

Abbod Ladhar waited at the bottom of the aisle, his back to the Osmaer Crystal. His fatherly smile, the expansive sweep of his arms, displayed nothing but welcome. "Cyne Colfre," he said, "you honor this Threshold. This is the young woman you spoke to me about?"

Cyne Colfre returned the smile. "Indeed, Abbod. This lovely child is Taminy-a-Cuinn."

"This lovely child," repeated Ladhar, his smile not altering, "is accused of heresy and practicing the Wicke Craft, if I am not mistaken."

The Cyne and Taminy continued to descend. "Wrongfully accused, I am convinced."

Leal stirred. That sound . . . like . . . like singing. He heard Fhada gasp, saw his arm out-thrust, toward the Shrine's Heart. He tore his eyes from Taminy's face and followed Fhada's gesture. A cry was lifted from his throat before he could stop it. "The Crystal!"

The Crystal pulsed at its core with a light that increased in steady, rhythmic increments — brighter, brighter. Fire traced its facets, jumped from point to point, while the sound of singing — or was it wind-chimes? — shimmered in the semi-darkness of the Holy Place.

Ladhar turned as swiftly as his bulk allowed and stared at the brilliant thing. His face, his eyes, glowed with astonishment — an astonishment which gave quick way to triumph. He swung back to face the Cyne. "Let the Crystal decide if she is wrongly accused."

He doesn't understand, Leal thought. *He doesn't see —*

He didn't see that Taminy-a-Cuinn's face glowed the same brilliant gold as the Stone she now gazed upon. He didn't see that that face wore an expression, not of fear or distress, but of pure joy. It was the face of a lover reunited with her Beloved.

The Cyne stopped halfway down the aisle, uncertain, but Taminy continued on, her eyes on the Crystal, feeding back its glory. She raised her hands to it and Ladhar sidled out of the way. The singing increased volume, a sound like a chorus of flutes and pipes and voices wrapped in and around a fine spring breeze and the Solstice peal of Cirke chimes. Eibhilin fire leapt from Stone to cailin and embraced her, twining her in its golden arms, spangling the still room with glory. It rose to the curved rafters, it painted the walls, it must surely have poured from the windows.

Leal forgot his invisibility Weave altogether and came to his feet, quaking. "Oh, it's true!" he said. "It's true!" He looked up at Fhada, who had also risen; the older Osraed's eyes streamed tears that turned to honey in the Osmaer gleam. He looked at the Cyne and saw a man frozen in disbelief. He looked at Osraed Ladhar and his companion cleirachs and saw men whose entire world had come undone.

Abbod Ladhar's mouth was open and above the singing of the Stone, Leal heard his voice raised in a shrill litany: "Away, daemon! Take her away! Take the daemon away!"

The cleirach who had begged to stay rose from his seat and advanced on Taminy who, oblivious within her now blinding cloak of Eibhilin gold, continued to caress the Stone. Leal tried to cry out, to warn her, but his throat made only a wild croak. The cleirach lunged. There was a flash of light, a sizzle of sound, and the man toppled backwards as if he'd collided with a solid wall.

A new sound invaded the room. It took Leal a moment to realize, incredulously, that it was laughter — the Cyne's laughter. Colfre Malcuim came down the aisle to the circular Shrine, circled to where Taminy could see him, and held out his hand to her. She shivered like someone shaking off a dream, glanced about, then took the proffered hand. The encompassing globe of Eibhilin light shattered like so much ephemeral glass and showered, in a myriad tiny, gleaming, silent shards to the floor. The golden aura faded, melted away into the flagged stones, under the benches, out of the air.

But Ochan's great Crystal still throbbed with a rhythmic aurora, dimmer than before, but still strong. It was like an echoed heartbeat, Leal thought, when he could think. He didn't need to ask whose.

Cyne Colfre led her away then; before the cleirach could rise from the floor; before his companion could find the courage to move to his aid; before Ladhar, his face convulsing in fits of disbelief and rage, could utter further condemnation. Light left the Stone in a receding tide. When Taminy left, she took the Light with her.

"My God," whispered Fhada. "What is she?"

Leal barely heard him. He stared at the Osmaer Crystal and wondered only how he might go and throw himself at her feet.

✧   ✧   ✧

"I am only saying, sire, that it might not have been wise to . . . "

"To push Ladhar's chubby face into his own ineptitude?" Colfre smiled, enjoying the memory of those fat jowls flapping like an empty bellows. *God, had anyone ever before rendered the man speechless?* He postured, puffing out his stomach and cheeks. " 'Let the Crystal decide if she is wrongly accused!' Well, it damn well decided something!" He dropped the pose and came back to sit on the couch across from his Durweard, his heart galloping at the mere *thought* of what she had done. "I tell you, Daimhin, she held that Stone in the palm of her hand. She *controlled* it! She made it *sing*! *Sing*! I swear by the Malcuim line, I have *never* heard it sing, and neither had our porcine Abbod."

Carried to his feet by that Voice singing, again, in his own blood, Colfre paced back to the garden window where Day could be seen to pull in her skirts; where Night spread hers out, layer upon layer.

"Sire," Daimhin said in the most diplomatic of voices. "Sire, I thought the point of the interview with Ladhar was to gain Taminy an ally. Do you think you succeeded in that?"

"Don't patronize me, Daimhin. Of course, I didn't succeed in that. So, he fears her. That may be better."

"Better?" Feich repeated. "My lord, had you no . . . control over the situation?"

Colfre laughed, exhilarated. "Not as far as that damned Crystal was concerned."

"I thought you said *she* controlled the Crystal."

Colfre shrugged. "That was the impression I had."

"Then, perhaps you should endeavor to control *her*."

Colfre turned to regard his Durweard with mild bemusement. "We *wanted* miracles, remember?"

"*Little* miracles. 'Oh-and-ah' miracles. Not stupefying, mind-boggling miracles."

"You have no sense of *mystery*!"

"And you have no — !" Feich turned his head and gazed momentarily at a muraled panel. He took a deep breath and looked back to his Cyne, smiling. "You have no idea, my lord, what the superstitious mind can make of such wonders. We are attempting to display a lovable Taminy, an *innocent* Taminy, not a fire-slinging hellion who knocks cleirachs about like rumble pins. Our purpose is to prove the Osraed to be inept and fanatical stewards of Caraidland's spiritual life."

"Our purpose *was*. I think that is changing. I think I see other possibilities."

Feich gazed down at the rich folds of his tunic. "I'm sure you do. I see . . . other possibilities, also. But if you terrify the Osraed, you risk uniting them. You can't afford to unite them now. United, and still a force in government, they will fight you tooth and claw over the situation with the Deasach, and they will never allow you to declare yourself Osric. Your greatest and best weapon against them is their own disunity."

Ah, damn, the man had a point. Colfre came back to the couch again, to sit and try to appear relaxed. Inside, he churned. "Well, Daimhin Feich, *Durweard*, what do you propose I do about it? Taminy-a-Cuinn performs ostentatious miracles completely at will. I couldn't have stopped her from healing that boy this morning. Nor could I have stopped what happened with the Stone. I saw what it did to that idiot cleirach, and I had no reason to believe it would show any more respect for a mere Cyne. So tell me: what can I do?"

"Try harder to control her."

Colfre nodded, mouth a-twist. "Oh, yes. I see. I'll have to book up on my Runeweaves."

"There are ways. I shouldn't need to remind you, my lord, that women — particularly very *young* women — find you most . . . winning. Win her."

Colfre, to whom such an observation was usually Sun to a seedling, could only stare at his Durweard in gut-tickling unease. "Absurd idea."

Daimhin Feich's surprise seemed genuine. "Why? Do you not find her attractive?"

Did he not — ? He pulled his arms about himself, suddenly chill. "She's beautiful. Lightning in flesh. She excites me in ways I didn't know a man could be excited."

Feich spread long delicate fingers. "Well, then . . . ?"

Colfre stood, putting his Durweard behind him. "No, I can't." He raised a hand. "Don't ask why. I couldn't invent an answer that would make sense. I can't because I saw her in the Shrine today making love to that Stone. Because I saw her in the street wearing a robe of blue glory and doing things no seventeen year old girl should be able to do. She is more than an embarrassment to the Osraed, Daimhin. She is their nemesis."

Colfre could almost hear Feich's eyebrows cresting. "Superstition, my lord?"

"Awe, my Durweard. You saw her this afternoon — a tired little girl. You didn't see her this morning when she was . . . I don't know what." He turned to intercept his companion's troubled gaze. "Lay it at the feet of my Hillwild mother. Perhaps it *is* superstition. And perhaps superstition is in the blood she passed on to me. Whatever it is, it *is*. I recognize, of course, that you're right. We must control her. We've befriended her; that's a start. But perhaps more is needed. You're a capable man, Daimhin. A more *reasonable* man than I am, obviously, and, I am told, as winning."

"My lord, I — "

"No, no. It's true. Perhaps you could succeed at what I will not even dare."

Feich inclined his head. "Yes, my lord. But in view of how you feel about the girl, how could I presume — "

Colfre glanced at him aslant. "You're a free man, Daimhin. Scion of a noble and powerful House. I may be Cyne, but I can hardly dictate your fancies, especially if they fall on a commoner."

He turned back to his darkened window, then. All color had drained from the garden as if lapped up by an invisible beast. He wondered if it was the same beast, sated, that now curled up in his stomach and slept.

She was exhausted, but sleepless, and felt like nothing so much as a woolly fleece sponge that had been wrung dry. *Or a riverbed,* she thought, *after a spring flash flood.*

Such had been the rush of Eibhilin energies through their human channel that she vibrated, still, from the Touch of the Stone. No, not the Stone, but the Stone's Mistress.

Channels. It took a series of them to filter the Messages of the Spirit that some men might hear them: Spirit to Meri, Meri to Osmaer-Stone, Osmaer-Stone to Taminy-Osmaer. And from Taminy-Osmaer to . . . ?

She shivered, recalling the face of the Abbod Ladhar, sweat-polished and wild-eyed. The Message could not be filtered enough for that soul to find it comprehensible . . . or acceptable. She could not reach a man like Ladhar, she could only expose him. She knew that after stepping into the embrace of the Crystal.

She knew other things, as well, of other souls. Of the two watching, unseen, from behind their simple Weaves, she knew earnestness and purity. Sharp contrast then, the cleirach's soul — a soul condemned by its own sense of worthlessness. A soul who fought that strangling emotion with the unlikely weapons of suspicion and self-righteousness. Those were the wrong weapons, but he had no others. That made Caime Cadder pitiful. It also made him dangerous.

A frisson prickled up the back of her neck. She rose swiftly from the bed, exhaustion forgotten, and moved with silent feet to the door. She opened it. The Riagan Airleas stood outside in the dim-lit corridor, his hand outstretched toward the door latch. Their eyes met in an almost audible collision.

Airleas lowered his, then quickly raised them again. "I would have knocked," he said.

"Oh? And why would you have knocked, Riagan Airleas? What can you want with me?"

He jutted his chin up and out, fixing her with a gaze he'd no doubt seen his father use on recalcitrant Eiric. "They say you did a miracle today in the Cyne's Way."

"Are miracles not permitted there?"

He blinked at her, looking, momentarily, like a little boy. "I . . . I suppose the Cyne must have permitted it. . . . Did you?"

"What am I to have done that was so miraculous?"

"They say you healed a little boy."

"God healed the boy. I was only an instrument."

"I don't believe it. I don't believe you can heal people. I want you to prove it to me." The brave little Riagan shuddered like a breeze-blown poplar, but stood his ground.

"And how may I do that?" Taminy asked.

"I have a friend — the son of my mother's First Maid. He's sick. Very sick. I'll believe you, if you can heal him." He glared at her, daring her to accept his challenge.

She felt her exhaustion keenly, then — a weight pulling at her, holding her to the stone floors of Mertuile. *Prove yourself, Taminy. Proof! Proof! For some there will never be enough proof. Are you one of those, Airleas Malcuim?*

"All right," she said. "Only let me get a coat. It's chill in the corridors."

Snug in a felt panel coat, Taminy followed the Riagan down half-lit hallways, up a long flight of stone stairs, to the level above the Royals. Into a darkened apartment he led, silent and secret, showing with gestures that he intended her to be as quiet. Finally, they stood in a small room in which a single candle burned. Odd, since the entire castle had the benefit of lightglobes. There were two in this room, both dark. On a bed beneath a narrow window, a small figure lay, covered with a mountain of blankets.

"That's my friend," murmured Airleas, his young face long and solemn. "He's got a terrible disease."

"Ooo-oh!" said the form on the bed, and shivered violently.

"If you're so magical, heal him." The imperious scion of the House Malcuim was back, peering at Taminy through glittering, slitted eyes.

She inclined her head. "Yes, sire." At the bed, she paused to look down at its occupant. "Are you in much pain?" she asked.

"Oh, ye-es!"

She listened carefully to the small, tremulous voice. "Where is the pain?"

"Oh, *everywhere!*" said the pile of blankets.

Airleas uttered a chuff of exasperation. "Can't you *tell* how much pain he's in? Can't you tell where it is? Isn't that part of the Wicke Craft?"

She turned her head to look at him. "But Riagan, I'm not a Wicke."

"So you keep saying. Very well, the *Art* then. Isn't that called a Heal Tell?"

"Yes, it is. And the questions I ask are part of that Tell." She lowered herself onto the edge of the bed. The blanketed child shivered harder.

"See," said Airleas. "He has a horrible ague."

Taminy stretched out her hands and pulled back the blankets a bit. A ghost-pale face peeked out at her from the folds, its forehead misted with perspiration. Feverless perspiration. "What's your name?" she asked.

The eyes, dark and clear, blinked. "Beag . . . mam."

"Well, Beag, it's not hard to see what's wrong with you. You've piled on too many blankets. Take them off and you'll recover quickly enough from this horrible ague."

"W-what?" asked Beag, and Airleas said, "But he has a fever! See how he shakes?"

Taminy turned to face the Riagan squarely. "That's fear, not fever. Your friend isn't sick. Nor is he really your friend. He's the child of your mother's servant which, to your mind, makes him *your* servant. You pressed Beag into service to test me."

Airleas looked like a landed fish, all eyes and mouth. Beag began to cry. Shrugging off his encumbering blankets he sat up and clutched at Taminy's sleeve. "Oh, mam, I'm sorry! But he told me I must. He's the Cwen's son — what could I do?"

"Lie beneath a pile of blankets and quake, it would seem." The female voice came to them from the doorway. It belonged to a shadow that, once in candlelight, became the Cwen Toireasa.

Beag whined and cowered. Airleas had the good grace to look contrite. Cwen Toireasa surveyed them both with bland bemusement. "To bed with you, Airleas," she told her son. "Taminy, you will accompany me . . . please." Both obeyed immediately.

The Cwen said nothing more to her as they navigated the resplendant halls and wound down the stairs to the level below. At the bottom of the stairs, Cwen Toireasa paused. "May we talk in your chambers? They would be more private."

Taminy nodded. "As you wish, mistress."

"My son," said the Cwen, when they had closeted themselves in Taminy's rooms, "trusts only the conviction of his own senses. I suppose he resembles me in that. Colfre is likely to believe what he has not seen and disbelieve what he has seen with his own eyes." She moved to seat herself on a low settle by the hearth. Firelight and lightglobes set her golden hair aflame, making her seem more Eibhilin than human.

Like the Gwenwyvar, Taminy thought. She seated herself across from the Cwen and asked, "What do you believe, mistress?"

"I'm not sure. I'll tell you what *don't* believe. I don't believe you're merely a madwoman or a zealot. Zealots and madwomen don't perform miracles. I was in the crowd today, along the Cyne's Way," she explained. "I saw what you did for the boy. I followed you on to Ochanshrine, too."

Taminy's surprise must have shown in her face, for the Cwen smiled and said, "You find that shocking? I don't trust my husband, Taminy-a-Cuinn. Or perhaps I should say, I trust him to follow his desires. He follows them all over Creiddylad and beyond. Sometimes he even exports them to the Abbis. I thought he was doing that this morning. It seems I was wrong."

Taminy said nothing, for she could think of nothing to say. She understood Toireasa's antipathy now, and that comprehension made her uncomfortable.

"I don't know if you are my husband's lover." Toireasa continued. "I do know that you're *more* than that. I might believe you," she added, "if you told me you were *not* his lover."

Taminy flushed. "I am not, mistress. I beg you to believe me. The Cyne has befriended me for reasons that have nothing to do with his affections."

Cwen Toireasa laughed. "How charmingly you put it! No, cailin. Colfre's affections are never involved in his plots and projects; only his passions are involved. And he has many of those. I think I know which one caused him to 'befriend' you — his passion to govern. . . . No, that's naive of me. Not to govern, to rule. And to rule by popularity. Colfre Malcuim fancies himself to be carved from the same wood as Buidhe Harpere or Liusadhe or, God help us, the Malcuim, himself." She shook her head. "The artist warrior. He would like to see himself as a bit of each of them. A strange admixture — gentle artistry, passionate zeal, a little blood-lust for spice — but pure Malcuim — golden-haired, visionary eyes the color of the sea."

Taminy smiled, knowing the Cwen was right. She could well imagine Cyne Colfre arrayed before a mirror that reflected fantasy instead of reality: a harp, a crown, a sword. That last, that was the danger in Colfre and it was nothing to smile over. Taminy sobered.

"Yes, it *is* funny, isn't it? That's why he married me, you know, in the hope of producing a golden Malcuim heir. But Airleas is darker than his father, which I, unable to produce another child, am not allowed to forget."

A chill glided down Taminy's back like a silken runnel of ice water. "Does he show Airleas that he . . . ?"

"Hoped for something else? Something other than a Hillwild throwback? Oh, yes. Not viciously, you understand, and not so much verbally as in those tiny, subtle ways that wound. Colfre did a family portrait of us once. He gave Airleas Thearl Malcuim's pale copper hair."

Taminy remembered that hair — how bright it had been in the sunny courtyard at Farewelling. "The Ambre Cyne, they called him," she murmured, "his hair was so bright. Poor Airleas."

"Colfre is not a forgiving man. He can't forgive his mother for being Hillwild or his father for marrying her; he can't forgive me for giving him a son who's more his than mine; and he can't forgive Airleas for just being Airleas. He named him, you know — Airleas, 'a pledge' — to remind me that somehow my pledge to him was broken." She looked down at her hands, clutched together in her lap. "To me, my son is a pledge that someday, when Colfre is gone, *he* will be Cyne. A better Cyne than his father ever dreamed of being." Her mouth twisted wryly and she raised her eyes to Taminy's. "No, Colfre has never dreamed of being a *good* Cyne, merely a popular and powerful one."

Taminy felt a wave of deep compassion for the Cwen of all Caraid-land and wondered at the confidences she'd revealed. "Why are you sharing all this with me, mistress?"

The Cwen studied her a long time before answering. "I don't know who or what you are, Taminy-a-Cuinn, but I know you can perform miracles. I hadn't believed in miracles until now. I suppose I dare hope you'll Weave a miracle for me." Toireasa rose then, shook out her skirts, and moved across the medallion carpet to the door.

"Perhaps I will Weave for you," Taminy told her. "Or perhaps you'll perform a miracle of your own."

Toireasa's smile was ironic. "Oh, I have already tried," she said, and let herself out.

CHAPTER 17

To what house can a lover go but the house of his Beloved? Where can he find rest, but in the arms of his heart's desire?

A lover lives in reunion and dies in separation. His spirit is impatient and his soul lacks peace.

A host of lives he would offer up to travel in the way of his Love or to lay his head at Her feet.

— The Song of Ochan

❖   ❖   ❖

"Why must you go, Saxan? Why must you? You aren't a pillar of the Hall. You've no voice there, no duty." Ardis-a-Nairnecirke flailed at her husband with haphazard words, her posture defensive. She didn't want him to take the downriver road to the capitol. She was afraid, as she had never been before, that he would come back changed, or not at all. It wasn't brigands she feared, or accident; it was this fever running through Caraid-land, a fever that no longer confined itself to Nairne.

"Who'll give lessons on Cirke-dag?" she pleaded. "Who'll say the blessing and lead the lays?"

Saxan did not even look up from his packing. "Ardis," he said, "I've a competant second in Aelder Culash."

"That doesn't answer me why."

"I've told you why. I can't just wait to hear. I want to be there. I'm entitled to be there. And, yes, I feel a duty to be there."

"Duty? To *whom*, Saxan? For God's love, it's out of your hands now."

He straightened from his satchel and looked at her. *Finally*, she thought. But his eyes had the glaze of someone who does not see what he looks at.

"Out of my hands," he repeated. "Yes, I suppose it is. But it's not out of my conscience . . . or my heart." His eyes focused on her face, at last. "Don't you feel it, Ardis? Didn't you feel it the first time you saw her?"

Ardis twitched, a frisson passing, ghostly, down her spine. Aingeal kisses, her mother called that. When she was a little girl, she'd turn quickly on her heel and kiss the air, hoping to catch the Eibhilin messenger and return its kiss. Ardis shook her head. "I felt something, God help me. I don't know what."

Saxan nodded, intent on her now. "But it isn't *evil*, is it Ardis? Wouldn't we know if it was evil?"

"Would we?"

"I've begged to know. An aislinn. A sign. An inkling. Anything. I feel *something* from Taminy-a-Cuinn, but I'd be the worst kind of liar — and a fool — if I pretended it was evil."

"If an aingeal fans your neck, spin about and kiss it back."

"What?"

"An old rhyme. My mother taught it to me . . . about those little tickles of-of something that make you shiver."

Saxan smiled and nodded. "I remember that, yes. I guess that's what I'm doing — trying to return the aingeal's kiss . . . or, perhaps, the Meri's kiss."

The chill Ardis experienced then was cold and unpleasant. "You don't believe her Tell, surely? Not *you*. By the Kiss, I've always believed you to be one of the most steadfast men the Meri had ever chosen."

He only looked at her, shouldering his pack. "I hope I am that. I *must* be that. And I must know about Taminy-a-Cuinn. Do you understand, Ardis? *I must know*."

She wanted to weep, but knew it would only add to the burden he already carried. "I understand."

He held out his free arm to her. "Then come kiss me good-bye . . . Aingeal."

She did, and found the affection comforting. They moved out into the upstairs hallway then, and Ardis called out to Iseabal to come bid her father a good journey. The girl appeared from behind her bedroom door too quickly and came, hang-dog, down the hall, her cheeks burnished rose. Ardis didn't confront her with her eavesdropping, but merely watched her hug her father's spare frame and scurry back to her room.

"She'll feel better by and by," said Saxan and kissed Ardis long and deep. "And so," he promised, "will you."

But watching him head off toward the river road, Ardis felt the promise to be empty. As empty as her house was without him.

"Aine! Aine-mac-Lorimer!"

"Here!" The redhead rose from behind a low shrub, brushing leaves from her breeches. "Did you have trouble getting away?"

"A little." Iseabal came the rest of the way into the river glade. Her skirts were tied up into her sash to ease riding astride, and her dark hair was bound into a fat plait that hung over one shoulder. "I told mother I was going to the Sanctuary to pray for father. That way I knew she wouldn't go looking for me." She shifted uneasily. "It didn't feel good to lie."

"So pray on the way to Creiddylad. Where's your horse?"

Iseabal gestured over her shoulder. "Tied to a tree back there. Where's Phelan?"

"He went back for Wyvis and Rennie."

"I thought they weren't coming."

Aine grinned. "Seems their mam found out about our adventure and thought they ought to go — not without *her*, though."

Iseabal's eyes felt as if they'd start from her head. "Mam Lusach is coming too? What about her shop?"

"She'll find someone to run it for her. Don't worry so."

Iseabal gazed into her palm, rubbing the faint, stellate mark there with her thumb. "I can't help but worry. I can feel her, calling me. She's lonely, Aine. And she's in danger."

Aine sobered. "I know. I feel it too. . . . " She paused to study the mark in her own palm. "Have you ever stopped to wonder what we're becoming?"

Iseabal shivered, but the chill was a delicious one. "I wonder every moment. But *she's* the cause of it. Whatever we become, we shall be better than we ever were."

"I never wanted the Gift," Aine murmured, then raised her head sharply. "Someone's coming."

It was Phelan. He had brought the Apothecary, her children, and Orna-mac-Mercer. All carried faint, star-shaped marks in their palms and a deep loyalty to Taminy-a-Cuinn in their hearts.

"The Cyne has spoken to you about the Assembly, of course." Daimhin Feich's smile came with an offer of tea.

She accepted the tea and nodded. "Yes, he's mentioned it several times."

"He's explained, then, that he wishes you to remain silent, and why."

"Yes. He wants the Osraed to appear fanatical and ridculous. And, of course, he wishes me to be found innocent of heresy."

"Both true. For you are innocent and the Osraed are fanatical and ridiculous. But, there's a bit more to it than that." Feich sat down next to Taminy on the stone bench she occupied in one of the castle's many pocket gardens. For a moment, he said nothing, but let his eyes roam over her face and hair. Her blush only made him smile more deeply. "How lovely you are — rose and gold. Like one of those." He gestured at the roses that stood sentinel along the wall. Then, he lowered his eyes and chuckled. "Forgive me. I was going to say that the Cyne has grown very fond of you. *I've* grown fond of you in the brief time you've been with us. We only advise you to your own good. Which is to say, for the good of Caraid-land. Cyne Colfre and I are aware, if no one else is, that the two things are inextricably connected."

"Yes, they are." She let her eyes rise to his.

He did not break off his gaze. "The Osraed are corrupt."

"Not all."

"No, but as an institution — "

"As an institution they have lost sight of their purpose. I'm here to remind them of it."

Feich stared at her. "I've never heard you speak like that before, of purposes — theirs or yours."

"You've never discussed the Osraed with me before. Not directly."

"So, you have a purpose: to remind the Osraed of *their* purpose."

"That's one of the reasons I'm here, yes."

Feich's brows rose. "There are more?"

She tilted her head to one side. "I see them, little by little."

"The Meri shows you, does She?"

"Yes."

"And what else does She show you?"

"Whatever She wishes me to see."

He was silent for a moment, studying her. "I am very loyal to my Cyne," he said at last. "Fiercely loyal. Perhaps I try to . . . compensate for my forebears." He smiled ruefully. "The House Feich is not well known for loyalty."

That, Taminy knew, was an understatement. In the long history of Caraid-land, the Feich were known to be loyal only to the Feich. Whether that put them in league with the House Malcuim or against it seemed not to matter. Until now, this man would have her believe. She gazed into Daimhin Feich's fox-eyes and tried to read the depth of his loyalty to Colfre Malcuim and his country. It was difficult, for the man's inner workings were complex and ever-moving. One thing was certain; he wanted what Colfre wanted — to weaken the Osraed and to invest their powers in a new institution. Daimhin Feich would make Colfre Osric, ruler by Divine Right.

"I must tell you this," Feich continued, flushing a little under her gaze, "so you understand my . . . motivation. I believe you can aid my lord in attaining what he desires and deserves."

"To be Osric."

He blinked. "Who told you that?"

She smiled, knowing the smile unnerved him. "You did.

Colfre did. Although not so much with public words as with private thoughts."

He laughed. "You toy with me, lady. Unkind of you."

"I have no desire to be unkind. Colfre wants to divest the Osraed of their administrative power and take it upon himself. You want to help him."

Feich hesitated, then moved closer to her on the bench, a urgency bristling from him. "Yes. Yes, Taminy. I *do* want that. You say, yourself, that the Osraed have forgotten their purpose. So they have. They've become enamored of temporal leadership and have failed to give spiritual guidance to the people of Caraid-land. Only when they are forced to concentrate on the spiritual will they cease to be distracted by the material. Colfre wants what you want, Taminy — for the Osraed to return to their spiritual duties. For them to look to you for their charter. The Cyne's ends and the Meri's ends are the same. Both will be served if your innocence is proved."

He moved closer still, taking on the expression of an instructive confidant. "When you are called before the Hall tomorrow, you must present a demure, child-like picture. The way you dress, the way you stand, the expression on your face, the tone of your voice when you speak — all will contribute to this picture. Convince the Assembly that you are that, and all the Osraed accusations will appear as so much dirty smoke."

He paused, eyes downcast, seemingly uncomfortable. When he lifted them again, they were overflowing with concern. He took her hand in his gently, firmly. "The Assembly must not see the Taminy-a-Cuinn who proudly announced herself to the Osraed Body — "

"That was not pride." Her voice was firm, if not sharp.

He floundered momentarily. "Well . . . well, then it was purpose. But *that* Taminy-a-Cuinn must not speak to the Hall." He looked deeply into her eyes now, his grip on her hand tightening. "Do you wish to be of service to Caraid-land, Taminy? Does your purpose have a place in it for that?"

Shivers of alien alarm raised the hair on her neck and arms, but she kept her eyes on his and made her voice steady and certain. "The good of Caraid-land is my ultimate purpose, Durweard Feich. For what other reason could I or my Mistress care what the Osraed do or do not? The Osraed were to serve this people and most have forgotten how. Worse, they strive to drag the newly Chosen into forgetfulness with them."

"Then serve Cyne Colfre and you will surely serve the people."

She pulled her hand from his and rose from the bench. "By remaining silent and making no claims?"

"Your actions speak more loudly and convincingly than any words, lady. The sweetness of your conduct, the mildness of your demeanor . . . Do you understand?"

She nodded, feeling his eyes along her back, flushing again at his regard. "I do understand, Durweard Feich."

"Surely, you can call me Daimhin, dear Taminy, when I have acknowledged my fondness for you."

She flushed more deeply and another unfamiliar tingle rippled through her. "Yes, Daimhin, I understand."

He rose and moved around to stand before her, capturing her hands again, holding them to his lips and kissing the tips of her fingers. In contact with its source, the tingle sharpened. He was vibrating with something akin to exhilaration, his eyes over-bright and dizzying, swarming with an energy that all but took her breath away.

He left her alone in the garden, then, to contemplate their conversation — alone, as she had been all week, except for her crowd-drawing tours with Colfre and her several visits with Toireasa and Airleas. The Riagan had apologized to her the night after his escapade, no doubt at the urging of his mother, and had stayed to ask her questions about the Meri — what She looked like and how She spoke and what it felt like to touch a person who was made of Light. She did not ask how he came to know of her claims, but merely answered his questions as best she could.

Bevol and Skeet she had not seen except in glimpses. They were not allowed to speak except in dreams where distance and walls made no difference. But, though that comforted her, it was not the same as seeing them face to face. Not the same as feeling Bevol's strong arms, protective, about her when her sense of isolation became too keen.

Taminy-Osmaer, of divine intent, was yet human and young. Loneliness sapped her in a way the constant parades and healings did not. Indeed, the daily "miracles" she had been called upon to perform revitalized her. Though she was uncomfortable with the parading and posturing, uneasy that the adoring crowds now connected her with the Cyne, it gave her the chance to Weave Healing and she was grateful. It also gave her the chance to make friends among the people of Creiddylad and its provinces. Friends she must share with Colfre for the time being.

The agitation Daimhin Feich had created in her passed as she roamed among the roses, reminding herself of the garden at Gled Manor. She was absorbed in their perfume when she heard the sounds of approach and paused, wondering if it was time for yet another parade of miracles. The Assembly members arrived day by day, and along with them more common folk who flocked to the city as if it were a site of Pilgrimage. It was not Ochanshrine they came to see, it was Taminy, the Wicke of Mertuile. And she, at her Cyne's bidding would perform for them, causing them to believe what they had only heard in rumor.

The Cyne was not alone when he entered the little garden; the Ren Catahn and Desary Hillwild were with him. Daimhin Feich trailed behind, his expression guarded. But Catahn's face held no such wariness, and his daughter's was eloquent with relief and joy. Together, they came to Taminy and fell to their knees at her feet. Both raised hands and she clasped them, palm to palm, fingers entwined. Her earlier uncertainty fled at their touch.

"My Lady," murmured Catahn, his head bowed, "you are safe."

"I am in the company of friends," she said, and could now be sure of it.

Catahn raised dark amber eyes to her face. "We are yours, Lady. What do you desire of us?"

Over the Hillwild's head, she could see Cyne Colfre's astonishment turn to glee. He glanced aslant at Feich, who merely raised his brows. She felt a prickle of anger. These people were pawns to Colfre — ciphers he would move about to obtain the sums he wanted. She pushed the anger down and smiled. "I have no desire that your coming here hasn't fulfilled. Only stay with me a while."

"Lady," said Desary, "I would stay with you forever. Take me as your lady's maid and companion. Let me serve you."

Taminy looked from one dark face to the other, feeling their devotion as a warm, living cloak about her. Such devotion awed her to the soul. "I don't want a servant, Desary, but I would dearly love a companion and friend." She raised her eyes to Colfre. "Cyne Colfre, with your permission . . . ?"

Colfre made a sweeping, gallant gesture, smiling his magnanimity at the three of them. "Of course. She shall have the chamber adjoining yours. And surely my kinsman, Catahn, can be persuaded to join us at table for the midday meal?"

Catahn rose and gifted the Cyne with a formal nod of his head. "I am persuaded, sire," he said and returned his gaze to Taminy.

"Delightful!" Colfre seemed ready to clap his hands. "We'll leave you to visit. Someone will fetch you for dinner." He turned to his Durweard. "Daimhin, to our business?"

Feich nodded, eyes wandering to the trio on the lush grass of his lord's garden. Then he followed the Cyne from sight.

"Lady —"

Catahn was halfway to his knees again when Taminy arrested him, laughing. "Please, sir, don't bow and scrape to me. I meant what I said," she added, putting an arm around Desary's shoulders. "I don't want servants; I want friends."

Catahn straightened, looking wild and dangerous among the Cyne's well-bred roses. "My Lady," he said, "you have them."

❖   ❖   ❖

"Was that wise, my lord?"

The Daimhin Feich and his Cyne walked briskly through the corridors of Mertuile enroute to the chambers of the Privy Council.

"What do you mean, Daimhin? Was what wise?"

"Leaving them alone together."

"What — will they now begin to hatch plots against me?"

"Catahn has been openly disrespectful to the Throne."

Colfre laughed. "You mean he's been disrespectful to *me*. His kin got along fine with my dear, gentle, malleable father."

"Sire, the Hillwild have always been rebellious."

Colfre shrugged. "When it suits them."

Daimhin felt irritation tickle his breast bone. "Sire, you do not give this the serious attention it deserves."

Colfre stopped walking and faced his Durweard upon the inlaid tiles of the castle's lower entrance hall, oblivious to the servants and courtiers who came and went about them, bowing without breaking stride.

"Daimhin, you amaze me. Didn't you see what happened in that garden just now? The mighty Ren Catahn humbled himself before that girl and *swore allegiance to her*."

"I saw, my lord."

"Then perhaps you didn't hear properly. 'We are yours,' he said. If he is hers, that makes him *mine*. He has pledged his allegiance to Colfre Malcuim with those impassioned words." He began walking again, missing the look his Durweard passed him.

Daimhin matched his stride. "I wouldn't be too certain of that, sire. You're right, the Hillwild *is* impassioned. But, I have learned not to trust passion. It tends to be fickle."

Colfre chuckled. "Poor Daimhin. A man who doesn't trust his passions? Such a sterile existence. Passion is *life*, my friend. To feel the blood singing in your ears because of a fast horse or a beautiful woman or a victory in battle. I paint my passion. I glory in it. As you should glory in yours."

"Now, sire, I said I didn't *trust* passion. That doesn't mean I won't indulge myself from time to time. But in this case, my lord, I must surely be expected to keep a cool head and a steady heart. I am your Durweard, after all."

"Cool and steady — not *dead*, Daimhin. If you are to

convince the lady Taminy that you're heart over head for her, you can't be nearly so methodical as you sound at this moment."

Feich smiled wryly. "Please, my lord. I fancy I know how to display properly to a young woman. Even this young woman, as peculiar as she is."

"Peculiar? I've heard her called exceptional, magical, rare, even dangerous, but never 'peculiar.'"

"She is, though. While most girls her age are thinking of the dances they will attend and the dresses they will buy, she thinks of Caraid-land and its spiritual malaise. Her passion is for your people, Cyne Colfre. Her longing is to heal your urchins and re-educate your Osraed."

"What? Can you expect me to believe there is no midge of womanly desire in her? Have we some sort of unnatural saint on our hands?"

The tickle in Daimhin Feich's breast moved southward; he could no longer attribute it to irritation. "Unnatural . . . yes, she is that, in her way. I do sense a certain . . . breathlessness in her when we touch, but it's an alien thing. One moment I believe she's like one of your roses; easily bruised. The next moment, I'm just as convinced the whole thing is a facade and . . . and I shall soon encounter thorns. Whichever — she is as I've said: she does things no seventeen-year-old girl should do. She thinks things no seventeen-year-old girl should think."

Colfre smiled, as if enjoying his Durweard's unease. "Are you admitting to me, Daimhin Feich, that you can't spark some desire in that young breast? Are you making excuses already?"

"She's a zealot, sire. Zealots tend to be single-minded in their purpose."

"A zealot? Is that all she is?" asked Colfre, echoing Daimhin's inner-most thoughts. "What was it you called her — 'a fire-slinging hellion?' I've never seen mere zeal sling that kind of fire."

"All right, then, she's a Gifted zealot or a Wicke, just as the Osraed suspect. But, she has her own purposes, sire. Her own agenda."

"Of course she does. And it's up to us to bring those

purposes into alignment with our own." Colfre put a hand
on his Durweard's shoulder. "Daimhin, she's a woman. Or,
if you please, a zealot in a woman's body. Given the right
temptation, that body will betray her. She vibrates the air
she moves through. Or can't you feel that?"

Daimhin laughed. "Oh, I feel it."

"Well, then. She can't be unaware of that. Nor can she
be immune to its effects if we are not."

Daimhin shook his head, puzzled. "That doesn't neces-
sarily follow. . . . My lord, can this be the same girl about
which you expressed such religious concern only days
ago?"

They had reached the council chamber and stopped
before its closed doors. Colfre turned to face his Durweard. "Daimhin, tell me, do you believe Taminy-a-Cuinn
is divine?"

Feich blinked. "You're serious."

"My question is a serious one, yes."

"Then, no. I don't believe it."

"Then do you believe she is the human expression of the
Meri's powers as latent in the Osmaer?"

"I'm not sure what that means, so I can hardly claim
belief in it. I'm not a religious man, as you well know."

"Well, then, do you believe she is a being who — how
can I put it — could in any way threaten your existence?"

"Politically, perhaps."

"Spiritually?"

"No, I don't believe that either. I'm not even sure what
'spiritually' means — if it means anything at all."

"Well then, you have nothing to fear from her. You have
no reason not to view her as a desirable, obtainable, politically
important young woman over whom you find it expedient to
gain control. I must trust you to use your own judgement and
not to violate my best interests. I can have no effect on your
beliefs, Daimhin. Nor can you have any effect on mine."

Feich grimaced. "Meaning," he said, "that if I were to
. . . engender her wrath instead of her love and she did
turn out to be divine or at least divinely powerful, you
could stand clear beneath the awning of your own piety
and bemoan my fate." He shook his head. "Oh, sire, I

wouldn't be so certain. It seems to me you lose out no matter what happens."

"How so?"

"Well, consider the opportunity — if she is *not* divine, you'll have no joy of her. I will. If she *is* divine, she has already peeked into the darkest recesses of your heart and will know that I'm only an amoral agent doing your bidding."

Colfre flushed to the roots of his hair. "You don't *have* to do anything," he murmured, glancing about as if suddenly aware of their surroundings. "I did not command you to seduce her, if that's what you're about. All I've asked of you, Durweard Feich, is that you help me obtain the girl's friendship and endorsement."

"Is her endorsement that important?"

"My friend, it is critical. Why do you doubt it?"

"Perhaps because I'm not sure that controlling her will be as easy as you think."

"I don't care how easy it is — or is not. She is our best and only tool for completely breaking the Osraed grip on Caraid-land. I can't put off the Hall's business indefinitely — not without an impelling reason that the people will support. Whether the Hall comes apart over this issue or whether they condone her or whether they condemn her, I will win the control the Throne should have — should *always* have had — *if she stands with me*. The majority of Osraed in the Hall are Tradists. They have always been my allies, but in this matter . . . " He shook his head. "The damned fools resist change and prattle about covenants and divine will. Osraed Ealad-hach will arrive in Creiddylad tonight. Tomorrow, he'll bring charges against Taminy. Every Tradist eye in the Hall will be on him. *They* will take him seriously simply because he has led them for so long."

"You fear he'll rally them?"

"I've given him no time for that, but he may confuse them, divide them against me. Then again, he may make such a fool of himself that none of them will want to associate themselves with his views. We're going to fill the public galleries with Taminy's worshippers, Daimhin. *That* is the crowd poor old Ealad-hach will play to. If he gets

support from his cronies, louder voices will drown it out."
Colfre smiled and inclined his head toward the double
doors of the council chamber. His Durweard moved
swiftly to open them.

The Cyne's Privy Council consisted of eight members
representing, equally, the noble Houses, the landed Eiric
and merchants, the Ministers, and the Osraed. As tradition
dicatated, Daimhin Feich represented his own House
there, in addition to being the Cyne's closest advisor. If the
rest of them were not Colfre's hand-picked men, they were
at least men who had never shown any sharp disagreement
with his policies. Except, of course, for Iobert Claeg.

There had always been a Claeg on the Privy Council,
dating from the time it was a Hall-appointed device to keep
the Cyne's behavior in check. They were a disagreeable lot, an
historically rebellious lot, and Daimhin Feich believed the
Claeg Chief was the only man on the Council who was not at
least somewhat intimidated by Colfre Malcuim.

His eyes sought Iobert Claeg as Colfre addressed the
Council. He was a fierce looking man, nearing middle age,
with steel in his soul that made eyes, voice — everything
about him — bristle like an armory. He continued to
bristle throughout Colfre's talk of Taminy's sweetness and
the kindness inherent in her miracles, of the fact that she
harbored no animosity toward those who had accused her
of Wickery and heresy. Finding the Claeg Chief unreadable, he turned his attention to Cyne Colfre's words.

"You, gentlemen," the Cyne was saying, "will now put
Taminy's case before your peers in the Hall. You will share
with them the written record of what I found in Nairne's
Osraed court. In a day's time, they will be called upon to
decide if Taminy-a-Cuinn is heretic or victim of funda-
mentalist prejudice. Let them know that their Cyne
believes she is the latter — an innocent victim."

"How — ?" began Ladhar and stopped, his face
coloring. "And if they ask how an innocent can perpetrate
such acts, show such signs as she does?"

"Perpetrate?" Colfre repeated. "We are speaking of
miracles, Abbod. I've seen them. *You've* seen them. The
people of Creiddylad have seen them." He smiled broadly.

"They love her, Osraed Ladhar, because she has befriended them. How can such a friend be suspected of heresy? Simply tell the Osraed of the Hall how very much she is loved."

Ladhar was silent after that, and all remaining questions came from Iobert Claeg. Between them, Daimhin and his Cyne answered them one by one, not expecting for a moment that the Claeg Chieftain believed any of it.

Outside the gates of Mertuile, Abbod Ladhar stood and let the sea breeze cool his heated face. He wished the chill would reach into his soul, but the fire there burned on, oblivious to tempering winds. He felt eyes on his face and knew the Ministers Cadder and Feanag stared at him, waiting for him to speak. "*Loved*," he said at last, making the word repulsive. "She is loved. Loved by a blind, irreligious mob. How badly we have done our work when people can love such an atrocity."

"She serves them up magical poisons," said Caime Cadder, "and they, gluttons, feast and thank her for poisoning them."

"But how does she do it?" asked Feanag, eyes doing a nervous dance between his two companions. "How is she allowed to do good, to call upon Blue Healing, to touch the Stone? I understand none of this."

"A test," said Cadder. "A trial of faith. This is a Cusp — such trials must be expected. Thank God that we see her for what she is."

Ladhar shook with rage. "What? *Thank God?* Will you stand aside, pious, and thank God while your countrymen are being led into darkness? While their ignorant souls rush, like helpless sheep, to their own destruction? While this Dark Sister wriggles her sweet way ever closer to our Cyne — to his heir?"

Cadder's eyes glinted at that — coals longing for fire; Ladhar was pleased to ignite them. "You saw how Colfre looked at her that day in the Shrine. That was worship in his eyes, Caime. Worship. And I've heard that she is a favorite with the Riagan Airleas, as well."

Cadder's voice was hushed and chill. "Worship is to be

given to God alone, and to His Scion, the Meri. Taminy-a-
Cuinn is an usurper — an abomination."

"An abomination," echoed Feanag.

"What do we tell our fellows in the Hall?" asked Cadder.
"Surely we can't speak as the Cyne bids us. Aren't we bound
to tell the truth? His so-called written testimony of the
Nairnian inquiry is incomplete. The claims of divinity Osraed
Ealad-hach alluded to in his letter are completely missing."

"Cyne Colfre asked only that we give his tell of her trial
before the Osraed Body and say that he believes her
innocent," Ladhar replied. "Other than that, we must be
bound only by our consciences. We will tell our peers what
the Cyne believes, then we will tell them what *we* believe."

Feanag seemed uneasy. "She hasn't won *all* the people.
Surely when Ealad-hach brings his charges — "

"She has won the Cyne," said Ladhar and added, "He
paints her portrait in his private chambers, so his servants
say. A portrait even the Cwen is not privileged to see."

He looked back over his shoulder at the castle rising
behind them. A late mist was twisting itself about the
ramparts and bright Malcuim banners, drabbing them in
funereal greys. Ladhar felt the two cleirachs with him
shiver and could not suppress a shudder of his own. Evil
had been planted in Mertuile and struggled to take root.
He felt, stronger than ever, his own divine charter — to
deprive that evil of existence.

Eadmund turned in his bed for perhaps the hundredth
time in the long, sleepless hours since he had lain down.
Truth was, he feared sleep now, for when he slept, *she*
would visit him to pick at his soul, to wear it away, to shock
it senseless. He couldn't close his eyes without seeing her
framed in the doorway of the Shrine, her face gleaming
with reflected Light, radiant, blinding. In that moment of
seeing, as he cowered behind the doorframe, his eyes had
betrayed him mercilessly. The Shrine had fallen away, even
the Crystal had disappeared, and Eadmund had gazed on
the face of the Meri. He'd all but swooned and, swooning,
had crawled away to his room to hide.

Oh, but not before filling his soul with her. Not before

etching her in his mind. She was there when he closed his eyes, so he couldn't close them . . . however much he wanted to.

He couldn't say what pulled him from his bed to the room's single large window or what caused him to settle there in the embrasure, staring out toward the estuary above which Mertuile sat astride her rocky cliff. But once there, his sleep-starved eyes gave him reason to stay. Above the towers and spires of the castle, an eddy of moonlit mist turned in a graceful spiral, inviting Eadmund's senses to dance. He smiled — his first smile in days — and followed the eddy gratefully.

When did he realize it had become something other than what his imagination made of it? He couldn't say. He could only feel cold and hot at once, could only blink his bleary eyes and will them to see ordinary mist. But the mist above Mertuile would not be ordinary. It took on an Eibhilin light, like the liquid in a lightglobe, and it found its own shape — a shape that suggested simultaneously a crystal and a rose.

Eadmund's tired brain boggled. Was it that the rose was made of crystal, or was the crystal cut to the shape of a rose? Then he realized the absurdity of his quandry, for surely a rose-shaped crystal and a crystalline rose were one and the same.

And there the thing was, floating over Mertuile as if it grew from her ramparts, and he couldn't say what it meant except that it filled him with the irresistible urge to laugh or sing. His singing voice being what it was, he chose to laugh. He laughed until tears ran from his eyes and his stomach hurt and his lungs burned. He laughed himself into an exhausted sleep and, in his sleep, he frequently chuckled.

Osraed Bevol gazed up at the night sky over Mertuile and admired his handiwork. Light chased light along the unfolding petal-facets of the aislinn and shimmered in the air around it, making the night glorious.

"Will it be seen by all, Maister?" asked Skeet from beside him.

Bevol smiled. "I wish it could, Pov. For if it were,

Taminy would not be here in this castle surrounded by suspicion and hatred she doesn't deserve."

"Then who will see it?"

"Only those who can."

"Oh, look!" Wyvis had stopped her pony and pointed at the crest of the next low ridge. She turned her head back toward the others straggling up the hill behind her. "Look, all of you! What is it?"

"It's a rose," said Iseabal.

"A crystal," said Aine at the same moment.

Phelan rode up between the two of them, his eyes shining with utter amazement. "It's aislinn. That's some Osraed's doing, for certain. God-the-Spirit! — I've never seen the like."

"Why do you suppose it's there?" asked Wyvis, saucer-eyed.

"It's a beacon . . . to show where Taminy is." The deep male voice came out of the light-sucking darkness beside the road and made everyone's heart shy sideways.

Mam Lusach brought her own mount to the fore and tried to present a formidable appearance. "Show yourself!" she demanded, but the man was already leading his horse out onto the road.

Iseabal gasped. "Father!"

"Aye. Father, it is," replied Osraed Saxan. "A father who thought he'd left his little girl at home, safe with her mother." He eyed up the Apothecary and said, with some amazement, "Dear woman, what in the name of God are you all doing here?"

Mam Lusach cracked a smile. "Following that there aislinn beacon, it would seem."

CHAPTER 18

Let this commandment be a Covenant between you and Me: have faith. Let your faith be immovable as a rock that no storms may harrass, that nothing can shake, that will abide to the cessation of all things. As your faith is, so shall your blessings and powers be. This is Harmony. This is the greatest Duan.

— The Corah, Book I, Verse 10

❖   ❖   ❖

Ealad-hach shivered, though the Hall was far from chill. Giant hearths radiated warmth on this fog-grey day, but it never reached the old Osraed in his witness box. He fumed a bit, still, about the lateness of his arrival in Creiddylad. He'd had time to speak to no one but Ladhar, who confirmed his worst fears: the Cyne had been engaged in a campaign of propaganda all week — a campaign to establish Taminy-a-Cuinn in the hearts of his people. He had primed the Assembly, as well, or at least a good half of it, with his own version of the Nairnian trials; only the Osraed and cleirachs knew, with any certainty, of the abominable claims the wretched girl had made at Halig-liath.

Ealad-hach's eyes drifted through the huge oblong hall from quarter to quarter. To the West sat the Osraed; to the East, the Ministers; to the North was the Eiric quarter, representing landowners and businessmen; to the South, the Chieftains of the noble Houses — Claeg, Graegam, Glinne, Cuilean, Madaidh, Skarf and others, even the Hillwild were represented by the elder Chieftain of the Hageswode, the Ren Catahn's blood uncle.

The old Osraed grimaced with disgust. There was much

shared blood among the Hillwild, for they rarely married out of the Gyldan-baenn. Small wonder such inbreds developed superstitious cravings for arboreal goddesses who would take up Hillwild causes and empower their fey leadership. His eyes roved the public galleries situated on two flanks of the hall between the Assembly quarters where others, who craved a supposed saint's benediction, jostled each other to receive her glance.

She came to her own box then — a flower-decked stall in the rounded northwestern corner of the Hall, situated at the right hand of the Throne. The Hillwild girl was at her side, as worshipful a pawn as her father, who sat in the southwestern gallery reserved for the Throne's special guests.

The crowd at the far end of the Hall, seeing their miracle-worker, went into a frenzy of adulation, calling to her, beseeching her, waving flowers at her — roses, all. And the Cyne — the stupid, dim-sighted young Malcuim Cyne — sat and grinned like a Prentice at Farewelling, confident *he* had a prize in his grasp. Whatever did he think — that with a powerful Wicke at his side, he could overthrow the spiritual institutions of Caraid-land and subvert its religion? Did he fancy the Cwen Toireasa, whose father sat in the Privy Council, would simply disappear while he pursued a relationship with this Dark Sister?

Ealad-hach glanced furtively at the Cwen, seated to her lord's left. Her face was composed, as always — smooth as pale silk. There was no indication that she sensed what her husband was about. Poor wretch. Surely the Meri would not allow it. Surely all things would work to ultimate good.

He heard his name called and realized the adoring crowd had been silenced. He moved to the circular speaker's box at the center of the room and timorously began to present his testimony. He told the story straight out, chronologically, from the time he first became aware of Taminy. He spoke of her oddness, the little miracles, the runebags and his initial suspicions. He told of how he'd tested her at Nairne Cirke and of Aine-mac-Lorimer's accident and of his aislinn and of the eventual trial.

All the while, he looked to Osraed Ladhar for support and found it readily given. Heartened, he began to give the details of the inquiry at Halig-liath when the Cyne stopped him.

"Enough. Enough for now. You have recounted her miracles — we, here, have seen many of those also, have we not?"

The crowd of observers, and indeed, some of the representatives to the Hall cheered at that, and Ealad-hach could only stare at them mutely, his eyes hopping from one eager face to another.

Dear God, his testimony had only made her more a goddess. These people gazed down on that fragile, flower-like face of hers and saw an Eibhilin personage — a Gwenwyvar, a Gwyr, even (Spirit help them!) the Meri, Herself. And how could they not, when that was exactly how she appeared — hair curried to a veil of pale gold, heaven-blue dress contrasting flesh like flower petals.

He wanted to commit violence on her at that moment. He wanted to rush the royal platform and throttle life from the Lie. He wanted to shake her until she dropped her facade and appeared as she surely must be — hideous, stark and colorless. More than that, more — he wanted to beat the beautiful face to horrible, bloody, truthful submission.

His eyes swept the three corner galleries, searching for any face that showed something other than whole-hearted acceptance of the Lie. What they found, instead, was the face of the iron-grey woman, the woman who had panicked him so at Halig-liath. Opaque, shuttered, her sheeny metallic eyes were depthless. Before, he thought he had only mistaken her for a Wicke, now he knew her to be one. And he remembered the name that went with that aging, ageless face — Lufu Hageswode. The Gifted daughter of the Hillwild Renic, Bana-Meg, she had been brought by her mother to Creiddylad's environs that she might be of service to the Osraed there. At the age of fifteen, she had become Mam Lufu, "Mother Love," called "The Solace of the Poor." A saint, some said — a Wicke, the Osraed had decided. All two centuries ago.

"Osraed Ealad-hach, are you ill?"

He woke his stunned being, whipped up his senses. "What, sire? Pardon. Pardon, sire. The noise. It . . . it disorients me."

"I asked you, noble Osraed, to lay forth your charges."

"My — ? But sire, I haven't finished with my evidence. You must hear —"

"We have heard enough."

"Sire, she claims —"

"Order, please!" Acting in his capacity as Durweard, Daimhin Feich stood and rapped his staff sharply on the polished wooden planks of the royal dais. "The Cyne has requested that you name your charges, Osraed."

Ealad-hach shook his head. Cold, frantic terror leapt to his throat. "Don't you see what's happening? Sire, we are surrounded by Wicke! In the gallery there," — he pointed — "I have seen yet another of them! A woman who — !" He cut off, realizing how absurd it would sound, and scrambled within to retrieve his dignity and control. They must not think him a wild-eyed fool. If they had not yet heard Taminy's claims, they would think his ridiculous.

"A woman who?" repeated the Durweard.

Ealad-hach glowered. "You would not believe me."

"Then, name your charges," Feich repeated.

"Very well, Durweard. I charge this young woman with practicing the Wicke Craft, with heresy, and with treason against the House Malcuim and the government of Caraid-land."

What had he expected? That they might applaud him? That they would hum and haw like ruminative wise men, then look calmly into his charges? He had not expected any of those things, yet neither had he expected a complete breakdown of order. That was what he got.

He withdrew amid a roar of hostility, thinking, *So few. So few there are who see.*

Osraed Eadmund was well-acquainted with fear. It seemed he renewed the acquaintance daily now, and he nodded at it again while Ealad-hach addressed the Assembly. Seated next to Bevol among the other Osraed representatives to the Hall, he had all but folded over in his chair when Ealad-hach turned to look at him — directly at him — and tried to catch his eye. He felt no better now, as the elder Osraed removed himself from the speaker's dais. The public galleries were alive with hoots and cat-calls, giving the great chamber an almost festive atmosphere, but through it all, Eadmund could feel Ealad-hach's hatred of Taminy unfurling behind him in a smoky black wake. He found the hatred frightening, more so because he knew it was a shared thing, being fed by some of the very men who occupied the Osraed gallery with him. He was amazed at his own sensibilities; he could almost see the emotion as smudgy tendrils reaching towards Taminy's box. He wished he could Weave a shield around it.

The Cyne called up his witnesses. They told of miracles great and small — so many, so frequently in the last week, the listeners must have been tempted to think, *Well, of course, she performed miracles! What else would one expect her to do?*

Cyne Colfre himself gave testimony as well, describing the Episode of the Rosebud, which Ealad-hach had related somewhat lop-sidedly as an attempt by Taminy to dupe the citizens of Nairne. And he related the events at Ochanshrine, making Eadmund break into a cold sweat and tremble like a newborn foal. He even called upon Abbod Ladhar to corroborate his story. The Abbod did so, but grudgingly.

Then, Eadmund heard Durweard Feich's voice making the ritual call to the Hall for fair judgement. The hearing was over. The young Osraed shifted in his seat, puzzled at the omission of Taminy's claims — claims he had heard as clear as Cirke-chimes at her inquiry, claims Ealad-hach had spelled out in stark clarity in his letter to the Abbod. He glanced sideways at Osraed Bevol and saw that the elder Counselor was already coming to his feet.

"Wait, lord!" Bevol called. "Should we not hear from the cailin herself? Should not Taminy be allowed to speak on her own behalf?"

The public approved this loudly and many Assembly

members added their overwhelming and curious assent. The Cyne hesitated. Then, with a smile that could have melted metal hearts, he gestured for Taminy to stand and address the Assemblage.

In the public gallery, people crowded against the heavy wooden balustrade, holding their breath. Durweard Feich, Eadmund noted, did more than hold his breath. He gripped his staff so tightly his knuckles showed white. His eyes were on Taminy, who rose as bidden and gazed around the hall, her own eyes seeming to touch each face as they had done that day at Halig-liath.

She spoke then, in a voice that was clear and sure. "I am Taminy-a-Cuinn of whom it has been said, 'She is a Wicke.' I am not a Wicke. I was a Prentice at Halig-liath during the reign of — "

Durweard Feich and the Cyne both moved to snatch her attention. She glanced at them and smiled. Eadmund almost smiled with her.

"I was a Prentice at Halig-liath," she repeated. "My father was Osraed and the Council allowed my studies to please him, somewhat against their best judgement. I am grateful to them for that. I was later expelled from Halig-liath by the Osraed Council before I could complete my Prenticeship."

The audience hissed and grumbled at this; Cyne Colfre smiled and most of the Osraed around Eadmund cringed and made sour faces.

"I went on a forbidden Pilgrimage," Taminy continued, then paused, face lowered as if in reflection. When she raised her eyes again, tears sparkled there. "My father returned alone and told the Osraed Council I had drowned, because they could not be told the truth."

Durweard Feich came swiftly to his feet. "A sad tale, dear cailin. We now see how you have suffered at the hands of the Osraed. Their cruelty does not bear further hearing."

Taminy turned to him. "But I've not finished my Tell."

"Let her speak," said Bevol quietly.

"Yes!" The Ren Catahn stood among the royal guests. "Let her speak. Let us all hear what she has to say."

"Really," interrupted Cyne Colfre, "it's hardly necessary. We can see she's innocent."

"Can we?" shouted Minister Cadder. "Let her speak!"

It became a chant. A chant Eadmund found even on his own lips. "Let her speak! Let her speak!"

Durweard Feich pounded his staff for order, but order could not be had. Friend and foe alike roared for Taminy to continue. Feich gave up and sat down to glare balefully at his Cyne. The moment he sat, the crowd quieted.

In the relative silence, Cwen Toireasa, who had been only a bystander, looked from her mute husband to his grim Durweard and shook her head. She gestured at Taminy. "Go on, Taminy. You said it was thought you drowned. Since that was obviously a lie, let us now hear the truth."

Taminy looked out at the Assemblage — the curious and the eager and the fearful and the hateful and said, "I am Taminy-a-Cuinn, daughter of Osraed Coluim-a-Cuinn, Cirkemaster of Nairne during the reign of Cyne Thearl. It was said of me that I drowned a hundred years past. I drowned only in the Meri's glory. I entered the Sea of Light only to become one with it. I, Taminy-a-Cuinn, became and was these hundred years, the Vessel of the Emerald Meri. I have returned as Taminy-Osmaer — Divinely Glorious. That is my new name. That is my Station."

The room erupted. Not a body remained seated; not a soul remained calm. Taminy-Osmaer brought a roar from the throat of the Hall that had never before been heard. The Assembly of Caraid-land was reduced to a boiling rabble.

Amid that turbulent sea, the Ren Catahn made his way from the southwest corner of the Hall to where his daughter and Taminy stood. His face was dark with anger and fear. His hand rested on the hilt of his sword.

It was Osraed Bevol who quieted them. He came to the speaker's dais and, climbing upon it, waved the crowd to silence. There was more than mere will in his gestures, Eadmund knew. He felt the fabric of the Runeweave, soft and silken. It sounded of pines playing the passing wind and smelled of summer meadows. The crowd let itself be lulled.

Then Bevol held up his hands and cried, "Have you nothing to say? Are you wordless, able to utter only animal sounds? Perhaps you are all bewicked, your mouths woven shut by this hideous creature?" He gestured at Taminy, who still stood in her box, her expression unchanged.

Osraed Ladhar rose ponderously to his feet and grasped the rail before him. "I will speak. Do you endorse this cailin and her claims, Osraed Bevol?"

"I do."

A murmur traversed the galleries.

"Then you are misled, Brother, for she makes a heretic of you."

There was some assent to that, but it had gained little momentum before Catahn Hillwild halted it. He took several long strides away from Taminy's box into the middle of the floor. "The Hillwild," he said, "stand behind the Lady of the Crystal Rose, ready to serve her. We, too, endorse her and her claims."

Eadmund's entrails clutched painfully as a sweep of vertigo passed over him. *The Crystal Rose!* That was *her* emblem emblazoned in this early morning's sky. And hadn't he known it? He vaguely heard the Osraed Lealbhallain and Fhada endorse Taminy, saw the two of them pale and sweating, step away from the press of bodies in the guest gallery. He felt his own body move, felt it rise to unsteady feet. What should he do?

"I don't understand her claims," protested the Eiric Selbyr, and from the Minister's northern gallery, the cleirach Cadder cried, "What need to understand them? They are pure, lying evil!"

Arguing broke out then, as Eadmund tottered among his peers. Sides and exception were taken in loud voices and words eloquent and ineloquent. Dizzied by the swirl of dissension, Eadmund made his way to the rail of the western gallery. "Please!" he choked, then cleared his throat. "Please!" Eyes turned to him, snarls died to growls. "Why must we do battle over this girl? The Covenant of the Meri is clear; we will not be left unguided in the face of evil. That same Covenant is equally clear on the nature of evil: evil cannot undertake the causes of good."

"Do you say," asked Ladhar from beside him, "that she is good?"

"I say," said Eadmund, and was sure he must melt under Ladhar's gaze, "that she has Woven miracles in the presence of many, myself included. If these miracles produce good results, then their source must, itself, be good. If they produce ultimately evil results, then, and only then, can we condemn their source as evil. Have her miracles produced good results or ill?"

There was some shoving in the public gallery and a woman's voice cried, "Good! She is good!" A chorus of other voices joined in.

Ladhar roared. "Her miracles have brought disunity and uncertainty to the members of this Assembly, to the members of the Osraed Body, to this entire country. That is pure evil!"

"But are those the ends?" argued Eadmund. "Are those the ultimate results of her work? Can we say, now, that she will not cause us to consider our own works and strive harder to perfect them? If she is of God, she must prevail, and in fighting her, we wrong her and we wrong God. If she is not of God, she will soon destroy herself, for evil does, ultimately, destroy itself." He made the mistake of glancing into the Abbod's face and his words failed him. "Please . . . can't we just leave her alone and — and wait to see what happens?"

From the floor, Bevol leveled a finger at him. "Feeble! Lukewarm! You vacillate, brother! You hide behind your fears!"

Yes, I do! cried Eadmund's silent spirit. *I do hide!*

Bevol continued to rebuke him. "Such half-hearted rejection is unworthy of the Meri's Chosen. Look at her, man!" He smote his fist on the balustrade of the speaker's box with a loud crack that caused the entire chamber to jump. "Study her. Interrogate her. Test her, if you will. But by the God of the Meri, *decide* about her!" He came down from the dais and strode the floor, reproving each of the four Assembly galleries. "Dismantle everything she has said and done," he told them. "Sift through it. Tear it apart

and put it back together again. *Then*, Pillars of the Hall —
THEN — either reject her — " he swung to point an
out-thrust finger at Taminy — "or accept her."

"Study her? *Test* her?" Caime Cadder launched himself
out of the Ministers' gallery and onto the floor, advancing
toward Bevol and Taminy. "Ludicrous! A waste of our
time! Pillars of the Hall, listen to me — Bevol distracts you
with rhetoric." He came face to face with Bevol before
Taminy's box. "Distracts you from the one pertinent detail
in which this girl is lacking." He turned to point a
trembling finger into Taminy's face. *"This girl bears no
Kiss! The Meri has never touched her!"*

The observation caused the room to erupt again, and
Cadder used the frenzy to bring himself closer to Taminy.
Before Bevol could interfere, the cleirach grasped her arm
and attempted to drag her from the box. "Look at her face!
Look at it! There is no mark there! There is no Kiss! She
lies! *She lies!"*

In the roar and rage of the crowd, Cadder's snarls were
lost. He shook Taminy harder, setting off a frenzy of
movement among her nearby supporters. But frenzy
exploded into chaos when, from the girl's forehead, issued a
flash of light — pale, emerald and too bright to look upon.

Cadder shrieked and stumbled backward to the floor,
rubbing his eyes frantically. The crowd cared little for him.
Their eyes were on Taminy, who stood on her dais, the stellate
mark on her brow shedding its Eibhilin gleam over all.

The chaos collapsed into a tingling, awful hush. No
voice spoke; no body moved to creak a bench, scuff a
heel, rustle a cloak. All watched as the light pulsed and
dimmed but did not vanish. No newly chosen Osraed had
ever had a Kiss so bright. Eadmund looked at it with
longing.

Bevol spoke. "It seems that Minister Cadder is wrong.
There is no detail in which Taminy is lacking, no sign she
cannot show you."

"Lies!" Cadder lifted himself from the floor, blinking
tears from his light-scalded eyes. "I will not believe her to
be divine!"

Bevol shook his head, then addressed the assemblage.

"What sign would you like to see next, before deciding about Taminy-Osmaer? She could perform *any* task if it would make you believe her Tell. But what good does it do? One test after another she passes; one sign after another she shows, and still you balk. Show us this, show us that! And when you are shown, you cavil and ask to be shown something more. These shows of miracles are useless. If they are proof, they are proof only to those whose lives they touch. Do not test Taminy-Osmaer with miracles and shows of power. Do not question her ability to show you greater and greater marvels. Test her spirit. Question her purpose. That, venerable Pillars, is *your* test." He gave the Cyne curt bow and left the Hall through the western doors.

Colfre came shakily to his feet. "Well," he said. "Well . . . We have seen . . . great wonders. But — but Osraed Bevol is correct. You," he raised his eyes to the galleries, "must compose your questions. Whatever questions you deem fitting to ask . . . this young woman." He turned to his Durweard then. "Daimhin, kindly dismiss the Assembly." He afforded Taminy one bemused glance before retiring from the throne.

"I thought you said she understood." Colfre did not wait for his Durweard to close the door to the salon.

"*She* said she understood." Feich's demeanor was cool and collected which thoroughly irritated his Cyne. "I believe she *did* understand."

"And merely forgot?"

Feich shook his head. "My lord, you saw what happened. She was silent until Bevol encouraged her. And she didn't . . . display that . . . sign until Cadder pressed her."

"Pressed her! The man attacked her! *In my presence!* Fanatical idiot." The Cyne paused to chew his lip. "It could work out for the best, though. Ealad-hach made the Osraed look ludicrous and Bevol, with his insulting sermonizing, simply added to that impression."

"Sire, I think you overlook an important point. *We* were not in control of that situation." He gestured in the general direction of the Assembly Hall.

The Cyne gazed at him, slow light dawning. "Bevol."

"Yes, Bevol. He played the Hall — and the crowd — like an expert hawker."

"But why? Is it personal power he seeks, or is he convinced he's doing the Meri's will?"

"Knowing his history, I should say the latter. Does it matter?"

Colfre clicked his tongue. "Now, Daimhin, you surprise me. Of *course* it matters. If Bevol is seeking personal gain, he can be bought or flattered into collusion with us. It's clear he has little personal regard for his institution. If he's doing the will of the Meri — or believes he is — he will not be dissuaded."

"Nor, my lord, will *she* be dissuaded from doing his will."

"You believe he controls her to that degree?"

"Isn't it obvious? We will not be able to control her as long as he does. I tell you, I had convinced her not to speak."

Colfre nodded. Osraed Bevol was, indeed, becoming a monumental nuisance. "What are we to do, then? Bevol is not likely to just go away and leave her to her own devices . . . or, should I say, to ours."

Daimhin twitched like a man who has just dreamed himself falling. "No. No, I suppose not."

They were interrupted then, by a courier who told them that the Hall was ready to reconvene. Colfre tried to ready himself for what that session might bring, but there was no way he could have been ready for the complete change in the demeanor of the Hall's members. Except for some indeterminate grumbling, they behaved most civilly toward Taminy as they asked her a battery of questions which bored their Cyne almost to tears.

What was the substance of the Meri? The answer: a twin spirit and a body of Eibhilin Light.

Was she spiritual or material? She was spiritual, her vessel was material. Together, they existed in a state that was both and neither.

Why did She communicate through these so-called vessels? Men could not withstand the glory of Her

Presence; Her beauty was too great to be borne. One soul in a generation could contain her, a female soul. That could change, Taminy added.

Why was she here? To remind the Osraed of their purpose and to establish a female order of Osraed; to purify the Osraed institution.

Why was that necessary? (Here, Colfre sat up and took note.) Decay, she said. The Osraed had become distracted. It was time for cleansing, time for reawakening, time for a Cusp and a New Covenant.

A New Covenant. Colfre liked the sound of that. He tried the words against his own impending proposal and liked it even more. His mind began to turn over the possibilities and the last few pieces of an idea fell into place.

He smiled. A New Covenant. He liked the sound of that.

In the jostle of people funneling from the Hall's public gallery, Aine somehow got separated from the others. Stretching and turning in the press of bodies, she struggled to see them, but found that sense inadequate to the task.

She was being pushed along on a slow current toward a door to the outer ward when someone stumbled against her. The touch sent a shimmer of awareness through her — a thrill of familiarity. She turned, expecting to see a friend and found herself gazing, instead, into the startled eyes of a stranger. The young woman stammered an apology and, hugging the child she carried to her shoulder, moved away into the crowd.

In due time, Aine was deposited in the outer ward and glanced around, seeking her companions. She found them, at last, standing in a tense knot beside a vintner's shop, and made her way over, dodging other members of the audience too deep in their discussions to care where they stepped.

"Aine!" Iseabal saw her and held out eager hands. "We feared we'd lost you completely."

Aine took the other girl's hands gratefully. "You'll never be half so lucky as that."

"I've never seen such a crowd," said Mam Lusach, checking Aine over as if a piece of her might be missing.

"It was like being caught up in a river current."

"Or a herd of sheep," Aine observed, then added, "Someone touched me."

Phelan laughed. "Well, I should think, in all that — "

"No, I mean, I *felt* someone touch me. Oh, stop laughing — you don't understand!" She looked to Osraed Saxan for some serious attention and got it. "It was so queer, Osraed. All these people were pressed in about me and I felt this . . . this Touch. As if one of you was there beside me. I thought it *was* one of you, but when I — " She stopped. There it was again, like the shivers she got from climbing out of cold water into the warm sun. It raised goose-flesh all over her.

She turned and saw the same woman standing across the shop-lined aisle and holding the hand of the little boy she'd been carrying earlier. She was clearly startled to have a group of strangers suddenly staring at her and began a shuffling retreat. She'd taken no more than two steps, though, when the child began to resist. She paused to listen to his chatter, shook her head, glanced at Aine, then, with a look of fearful resolve, allowed the little boy to lead her to where the others stood watching.

The child spoke first. "Are you friends of the Lady Taminy?"

Aine was too startled to reply. The Osraed Saxan was not. "Yes, we are. We're from Nairne and we've come here to be close to her."

The boy craned his neck to look up at his mother. "You see, Mama, we weren't being silly, after all. They're friends, too."

"You know Taminy?" asked Iseabal.

The woman nodded, smiling diffidently. "She healed my boy, Losgann. And she . . . she gave me this." The woman opened her left hand, exposing the palm. Drawn there, as if in faintly glowing ink, was a star-shaped rune.

Aine gasped and heard the sound ripple through the group around her. She displayed her own palm, as did Iseabal and Wyvis, Rennie and Phelan, Orna and even Mam Lusach.

"My dear God," murmured Osraed Saxan and stared into his own palm. "I didn't . . . I didn't realize . . . " He looked at their new acquaintance. "Mistress, we've heard rumor that Taminy has been working miracles in Creiddylad all the week. Is that so?"

"Oh, aye." The woman nodded, her little boy echoing the movement.

"Then there must be . . . Are there others . . . like us?" He indicated the star-decked palms outstretched between them.

"Oh, aye," was the answer. "As many as her miracles, I reckon. Would you like to meet them?"

Saxan smiled. "Mistress, there is nothing we'd like better."

Daimhin Feich let himself into the Privy Council's chambers and paused by the door, looking perplexed. "Gentlemen, I'm surprised to find you here. Can you be finished with your deliberations so soon?"

The two men there shifted guiltily before Minister Cadder said, "No, Durweard, but nearly so. We are here because the deliberations have taken an unhappy turn." There was no hint of respect in the man's voice.

Feich ignored that and, smiling, spread his elegant hands. "Then wouldn't your peers benefit from your opinions?"

"Our peers are asses," replied Cadder and drew a censuring *shush!* from his companion, Feanag.

"And what has caused this sorry metamorphosis?"

"Need you ask, sir? It's that damned girl. She seduces them, as she has seduced your lord . . . and yourself, it would seem."

Now, Feanag's thin lips disappeared completely and Feich laughed. "Oh, she is a mighty seductress, that one, I agree. The beauty of her face, the calm, sweet, reasonable music of her voice. And you're right — Colfre is quite smitten."

Cadder narrowed his eyes, studying the Cyne's Durweard as he might an oozing sore. "And you are not?" No belief there, only ridicule.

Feich shook his handsome head. "I'm a dense individual, Minister Cadder. Dense and suspicious. Taminy-a-Cuinn wastes her efforts on me. But the Cyne — that's another matter."

Cadder came several paces nearer the younger man, still examining him. "You sound so casual — so unconcerned. Have you no reaction to her miracles?"

"I suppose I am amazed by them — when they first occur."

"And do believe their source to be divine?"

Feich smiled. "No."

"Then have you no fear for the soul of your Cyne?"

"I can't say that I fear for his *soul*, Minister. I'm not certain he possesses one. Why should I waste my fear?" He ignored Feanag's hiss of disbelief and continued. "I do, however, fear for his life and his throne and his people. Yes, I do fear for Colfre. I don't like to see him manipulated by a shrewd magician."

"A magician? Is that what you think of Taminy-a-Cuinn?" Cadder's scorn was palpable. "Believe me, what she did with the Osmaer Crystal was no mere magic."

"Ah, but I didn't see that. I have only a second-hand tell. I never believe hearsay. Besides, I was not thinking of her so much as that peculiar Osraed of hers."

"Bevol?"

"Aye, Bevol. Now, there's a grand manipulator."

Cadder moved even closer to Feich, his body and face speaking the language of conspiracy. "You disliked what you saw of him today in the Hall?"

"I did. Heartily. But I can hardly disregard the desires of my Cyne and pursue my own opinions. I can advise Colfre; I cannot command him."

"And if you could, would you . . . put an end to this manipulation of the throne?"

Feich nodded, his face completely sober. "Most assuredly."

Cadder studied that face for a moment then glanced at his tight-lipped peer. "Then, you would be pleased to see the Wicke destroyed?"

Feich blinked. "The Wicke? Why destroy her?" His emphasis fell gently on the last word.

"She's evil. She's the manipulator of our Cyne, whom you — "

Feich was laughing. "Open your eyes, cleirach. It isn't

Taminy who is evil. It isn't Taminy who manipulates. I doubt she even authors those so-called miracles that so impress our unlettered brethren. She's a toy, gentlemen. As Colfre is a toy. As the Cwen and the Riagan and, yes, your dear Abbod are toys." He held up a finger. "The player, gentlemen — the player is Bevol." Feich paused, glancing from one cleirach to the other, then said, "I must be going. This is hardly the time for frivolous conversation. I adjure you, Ministers, do return to your Pillars and attempt to sway them to the right way. We tread a dangerous path."

He slipped out as he had come in — swift and quiet — leaving a silence behind him that was as tightly woven as any inyx.

The cleirach Feanag swallowed noisily, straining silence's fabric. "Is he right? Is Osraed Bevol that powerful — that evil?"

Cadder's hooded eyes forfeited nothing of his thoughts. "It makes a certain sense. Think, Feanag. The power she's displayed are those of a consummate Weaver, not a child barely old enough to be out of Prenticeship. Not a female. Even a Wicke shouldn't be able to field such power. But an Osraed . . . "

"An Osraed mighty and learned enough to be at Apex," added Feanag.

"Yes. I believe he may be right."

"What do we do?"

"We do what the Durweard suggests; we attempt to sway our *peers*." He clapped his associate on the shoulder then, and hurried him from the room.

In a seaward window embrasure, the curtains kicked as at a swift breeze. But it was not a breeze that descended, on four feet, to the floor.

Airleas, his face pale, turned to his companion, quivering a little in fear-dappled rage. "What does it mean, Skeet? What was Daimhin saying?"

The older boy's mouth was set in a grim line. "Nothing but what he wanted those two to understand."

Daimhin Feich watched his Cyne for several seconds

from the shadowed doorway before making his way out onto the bridge to the Blue Pavilion. He knew Colfre well — better than anyone else did, including Cwen Toireasa. They had been raised almost as brothers, for Colfre's father, Ciarda, had been an egalitarian monarch, loath to separate his son from the children of the noble Houses. Because of his father's duties as Chancellor, Daimhin's family had lived at court; the two boys had chased through the same gardens, eaten at the same table, and played the same games.

Daimhin Feich looked at Colfre now and wondered if that was still true or if the game had changed . . . or if they had. And when? Could he trace Colfre's erratic behavior to his meeting with Taminy-a-Cuinn, or had it begun when he first conceived of himself as the first Osric of Caraid-land? And at what point had Colfre Malcuim begun to have secrets?

Daimhin crossed the bridge, drawing a smile from his sovereign. *And what is going on in the royal head now, my lord?* He did not return the smile. "Sire, the Pillars of the Hall seem to believe they have come to some decision."

Something like fear flickered momentarily in Colfre's light eyes but the smile barely faltered. "They've reached agreement? I suppose I can't be surprised."

"Agreement? I think not. But I'm told they've come to terms."

Colfre shrugged, not quite able to make the gesture nonchalant. "With?"

"They won't discuss that with us, sire. Why break centuries of tradition because of one unprecedented event? They'll announce in chambers."

Colfre said nothing, merely nodding his head like an old woman, again and again. Frustrated with his silence, Daimhin asked, "What if they condemn her?"

"Does it matter? The people will condemn them, I will do likewise, and she . . . she will do whatever she does."

"And if they endorse her?"

"Then she will endorse me."

"And the Osraed?"

"And the Osraed, and the Osraed. What do I care for

the Osraed?" Colfre leaned forward on his bench, fist clenched before his face. "I have them, Daimhin. Either way, I will remove them from power."

"You believe Taminy will confirm you as Osric?"

"Of course she will."

"If Bevol desires it."

"Whether or not Bevol desires it."

Daimhin studied his lord for a moment, uncertain he wanted to ask about this sudden certainty. But he did ask. "And what fills you with such certainty?"

Colfre's smile widened to a white gleam in the slight duskiness. "I have dreamed."

Daimhin was sure his face must look at least as blank as his mind had become. "Sire?"

Colfre rose to face him, his face alight with a strange, eager, sweating wonder. "Last night I dreamed. I dreamed I was walking in my gardens and saw a rose growing there that surpassed all others in beauty. Its petals were clear, transparent and golden. I went to pick it from the bush, but a raven flew down and tried to pluck the flower from me. Before I could chase the wretched creature away, the rose burst into flame. And I . . . I was transformed into a dove — my namesake. I spread my wings and flew above Mertuile. Then I woke. I didn't realize what it meant until the Assembly met this morning. I was afraid at first. I'm not ashamed to admit it. But then, I realized it was supposed to happen that way. The Rose burst into flame today, Daimhin. I will soon soar in the updraft of those flames. I have but to let Taminy-Osmaer work her will, and I will be Osric of Caraid-land."

Daimhin did not need to ask if he truly believed that — the answer was written plainly in Colfre's face. Whether he really believed it or not, he wanted to and therefore would.

Colfre rubbed his palms together. "Shall we hear their decision?"

"Sire, in view of what you've told me, I think it might be a good idea if we waited until morning."

"Why so?"

"We should formulate how we will respond in each eventuality. And we should discuss the options with Taminy."

"I told you, Daimhin, we don't need to do that. She'll know what to do. We've only ourselves to worry about."

Daimhin bit back his frustration. "Of course. Then we shall plan only for what we need to say and how to say it. There is, too, a third possibility — by far the most likely. And that is, that the Pillars will agree within their respective groups, but not as a whole."

"So much the better. Divided, they look like a directionless rabble. It will be obvious that the Spirit does not guide them."

Daimhin nodded. "I see, lord. Yes, of course, we must prepare for that eventuality also."

"We will be prepared for *any* eventuality, Daimhin."

Daimhin Feich nodded again and managed a conspiratorial smile. He left his Cyne's presence knowing that if they were to be prepared for any eventuality, he would have to see to it.

Bevol folded his stole onto the foot of the bed and coiled his prayer chain atop it. The crystal caught fire from the bedside lightglobe, winking into the semi-darkness of the chamber. "I'll take a walk before I retire, Pov," he said.

"Yes, Maister." Skeet bobbed to his feet.

Bevol smiled. "Alone."

The boy's lips compressed. "Then you'll be taking your crystal, surely."

"No need."

Dark eyes flitted to the window and back. "Maister . . ."

"Pov-Skeet, you've acquitted yourself well these years. My Weard and companion, worthy protegé . . . son. Strange, the way the Meri answers prayer. Childless, I have had more sons and daughters than most two men. You" — he pointed at Skeet's nose — "were a particular surprise." There was no answering grin. He didn't expect one. "You've made safe those papers, have you?"

"Aye."

"Good. I wouldn't like to think someone could sneak in here and snatch them while I'm out strolling. This castle isn't a friendly place. Still, you know who your friends are."

Skeet didn't reply, but merely looked at him with unreadable eyes. He sighed and held out his arms. The boy flew into them and clung, reminding Bevol — if he needed reminding — that there really was a boy, after all, beneath Skeet's peculiar poise.

Anomalies — I am surrounded by them.

"Be safe, Maister." The voice was muffled against Bevol's robe.

He chuckled. "I am always safe, Skeet. Always."

He closed the door behind him, but did not, for a moment, imagine that it would create a barrier to Skeet. Those eyes would be on him, regardless of walls or doors or circumstances.

He eschewed the floral gardens this evening and made his way leisurely along the battlements on the seaward side of the castle. He was in no hurry; the sea air was to be savored. The sky was still red to the West and he was no more than a silhouette against it — a shadow drifting toward absorption by the coming night.

He sensed before he heard the approach of others. They came along the walk from the shadows of one great tower, stealthily, they imagined.

"Good-evening, gentlemen," he greeted them, and couldn't help but chuckle at the surprise in their half-masked faces. "Will you join me in my walk?"

CHAPTER 19

Has My patience made you bold and my mercy made you careless? In search of fire, you follow your passions along treacherous paths. You eschew the Sun in favor of a manmade flame. Do you think Me unaware?

— *The Book of Pilgrimages (Osraed Aodaghan)*

❖   ❖   ❖

The house was neither spare nor lavish, its neighborhood neither poor nor rich. Both were unremarkable, but Iseabal was thrilled, nonetheless, by the thought that, here, she would meet others who believed in Taminy-Osmaer. They went to the front door, which surprised Iseabal. Somehow she thought they ought to be sneaking through darkened alley-ways to secret chambers.

When the door was opened to them, their escort, Haesel, held up her left hand, exposing the palm to the master of the house. A greeting was given and, one by one, the Nairnians passed through the portal, each showing his or her palm to the doorkeep. That turned out to be a portly, greying gentleman with a ruff of wiry beard and a distinct twinkle in his eyes. He told them his name was Grimnis. Iseabal liked him on sight.

The others were in a large inner room still lit by candle and wick. They seemed unsurprised that Haesel Sweep had brought new faces with her, but only looked up with friendly curiosity when she and the master of the house led them in. Of great surprise to Iseabal was that the leader of the group, or at least its present focus, was an Osraed. The man was younger than her father, but similar in build and carriage. He greeted them cordially, seeming especially pleased to see another Osraed, then introduced them around the group.

There were eighteen of them, all told — old, young, rich, poor and in-between — and Iseabal felt as if she knew each and every one of them and had for a very long time. It was an odd feeling; though her eyes told her their faces were unfamiliar, her spirit informed her otherwise.

The tall, spare Osraed, Fhada, explained that they awaited a decision; the Hall would confirm that it believed Taminy to be Osmaer, or it would reject her.

"And if they reject her?" asked Saxan. "What will you do then?"

Fhada smiled. "We don't know. But we're sure to receive guidance. Each of us, from the moment She spoke to us, has received guidance. If not for that, we would never have been able to find each other."

A commotion from the hallway preceded the arrival of the Osraed Lealbhallain. Iseabal and her companions had little chance to react to his unexpected presence, for everyone else in the room at once clamored for him to speak.

He did speak, blinking in disbelief at the familiar faces he saw. What he said was, "There's been no decision. Osraed Bevol has disappeared."

"I'm very sorry about your friend." Cwen Toireasa trailed elegant fingers over the marble balustrade. Her eyes, shadowed with concern, searched the grain her fingertips traced as if the answer were there. "With your Gift, can't you tell what happened to him?"

Taminy shook her head, not quite rousing herself from her own contemplation of the glen where they strolled — a place with a tiny stream and a fish-filled pond that reminded her of her forest glen at home. But this glade was enclosed within tall grey walls; only the air here was free. "It's as if a door closed, cutting off all light and sound. He's gone."

The Cwen's face paled. "Do you think he's dead?"

"I don't know. I've never felt another person's death

before — not really. Before, when I was . . . the Vessel, death only made people clearer — stronger."

Toireasa gazed at her with wonder. "Death is not an end?"

"Not to the Meri. Not to the Spirit." She watched her fingers twist the sash at her waist. "My parents died while I was in the Sea. I felt them each grow in brilliance at the moment they fled their bodies. I felt them touch on me with joy. I was joined to them, linked — indissolubly, I thought. Until I stepped out of the Sea. Then they were muted to whispers and I was alone. Except for Osraed Bevol and Skeet and Gwynet. Now, there's only Skeet, and the Cyne won't let me see him."

The Cwen laid a hand on Taminy's shoulder. "Do you know who has done this? Is it . . . my husband who's caused Osraed Bevol to disappear?"

Taminy shook her head. "I don't know, mistress. I sense hostility beyond the walls of Mertuile . . . and within them. I don't think any one man is responsible."

The Cwen nodded. "I'll arrange for you to see Skeet. Colfre need not know — nor Daimhin Feich." She glanced across the glade to where servants prepared refreshment beneath the carefully supported boughs of a gnarled conifer. "Tea's ready now," she said, and turned.

There was a shout from somewhere above them — a commotion high up on the inner wall. Distracted, Taminy turned, shielding her eyes against the Sun. There was movement amid the bright light, venom amid the movement. Something whistled through the air and Cwen Toireasa screamed. Taminy's world tumbled suddenly end over end as someone hit her, knocking her to the ground. Sound warped into a cascade of shouts and screams. Then she was being dragged bodily toward the castle.

She had Woven a Ward without thinking about it. Now she strengthened the shield, making her assailant gasp and let loose of her.

"My lady!"

In the lee of Mertuile's sheltering haunch, she turned and found herself face to face with Daimhin Feich.

"My lady, are you all right?" His eyes were over-bright

and his flesh ashy, though color burned in his cheeks.

"What happened?" she asked. "Why did you — ?"

Cwen Toireasa was between them then, grasping her shoulders. "Someone shot at us from the inner curtain. A bowman. Are you all right, Taminy? He didn't — " Her eyes fell to Taminy's skirts, widening in her blanched face.

Following them, Taminy saw at once the cause of her fright. A crossbow bolt was lodged in the heavy fabric over her right thigh, its murderous barb shot clean through and out again like a giant's sewing needle.

Daimhin Feich gave a strangled cough. "Cyne's grace, Taminy! You were near hit." He took her arm again, shepherding her up onto the broad stone verandah that adjoined this side of the garden. There, he seated her on a padded bench, dropping down beside her, his eyes drowning her in anguish.

Taminy glanced over his shoulder at Toireasa. She could not have read the other woman's face, but the feelings behind it darted this way and that around a central core of steely conviction. "I'm going to speak to the Captain of the Guard," she said. "I want to know how this could happen."

Bending to remove the bolt from Taminy's skirt, Daimhin barely seemed to note the Cwen's departure. Taminy gazed down on his dark, gleaming hair and found herself courting the most peculiar array of emotions. As if he sensed her regard, the Cyne's Durweard raised his head and caught her in his eyes, dizzying her. Her heart pounded against sudden restriction and heat rose in her cheeks. She did not comprehend what she felt, could not say, "This is good," or "This is bad." She could only stare at the man, mute and perplexed.

He took her hand, fanning the blaze in her cheeks, making her skin creep pleasantly. "Taminy," he said, his voice a whisper. "Dear Taminy, how close I came to losing you. If that bolt had found its mark — " He bent his head, pressing lips to the back of the hand he possessed, then turning it to kiss the palm.

Choruses sang in Taminy's ears, chill-hot dancers pirouetted up her spine, while a sensation that was not quite pain awoke in the place from which Healing flowed.

She thought of a sharp-clawed bird stretching its wings within her, pressing at the confines of her body. Something was being born within her, and she knew it to be desire. She did not thrust it away, but touched the new sensation, explored it, turned it over in her soul. Her left hand, still her own, moved to rest on Daimhin Feich's glossy hair. It was thick and she twined her fingers in it, feeling heat from the flesh beneath, feeling her own heat rise. Was this the beginning of love?

He raised his head again, his eyes bright and exultant. *They Weave*, she thought. *They Weave webs about me. Webs like hot silk*. She wanted to wear that garment, wanted to wrap it about her and feel it glide warmly against her skin.

As if he read her thoughts, he brought his lips up to brush hers in the merest, teasing whisper. He withdrew slightly to look at her then, to let his pale eyes Weave out more web. Satisfied with what he saw in her face, he raised his hands to her hair and pulled her gently to a second kiss, his tongue parting her lips and running lightly over her teeth.

The fiery bird within Taminy's body dug in its talons and beat at the confines of her womb. Liquid fire flooded her, hot and moist. She trembled and, feeling her tremble, Daimhin pressed his kiss home, tangling his hands in her hair, driving the breath from her lungs.

A sound from down the verandah caused him to free her and move away, hastily adjusting the folds of his tunic below its wide leather belt. He glanced up at her from beneath dark lashes. "Forgive me, lady," he said, but there was no regret in his eyes. He turned as a pair of guards hurried toward them, looking fierce and efficient.

He took them aside to confer in hushed tones while Taminy stared at the crossbow bolt that lay at her feet. She picked it up and turned it in her hands, puzzled by what it told her. Gradually, her trembling eased and was replaced by the memory of why she was the target of such a thing.

"The guards regret that the man who fired that fell from the curtain and was killed." Daimhin stood looking down at her, his lips curled wryly. "Most likely it was some religious fanatic —"

She shook her head, stopping him. "The man who fired this was paid to do it. There was no passion driving him."

Daimhn Feich's brows scaled his forehead. "A paid assassin? How do you know?"

"I can tell much in a touch," she said. *Except yours. I can tell nothing from your touch except that it burns me and makes me want to worship the fire.*

He smiled at her and held out a hand. "You must change those ruined clothes, my lady. Let me escort you to your chambers."

She did let him. He was visibly disappointed to find Desary Hillwild there, but Taminy was glad. Glad to slip out of his silken webs, glad to silence the clamor of her body. But when the door of the chamber closed she was assailed all over again by Desary's impassioned anxiety.

"I should have been there, Mistress!" the Hillwild girl protested. "Whatever was I thinking?"

Taminy managed a smile. "That your father might like to see you?"

Desary shook her head, sending a cascade of dark hair over her shoulders. "I should have been with you, Taminy. I won't leave your side again, I promise."

Taminy was grateful for that, but Desary's promise was put almost immediately to the test. Called to an audience with Cwen Toireasa in her ground-floor salon, the two girls were intercepted by Daimhin Feich who insisted that Desary go on ahead while he spoke privately with her mistress.

"I spoke to the Cyne," he told her as they strolled slowly through the broad corridors toward the castle's seaward side. He did not touch her, but moved along only a breath away. She felt static rise between them and prayed she might stay grounded this time. "He is mightily distressed and bids me tell you we will find whoever hired the assassin and punish him before the eyes of Creiddylad. The Cyne is very fond of you, Taminy. Though not, I think, as fond as I am."

She glanced up to catch his smile. It flooded her with heat. She looked away.

"Wait, lady!"

He turned her to him, hands firm on her shoulders. From the tail of her eye she saw Desary pause far ahead of them. The girl didn't turn, but merely stood, waiting. She gave her eyes back up to him and he seized them.

"Your manner tells me you are uncertain of me. I apologize, again, for my behavior earlier — I would apologize a thousand times if it would soothe you. But I must tell you — yes, I *must* tell you — that I am driven only by my attraction to you, an attraction I am at a loss to fight or fathom." He raised a hand to tilt her chin upward and studied her face, stroking her lower lip with his thumb. "Tell me I needn't fight, Taminy. Tell me that the fires within you are as fierce as the ones that light my soul. Do I see that same attraction in your eyes or do I only wish to see it?" He shook his head, anguish in every feature. "No, I'll not be a coward in this. Let me bare this soul to you, Taminy-a-Cuinn. Let me tell you I am driven by love."

She quivered under his touch — waiting, breathless, for the stroke of his lips, the dart of his tongue. She had a sudden desire to press herself against him, to know what it felt like to meet him body to body, to be clasped in his arms.

He lowered his head, but did not embrace her. "By the God of all things, I would die to show you love's ways. I would die of sheer joy if we could live, side by side, submerged in each other till the end of time. But . . . " He dropped his hands to his sides and stepped away, leaving her to sway like a mast stripped of supporting lines.

Dear God, the wind is so strong here.

He gazed at her from too far away. "But, this . . . situation . . . Everything is so uncertain. Caraid-land is being torn apart by the forces that control our lives. Colfre struggles to hold it together, but I feel the fabric being rent. You feel it, too."

I am being rent.

"The Assembly is wracked with indecision, the Osraed have been discredited and Caraid-land reels in search of spiritual direction. With Osraed Bevol gone, with no heir to the position of Apex, how can they find it?"

There was a tiny explosion of light in Taminy's head.

"But that's why I . . . that's why I'm here. For direction."

He grasped her hands in his. "Yes. I know that. You belong to this people. And believe me, Taminy, their eyes are on you every moment. They pray for your glance, for your smile. They wait for you to give them direction. I fear only that — " He lowered his eyes.

"Only what?"

"That the direction you choose will carry you away from me, along a different path. I must stay with my Cyne. No matter what, Taminy, I must be at Colfre's side to guide and protect him. But I would rather, with all of my heart, be at yours." He narrowed the gap between them again, standing mere fingers' breadth away. "Only you know which it will be. Only you can decide whether we are together or apart."

Taminy all but held her breath while frissons of awareness scattered over her, tingling on the tips of her breasts. She looked up at him, struggling to read him. *Why is it so difficult? Does love block the Touch?* She had never known that to happen before. And she had only this much knowledge of desire. "How can I?"

He shook his head. "I can't ask it."

"Tell me, please, sir."

He looked anguished again. "No, no! Speak my name."

"Daimhin," she said.

"Ah." He groaned as if the sound burdened him.

"Tell me."

"The Osraed can no longer guide Caraid-land; only Colfre can. He has been visited by dreams — aislinn which tell him *he* is the one the country must look to for leadership. Now, he is forced to share that burden with lesser vehicles — the Assembly, partisan as it is, and the weak and corrupt Osraed. But if their responsibilities and duties were laid upon him alone, if he were Osric — Cyne by Divine Right. He could take the reins of government in strong hands — hands guided by the Spirit and the Meri. Colfre believes only you can bestow that station on him."

"He believes I am Osmaer?"

"Yes, he does."

"And you, what do you believe, Daimhin Feich?"

"I believe I love you."

"And if I endorse Colfre as Osric — ?"

"Then you would be spiritual allies, cojointly caring for the souls of Caraid-land. The infighting of the Houses, the greedy plunder of the Eiric, the fanaticism of the cleirachs, the corruption of the Osraed — all set to naught. By you and Colfre."

"And you would be at my side?"

"Forever."

A movement in the tail of her eye reminded Taminy that another had made that promise and now kept it, if from a distance. "Others have also made that pledge. Can I trust you to keep yours?"

"You wound me in asking," he said and kissed the palm of her left hand. He let go of it rather suddenly, and stepped back from her, eyes searching.

She smiled at him. "The Cwen will wonder why I am less than obedient in answering her summons." She started to walk again toward the waiting Desary.

"She does not summon you, lady," Daimhin told her. "She requests your presence."

He left them at the door to Toireasa's salon, not by choice, but because the Cwen's Maid refused to admit him, insisting that her mistress was "indisposed." The real reason for the Cwen's reticence met them as soon as they entered the room. It was Skeet who greeted them, Skeet who informed them soberly that he couldn't tell them where Osraed Bevol was or what had happened to him.

"Then, is he dead?" Taminy asked. "Have they killed him?"

"I can't answer you that, Mistress," Skeet said.

"Then there is no spiritual heir to the Apex. The Osraed will have to elect. And that will take time." *Time in which Caraid-land will wallow without direction, for at this moment, I have none.*

"Oh, but there is an Apex already appointed, mistress," Skeet told her, his eyes glinting oddly. "Osraed Bevol left his testament with me."

Taminy felt amazement all the way to the core of her soul. All the while she had been assaulted with the distractions of Mertuile, Bevol had kept his eyes wide open, had known danger surrounded them, and had taken precautions. "While I slept," she murmured and felt as if, drowning, she had just pulled her head clear of the water.

"What, mistress?" Desary asked her. "What did you say?"

"I said I've been asleep, Desary. I pray God I am at last awake." She turned back to Skeet. "Who is it, Skeet? Who is the new Apex? We must summon him."

Skeet smiled. "Why Osraed Wyth, of course, mistress. And I've already seen to his summoning."

CHAPTER 20

This is the hour of dawn. The light of the Sun is not yet at the height of its power. When the Sun has ascended to its midday station, its flames will blaze so hot that they will excite even the crawling things under the earth. Though they cannot perceive the Light, yet they will be set in frantic motion by the heat.

— *Testament of Osraed Bevol*

❖   ❖   ❖

"Osric?" Iobert Claeg spoke the word as if he'd never heard it before. "And what in the Name of the Spirit shall we want with an Osric? There's never been such a thing in the history of Caraid-land."

"Ah, not so," Colfre corrected him. "Malcuim the Uniter was Osric before Ochan gathered up the Osraed and established that sacred institution at Halig-liath. There was no official Assembly then either, if you recall. Merely a rabble of House and village representatives who fought over land rights and whether or not to give their young men into Malcuim's army."

"Aye, well I don't recall, sir. I ain't that old." He glared at Colfre, then took a stroll from one end of the Cyne's dais to the other.

Bristling, Daimhin thought. *A Claeg through and through.*

"Tell me why my House should support this Osric nonsense. What do the Claeg — or any other House," he added, glancing at Daimhin Feich, "have to gain by your becoming divinity?"

"Not divinity, Claeg," Colfre corrected, rolling the

chalcedony ring about on his finger. "No, sir. The only divinity at Mertuile is Taminy-Osmaer. I'd be merely Cyne by Divine Right."

"Merely, eh?" The Claeg Chief cocked his greying head. "By *her* say-so?"

Colfre nodded. "By her say-so. If I am Osric, she will be at my side. And with her at my side, it will be springtime in Caraid-land eternally. Miracles, by God, every day of the year."

"But why should the Claeg support such an idea? If you mean to disband the Hall —"

Colfre raised his hand. "Not disband it, merely limit its capacity to advisory. And the Claeg will forever be represented on the Privy Council, which will retain its consultative status."

"The Hall and the Osraed were for checks and balances, Cyne Colfre," Iobert reminded him. "What's going to check you if you get some squirrel-brained notion about warring on the Deasach or taxing the breeches off the Houses?"

"Taminy-Osmaer."

Daimhin watched the Chieftain's face as he chewed that idea. *Love-struck old fool. Softening that iron heart is one of her finer miracles.*

"Why are you in such a hurry with this, Colfre?" the Claeg asked finally. "Why can't the Hall wait until a new Osraed has been elected to Apex?"

"What? Shall Caraid-land hold its breath while every Osraed within its borders is visited by dreams and visions? While the Osraed Council sifts and ponders and prays itself to a divine revelation? Shall Taminy go unvindicated while they regroup? Do you not understand what is happening, Iobert? The cup of revelation has passed from their withered lips to her young and vital ones. She — and not the Osraed — represents the Meri in Caraid-land. There is a new order coming into being and Taminy-Osmaer is its mother."

Iobert Claeg snorted mightily, but Daimhin could tell he was not unimpressed. "Making you its father?"

Colfre merely inclined his royal head.

"Aye, well, you are the Malcuim. I suppose we can do no better."

"I was the first to recognize her," Colfre reminded him. "Except of course for Osraed Bevol."

"Aye. And he's dead, most likely. Meanwhile, you've let someone's henchman get a shot at her, too."

"My Durweard was there to protect her. And the would-be assassin paid with his life."

The Claeg glanced at Daimhin, then, a wry twist to his mouth. "Your Durweard protect Taminy-Osmaer? I saw that woman straighten a man whose back was crippled with pain. I saw her ward off that idiot cleirach, Cadder. And I heard what she did to him in the Shrine. I'd not be too sure your Durweard had aught to do with it." He made a gesture of dismissal. "Never-the-less, I'll carry your politicking to the Houses. Good luck with the Osraed."

The Claeg had nodded a curt dismissal and turned to leave when a lackey in Malcuim colors scurried into the room with tidings that obviously could not wait. He spilled them before he'd even come to a stop before the throne.

"My lord, there's an Osraed Wyth just outside in the vestibule. He claims he's the new Apex of the Triumvirate."

The Hall was to reconvene. With a new Apex, duly confirmed in a testament produced by Taminy herself, there was little that could be done to stall. The unexpected appearance of the young Osraed put Colfre in such a high state of nerves, Daimhin could scarcely maintain his patience. It was idiotic; barely a month ago Colfre had assured him the young Counselor was too uncertain of himself to warrant worry, and now he was mumbling about acts of God and watchful demons.

"Did you not dream?" Daimhin asked him the eve of the Assembly. "You told me you dreamed that you were to be Osric. If that's so, then why should the appearance of this boy unnerve you?"

"The circumstances," muttered Colfre. "He must have started from Nairne the very moment that Bevol . . . went missing."

"Sire, he is endorsed by Taminy. As are you. How could

he be a threat to you? Surely, if she is an ally, he is one also."

Colfre could not dispute the logic of that. "You're certain she will endorse me? She will confirm that I am to be Osric?"

Daimhin smiled a smile that went all the way to the core of his being. "I'm certain, lord. I have spoken of love to her — of spending eternity at her side. I have all but worshipped her. And I now know that we possess no unnatural saint. There is fire in that young body and I have warmed myself in it."

To his surprise, Colfre paled. "What have you done? You haven't . . . violated her?"

"My lord! I courted her. I saved her life, regardless of what the Claeg would have you believe. We've kissed, nothing more. Rest assured, I will not 'violate' her, as you so politely put it. When she capitulates to me, she will do so of her own free will. Where is the victory, otherwise?"

"Victory?" Colfre clutched at the collar of his tunic as if it had suddenly grown too tight. "She is Osmaer," he whispered. "You cannot mean to — to conquer her."

"Is that not what you meant to do, sire?"

"No! Never that. Never!" Agitated, the Cyne paced away from him down the length of the Taminy mural he had recently begun. He paused below the panel wherein she emerged from the Sea, naked and streaming ocean froth.

Daimhin's eyes were drawn to the half-finished likeness and he wondered how close Colfre's imagination came to reality. Shaking off the heat that evoked, he dragged his eyes back to his lord's ashen face.

"I meant to gain an alliance," Colfre was saying, "a meeting of minds and hearts. My intention was friendship, not conquest."

"Ah. Forgive me. I mis-spoke. But no matter." He smiled brightly. "We have a friend. And we have made friends for her, too, have we not?"

Colfre nodded. "Yes. Yes, and she will remember that, won't she? There are those who hate her, but surely she realizes we did not mean to make enemies for her — "

"Sire, she understands that the enemies she has made

are enemies because *she* threatens their authority. She doesn't blame us for Ladhar's implacability or Cadder's histrionics. After all, look at her claims."

Colfre visibly calmed himself. "Yes. Yes, of course, you're right. She knows what's in our hearts, after all. She knows I love her. As flesh may love the divine," he added.

Daimhin smiled indulgently. So much for his fear that Colfre would be jealous of his own dealings with the lady. *Your flesh may love the divine as deeply as it wishes. Mine desires its like.*

It was desire that led him to Taminy's door later that same evening. That and a hope that she might capitulate to his desire. He found her with company. Not only Desary Hillwild, but the Osraed Wyth and Skeet and, most surprising of all, the Riagan Airleas. There were candles and tiny lightglobes set in a circle about the carpet of her room and he thought they must have been praying for their lost Osraed.

After a moment of discomfiture, his composure returned and he begged the lady's indulgence and a brief audience with her. Her eyes like jewels in the unsteady half-light, she bid her companions leave her. He waited, smiling, looking like a young man in the throes of first love. He watched his own reflection in her mirror and was pleased by what she would see when she closed her door on the others and turned to look at him.

Heat licked up his spine when her eyes touched him. It was the light. It spun a sun-halo around her head and made her face seem gilded. She was dressed in a soft robe not fit for day wear; gone were the layers of skirts and laced up sous-shirts. He could make out her form beneath the fabric and it prompted the absurd thought that Colfre's paintings were products of cowardice. A man with any blood in his veins would choose to sculpt.

He took her hands. "I had to see you once more before the great and glorious day. Tomorrow, Caraid-land receives direction."

"Yes." She nodded, her eyes never leaving his face.

He smiled. "I thought your eyes were jewels. I was wrong. They're seas. Let me drown in them."

"I drowned once," she told him, "in the will of the Meri. In the glory of God. I live to immerse myself in that. I *am* immersed in that at every moment."

He kept his smile in place, though her words annoyed him. "Of course."

"Of course," she repeated. "Of course, he says, as if he understands what he does not believe."

"Believe? Taminy, beloved, I believe in you."

"And do you then believe in the Meri? You once seemed unsure."

"I suppose I am coming to belief."

"I tell you She exists and that She expresses Her will to me now, as we speak. Do you believe?"

He nodded. "If you say it."

"If I say it? Because you believe in me, you will believe in Her?"

"Yes."

"And do you then believe in God, the Spirit of This All?"

"I . . . if you say it is so."

"I say it is so. I am the expression of That Will. I do That Will. Will you also do it?"

He wanted to drop her hands but found he could not. "What do you mean?"

"What if it is not the will of God that there be an Osric this generation?"

"What?"

"What if I tell you it is not God's will that Colfre Malcuim be Osric? What would you say?"

"Why would it not be God's will? Colfre has had aislinn visions — "

"Colfre has dreamed what he wishes to dream. And he plots. And you plot with him."

"I? No, Taminy, believe me, I . . . You mistake me — "

"No, but almost." She let go of his hands, leaving him oddly bereft.

"Tell me, Taminy, tell me why Colfre may not be Osric. Tell me and I'll try to understand." The anguish he heard in his own voice surprised him. He prayed his Feich ancestors that it was convincing.

"Colfre is weak. Weak of spirit and conviction. Weak even, in his own avarice. His mind struggles against the real and seeks compromise where compromise should not be sought. He must not be Osric of Caraidland. To place such power in his hands would be the undoing of everything that has been accomplished here."

"You . . . you will not confirm him?"

"I do the will of the Meri and the Spirit. Whose will do you do?"

"Don't ask me to betray my Cyne, Taminy. It's too much, even for your sake —"

She shook her head. "Not my sake. Yours. You try to seduce me to your will —"

Startled, he threw himself to his knees before her. "Yes! Even if it damns me, yes! And I'd do it again." He held out his hands to her. "I am nothing but desire for you. I look at you and loyalty becomes only a word, a vague and pious concept, a shadow. Touch me," he demanded. "Touch me and feel the truth of my words. Touch me and your will is mine."

"I don't need to touch you, Daimhin Feich. I can feel you from here, pulling at me. I've never known desire before," she added, her voice a murmur.

He smiled, engagingly, he hoped. Was that vulnerability he saw in her eyes? "Am I to be damned for awakening in you what you also loosed in me?"

She was silent, gazing at him, her eyes in shadow. She shook her head. "No, not for that."

His hands quivered between them, still reaching for her. She seemed to study them for a moment and then, with deliberate langor she reached out and brushed her fingertips across his. The shock that tore through his body stunned him almost witless. He felt scalded and frozen, certain only that that had been no mere discharge of stray static. He tried to take her hands again, to draw her to him, but she would not allow it.

Instead, he grasped the folds of her robe and pulled her into his arms, pressing his face to her abdomen. "Taminy!" He made the name a duan of desperation, crying it against her, willing it to burrow into her, to strike her core. Hands on his shoulders, she pushed him away.

He was tired. Tired and stunned to have misjudged her attraction to him so badly. He rocked back on his heels and sat looking up at her, watching her hand find the place his face had rested, the place where his tears of frustration had stained her robe. "Is this my punishment, mistress? Do you punish me?"

She shook her head, no longer looking at him, looking beyond him. "No, Daimhin Feich. You punish yourself."

He pulled himself to his feet then, and found his way unsteadily to the door. In the mirrors he looked utterly defeated and dejected. That was good. He paused with his hand on the door latch. "What must I do to win back your trust, Taminy-Osmaer?"

She did the most confounded thing then — she laughed. It was a bright, cold sound like a shard of crystal, and it cut. "But I do trust you, Daimhin Feich," she said, and turned away from him.

He watched her in the mirrors until the door closed.

Osraed Wyth could not help but be awed by the size and grandeur of the Hall. Floors of native stone and tile glistened, the wooden galleries gleamed, chandeliers composed of myriad lightglobes added their own radiance to the warm splendor of the waning Sun that cascaded from high mullioned windows.

Everyone had spent the day in preparation. The servants had scurried and polished and cordoned and laid out food and drink in the Throne Room for what Colfre expected would be his very own jubilee. Taminy and her companions had spent the day in meditation and prayer.

Wyth would have been among them had he not now been on the Assembly. They had deliberated for some hours both in their constituencies and with the general membership, carefully drawing up their responses. And their responses were two-fold; for the Hall was split over Taminy-a-Cuinn and no amount of miracles or consultation or doctrinal exposition would mend the breach. Wyth's testimony of the Meri's nature and of Taminy's claims served only to confirm the already confirmed. Those who believed her to be both Wicke and heretic were not at all impressed.

While the clear majority affirmed that Taminy possessed powers and insights which could only come from the Eibhilin realm, they were not an overwhelming majority, and the opposition could hardly pretend to be neutral. When all was said and done, there were two implacable camps. Iobert Claeg would speak for the assenters, while Osraed Ladhar represented the dissenting view.

By sunset the the Hall was aswarm with people and aswim in the warmth of their bodies. The audience had been allowed to expand onto the floor between the Assembly Galleries, leaving only a portion of the floor area before the royal dais for the Speaker's box.

To Wyth Arundel, the babble of voices sounded like the utterances of the Bebhinn many times amplified. They hushed as the Cyne appeared with Taminy at his side, the royal family, his Durweard, and Desary Hillwild following.

Durweard Feich called the Hall to order and gave a summation of the case of one Taminy-a-Cuinn, claimant to the station of Osmaer. There was no one to whom the Durweard's words were news, and the faces turned up to him from the floor of the Hall were eager for the proceedings to reach their climax.

As was traditional, a spokesman for each group within the Hall rose and presented the view of the constituency. Only tonight, the refrain was different. "We are divided," said the Osraed Ladhar. "We are divided," announced the Minister Cadder. "We, too, are divided," agreed the Eiric Selbyr.

The last to stand was Iobert Claeg. Clutching the hilt of a sword whose only purpose was supposedly ceremony, he rose and glanced at the watchful faces in his gallery. His eyes rested longest on Catahn Hillwild, whom he had invited to sit next to him, then he turned to the Throne and announced, "We, the Chieftains of the noble Houses of Caraid-land and of the free kindred of the Gyldanbaenn are not divided. We offer up our lives and our loyalty to Taminy-Osmaer — with one accord."

And so a Claeg, for not the first time in Caraidin history, brought down the roof of the Assembly Hall. The crowd, by and large, was jubilant, and the royals were obviously pleased. Those who had reason to be uneasy, were, and Wyth could not help but notice that Daimhin Feich was among them.

Iobert Claeg remained standing during the uproar, waiting with rock-like patience for the room to quiet. When, at last, it did, he continued. "I, Iobert Claeg, speak now as representative of a clear majority of the General Assembly of Caraid-land. We hereby declare that to the best of our determination, Taminy-a-Cuinn's claims as to her existence and nature are authentic and faithful. We recognize her as Taminy-Osmaer, Voice of the Meri, and we await her good-pleasure." He then offered Taminy, seated at the Cyne's right hand, the deepest bow anyone had ever seen a Claeg perform.

To the crowd and the Throne, this was reason for further celebration. People on the floor had risen and, forgetting that there was another quarter unheard from, began to dance about and sing. At this point, the Osraed Ladhar rose ponderously to his feet and began to stamp in a slow, measured cadence. Other members of his constituency followed suit until the great chamber echoed with the sound of his army's stationary march. Everyone in the Hall turned to look at the dissenters; everyone quieted and waited for the march to end.

When it did, Ladhar trundled to the lip of the Osraed gallery and addressed the crowd. His face glistened with sweat, but the light of righteousness was in his eye. Wyth, standing near him, saw clearly that he was a believer in his own cause. The younger Osraed could hardly despise him for his words.

"I, Osraed Ladhar-a-Storm, represent the minority of the General Assembly of Caraid-land. We hereby declare that, to the best of our determination, Taminy-a-Cuinn's claims as to her existence and nature are incredible and insupportable. We deny that she has any station that we, as members of the Assembly, should recognize, and do declare that we believe her to be both Wicke and heretic and the majority of this Council to be misled."

Ladhar's pronouncement was met with a barrage of jeers. The Cyne, obviously pleased by that, rose languidly from his throne and came to the edge of the royal dais, his hands raised as if to bestow a benediction on the teeming crowd which, seeing him, quieted respectfully.

Colfre smiled and spoke out in a loud voice. "Friends! The Osraed Ladhar and his constituents have a right to their beliefs, however much they depart from ours. There is but one more quarter to be heard from. The Lady Taminy-Osmaer will now address this assemblage."

There was silence as Taminy rose and came to stand at the lip of the Cyne's dais. All faces turned toward her, faces of both friend and enemy. All waited eagerly or anxiously to hear what she would say. Pulled as if by a magnet, Wyth slipped from the Osraed gallery and moved toward the head of the Hall. He dimly perceived movement elsewhere, as well, but his eyes were for Taminy this moment, and would not be pulled away. She looked out over the crowd, and Wyth knew that each person in the room would feel that he or she had been the special recipient of her gaze. Then she spoke.

"People of Caraid-land, your Osraed have told you that we are in a Cusp. They have not lied. This is the Golden Cusp, a time of challenge and of change. A time when discerning truth from error is nearly impossible. A time when men's hearts have grown tepid and their minds are caught in the snares of tradition and complacency. A time when mortals reach out their hands and attempt to wrest sovereignty from the Eternal." She glanced back over her shoulder toward Durweard Feich, who had straightened, gripping the arms of his chair. When she faced the crowd again she said, "I am Osmaer, living symbol of the New Order, center of the Covenant between God and Meri, Meri and Man. My purpose among you is to refresh and renew and protect your faith, to clear the dross from the mirrors of your souls.

"There are some among you who doubt that purpose. I am saddened by that, but I cannot judge you for what you truly believe — the Spirit will judge the depth of your faithfulness. There are others among you who would subvert that purpose and use it to your own advantage. I cannot judge you for your lack of belief — the Spirit will judge the depth of your faithlessness.

"There is a man among us," she said, and both the Cyne and his Durweard leaned forward in their seats, "who aspires to share my purpose. Who desires to stand beside me and guide the souls in this room and beyond. Who wishes to hold Caraid-land in the palm of his hand, like the jewel it is, and to possess it."

She turned and pointed to the throne and the man in it, the yards of pristine silk in the cloak-sleeves of her gown making her look like some white, winged being stretching itself toward flight. "Cyne Colfre is the man. He is now Cyne of Caraid-land, lord of the House Malcuim, descendant of Cynes, but he would be more. He would be Osric — Cyne over you all by divine right."

She gave the crowd a moment to assimilate that. Behind her, Colfre beamed. He came to his feet amid the growing swarm of murmurs.

Then Taminy raised her hands, bringing the crowd's attention firmly back to herself. "People! Listen to the words of the Meri: neither Cyne Colfre nor any other man shall be Osric of Caraid-land!"

Colfre's smile froze in place, then shattered as if struck from his mouth. He came to Taminy's side on uncertain feet.

Wyth felt his muscles coil and he edged closer to the dais.

"What? Why? *Why* have you done this? Have I not been faithful? Have I not believed? Have I — "

"DAEMON!" The shout came from Daimhin Feich's throat. He rose from his chair, face radiating red fury, finger pointed at Taminy. "Foul daemon!"

Wyth's body was a pillar of ice. The cry was suddenly in the air all about the hall as people darted out of the crowd toward the dais — toward Taminy. There was hatred in their faces; more terrifying still, there were weapons in their hands. Wyth had none. Empty-handed he leapt to

Taminy's defense, praying he would reach her before that maddened cleirach with the pike.

Cries of outrage rose all about him, the chamber seemed to spin and the floor to shrug under his feet. He cut in front of the cleirach, certain that any moment the pike would be buried in his back. But it wasn't, and he reached the dais without harm. Desary Hillwild was there before him, struggling with Daimhin Feich, who was trying to push her over onto the floor several feet below.

Then a hand overshot Wyth's shoulder. It belonged to the wild-eyed Minister. Grasping for Taminy's arm, he caught the folds of her sleeve and, for a sickening moment, Wyth feared he would wrench her from the platform. He reached up his own hands, struggling to break the hold the other man now had on Taminy's wrist. He could feel the other's weight upon his back, hear his hoarse yelling in his ear. "Daemon! Die, daemon!"

People milled frantically about them while, above them on the royal dais, Daimhin Feich turned hate-filled eyes on Taminy and raised his staff to strike her.

Light, sharp and clear and painful, exploded from Taminy's body, and from her forehead the Meri's Kiss shone like a great, blinding jewel. Feich dropped his staff. The cleirach wailed in agony and fell away from Wyth's back. In the confusion, Wyth was able to drag himself up onto the dais, where he stood shoulder to shoulder with Desary Hillwild and others that appeared like wraiths about them. He glanced wildly about, squinting in the glare of Taminy's glory; there was Aine-mac-Lorimer and Iseabal-a-Nairnecirke and even her father, Saxan. There were others he knew and more he didn't know, and all were coming to stand in the radiance of Taminy-Osmaer.

Their enemies, seeing this, raised their weapons and pressed forward, trying to shield their eyes. The cleirach with the pike clambered onto the dais and raised his weapon over his head. The Ren Catahn appeared behind him, sword drawn, his arm cocked for a strike.

"NO!" Taminy's voice washed over them as if in chorus. "No, Catahn, there must be no blood spilled on my behalf!"

She raised her left hand. Beside her, Aine-mac-Lorimer echoed the movement, and from her palm, shot another agonizingly glorious beam of light. It smote the cleirach in the eyes and all but felled him. The others followed suit. One by one, they raised their left hands, one by one they added to the streams of glory until the royal dais gave birth to a sunrise.

Wyth, amazed by the sight, tentatively raised his own hand. Exquisite energy coursed through him, bringing tears to his eyes and a cry to his lips.

"Here! Here!" He heard the shouts and tried to discern their source.

From a doorway at the back of the royal dais, a man in dark leathers beckoned. The Ren Catahn, seeing him, called out, "Lady, to the door!" And to his daughter, "Get her to the door!"

Their response was immediate. Still encircling Taminy, her little group of followers began to press backward toward the exit. As they retreated, the people on the floor came on, friend and foe alike. They crowded the edge of the dais, reaching their hands out as if they could feel the substance of Taminy's glory.

Seeing them advance, Cyne Colfre raised his royal skirts and disappeared behind his throne. His wife, the Cwen, and his young heir, remained seated, watching. But Daimhin Feich was not willing to either flee or stand aside. Eyes streaming, he glanced wildly about, until his search was rewarded. Flanking the Cyne's throne were two bowmen. Feich leapt upon the nearer of them and wrested his weapon away. Whirling, he brought the crossbow up, seeking a target among the bodies surrounding Taminy-Osmaer. Taminy willingly gave him one. Cleaving the ranks of her companions as if they were the waves of the Sea, she brought herself into Feich's sights.

Unbelieving, he lowered the bow. "What are you?" he asked. "Tell me that before you die."

She spread her arms wide as if to embrace him. "I am your Beloved, Daimhin Feich."

He raised the bow again, sliding away the safe-latch. But something drew his eyes upward toward the darkened windows. His face paled, and horror scrolled across it. Lips drawn back in a snarl, he roared aloud and fired his bolt at the empty air. High above, a window shattered. Daimhin Feich dropped the crossbow and ran.

Beneath a shower of glass, Wyth and his companions fled. With Ren Catahn and a phalanx of armed Chiefs as their rearguard, they funneled through the open doorway, finding their path lined with fierce-looking men in the colors of the House Claeg. The grizzled warrior who led them was Iobert Claeg, himself. They were escorted swiftly through to the outer ward where a teeming crowd had gathered — a crowd which even Mertuile's Great Hall could not hold.

Impatient to hear of Taminy's acceptance, people pressed upon the gates of the inner ward hoping to hear a word from those more privileged. Instead, they saw the object of their desire whisked into their midst surrounded by armed men. Crying out, they put out hands to touch her, strained to catch a glimpse of her radiant face as she passed by. "What happened?" they asked her escort, and the reply set up an outraged refrain: "They tried to kill her! The Cyne tried to have her killed!"

The crowd became a mob, howling over the treachery. Some of them followed Taminy from the castle, some of them turned to assault the gates of the inner curtain.

From the midst of the empty Cyne's Market, the Ren Catahn looked back over his shoulder at the wild scene framed by Mertuile's outer gates. Wyth saw his teeth flash in a great brilliant smile. "By the Kiss! I'd not ask for a better rearguard than that."

They moved on then, swiftly, into the dark eve of the Cyne's jubilee.

CHAPTER 21

Know that each soul is molded in the nature of the Spirit; that each being is pure and holy at its birth. The souls will vary only as they acquire virtue or vice in the World of Shadow and Light. Yet, at birth are all souls are pure.

— *Prayers and Meditations of Osraed Ochan, Number 19*

✧　　✧　　✧

Cyne Colfre Malcuim closed the window of his salon and drew his jacket more tightly around him. Watching him, Daimhin Feich mirrored the movement. Normally, he would have savored the landward breeze, for at this hour, it carried the scents of the marketplace — baked goods and ciders and spices. This morning, it bore only the ragged sounds of protest, the sounds of the mob that snarled at their gates. Through the night they had been there — hounds at a hare's hole — while their Cyne cowered within.

"How did it happen, Daimhin? Explain to me how this happened."

Feich, his eyes sunken hollows in his snow-field face, did not look at his Cyne. "If you'd be more specific, sire —"

"How did she betray us? You said you were certain of her."

He made himself smile. "I thought I had convinced her of my love. I thought I had convinced her of her own desire. (I *had* convinced her.) She rejected both. Obviously, she felt this creature she worships to be more important than those things."

"The Meri is not a 'creature,'" Colfre said quickly and glanced about him as if expecting daemons to erupt from the floor. "She is divine. How much more proof of that do you need?"

"No more, I think, if by divine you mean supernaturally powerful."

"And yet you tried to kill her." Colfre muttered. "You set that pack of — of fanatics on her."

"They set themselves upon her. And after she denounced you, after that demonstration of her power . . . I was afraid. Afraid for your life — afraid for all our lives. I believe she may live closer to chill hell than the Eibhilin realm."

Colfre ogled at him. "Don't say that! Dear God, she might still be able to hear you. Why do you say that?"

"What I saw." He shook himself, remembering.

"What?" asked Colfre. "What did you see?"

"A door into hell. A bright, horrible portal into — " He shook his head, lacking words.

A noise interrupted, and a lackey entered the chamber, bowing. "Pardon, sire, but Cwen Toireasa wishes to confer with you privately. She's in the lower hall."

"The lower hall?" Colfre repeated. "Why there? That's hardly private."

The lackey bowed again, nervously. "I don't know, sire. That's what she said — the lower hall."

The Cyne nodded. "I'll come directly."

The lackey bowed a third time and left the room.

"What do we do now?" Colre asked. "You're my Durweard, advise me. What do we do?"

"Let me think. Speak to the Cwen. When you're finished with that, perhaps I'll have some advice to give you."

Face bleak, Colfre went to his Cwen.

In the lower hall, Colfre found, not only the Cwen, but Airleas. Both were dressed for travel, and through the open front doors of the hall he could see a waiting carriage.

"Airleas and I are leaving Mertuile," Toireasa announced. Her voice trembled slightly, but Colfre didn't wonder at it. With the castle surrounded by a rabble, she might well be nervous.

He nodded, feeling just a little bleaker. "Yes, I agree it would be a good idea for you and Airleas to be elsewhere until this situation is . . . in hand. Where do you propose to go? Ochanshrine would no doubt welcome you."

The Cwen's smile was ironic. "I doubt that. I propose to go to go Nairne or, if not there, wherever it is Taminy has gone. I don't intend to come back."

Colfre felt as if every drop of blood had been squeezed from his body. "What? What are you saying?"

In answer, she raised her left hand and showed him her palm. The mark was there, star-shaped and slightly aglow — the same mark those others had shown with such disastrous results. There was not enough air in his lungs for a gasp; instead, he swayed and wished he could sit down. "You're . . . you're one of them. A — a Taminist."

"If that's what you would call us, yes."

"And Airleas?" He looked to his son with fear clogging his throat. The boy displayed his palm and Colfre's legs began to quake. "No. Dear God, no. Not Airleas, too."

Toireasa took a step toward him, putting herself between him and the boy. "You could join us, if you would."

"I can't. I am still Cyne of Caraid-land — "

"How much longer? So many of your people hate you. So many distrust you. Whose side were you really on? You befriended Taminy, all the while ingratiating yourself with Ladhar and his pack of trained wolves. What in the name of the Spirit where you thinking?"

He swallowed painfully. "That I could be Osric."

"You care so much for that?"

"The system tied my hands. I couldn't rule the way I wanted to. The way my Ancestor ruled — "

"That was six hundred years ago! Malcuim was a barbarian. It took the Meri and Osraed Ochan to tame him, tutor him, make him the Cyne he became. Before that, he was no more than the most powerful of a clutch of petty Chieftains. That, I think, because he built his castle in a more strategic location."

He gaped at her. "What do you know about any of this? You're a woman. A Cwen. What possesses you to fill your head with such things?"

"The desire to know — to understand." She smiled, viciously, he thought. "I know Taminy-a-Cuinn. I've seen what a woman can do."

"And so you'll become one of them. An outlaw. A heretic."

"I'm already one of them. And heresy is a matter of viewpoint. You believed in her."

He still did. The realization made him quake. "Yes, but —"

"Come with us, Colfre. Reconcile yourself with her. Beg her forgiveness for what you allowed Feich and Cadder to do. She'll accept you. And Caraid-land will still accept you as its Cyne."

A part of him wanted to do that. But it was a small part, trapped within a cage of habitual desire. Colfre set his jaw. "Under her regime, the station of Cyne would have little meaning. I would not rule. I'd be a mere figurehead . . . like my grandfather. Everyone would know I was a mere puppet — a toy." He would do anything to avoid the humiliation of that — to be Cyne in name only, nurse-maided by a committee, directed by another's will — no, that was not acceptable. "I must be Cyne of Caraid-land. I want no other existence."

"Then there's nothing more to be said. Good-bye, Colfre. You'll no doubt wish to divorce me; I've left my written agreement to that in my chambers." She turned to their son, who had watched the encounter with un-child-like solemnity. "Come, Airleas, it's time for us to go."

"They won't let you out," said Colfre.

"Your soldiers?"

"No, the mob. They'll kill you. They'll kill Airleas."

She shook her head. "No, Colfre. They won't harm us. We bear the mark. We're of the New Covenant. They'll let us pass. But you *are* trapped here. By your own will." She turned away then, gathered Airleas to her side and left him.

The boy turned his head for the briefest moment as he stepped through the door, fixing Colfre with his dark Hillwild eyes. "Good-bye, father," he said, and was gone.

I won't let you! I won't let you take my son! He wanted to scream those things aloud, but there was no strength left in him. The quivering of his legs increased, forcing him to sit. He sank to the floor in the center of the Malcuim crest, head to his knees. Servants came and went. None stopped to ask him if he was all right or why he hunched there, rocking like a drowsing infant. It was there that his Durweard found him hours later.

❖   ❖   ❖

"The course is clear, sire," Daimhin Feich said, "you must show strength, now, or all is lost." He couldn't be sure he was getting through, for Colfre would not look at him, would not take his eyes from the cup of wine that had been set before him.

"I hated Toireasa when she gave birth to Airleas," he said at last. "And, at times, I convinced myself I hated the boy as well. Did you know that? Did you suspect that your old friend was such a monster that he could hate his own wife and son?"

Taken aback, Daimhin could only murmur, "No, lord. I had no idea."

"I looked at him and saw my mother — saw the taint of Hillwild blood that infects the Malcuim line. Ciaran was a fool to sell his unborn sons' birthrights for peace. The Hillwild should have been eradicated or driven so far into the Gyldan-baenn that they'd never come out again. Let them pollute Deasach blood." He paused, ruminating. "But it wasn't her fault, you see. It wasn't Airleas's. It was me." He poked a thumb at his chest. "I was the one with the taint. Not Toireasa."

"The Hillwild are a rebellious people," Daimhin agreed. "A hard people, and wild. But they are fierce in battle, and have their own honor. You could ask for no better soldiers in the field."

Colfre gave his Durweard a wry glance. "So your great experience in battle tells you, eh, Daimhin? It's been two generations since Caraid-land has had blood spilled on her soil. What would you know of Hillwild valor?"

"What my father and grandfather have told me."

"Hm. And now you'd have us raise an army to go off and fight those wily warriors in their own territory? Where are you going to raise this army, Durweard Feich? Out of the Sea? Out of the graves of our ancestors? The people outside those gates will not suffer an army to be gathered."

"We have the royal guard — "

"Many of which have defected."

Daimhin was losing his patience. "I'm aware. There are yet enough to mount a fighting force."

"To what purpose?"

"To go to Halig-liath and bring back the Riagan and the Cwen."

Colfre shook his head. "No. It's futile. Halig-liath is a fortress nearly as impregnable as Mertuile."

"Not if we attack from the ridge. We can raise an army from the House Feich, alone. Not everyone is in thrall to Taminy-Osmaer. We must bring back your heir."

Colfre's head drooped toward his wine cup. "I have no heir. I have no Cwen. I have no life."

"Sire!" Daimhin threw back his chair and stood, all but pounding his fists on the table. "I can't abide this talk! You are Cyne Colfre Malcuim — *Malcuim*, damn you! You are still the sovereign ruler of Caraid-land, still in power in Creiddylad, still in residence in Mertuile. Supporters will flock to you — already, they are doing so. You saw the vote — there are Eiric loyal to you, Ministers and even Osraed. The Ministers, alone, should be able to raise up an army to march on Mertuile." He didn't mention that he'd already commissioned them to do so.

Colfre shook his head. "No army. I will shed no blood."

"You were ready to shed Deasach blood. What of your bold campaign to press her borders?"

"A madman's daydream. That was a different Cyne Colfre."

"No. I'll not hear you speak that way of yourself."

When Colfre made no reply, Daimhin went around the table to his side and bodily pushed back his chair. Dropping to one knee before his Cyne, he boldly grasped the royal's arms and shook him. "Colfre Malcuim, you have been my Cyne, my lord, my mentor and, above all, my friend. It bleeds me dry to see you like this. That woman has sucked the light from your soul. Do you need any further proof of her evil?"

"That woman? Do you speak of Toireasa or Taminy?"

"Taminy, of course. Toireasa is merely bewicked by her. If we could eliminate the evil — "

"You can't eliminate her, Daimhin. *They* won't let you."

Daimhin stared at his Cyne's ravished face. Damn, but he had sunk so far . . . "Perhaps *They* have nothing to do with it. If she is evil — "

Colfre tried to cover his ears. "Stop! Cease chattering to me about her evil. She isn't evil. She's light upon light. Only I — *I* am too much a creature of darkness to be able to look on her. She blinds me, burns me, withers me."

"You cannot let yourself fall into despair."

"Too late. I have fallen. Leave me."

"No."

Colfre surprised him, breaking his hold and pushing him forcefully away. "Leave me alone, Daimhin. Go away. I need time to think."

Shaking with rage and frustration, Daimhin did as bidden. He, too, needed time to think.

Silver-tailed clouds galloped the skies, driven by a brisk whip of wind. The tallest peaks of the Gyldan-baenn tried to snare them as they passed, but only a few paused to graze the high slopes. From her window on the southern side of Halig-liath, Taminy watched them. They carried autumn on their backs, late summer thunder in their hooves. She smiled. She liked autumn.

"Good to see you smile, Lady."

She turned. The Ren Catahn stood just within the door. He was one of the few people who could catch her unawares, and only if he put his mind to it.

"How long have you been standing there?" she asked him.

"Not long. I didn't want to interrupt your thoughts."

She beckoned him to sit with her in the broad window seat. He did with some timorousness which, in a man of his stature, was amusing. She smiled again, watching him. When he had made himself comfortable at as respectful a distance as the seat would allow, she asked, "What news?"

"There's been no movement of troops from Creiddylad. The Cyne's been in seclusion since the Flight. Rumors tell of his failing health — the Cwen and Airleas have left him."

"Yes, I know. They're coming here."

Catahn grinned. "Of course, you know. Ah, but did you know I sent an escort to meet them?"

Taminy laughed. He liked to try to catch her out. It made her feel as if he was actually her protector. Well, he was that — the Meri had granted him the station in an

aislinn. "A Hillwild escort?" she asked. "Her poor driver
will be petrified."

"I sent along an Osraed for good measure."

"Wise of you."

"Meanwhile, another group of pilgrims have arrived.
They offer their children into your service."

"Only their children? What of themselves?"

"They say they are too old to be of any use."

"I shall have to speak to them about that."

"It would please me. They're Hillwild — all the way
from Moidart."

Something grey whispered at the fringe of Taminy's
awareness. She frowned. "How large an escort did you
send for Toireasa?"

"Seven men, including the Osraed. It was Osraed
Tynedale's opinion that I had overdone it."

Taminy shook her head. "They're two days out still. The
escort will meet them — ?"

"Tonight, I should imagine, Lady. Why?"

"They're traveling by carriage, stopping at night. A fast
company of horsemen could overtake them."

Catahn's glossy black brows scudded up his broad
forehead. "You fear retaliation from Mertuile? They've
done nothing."

"Nothing overt."

"The Cyne may yet come to believe in you, Lady."

She contemplated that for a moment, then nodded.
"Yes, though perhaps not in this life. You sent Osraed . . .
Eadmund."

He nodded, awed by her growing abilities.

She would someday tell him that she knew him inside and
out, heart and soul — but not today. "I'll touch him. They must
hurry back to Halig-liath. Something is moving at Mertuile."

Catahn frowned. "I don't like the sound of that, Lady.
Shall we arm more guards?"

In answer she merely looked at him, humor tugging the
corners of her mouth.

He actually blushed. "Forgive me. I forget we have
other defenses than bow and sword." He stood. "Osraed
Ealad-hach wishes to see you. He's outside."

She gave him a look of mock reproach. "You made him wait."

Catahn grinned. "He deserves to wait." The Ren strode to the door and ushered the old Osraed in. "Shall I stay, Lady?" he said, growling a little for Ealad-hach's benefit.

The old man cowered and Taminy felt pity well in her throat. "No, leave us. It's all right. You wish to speak with me?" she asked Ealad-hach when they were alone.

"I wish to leave Halig-liath," he said and refused, as always, to look at her face.

"Are you being mistreated here?"

"You know I am not. I simply find my position here untenable. To all intents, the Osraed Council no longer exists. Indeed, the Osraed Body no longer exists, as a body. You've seen to that."

"Destroying the Osraed Institution was not my intention, but merely to renew its spirit."

"You have brought chaos to Caraid-land, Lady Taminy." He made the words a curse.

"Don't call me that. 'Cailin' or 'girl' or even 'Wicke' would be more acceptable from your lips."

He inclined his head. "As you wish, Wicke."

She flinched. Hatred would always wound her and she must always lay herself open to it.

He smiled a little, seeing that. "Pain, Wicke? It amazes me that anything I do could hurt you."

"Everything you do hurts me, Osraed. I wish I could make you see me for what I am. I wish you could believe."

"If you're what you claim to be, then that should be well within your powers."

She smiled ruefully. "Within my powers, yes. Within my nature, no. The Meri did not force young Ealad-hach into Halig-liath. He came here of his own free will. He saw the Gwenwyvar in a dream, woke beside Her pool, and knew not how he'd gotten there in the middle of a summer night. After that he was in love. So very much in love that every breath he breathed and every word he spoke was of the Eibhilin worlds. Halig-liath was heaven to him. And now, he wishes to leave heaven."

The old man stared at her, trembling as if with palsy.

"How do you — ? Oh, wicked. Wicked wonder to use that against me now, when I am so weak."

She stood and moved to stand before him, eye to eye. "Ealad-hach, who do you think it was that called to you that night? Whose duan sang you from your room out onto the hills, out into the woods, down to the Gwenwyvar's pool?" She pressed her fingertips to her breast. "It was I, your Beloved, who called to you. Why do you not recognize me?"

His trembling increased twofold and his eyes overflowed with tears. He went to his knees before her, hands beseeching. "Please," he sobbed. "Please, release me from this prison."

His pain smote her like a blast from a blaec-smythe's forge, nearly felling her. Dear God, how horrible it was to be Ealad-hach, to be so torn and twisted that day looked like night and night looked like chill hell. She gazed into his soul and knew what he asked and knew what she must give him for his pain. *Spirit, forgive me for my presumption.*

Dropping to her knees, she reached out and took the gnarled hands in her own. Wracked with sobs, he could not resist, but merely gazed at her from teary eyes. "You are released, Osraed Ealad-hach. And with Our blessing." She lifted her left hand to his forehead placing there, a tiny flower of light.

His eyes widened and the sobs stopped in his throat. Something trembled on his lips — words that rushed up from his heart of hearts to overwhelm him.

Yes, now you see.

A quivering hand rose to her cheek and found a tear there. The old man smiled. "Beloved," he said and collapsed into her arms.

She cradled him there for a time, only gradually becoming aware of Catahn's presence in the room. She looked up, tears still coursing down her cheeks.

Seeing them, the Ren came to her side. "My Lady, what has happened?"

She stroked the old man's brittle hair. "The Osraed Ealad-hach is dead, Catahn. His soul is in the arms of the Meri."

❖   ❖   ❖

"What did the doctor say, lord?"

"What else could he say? He said my health is failing."

Daimhin Feich came across the room and dared to sit on the edge of his Cyne's couch, facing the wasted man who lay there. "Then he will have medicines for you. You will be tended night and day. I'll handle these problems of state until you're recovered and — "

The Cyne uttered a wheezing laugh. "Daimhin Feich, one-man diplomatic corps. Problems of state. My realm is crumbling, I will die heirless and you sum it up as problems of state. Such an optimist."

"You will not die. Let alone heirless."

"Well, I can't father a child in this condition. Nor have I any desire to, even if any sane woman would have me. I could adopt an heir, I suppose."

"You'll need no adoption. We'll get Airleas back. I promise. I've raised a force of men. They ride in two hours."

"Ride? Ride where?"

"Toward Halig-liath. At flank speed they may be able to catch the Cwen and Riagan before they make the fortress, if not, we'll take a larger force and lay seige. I'll go myself if I have to, but I will get Airleas back."

"For me. You'd do all that for me?"

"Anything. Anything for you, sire."

Tears sprang to Colfre's eyes. "Dear God, you are a loyal friend. The most loyal friend a man could find."

Daimhin bowed his head deeply. "Thank you, lord. You do me honor."

"No. You do *me* honor by standing so close beside me through all this. Lesser men would have deserted me. As did my Chancellor, half my Privy Council — "

"Don't think of it, sire. Think of getting Airleas back. The Malcuim line will continue."

Colfre nodded. "You must be Regent. Toireasa is not to be trusted."

Daimhin flicked his eyes wide open — his mouth as well. "I, sire? Regent?" He ducked his head again. "You drown me in honor."

Colfre was nodding more fiercely now. "Yes, call the

Osraed Ladhar. He must witness and counter-sign. I will make you Regent now. Immediately."

Daimhin lifted the Cyne's hand to his lips and kissed it. "At once, sire."

He had to use the seaward cliff passage to leave Mertuile — the same passage Cwen Goscelin had used in her heroic escape over a century before; the same passage young Cyne Paeccs, son of Malcuim, had used to flee the Claeg and Feich, who were attempting to overthrow the Malcuim line. Ironic, that. But he would enjoy the irony later; now, he had to bring Ladhar to Mertuile.

He did it in record time, though the cliff path was slippery with rime, though the boat, hidden in its tiny cove, was so long unused that the mooring line had to be cut, though he was a poor oarsman. He resented the fact that, on the return trip, the Abbod could not be imposed upon to row a lick.

They were in the halls of Mertuile when he'd regained his breath enough to speak steadily. "I will now tell you why you've been brought here."

Ladhar shot him an acerbic glance. "You told me Colfre was dying."

"I exaggerated. I needed you to come unquestioningly. He wishes appoint a Regent to Airleas."

"Airleas is gone."

"Yes, but I've mounted a campaign to get him back."

"Ah, is that what that was all about? I was informed something was going on out at Selbyr's estate. It was a conscription."

"It was loyal volunteers rallying to the aid of their Cyne and country."

"Yes, well . . . So, Colfre will appoint Regent to his Taminist brat. He *is* a Taminist, you know. Toireasa sent over two formal self-worded testaments in which they both denounced the 'old order' and embraced the 'New Covenant.'"

"Poor child."

"Yes, poor child. So he's to be dragged back to Creiddylad and made to recant his pagan ways, eh? Think it'll take?"

"I don't know. It's doubtful, I suppose."

"So, who's to be Regent?"

"I am."

They were outside the Cyne's salon now. Ladhar stopped and lowered his voice. "You? Rumor has it you were courting the Dark Sister."

"I was attempting to inveigle my way into her good graces, hoping, for Colfre's sake, it would make her more tractable."

"Ah. Failed miserably, didn't you?"

Daimhin bit back his sudden anger. "Yes, miserably. I am not a Taminist, if that's what you're thinking. Frankly, I'd like to see the bitch tied to a log and put out to Sea." *But not before-time.*

"Tied to a tree and burned," Ladhar said. "Burning leaves nothing to chance." The old Abbod cocked his head to one side. "Airleas would be a poor Cyne. Surely, he might be persuaded to give up his dark faith, but there's no guarantee he won't go back to it the moment the Circlet is on his head."

"No guarantee at all."

"And if Airleas won't recant, and Colfre dies, then we've no Cyne at all. Colfre should do more than appoint a Regent. He should appoint a Cyneric."

Daimhin frowned. "A Cyneric? Is that wise? Doesn't that rather make him and Airleas targets for foul play?"

"Not if the Cyneric is someone we can all trust." Ladhar tapped lightly on the Cyne's door and, receiving permission, preceded Daimhin into the room.

Ten minutes later, Daimhin Feich was Regent to Airleas — to be Cyneric if Airleas were to die or abdicate. A testament was signed by all three attending parties and lackeys were sent to post the public bans.

Not, Daimhin thought wryly, *that anyone would care.* Word had spread far and wide that he was the man who had taken a crossbow and aimed it at Caraid-land's new Beloved. He would not be a popular figure, but he would at least be a powerful one.

"Daimhin, is that you?" Colfre turned from his writing

and squinted into the darkness beyond the glow of the lightbowl mounted on his desk.

"Yes, sire." Feich stepped into the half-light, raising his hand. Bits of fire gleamed off the metal goblet in his hand. "I saw you were up late and brought you some hot cider." He smiled. "It's so good to see you feeling better, friend."

Colfre smiled in return. The very sight of Daimhin Feich filled him with gratitude. Loyalty. There was no price you could put on that. The man should have been his brother, so much alike were they. He held out his hand for the cup. "Thank you, Daimhin. I am feeling better. You've handled this 'problem of state' very well." He took a sip of the cider, then set the cup on his desk. "Mm. Very good. I notice the rabble is gone. Did we wear them out?"

"Some. I had them barred from the Cyne's Market. There will be no one but merchants there in the morning."

"Where did you get the men to accomplish that? I thought you sent them all after my faithless wife."

"Feich is a populous House, my lord. And one which commands great . . . respect."

Colfre laughed. "Yes. Yes, it does. Especially from its enemies."

Feich bowed deeply. "It does me good to hear you laugh, sire. Even if my family's legendary treachery is the cause."

"Forgive me, friend. I shouldn't make a joke of that."

Feich merely inclined his head, then left the Cyne to his writing. Colfre sighed. He really did feel better. Airleas would be brought back and the Malcuim line would continue. Daimhin Feich had promised it and therefore it would be done.

Colfre took another sip of the cider and bent back to his testament.

CHAPTER 22

The mystic Beloved, before concealed by the veil of words, is now revealed to the eyes of men.

I bear witness, my friends, that the benediction is complete, the testimony fulfilled, the proof demonstrated, the sign given. Let all now see what your efforts in the path of the Meri will unveil and accomplish.

Divine grace has been bestowed on you and on all that dwell in the Land of Shadow and Light. Sing duans of praise to the Spirit of All Worlds.

— Testament of Osraed Bevol

❖   ❖   ❖

Blood thundered in his ears. Daimhin Feich listened, heeding its siren call. He wondered at the strange visceral elation he felt just strapping on this sword. He had never worn one, save for ceremonial purposes, and this was no ordinary sword — it was a Malcuim sword, worn, so legend said, by the Malcuim himself. It was a sword intended for fighting and Daimhin Feich had every intention of putting it to that use.

He strode the corridors of Mertuile with a new vigor this morning. A vigor the black banners and bundles of dead flowers that festooned the halls could not dampen. He was Regent to Airleas Malcuim, Cyneric if Airleas failed to take the Throne. Dark joy bubbled in his breast, threatening to make him laugh. That would be inappropriate now, with Mertuile in mourning; he would laugh when he stood before the Stone and felt the Circlet on his head. A Feich on the Throne! He began to whistle a tune, but Mertuile's empty interior threw it back at him misshapen. He stopped whistling.

In the lower hall, the Abbod Ladhar met him, along with his own cousin, Ruadh, commander of his fighting force. One was dressed for travel, the other for battle.

The Abbod's face was screwed into a disapproving mask and he glowered fiercely. "Why do you insist that I accompany you on this war crusade? My place is here."

"To comfort the mourners?" Daimhin asked. "To pray for the soul of your poor dead Cyne? His soul is wherever it deserves to be, Abbod. With the souls of other men who have taken their own lives. Your place is with those living, those who will march to free the Cyne's heir from the clutches of the Taminist evil. Your place is beneath the banner of the Meri, facing that evil. Or do you fear facing it?"

"I fear no man, nor woman, nor Wicke. But the period of mourning is not passed. It has barely begun."

"Mourn on the road, Abbod. Now, we ride to Halig-liath." He passed through the door his cousin held open for him, out into the morning Sun that slanted over Mertuile's landward wall. The gates to the outer ward were open and, through them, he could see the ranks of horses and men that were now at his command. He smiled, letting his earlier elation rise to a boil within him. Sensual, it was. He felt heat fan out from his groin and listened, again, to the song of blood in his ears. A quest. A crusade. And it would end at Halig-liath.

It was not Airleas Malcuim he thought of as he and his hundreds rode east.

The Feich forces were arrayed before the gates of the Holy Fortress. Cyneric Daimhin Feich rode at their head with Ruadh Feich at his side. Behind them, the Abbod Ladhar glowered from the back of a sturdy horse, the Malcuim standard fluttering overhead. Beside it, on a second staff, the Star Chalice was borne aloft. It was a bit of grandstanding that did not sit well with the Abbod, but to Daimhin Feich, it added a twist of historical irony to his crusade. Centuries before, another army had rallied to face down another Malcuim heir, using the same holy relic to confound his forces. And now, as then, hundreds had rallied. Not only Feich, but Feich allies — southern Eiric, for the most part, to whom the Osraed were a nuisance and the idea of supernatural intervention, an anachronism. For the Feich it was a return to the glory days. The days when the great House was a thorn in the side of whatever Malcuim happened to sit upon the Throne.

Daimhin Feich, Regent and would-be Cyneric, turned to glance up at the standards aloft behind him. He would tear down that Malcuim emblem soon, replace it with his own. But for now, the Feich crest appeared only on the arm bands of the troops massed behind him.

He moved his mount forward, all the way to the shadow of Halig-liath's gates. The heavy oaken doors were open, but the portcullis was down. The Ren Catahn stood behind it, Iobert Claeg at his side. Feich spoke to the lowland Chief. "A twist in history, this, old friend — that Feich and Claeg face each other across defenses."

"Aye, well, it was inevitable. The Claeg do what they believe is right. The Feich do what they think is profitable."

Feich chuckled. "Barbed words, Claeg."

"May they draw blood."

"I must speak to the Cwen Toireasa and the Riagan Airleas."

From behind the sill of the gate, Toireasa Malcuim heard the words and shivered. Grasping her son's hand, she willed her feet to move her forward. They behaved as if rooted to the cobbles. Someone took her other hand, flooding her with strength. She smiled. *Oh, to feel this strong and resilient, always.*

With Airleas on her left and Taminy on her right, she went out to face Daimhin Feich. His eyes gleamed when he saw them, and he dismounted, coming to stand before the portcullis.

"This is absurd," he said. "I merely wish to reason with you, mistress. Can't we do without further barriers between us?" He gestured at the heavy wood and iron grille that separated them. "Your men have their bows aimed and ready. What could we do against them?"

Taminy turned her head and glanced behind her. The portcullis rose ponderously.

"Thank you." Feich dropped his gaze to Airleas. "I bring you sad news, Airleas. Your father, Cyne Colfre Malcuim, is dead. You are now Cyneric of Caraid-land."

The boy's face paled, but he showed no other sign of emotion. "We know," he said. "We felt him die."

Feich moved his narrowed eyes to Toireasa's face, fighting the urge to look at Taminy. "I regret to say that he died by his own hand. Your desertion destroyed him, madam."

The Cwen shook her head. Her gaze on him was hard and cold. "I destroyed nothing, Daimhin Feich. It was you who destroyed him. You who deserted him. You who passed him the cup of betrayal. This" — she nodded toward the soldiers arrayed behind him — "this is forever and always what you have wanted, is it not?"

Feich's insides cooled at her words. What did she know of a "cup of betrayal?" He only just kept his eyes from seeking Taminy's reaction. "You mistake me, mistress. I had nothing but the good of my Cyne at heart. And the good of Caraid-land. That good can only be served by the return of the Cyneric Airleas to Mertuile to be set before the Stone."

"Under whose regency?"

"Under my own. By the Cyne's decree. Ask Osraed Ladhar, if you don't trust me. He witnessed the act and counter-signed the document. For the sake of this land, which we both love, I beg you, Cwen Toireasa — let Airleas return to Creiddylad with me. Let him be set before the Stone as is his right."

Toireasa smiled wryly. "Ah, Goscelin's dilemma. To be parted from her child, or to hold him fast to her side."

"Goscelin had no choice, mistress. You do. I offer it to you."

"And the alternative?"

Feich gazed around him at the hills above, the town below, the long slope, meadows and woods behind. "This land is divided, torn by dissenssion and strife. Blood flows. Lives are lost. Mistress, Airleas is a symbol of Caraid-land's unity. If he is not at Mertuile, Caraid-land is a headless corpse, thrown to merciless eaters of carrion."

"Then let him return to Mertuile with me. Let Taminy Weave her will in Caraid-land and let its wounds be healed. Let Taminy complete her purpose — to renew and unify Caraid-land as it has never been unified before."

Feich did look at Taminy now and the hatred that had collected in him over the weeks roared for release. Her face blanched as his eyes touched it, and he knew without doubt that she could feel the black emotion roiling within him. Something else sprang to join it, something that burnt its way up from his groin, scorching him. Self-disgust followed — disgust that his own body could betray him so thoroughly. He knew what she was — anathema. "She will Weave her will in chill hell and nowhere else."

"Then you return to Mertuile empty-handed."

"You deny your son — Colfre's son — his birthright. He is a Malcuim —"

"Yes, and so am I. And I shall behave like one. Cowardice ill-befits a Malcuim Cwen. I will not give my son and Colfre's into your hands, Daimhin Feich. In your hands he would become a pawn . . . as Colfre was."

Beside Toireasa, Taminy stirred, returning Feich's gaze. His innards squirmed. "Then you shall be declared outlaw — all of you. Heretics like her." He pointed at Taminy, and sought the faces of those behind the trio in the archway. "I'll have you declared Wicke. You'll be hunted down like vermin wherever you go. Fed to the waves or the flames. You'll watch your husbands and wives and children die horribly before your eyes. Is that what you want? Cyneric Airleas, is that what you want for your mother?"

The child twitched as if Feich had poked him. He glanced from his mother to Taminy, then set his eyes on Feich's face. "If we deny Taminy-Osmaer, we'll *live* horribly. A Malcuim does not poison himself."

"Your father did. Day by day his soul writhed in torment because he believed in *that*." His finger pointed at Taminy again. "It tore him asunder in the end." He glanced at the Ren Catahn, standing just behind the three. "Perhaps it was the Hillwild blood in his veins that made him susceptible to pagan goddesses — that made him weak of will and shallow of mind."

"Or perhaps it was having a fox for a Durweard," Catahn growled.

"My father worshipped power," said Airleas. "That's what made him weak. And you knew it. I don't care if you call me a Wicke or a heretic. I love Taminy and I love my mother. I won't leave here no matter what you say. Go away, Durweard Feich, and leave us alone. You can have the Throne and the Circlet if you want them so much." He looked up at his mother. "Can I go now? I don't want to talk to him any more."

Toireasa smiled into Daimhin Feich's face. It was a smile fierce with pride. "You've heard the Malcuim. Leave us."

She turned her back on him then, and prepared to usher Airleas away. Desperate, he leapt forward. "Airleas! Come to me! These women deceive you! They've poisoned your mind. Your father made me your Regent. Trust me, Airleas, and come to me!"

Airleas turned back to give his father's Durweard a scathing look. "You stink," he said.

Feich made a move to draw his sword and follow the royals into the courtyard. Before he had tightened his grip on the hilt, the portcullis crashed down again, digging its sharpened tines into the earth. Feich jumped clear, swearing. When he regained his poise, the Cwen and Airleas were gone and only Taminy faced him from the other side of the grille, Catahn hovering warily behind her.

"You — !" Feich moved forward again. He stopped at little more than arm's length from her, the portcullis bars creating a thick frame about her head and shoulders. "You are a dagger in the heart of this land."

"And you are the man who directs the blade. Stop this now. Let Airleas and Toireasa return to Creiddylad free. Let me pursue my mission in Caraid-land and the wound will quickly heal."

He gazed at her a long moment, then nodded. "All right. I see that what you say is true. My actions are a determining factor in what happens here. Yes. You may return to Creiddylad a free woman."

Taminy smiled while, behind her, the Ren Catahn laid a

hand to his sword hilt. "I have changed since we last spoke, Daimhin. Then, I was caught at a crossroads, stranded in a state of transition. Powers ebbed and flowed, awareness informed me only fleetingly. I am past that now. And because I am past that, I know that you lie. If Airleas were to pass into your hands, Regent Feich, he would become, as his mother said, a pawn. As it seems his father was, as you intended me to be. There is still pain in that memory. How close I came to allowing my purpose to be consumed by yours. And for what — a flash of white heat, a touch of warm flesh? That was an ordeal by fire, Daimhin. And I still ask, 'Did I pass?' Or did Osraed Bevol rescue me?"

Feich jerked. "Bevol? Bevol is dead."

"After a fashion. And yet, he lives, after a fashion. You wouldn't understand." She shook her head and he felt her sigh rush through him like a cool breeze. "I want so to appeal to your spirit. I want so to speak to your conscience. But by all the powers that vibrate in this great rock, I cannot reach either."

Talk of spirits and consciences made him squirm. "Enough nonsense. I have no choice but to return to Creiddylad and have myself declared Cyneric."

"You already think of yourself as that."

Feich hurled himself against the barricade. It rattled only slightly, though he threw his whole weight into the motion. "Bitch! Stop pretending to read my mind!"

Catahn's sword was out as he came to Taminy's shoulder, ready to run Feich through — if Taminy would allow such a thing, which she wouldn't.

"Afraid of me, Wicke? Does your trained bear dance attendance because you fear me?"

"Lady?" Catahn's intent was clear in his voice. He wanted to put an end to Daimhin Feich. Yes, of course — he wanted to keep the Crystal Rose for himself.

"I'm not afraid of you," Taminy said, and Feich scoffed.

"Then send your bear away."

Taminy knew Feich's demand posed no mortal danger. She looked up over her shoulder into Catahn's dark face. "It's all right, Catahn. Stand down. He can't harm me." *I must be certain he can't harm me.*

Reluctantly, the Hillwild removed himself from Taminy's side, fading into the shadows beneath the arch. Taminy moved close to the portcullis.

"You feel nothing for me, Taminy?"

"I feel pity."

"Prove that. Give me your hand."

She put her left hand, palm up, through the grille. The star, golden, gleaming, shone at him. He started to take it, hesitated, and jerked away when their fingertips brushed. His face burned red and he wriggled as if ants crawled upon him.

She withdrew the hand. "Now who is afraid?"

"I will return to Creiddylad and I will, myself, be set before the Stone."

"While Airleas lives? Then you will be Cyne of a land divided completely. Your only chance of maintaining Caraid-land's unity is to have Airleas at Mertuile."

"Half a country is better than none at all. I *will* be set before the Stone, and the Throne and Circlet shall remain in my possession and be passed down to my sons. The Osmaer Crystal will be in the hands of Feich from this day forth. And no Malcuim shall ever take it from us. And as for you, dear lady, I shall hound you and yours until I have eradicated every last one of you. These hands" — he held them up before him — "These hands caressed you and drew such passion from you not that long ago. Today I would cheerfully use them to strangle you. But I think you're worth more to me alive. The people love you, Taminy-a-Cuinn."

"And I love them."

Calm — she was too calm. He spoke to her with passion threatening to tear itself loose and devour him, and those green eyes gazed back with the coolness of sea water. He quaked with the effort it took not to scream at her — not to thrust his hands through the grille and tear at her throat. *Why did she not love me?*

"You can't receive what you refuse to give," she murmured, and there was nothing left to do but stare at her, hating and wanting, until he could make himself turn away from her gaze and return to his horse.

When he was Cyne, he thought, as he turned his troops about, things would change. He would hold the Crystal and, with Ladhar's help, he would learn to wield its power. He had always been fey, though he'd kept it well-hidden. Then, as Cyne — no, as more than that, as Osric — he would let that Gift come to the fore. Caraid-land would find itself possessed of a very powerful leader. First, the Taminists would be eradicated, then the Deasach would be made to tremble.

He turned in the saddle just before the trees obscured the gates of Halig-liath from sight. She still stood there, watching him, looking small and vulnerable and absurdly young. Heat licked up his spine, irritating him. He dug his heels into his horse's flanks and rode to the head of the long column.

Taminy felt Catahn's presence at her side as a spot of soft warmth in the cold, iron shell about her. She allowed the shell to melt away into the earth and sagged back against the Hillwild's comforting bulk.

There was a creak of leather and one large hand came to her shoulder. "He will return, Lady."

She nodded, thanking the warmth that spread from his hand to suffuse her. "He will return when he realizes that Airleas is Cyne of Caraid-land's heart and that to possess that heart, he must possess Airleas."

Catahn snorted. "He'll be happy enough with the body for a while."

"Not long."

"And when he returns, will he find us here?"

She shook her head. "No. With us here, the people of Nairne are in danger. We must be elsewhere when Daimhin Feich revisits Halig-liath."

She turned and re-entered the courtyard, Catahn maintaining his place beside her. She ignored the questioning faces that greeted them for a moment, and paused to gaze up and over the high eastern walls. The five of the seven peaks of the Gyldan-baenn marched away toward the south. Far and away, she could see the snow-capped thrust of Baenn-ghlo, for once, not wrapped in the mists that gave it its name. The smaller summit of Baenn-an-ratha stood out in stark relief against its bright, massive flank. Somewhere among those crags and forested passes Catahn's stronghold, Hrofceaster, snuggled in near-inaccessible safety. It would be a difficult place to winter for those used to milder climes, but there they would be safe, and there they would not be subject to seige.

Catahn had followed her gaze to look lovingly and longingly on those same peaks. "Shall we begin preparations for travel, Lady?"

She smiled and squeezed his hand where it still rested on her shoulder. "Thank you, Catahn," she said and moved to where Cwen Toireasa and Airleas waited in the midst of a cluster of other believers.

Catahn watched her till she was absorbed by the group, then pulled his eyes back to the Gyldan-baenn. His heart swelled with a surge of something big and fine and warm. He would go home soon, and he would bring the Lady of the Crystal Rose with him.

The Cynes of Caraid-land

Malcuim the Uniter—first Cyne of Caraid-land
>> ((First Manifestation of the Meri: Golden Aspect
>> 5th year of the reign of Malcuim))
> (Osraed Ochan, Father of all Osraed is at court)
> [Establishment of the Hall of General Assembly]
> [Houses Claeg and Feich unite against the House
> Malcuim]

Paeccs the Peaceful
> [Dorchaidhe Feich leads an uprising against Paeccs; the
> royal family flee to Halig-liath]
> [Feich usurps Paecc's throne]
> [Popular revolt; Feich is overthrown; Paeccs retakes
> Mertuile with the help of the Hillwild]

Cai (brother of Paeccs)
Bitan-ig
> [Claeg and Feich uprising continues — The Battle of the
> Chalice and the Skull, Year of Pilgrimage 102]
>> ((FIRST CUSP: Crimson Aspect, YP 102))
> [Foundation of the parish system by Bitan-ig and the
> Osraed Abhainn]

Niall Cleirach
Kieran the Dark (wed to Ailis Graegam)
> [The Claeg insurrection]
> [Establishment of the Cyne's Cirke]
> [Claeg domination of the House Malcuim]
> Buchan Claeg, Usurper
> [The First War of the Crystal, YP 160]
> [Bearach Malcuim seizes the Osmaer Crystal]
> [Buchan murders Cyne Kieran, captures Buchan's
> counselor, Osraed Gartain]
> [Gartain murdered]
> [The Feich betray the Throne; Bearach Malcuim
> executes the Feich Chieftain at Storm]
> [Bearach Set before the Stone at Halig-liath with
> Buchan Claeg still in control at Mertuile]

Bearach Spearman (son of Kieran)
> [Alliance between Bearach Malcuim and the Renic
> Garmorgan Hillwild of Moidart, YP 168]
> [Bearach seizes the Claeg estates]

[Buchan Claeg dies and his son Gery surrenders
   Mertuile to the Malcuim]
Readanor
     ((SECOND CUSP: Violet Aspect, YP 197))
Buidhe Harpere, Bard and Poet
Drew Golden Wynn Golden
Earwyn the Warrior
     [Little War of the Fishes, YP 305]
     [War ended by disaster—Earwyn's fleet destroyed]
       ((THIRD CUSP: Blue Aspect, YP 307))
Seosaidh
     [Consolidation of the Hall as governing body]
Robartach
Todd Eachan (age seven)
     [The Gentle Age]
Liusadhe the Bard (grandson of Todd Eachan, age 13
     [Expulsion of Wicke (and Feich) from Creiddylad]
       ((FOURTH CUSP: Silver Aspect—[Lufu
          Hageswode, called "Mam Lufu"], YP 419
          NOTE: This Cusp took place out of Pilgrimage
          Season. One Osraed, Aodaghan, was chosen,
          followed by a five year dearth.))
     [Liusadhe reigns from Ochanshrine with counselor,
       Osraed Aodaghan, at his side]
     [Enlargement of the Abbis at Ochansrine, founding of
       Wynecirke]
     [Purge of Osraed at court, divine establishment of the
       Hall as permanent instrument of government, equal
       to Cyne and Osraed]
Saeweard Steward
     [Permanent inclusion in Hall of House Chieftains]
     [Station of Minister officially recognized—Ministers
       elected to the Hall from the ranks of the cleirachs]
     [Institutionalization of tax upon commoners to enlarge
       Cyne's Cirke]
Siolta the Lawgiver (wed to Goscelin the Just of Nairne)
     [Hillwild unrest—Haefer Hillwild torments the Throne]
     [Surrender of Haefer Hillwild at Cyne's Cirke]
     [Siolta assassinated by Ruanaidhe the Red, who
       commits suicide in shame]
     [Pilgrimage of Haefer Hageswode (Hillwild) at age

          50—he becomes the first Hillwild Osraed]
Triune Regency (Harac Glinn, Diomasach Claeg,
     Goscelin Malcuim)
     [Struggle for control of Thearl]
     [Goscelin prevails and removes Thearl to Halig-liath]
The Regency of Goscelin the Just
Thearl the Stern (wed to An-a-Cleon)
     [Murder of the Eiric Cleon by the Claeg]
     [Murder of Warein Claeg by brothers of An-a-Cleon]
     [Claeg and Hillwild uprising—Seige of Ochanshrine]
          ((FIFTH CUSP: Green Aspect [Taminy-a-Cuinn],
          YP 490))
     [The Meri silent for five Seasons—Osraed Lin-a-
          Rumenea advises Cyne Thearl to make peace with
          the Hillwild]
     [Thearl dies during negotiatios at Hrofceaster]
Domnhall, Pursuer (wed to Eadaoine)
     [Domhnall killed in seige of Claeg stronghold]
The Dearan Regency
     [The Reconciliation of House Malcuim with Claeg and
Feich]
     [Libraries and schools established nationwide]
Ciaran (wed to the Hillwild, Aelf Hageswode)
     [Ciaran suspected in death of brother Modraed and exile
          of brother Donabhan]
     [Puppet rule of Ciaran under the Hall and
          establishment of the Privy Council led by Hurst Claeg]
     [Battle of the Banner—Ciaran embattled against
          Claeg and his own son, Ciarda, on the plain beyond
          Tuine]
     [Ciaran flees the battlefield and dies at Tuine]
Ciarda, Friend of All (wed to Brann Hageswode)
     [Second Little Battle of the Fishes—ended
          peacefully with the counsel of Osraed Bevol]
     [Rule of Peacefulness]
     [Ren Fasgadh marries Ciarda's sister, Fioned
          Malcuim]
     [Rise of Tradist Fundamentalism among Osraed]
Colfre, Peacemaker (wed to Troireasa Selbyr)
          ((SIXTH CUSP: Golden Aspect [Meredydd-a-
          Lagan], YP 605))